Useful

Debra Oswald is co-creator/head writer of the TV series *Offspring* and a two-time winner of the NSW Premier's Award. Her stage plays have been produced around the world and published by Currency Press, including *Gary's House*, *Mr Bailey's Minder*, *Sweet Road* and *The Peach Season*. Debra has written four plays for young audiences – *Dags*, *Skate*, *House on Fire* and *Stories in the Dark*. She is the author of three Aussie Bites books and six novels for teenage readers.

For Matthew Kalitowski

DEBRA OSWALD

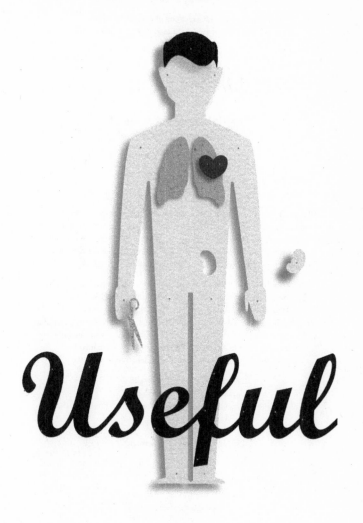

Useful

PENGUIN BOOKS

PENGUIN BOOKS

UK | USA | Canada | Ireland | Australia
India | New Zealand | South Africa | China

Penguin Random House group of companies whose
addresses can be found at global.penguinrandomhouse.com.

First published by Penguin Group (Australia), 2015
This edition published by Penguin Group (Australia), 2016

1 3 5 7 9 10 8 6 4 2

Copyright © Debra Oswald 2015

Cover design by Alex Ross © Penguin Group (Australia)
Text design by Samantha Jayaweera © Penguin Group (Australia)
Illustrations by Alex Ross © Penguin Group (Australia)
Typeset in Adobe Garamond by Samantha Jayaweera, Penguin Group (Australia)
Colour separation by Splitting Image Colour Studio, Clayton, Victoria
Printed and bound in Australia by Griffin Press, an accredited ISO
AS/NZS 14001 Environmental Management Systems printer.

National Library of Australia
Cataloguing-in-Publication data:
Oswald, Debra, author
Useful / Debra Oswald

ISBN 9780143573739 (paperback)

A823.3

penguin.com.au

Part One

1

A fall from the twenty-third floor would be more than enough to do it.

Access to the rooftop of a multi-storey building turned out to be surprisingly easy. Sullivan had prepared a story: 'I'm a location scout, wanting to suss out this rooftop as a possible film location.' But in the end he didn't need to bullshit anyone.

The door to the roof stairs did carry a sign – 'No unauthorised access' – but as Sullivan approached it, the door swung open from the outside. A handy piece of luck.

A guy heading back inside leaned his weight against the heavy metal door, holding it open so Sullivan could get out.

'Thanks, mate,' Sullivan said, shuffling through the gap, his Hawaiian shirt lightly brushing the other man's stripy business shirt. That close, the smell of the guy was notable: just-smoked cigarette plus the sour stink of last night's fags seeping through his pores. The man pressed his lips together in a sort of smile, a smile of mutual shame, assuming Sullivan was going outside to smoke too.

As Sullivan stepped onto the rooftop, hearing the door thud closed, it occurred to him that the sad smoker was the last human being he would ever encounter.

Around an air-conditioning duct was a small midden of cigarette butts and a dark stain on the concrete, tacky enough for fluff and grit to stick to it. The smell of urine hit Sullivan and he pictured a semi-circle of miserable men in striped shirts pissing onto that sticky patch while they sucked on cigarettes.

He felt a bit of sick come up into his throat, stinging yellow bile. It could be the stench of urine and fags making him nauseous. It could be after-burn from the half a bottle of cooking marsala he'd found in the cupboard. It could just be nerves. Didn't matter. He had to get on with this task.

Sullivan checked that his driver's licence was easy to locate in his wallet, alongside the note that stated his desire to be cremated or somehow disposed of with no funeral. He didn't want anyone to go to any expense. He then shoved the wallet deep into his back pocket. When they found him at the bottom, they would need ID. So they'd know it was Sullivan Moss.

He wasn't sure who qualified as his next of kin now his mother was dead. He was an orphan now. Could a person consider himself an orphan at thirty-nine years old? He wondered if people who had children of their own felt like orphans when their parents died.

Thinking about dead parents was a stupid mistake because it got him thinking about his mother – a benign woman who deserved better from her only child than hurried phone calls made while waiting in kebab shops or Centrelink queues. She deserved better than a dozen promises he'd visit her in hospital, promises sincerely made in the moment but thoughtlessly broken in some other moment. And then there was Pete.

When Pete lay dying in hospital, Sully had never made contact, too ashamed to face him – a steadfast friend who'd put up with Sully's shit for decades, a truly good man who'd spent part of every year doctoring in remote desert communities, humble, tolerant, generous . . . Bloody hell, the guy probably got the melanoma that killed him because he'd worked so much under the desert sun curing the sick and saving lives. How could Sullivan have walked into that hospital room and said, 'Well, Pete, you – an unquestionably valuable addition to the planet – are about to die while I – a fucking waste of floor-space – will live on'?

And here it came again: the disgust flushed through Sully's body, sucking with it every bad thing he'd ever done, every failure, every crime – nothing big enough to be glamorous or worthy of anti-hero respect . . . Just an endless stream of tawdry stuff, petty betrayals and selfishness. The sticky shameful things adhered to each other to form a toxic lump in his insides.

Sullivan didn't want to feel that any more. Which was the whole point of coming up to this rooftop.

He stepped over to the section of the roof where only a one-metre wall guarded the edge. He'd picked this method because he figured if he could summon the courage to pitch forward at a sufficient angle, then he'd have to succeed. His customary cowardice and inability to see things through to a proper conclusion wouldn't get in his way. He'd just be falling with no choice in the matter and the thing would get done.

Sullivan stepped up onto the low wall and peered over the edge. The job of obliterating himself shouldn't be a huge effort, considering he'd made so little meaningful impact on the world. He looked down at the bitumen surface of the car park one hundred and fifty metres below.

Was his torso like a skin bag full of blood and organs, a bag that would split open on impact? That's not how they usually showed it in movies. But movie versions of things couldn't be trusted. Not the way a fall from the twenty-third storey could be trusted to achieve a certain result.

His legs were trembling. The yellow bile oozed up his gullet again. The temazepam he'd taken to steady himself kicked in and he felt himself keel over. He was falling, feeble and boneless, unable to hold himself upright even if he were to try.

2

The second-best time in Natalie's day was the last chunk of the breakfast shift. Between seven and eight, Heather, the presenter of the radio show, was warmed up, in the flow of it, and so was Natalie. In her producer's booth, Natalie wrangled talk-back callers, lined up the phone interviews, typed notes on the screen for Heather, slid concert tickets into envelopes to send out as listener prizes, kept an eye on the TV monitors, checked the run-down sheet and still found moments to glance up through the glass and laugh at some witticism Heather had made. In Natalie's experience, presenters thrived on a bit of visible amusement from a producer, given that they couldn't hear the audience responding to their efforts. Nat thrived when she worked at precisely this rate of busyness – too engaged to second-guess herself or agonise about anything but not too busy to spark up the occasional creative idea.

This morning, at 7.12, Natalie put through the next caller, then typed a brief note: *Line 3, Pauline, funny.* Meanwhile, with her spare hand, she tapped the button to answer another call.

'Hi, this is the breakfast show,' said Natalie. 'What do you want to say to Heather?'

There was no voice on the other end – just a couple of shaky breaths.

'You there? Sorry, this must be a bad line.'

'Am I speaking to Natalie?' A female voice, middle-aged, the spongy consonants of an accent.

'Yes. I'm Heather's producer. Did you want to chat on-air about circumcision?'

'No. I need to speak to you.'

'Me?'

'This is Gordana.'

'Oh. Gordana. Hello.' Natalie had met her – the Croatian woman who lived in the flat across the hallway from Nat's father, Frank. They'd exchanged greetings a few times on the stairs. 'We're live on-air right now,' Natalie explained, in the cheerful but please-hurry-up voice she used with the loony or dud callers. 'Can I call you back when —'

'I need you to come here to my unit. There's a problem with your father,' said Gordana bluntly.

Natalie felt a sting of panic through her ribcage. 'Is he all right? Is it something urgent?'

Gordana cut in. 'At what time do you finish on the radio?'

'We're off-air at eight but then I have to —'

'It will be okay if you come to my unit as soon as you finish on the radio,' Gordana declared and hung up. Natalie flinched at the abruptness but at least her momentary panic had been defused. It was obviously not a medical emergency.

Natalie contemplated ringing her dad to suss out what was going on, but since his retirement, he slept at erratic times. She didn't want to phone this early and yank him out of some precious pocket of sleep. She didn't have Gordana's number to call back and decline the invitation or request more information. Maybe she should ignore the phone call entirely. Then again, if there was a chance her poor dad was embroiled in a conflict with his odd Croatian neighbour, he deserved some assistance.

At eight, Natalie postponed the post-show meeting. It wasn't far from the studio to Frank's flat in Glebe. She could sort out Gordana's problem and be back in the office in an hour or so.

As she drove, Natalie compiled lists in her head. Fix new promos for show, persuade marketing people to ditch unintelligible competition, check writers' festival press release to bags the best authors, talk to Neil about decision on casual junior producer, buy new school shoes for her eight-year-old son, Louis, check out flights for Louis to visit his father in Kuala Lumpur, get Louis a haircut, get herself a haircut, order that thing from that place for her mother's birthday, make time to see Shelley before her next round of chemo.

If the list of jobs threatened to grow too long, long enough to generate anxiety, Natalie reordered the jobs in terms of priority, picturing items in different fonts and type sizes. She quarantined Louis stuff from work duties, then allocated each task a timeslot in her week and successfully calmed herself.

Natalie jogged the five hundred metres from her parking spot to the front of Frank's building, telling herself she was efficiently utilising this errand for exercise too, but when she reached the entrance, she realised she was an idiot. Now she was breathless and a bit sweaty. Better to be composed and quietly formidable when facing whatever problem Gordana had conjured up, rather than presenting as a flustered noisy-breather.

She pressed the button for Gordana's flat, 1D, and the locked main entrance buzzed open. There were four apartments with courtyard gardens on the ground floor. She considered knocking on Frank's door, 1A, to get his version of the supposed problem. But then behind her, the door of flat 1D suddenly clunked open, making Natalie jerk with fright.

'Thank you for coming,' said Gordana and ushered her inside hurriedly, almost furtively.

Gordana was wearing jeans and a geometric-patterned shirt. She was late forties, stocky and square-bodied with assertive dark eyes, heavy eyebrows and hair dyed a lurid chemical orange.

'Natalie,' she said. Every word Gordana spoke landed on the floor between them like an unapologetic lump. 'I must ask for your help.'

'Well, if I can,' Natalie said. 'Do you have a problem with my father?'

Gordana nodded briskly and swept her hand towards the main bedroom. Natalie hesitated. Was she supposed to go in there? Gordana repeated the sweeping gesture so Natalie followed the firm hand signal into the bedroom.

Frank was on the bed. He lay flat on his back wearing a T-shirt, with the sheet pulled up to his chest. His lips were slightly parted as if about to speak but Natalie instantly knew he was dead.

'Oh Dad . . .'

She stepped closer and placed her hand on his wrist. It was cool and papery.

'A heart attack,' said Natalie.

'Yes.'

'Did you call an ambulance?'

'There was no point to call. When I woke up, he was already cold.'

Natalie's eyeballs burned and her throat constricted, ready for the tears to come. But before she could draw in enough breath to cry, Gordana's flinty voice cut through the air in the room.

'This is very sad,' said Gordana. 'But right now there is an important thing I must ask. My husband will come home from work soon. So I need you to help me carry your father into his own unit.'

'Sorry?'

'Mirko does not know about this. You can agree it is better that he doesn't know. I am sure we can carry your father together.'

'What? What are you saying? You expect me to help you move his dead body – oh . . .'

'You are upset. Of course. I am upset,' Gordana said. 'But it is not necessary for there to be more trouble than . . .' Her voice broke, like a fissure suddenly cracking through a brick wall. She took a breath and Natalie saw her gulp away the urge to cry. 'I don't want Mirko to be upset if he finds Frank here. Mirko will be home in thirty minutes.'

'Gordana, I don't think . . . I mean, this isn't . . .'

'Who else can I ask?' She addressed Natalie with such a logical tone, it seemed to suck the strangeness out of the request.

Gordana lunged forward to tuck the top sheet around Frank's body. She placed his other clothes, neatly folded, onto his belly. Then she looked at Natalie, direct and desperate.

'Please.'

Maybe the urgency of Gordana's predicament trumped grief. Certainly, the pain in the woman's voice, for just those few seconds, was undeniable, so it couldn't be ignored. And her plan was oddly sensible.

Natalie found herself helping Gordana lift Frank's body, using the yellow fitted sheet like a hammock, with the elastic corners bunched up to form handles.

Frank was a substantial man – six one and he'd packed on weight since he retired – so carting the sheet-sling was awkward. Gordana took the head end, the heavier end. She was strong – her stocky frame seemed to be entirely made of muscle, like a wombat.

The two women moved slowly and deliberately through Gordana's flat. Neither spoke, so the only sound was the scuffing of shoes on carpet. Natalie was surprised to feel a small surge of power in herself. She and Gordana were doing what needed to be done, like people in wartime. They were taking control of the circumstance in which they found themselves with a decisive practicality that sliced through the doubts piled around this whole manoeuvre.

By the time they reached Gordana's front door, the weight of the body in the sheet was creating a pendulum action. The sheet swung sideways and Frank's left hip thumped against the doorframe. Natalie flinched as if they'd hurt him, and the sound – a meaty thud – made her guts lurch. That was her father they had just whacked into a doorframe like a piece of unwieldy furniture.

To avoid more such thumping, the two women adopted a shuffling gait as they moved into the communal hallway, trying to keep their elbows locked so the body didn't swing too much. Natalie's decisiveness crumbled and she was flooded with regret. This was surely a disrespectful and shameful thing to be doing to her dad but how could she reverse the decision? She couldn't insist they carry the body back to Gordana's bed. There was no choice now but to carry on.

When they reached Frank's door, they lowered the sheet to the floor so Natalie could fish the key out of her bag. That pause – which could only have been a few seconds – felt excruciatingly long. Natalie was panicky – what if one of the inhabitants of 1B or 1C chose this moment to head out the door for the day? She scrambled to think of the explanation she could offer curious neighbours but her brain was too jammed to function.

Nat and Gordana made brief eye contact to coordinate picking up the body again in unison in order to shuffle into the flat.

The moment they got inside and let the door thunk shut, the growling started. Frank's dog had stationed himself between the dining table and the sofa.

'Hi, Mack,' said Natalie in the perkiest voice she could manage.

But Mack wasn't interested in her. His eyes were fixed on Gordana, keeping up a low warning growl.

'It hates me,' said Gordana, terrified. 'It is because of this dog that me and Frank must always go to my unit.'

Always. So Frank and his neighbour having sex was not a once-only thing. Natalie remembered that Frank's neighbour Mirko worked nights as a security guard. Maybe the sex had been a regular event. Natalie shook the thought out of her head – she didn't want to envisage that right now.

Head low, shoulders flattened, the dog stalked closer to Frank's body and sniffed. Gordana shrieked and dropped her end of the fitted sheet.

'It's okay, Gordana.'

Natalie hustled Mack into the bathroom and shut him in. 'Good boy, Mack. You wait in there, mate.' He was a thirteen-year-old kelpie cross, black and tan with swatches of mottled grey. One eye was gone,

sewn shut, thanks to the Mack truck that had skittled him on the Hume
Highway. When Frank had taken in the damaged puppy, he'd named
him in recognition of the truck.

The two women carted Frank into the bedroom and lifted him
onto his own bed, then rearranged the bedding to look plausible.

'You should go back to your place,' said Natalie.

'Yes. Thank you,' said Gordana in her leaden tone and hurried
back across the hallway with the yellow sheets bundled in her arms.

Natalie perched gingerly on a bottom corner of the mattress. It
hit her that Frank Dennis as an entity was gone. She felt a rush of tenderness for the corpse lying there in the bed but the corpse seemed
to have very little connection to Frank himself. She'd heard people describe this experience – that when the spirit leaves, the body
becomes a meaningless shell.

What was wrong with Natalie that she wasn't crying? Her lovely
dad. She loved him. He was only in his sixties. This was terrible. Was it
the suddenness that left her stranded numbly in this moment? Or was
it the weirdness with Gordana that had thrown Natalie's responses off
the normal rails into some dry tearless ditch? Christ almighty, what
had she agreed to do? She'd just done something peculiar, possibly
immoral, certainly illegal. How could she ever explain to another person why she'd made that choice? She couldn't. She would never tell
anyone about moving the body.

Natalie rang Frank's GP and found herself able to lie quite fluently.
'Dad didn't answer his door. I let myself in and found him in his bed.'
The doctor arranged to come in an hour to issue a death certificate.

She tried to ring her brother, Nick, in Melbourne but he wasn't
picking up. It'd be better to contact him later rather than dump this
news on his voicemail.

She put off the job of ringing Judy, her mother. Nat couldn't bear
to hear any hint of judgement of Frank in her voice, couldn't risk that
Judy might slide one of her serrated comments into the conversation.
Not right now, when her dad was lying there unprotected.

Natalie closed the bedroom door, then let Mack out of the bathroom. He zigzagged through the flat, nosing around. Was he looking for Frank? Exorcising Gordana?

'Hey, Mack. Hey, gorgeous,' Natalie cooed and Mack came to her cheerfully. As she squatted down to give him a neck rub, it occurred to her that the dog might need a walk.

There was an hour until the doctor was due to arrive. Other calls could wait. It did feel weird to leave Frank alone in there but that was silly thinking.

Natalie took Mack to the closest spot – a small park where the ground was moist and the seats were mossy because the surrounding terrace houses kept out most of the sunlight. She let the lead go slack in her hand so the dog could wander and sniff.

Natalie had found her father dead in the neighbour's bed. Should she be suspicious? Television and crime fiction had trained everyone's minds to look for twists and intriguing explanations. But usually in real life – and surely in this case – the explanation was the banal and likely one: a man with known cardiac problems suffered a fatal heart attack during the hours sometime after sex. If there was any twist involved it was the fact that he had been having sex with an orange-haired, blunt-voiced woman like Gordana. That was twisted enough.

Natalie's sixty-five-year-old father – divorced, retired, mildly depressed, almost a hermit in his social habits – had probably been having frequent sex. Meanwhile Natalie – a thirty-five-year-old woman, not untouchably hideous, supposedly in her sexual prime – had not had sex for two years. She masturbated at night to get to sleep but for two years that had been it. She shuddered with disgust at herself – how could she think about masturbation when her father was freshly dead in the flat two hundred metres away? She shouldn't.

Instead, Natalie compiled a mental list of the jobs she should do. Ring everyone who would need to be rung. Organise the funeral. Sort out a home for Mack – with some loving person who didn't suffer from allergic asthma like Louis. Figure out the way to break the news about Grandpa Frank to Louis and prepare answers for his likely questions. Try to obliterate all memory of Dad in Gordana's bed. Try to have sex with another human being in the next twelve months.

Natalie suspended her list-making when she saw Mack do a poo. As she grabbed a plastic bag from her pocket, the rustle of the plastic triggered the thought: *Dad will never do this again. He'll never walk Mack in this park again. My dad's gone. I've lost my dad.*

The tears came. Big heaving sobs. Stupidly, she didn't have a tissue so she had to wipe her face on her sleeve. She cried loudly enough that people walking past glanced over. Mack nudged at her legs, curious but patient. She cried for a long time until the sobs turned into hiccups, then into little shuddery breaths and finally eased.

3

Sullivan's head was a great slab of volcanic rock. He was an Easter Island statue. An Easter Island statue with an almighty headache.

Sometime later – he had no measure of how long – his stone head felt hollowed out but still too weighty to lift. Inside his skull, the contents were soupy, unable to congeal into a thought, except to register that he was alive and he had a headache.

During the next phase, Sullivan became aware that his head was attached to a body lying on a bed but the limbs seemed unrelated to himself, the way his arm had felt being stitched up under local anaesthetic. He had needed those stitches after falling through his mate Tim's glass coffee table. (Tim had been very good about it, considering it was entirely the fault of Sullivan's drunken gyrations, several people having already steered Sully away from breakable items.)

As with the local anaesthetic, right now in this hospital bed, Sully was experiencing lack of proprioception – the sense of one's own body in space. If he could retrieve a word like proprioception, he probably hadn't fallen twenty-three storeys. What had happened on that rooftop? He rummaged around in his brain for a relevant memory but then sank back into unconsciousness again.

The next time Sullivan opened his eyes, he saw a nurse with freckled arms checking the drip attached to his hand. He followed the arms up to her face – creamy skin, sprinkled with caramel freckles, pale eyelashes and hair the colour of golden syrup. Lovely, as if she were made of ice-cream.

'Did I fall?' asked Sullivan, surprised to find he could utter audible words.

'You fell and hit your head,' answered the ice-cream nurse. She was Irish. 'You were found unconscious on the roof of the building.'

He'd fallen *on* the roof rather than off the roof. The guy in the stripy shirt might have found him on his next smoke break.

'Am I okay?'

'More or less,' she said. 'But you have a serious concussion. The doctors did a scan to check for head injury and they're keeping you here for observation.'

For a moment, Sullivan hoped that the doctors assumed he'd been up there for a cigarette and had taken an unexpected innocent tumble. But then the Irish nurse said, 'You're more okay than if you'd jumped.'

So the medical staff did realise he'd gone up to that rooftop to kill himself. Not surprising since there was a note in his wallet with instructions about disposal of his body, introduced by block letters: *I'M SORRY. Sullivan Moss.*

'How's the pain?' the nurse asked.

'Powerful.'

'I'll get the registrar to write you up something.'

A day later, when the clanging in Sully's head dulled to a bearable ache, he began to reconnect with his body again. His body was being looked after with such care and skill. Brain scans, analgesics, blood-pressure readings, clean white sheets smoothed across legs, charts with precise notes about every physical function. The drip was quietly but reliably delivering good things into his veins. An earnest young doctor tested Sullivan's reflexes and peered at his pupils. Senior doctors came and checked him over. And all the time, the luscious Irish woman and other nurses were flitting in and out, tending to this body with their capable hands. Was he worth all this attention and skill?

Sullivan regarded the shape of himself in the bed. Despite

twenty-odd years of his reckless attitude to personal health, this body still functioned more or less well. He had planned to smash it onto bitumen with whatever violent force a fall of one hundred and fifty metres generated. What a shame to destroy healthy working organs just because there was something wrong with the brain that was attached to them. It would have been a waste. A shameful waste. Would this be yet another thing to feel ashamed about?

Just as this thought threatened to wash over him and carry him away to a bad place again, the Irish nurse appeared at his bedside.

'Good morning, Sullivan Moss.' The skipping melody of her accent gave him a sudden stab of pleasure, even in his groggy state. 'How are you going with your waterworks?'

He was confused. 'Waterworks?'

'Pissing,' she explained. 'We need to be sure your bladder and kidneys are doing their job.'

And that was when Sully realised what he could do. He was a person with a torso full of functional organs, including two kidneys. Now highly trained people were taking good care of these organs he had been prepared to squander so thoughtlessly. There was no need to squander everything. People donated one of their kidneys to relatives as standard practice. Sullivan didn't happen to have a relative in need of his kidney, but it must be possible for doctors to find a stranger who could use it.

That was it. He would donate a kidney. He would be useful.

4

Juliet preferred to have an orgasm immediately before she and Tim fucked. Sometimes she would suck his cock for a while first, sometimes not. Tim had always loved going down on her but in the last few years Juliet preferred him to use the vibrator.

If there was a certain routine to the sex, that didn't bother Tim. After fifteen years together, a couple developed a kind of efficiency – knowing what each other liked, knowing what worked.

Tim had adored Juliet's body when she was fleshier, after the twins were born. When the twins started school, she threw herself into distance running, and now her body felt very different – sinewy, dense, as if she were packed tight inside a casing of muscle. But he enjoyed her body like this too, relished getting his hands on her.

He loved watching Juliet orgasm, her whole body taut and completely overtaken by the sensation. The instant after she came, she would yank Tim around on top of her.

Juliet had always enjoyed fucking and Tim loved that. Not just for the physical pleasure – although that was intense – but also because he felt he was connecting with her. He wanted to mash his body against hers as if they could truly bond that way.

As soon as Tim finished, Juliet slipped out of bed and into the bathroom. Originally, she had adopted the habit of having a quick wee to avoid post-coital cystitis. These days she stayed longer in the bathroom. Tim knew it was deliberate. Juliet was separating herself from him, reclaiming her body as hers alone, so that by the time she came back into the bedroom, any connection Tim felt from the sex was dissolved and flushed away. This morning, Juliet didn't get back into bed and she avoided eye contact.

Their bouts of carnal activity usually happened first thing in the morning. After a few hours of sleep, a modicum of innocence still seemed possible. In the evenings, there would be red wine and lacerating remarks and Juliet would sigh, each sigh poison-tipped – well, then the air between them would become far too noxious for sex to occur.

And anyway, the sex was rare now. Once every three weeks. Sometimes even less.

In the molten core of one of their more vicious arguments, Juliet had hissed: 'I only fuck you so you can't say I don't.' Tim pushed that out of his mind, kidding himself she didn't mean it. What else could he do?

He lay on the bed watching Juliet dress to go running. In January it was too hot to run except in the cool of the morning or evening. The time it took to have sex with him this morning had cost Juliet some of that precious exercise window and Tim knew that once she started sweating along the cliff-top jogging path, she would resent him for it ferociously.

She hauled on the Skins gear she liked to wear – black compression leggings and a shirt that packed her lean body into a tighter parcel.

Even when she dressed up, his wife favoured fitted stretchy garments – like stylish bandages. Last Christmas Tim overheard his sister commenting that Juliet looked like a 'piece of gristle in a very expensive dress'.

She ran long distances, almost every day. Tim was certainly not a slob – he jogged and played squash. He was a competitive person who liked to do things full bore. But his fitness regime was nothing like Juliet's running. She ran as if it were her job. As if something in the world would collapse or cease working if she stopped running. Maybe in her mind she was running away from him, from the twins, from this life that made her unhappy.

The occasions Tim heard Juliet sobbing in the garage were the worst. Feeling it was his fault his wife was so very, very unhappy.

As the sobbing continued, he would be hit by a wave of resentment. How was it his fault? He earned heaps of money for this family. He'd never been unfaithful. He had supported Juliet in every choice she'd made. If she wanted to work or not work, travel, have therapy, study, start another business – whatever she considered the right path – Tim would back her. But it seemed nothing would make her happy.

When the sobbing dragged on even longer, Tim's guts would twist, actively hating Juliet for being miserable. He despised her for making him feel responsible for her happiness and making him feel guilty that he couldn't fix it. By the time she came in from the garage with puffy eyes, he'd have built up such a reservoir of anger that he'd say something cruel. Then he'd feel bad about the words coming out of his mouth and he would hate her even more for turning him into a guy who said horrible things like that to his wife.

Apart from arguments, most of their interactions involved the making of arrangements. That was how it was this morning as Juliet put on her running shoes.

'Remember we're supposed to go to that dinner on Friday,' she said.

Tim nodded. 'Let me know what day you want your car in for a service.'

'I've made an appointment time with the school counsellor. Details are on the fridge.'

Before she left the room, Tim said, 'By the way, let's not use that pool company clown to fix the filter again. He fucked it last time.'

Juliet looked up and nodded. Then she was out the door.

Flaked out on the bed, he listened for any sounds from down the hallway. Should the twins be awake and getting ready for school? No, because it was still school holidays. He should have remembered that. Juliet would see it as evidence of guilt that it took him a minute to remember, a sign that he wasn't engaged enough with his kids.

Pia and Justin were fifteen now. They would mostly likely sleep until midday, then hang around shopping centres or cafes or some other private-school kid's opulent home until it was time to phone Juliet to pick them up.

The twins had been so great when they were tiny – he'd be intoxicated just watching them rumble on the carpet like lion cubs, looking up at Tim with their open little faces. But something had happened in the years since and now they felt nothing but contempt for their father. They appeared to hate Juliet and each other too but that was no consolation. They didn't seem like very nice people. Maybe they were pleasant, even loving, with their friends. Tim hoped so. He fervently hoped he and Juliet were not responsible for raising two people as selfish, sullen and passionless as Pia and Justin seemed to be.

At work, Tim Wozniak was seriously fucking good at his job. His section at the bank – he ran the bonds desk – was one of the most successful. By some measures, the most successful. He'd earned obscene amounts of money for a number of years and ridden the crises more adeptly than most.

At the end of the work day, the team ruled a line under the day's trades. 'Let's mark it.' There was a clear result – good or bad – like sport. In Tim's case the result was usually good because he knew what he was doing. If he or one of his traders made a mistake, he had an idea how to rectify it or recover from the setback.

Then he'd leave the office and drive home to this house where nothing he did was right and he had no idea how to rectify anything.

Tim's mobile rang on the bedside table and he saw *Astrid* on the caller ID. Astrid was the ex-wife of his ex-friend Sullivan. He'd seen her a month ago at Pete's funeral. Tim had always liked Astrid. Certainly, she could be bossy but she was smart and good-hearted.

Quite sexy in a schoolmistress way. Too good for Sullivan.

'Hi, Astrid,' said Tim. 'How are you?'

'Good thanks, Tim. Listen, a social worker from RPA Hospital just rang me. About Sullivan.'

'Oh yeah,' said Tim warily. 'I'm officially not interested in whatever mess Sully's got himself —'

'He tried to kill himself.'

Tim was silent for a moment. There was no way that piss-weak bastard would ever do anything as definitive as a real suicide. Even so . . .

'Shit.'

'He's okay, apparently,' Astrid explained. 'Concussion and minor injuries. But the hospital wants to make sure he has somewhere to stay when they discharge him.'

'Well, I assume he's still living in that rat-hole in Ashfield.'

'They seem to think he has nowhere to go. That's why they rang me. But I can't deal with him,' Astrid said firmly. Fair enough. The woman had already endured more crap from Sullivan than any person should. 'I thought you could —'

'No. No. No way. He can get fucked.'

Tim had bailed Sully out so many times – given him money, set him up for jobs. He might well have continued being the useless dickhead's benefactor indefinitely. But then when Pete got sick, Sully behaved like such a low-life that Tim couldn't stomach him any more. The day Sullivan failed to show up at Pete's funeral – their best mate's funeral – and then created an appalling scene at the wake, Tim ruled a line under their friendship.

'I understand why you feel like that, Tim,' said Astrid. 'I'm not sure what options Sullivan has left at this point.'

5

Sully had no clothes. His Hawaiian shirt had been encrusted with vomit when he was found on the rooftop and his jeans had torn on a jagged bit of pipe when he fell. Both garments had been chucked out in the emergency department. On the morning of the rooftop day, Sullivan had shoved the rest of his wardrobe in a charity bin outside a supermarket.

So now he had no choice but to pad down the corridor in a hospital gown and disposable paper undies. The drip was out so he didn't have to wheel a drip stand but they'd kept the cannula in his hand just in case.

Sullivan scanned the directory on the wall opposite the bank of lifts. *Renal Unit. Level Seven.* That was the place to start this quest. He stepped into the lift alongside a woman holding a bunch of cartoon-bright red gerberas. When the lift stopped on level seven, Sully flashed her a business-like smile, as if she would somehow appreciate that she had been travelling in the lift with a man on a selfless mission.

The glass doors to the renal unit opened directly onto a waiting area with rows of chairs covered with the kind of insipid pastel fabric favoured by hospitals. Two people were sitting there – a scrawny guy with his head tipped back and a puffy-faced woman flipping blankly through a magazine with the resignation of a person who'd become used to waiting. Is this what people with renal failure looked like?

Sullivan contemplated giving one of them his kidney, transforming their lives, seeing them skip out into the corridor with a surge of new energy and hope.

That image gave him the kick he needed to front up to the desk where a tall woman in a hospital uniform was talking on the phone, checking a computer screen.

As she finished her call and turned to face Sully, he was able to read her name badge. 'Diane Milton, Transplant Coordinator.' Perfect.

'Hello. I'd like to talk to someone about a kidney transplant,' he said, holding his voice steady in order to sound unquestionably sane.

Diane Milton was confused. 'Sorry, Mr —?'

'Moss. I was hoping to —'

'Are you a patient with this unit?' she asked, scrunching her eyes.

'Oh no, sorry, sorry.' Sully laughed and waggled his fingers at the hospital wristband, the blue gown. 'I can see why you'd think – no, I don't need a kidney. My kidneys work fine. I have a minor head injury – well, not even a head injury really. I just hit my – anyway, I'm here to *give* someone a kidney.'

'Oh, I see.'

'Sorry to turn up not properly dressed. Then again, since I'm already in a gown, cannula inserted and ready to go, you could whizz me straight into an operating theatre and whip out my kidney.'

'That's not how the process works.'

'Oh, I know. Joking.' Sullivan bunged on a winning smile. 'I just figured – since I'm in the building – we could get the process cracking.'

Diane took a breath, patient. 'Well, when someone is considering donating to a family member or friend, we usually ask —'

'There's no family or friend. I want my kidney to go to whoever needs it. To a stranger,' he explained, his volume rising as his enthusiasm for the plan solidified.

Sullivan saw Diane Milton flick her eyes past him to glance at the two people waiting on the pastel chairs. Was she worried they'd heard his offer and were about to lurch forward to claim Sullivan's kidney right now? Maybe fight over who would get it in an undignified fashion?

She pointedly lowered her voice, making it clear Sullivan should do the same.

'Look, Mr Moss, I'd suggest you concentrate on recovering from your head injury.'

'Are you allowed to donate one to a stranger?' asked Sullivan in his best indoor voice.

'Yes. It's less common but we do have cases where —'

'Great. Sign me up.'

'The best thing is if I get you some material to read,' she said.

Diane turned to a display rack of pamphlets and selected a few. Sully was six foot two but Diane, in heeled shoes, almost matched him. She was in her late fifties, handsome, with short, slate-grey hair and a large prow of bosom that she held upright, so when she sailed around behind the desk, there was something stately about her.

Diane collected together a wad of brochures and information sheets.

'Why don't you take these home to read?'

'Yes. Thanks,' said Sully. 'But believe me, whatever's in the pamphlets – I mean, I will read them of course – but either way, I definitely want to do this.'

Diane gave him a small cautious smile. 'We have an information day for living donors coming up, if you'd like to leave your contact details.' She swung a notepad round for Sully to fill out his details.

'Right. Terrific. I can put my email address,' he said. 'I don't have a residential address at the moment.'

'Before any serious consideration, we suggest people discuss the idea with their partner or family members.'

'No problem there,' Sully jumped in helpfully. 'I don't have a partner or any family to be bothered one way or the other.'

Diane scrutinised Sullivan for a moment then went on, doing her routine spiel in a calm tone. 'Well, you might need to discuss it with your employer, because for people who go ahead with this, it's a big commitment.'

'I'm not currently in employment.'

Diane nodded. It was dawning on Sullivan how he must look to her. A homeless, unemployed, unloved man, overweight, under-muscled, greasy-haired, pasty-skinned, his forehead scabbed and bruised from the fall, one eyeball stained red thanks to a burst blood vessel, wearing paper underwear, over-eager like a panting labra-dor, babbling at her about giving his kidney away to a stranger. Why would anyone accept an organ from such a man?

That thought paralysed Sullivan for a couple of seconds but then he pressed on. This was all he had. So he had to press on.

'I understand I may seem like a time-waster to you. I'm not a time-waster. Well, yes, look, I have been a time-waster in my life but I've reached a certain – a certain watershed. Anyway, this is something I'd like to do. To be useful to someone who needs this.'

It struck Sullivan that Diane Milton *knew* he'd sustained a con-cussion while preparing to commit suicide. Did she know? She couldn't know. And it was better not to tell her. In fact, it was crucial that he not mention the suicide part. They might not want a kidney contaminated by suicidal thoughts. He definitely wouldn't tell her that part.

But Diane was looking at Sullivan as if waiting for some further explanation. Controlling his mouth had never been Sully's strong suit.

'Oh, look, I should say that I had my recent fall while – well, when I was in the process of committing suicide.'

Diane nodded as if this were no more remarkable a piece of infor-mation than his age or occupation.

'Does that rule me out?' he asked.

He held his breath, feeling Diane's eyes on him, when a nurse called from a treatment room. 'Are you ready, Diane?'

Diane signalled 'one second' to the nurse, then turned back to Sullivan. 'I'm sorry, Mr Moss, I have to go.'

'Oh no, don't apologise. You go. You're busy. Important stuff to do. I'll get out of your way.'

She pushed the pamphlets across the counter into his hands and then nodded a goodbye, clearly never expecting to lay eyes on Sullivan Moss again.

On the way back down to his own ward, Sully felt dizzy, his legs feeble. He had to lean against the wall of the lift, holding tight to the wad of kidney pamphlets.

6

Natalie parked in the five-minute patient pick-up zone outside the hospital entrance but then turned off the ignition and sat in the driver's seat. She wasn't convinced being here was a good idea.

Her friend Astrid had been supportive in the days since Natalie's dad died. Astrid had arranged funerals before so she could advise Nat on the best way to go about it. She'd also offered her own bracing brand of get-on-with-it emotional reinforcement which could be helpful at the right moment.

Last night Astrid had phoned, unusually flustered, blurting about her ex-husband Sullivan. He'd attempted suicide – well, positioned himself on the top of a tall building with that intention – then tripped over and ended up with concussion. The hospital was discharging him today.

Sullivan had burned through his friend credit with everyone he'd ever met and no one would offer him a temporary bed. Even adjusting for Astrid's angry-ex-wife prejudice, it sounded pretty dire.

On the phone, Astrid had rattled off her proposal: her suicidal ex-husband should move into Natalie's dead father's flat to take care of the dog and house-sit until the property was sold. This idea struck Nat in the same way as Gordana's request to move Frank's body – unsettling and peculiar but the logic of it was clear. Natalie thought of herself as a practical person but these two women left her in the dust when it came to unsentimental solutions to awkward problems.

'Sullivan loves dogs,' Astrid had assured her. 'I'm sure he won't accidentally kill the dog.' Lord, was it likely he'd accidentally slaughter other living creatures?

The guy was a stranger to Natalie, a man with a history of boozing and general mismanagement of life. When she and Astrid had first become friends two years ago, they'd bonded over the fact that they had both been cheated on during their marriages. Now Astrid was suggesting her unfaithful ex-husband as a house-minder.

Natalie knew she was being railroaded into this arrangement by her friend. Astrid had a hearty way of bossing people into things and Nat often found herself manoeuvred into positions in which she felt mildly exploited. Was she foolish to invite a person like Sullivan Moss into her life even in a limited capacity?

Then again, it would be a relief to know Mack could stay in his old familiar home for a while until Natalie found him a new one. Her dad's flat had a comfortable bed and here was a person who needed a bed desperately. It was a matter of basic human decency. Frank himself had always been a soft-hearted man, and extending kindness to a stranger could count as a tribute to her dad.

Anyway, given Sullivan Moss's past flightiness, he probably wouldn't stay long. Soon enough, Nat would find a permanent home for the dog and she wouldn't be in such urgent need of a house-sitter. And she could always call a halt to the arrangement if it felt uncomfortable or proved problematic to have him in the flat. Yes, she could always turf the guy out if necessary.

Natalie pulled her keys out of the ignition and headed through the automatic doors. Astrid had shown her photos of Sullivan during the show-and-tell phase of initiating their friendship. In photos, he was always smiling, hair flopped over his face, rumpled as if he'd just been pulled out of a bag.

She scanned the foyer – past the anxious people with giant radiology envelopes and the anxious people with newborn baby capsules – until she spotted a man on his own, staring at the gift shop display window. Natalie recognised the profile and the dark hair from the photos. He was taller than she expected but the height was reduced by his boneless posture. As Astrid had described with worried disapproval, Sullivan was overweight, with a distinct belly and a chubby face. The clothes he was wearing didn't fit him, the trousers slightly too short and the shirt buttons straining over his paunch.

He looked harmless enough. Natalie strode up to him.

'Excuse me. Are you Sullivan?'

It was only when he turned that Nat saw the other side of his face – the bloodshot eye, the scabbed forehead, the yellowing bruise from cheekbone to hairline.

'Yes. I'm Sullivan. Are you Natalie?'

Natalie nodded and Sullivan did an awkward bow of acknowledgement. He was the kind of guy where you could still see the blue-eyed little boy inside the grown man's face. That might have been endearing when he was twenty-three. It was pretty sad at thirty-nine.

'I'm so sorry about your dad,' he said.

Many people had said those words to her in the last few days. Most had spoken sincerely but with that polite distance which allowed Natalie to absorb the condolences in a neutral way, with no chemical reaction in her. But something about the way Sullivan said the words took her by surprise, making her feel suddenly raw. She fought the urge to cry by pulling down the sides of her mouth and turned away to fiddle with her phone.

'Do you have a bag or anything?' she asked him.

'No. Just the clothes I stand in. Clothes the hospital donated to me. I've freed myself from the chains of materialism.'

Sullivan offered a jokey smile so Natalie responded with a small laugh. When a person was in as wretched a position as this man, you should laugh at any joke-shaped thing they said.

*

As they drove the short distance to Frank's flat, Natalie gave Sully a run-down about Mack and his routine, diet, foibles. At traffic lights, he could feel her sneaking glances at him.

Sullivan had noticed Natalie grimace and turn away when he said he was sorry about her father. He couldn't blame her. He could see, from her point of view, there was something faintly obscene about being offered condolences by a man who'd just tried to kill himself. *I'm sorry your dad's dead even though I have recently sought to be dead myself.*

Anyway, Astrid would surely have told Natalie enough for her to regard him with general disgust. Sullivan was used to bad press preceding him. It made it all the more remarkable that she was allowing him to stay in the flat.

Natalie parked outside the entrance to the apartment building – a modern place surrounded by Glebe terraces. As Sully followed her up the front steps past the mailboxes, his eye fell by chance on the point where her waist curved outwards to her hip. She was one of those women with real swelling hips. Natalie herself probably hated them, in that way so many women didn't appreciate their own loveliness. Sullivan found most female persons attractive but those round hips swinging up the steps in front of him were especially gorgeous, almost heart-stopping.

Sullivan was surprised to find himself having a libidinous thought, however mild. In the last few months, his libido had atrophied, apart from the occasional joyless wank. Was a possible reanimation of his groin a good thing? Maybe not. His sexual impulses had ended up causing people a lot of misery over the years.

As Natalie was unlocking Frank's flat, the door across the landing opened and there was a woman's voice. 'Hello.'

Sullivan turned with a polite smile ready on his face but when he saw the neighbour's radioactive orange hair, he made a strangled throat noise to avoid yelling out. The woman's hair was the colour of rust on the hull of a container ship.

Natalie was polite to the neighbour but without making eye con-tact. 'Hi. How are you?'

'How are *you*?' asked Gordana, squinting at her.

Natalie acted as if she hadn't heard the question. 'Gordana, this is Sullivan. He's going to be staying in Dad's flat for a while, looking after the dog.'

Sullivan lunged across to shake her hand. 'Pleased to meet you, Gordana.'

'Yes. Hello,' Gordana replied with a thumpingly flat intonation. 'I am here across the hall if you have questions about the building or you need any —'

'Thanks, Gordana.'

Sullivan noticed how awkward Natalie was with her. He tried to lighten the mood by flashing a smile at the woman. 'I'll be a good neighbour and keep the bagpipe-playing to a minimum.'

'What?' asked Gordana.

'He's joking. There are no bagpipes,' said Natalie as she hustled Sullivan away.

Inside her dad's apartment, Nat strode straight across the living room to open the sliding glass doors that led into the courtyard. The dog galloped in to greet her, his entire body squirming with joy.

'Hello, mate. Hello, beautiful,' she said, squatting down to rub Mack's chest. 'This is Sullivan. He's going to be looking after you for a while.'

'Hi, Mack,' said Sullivan, offering his hand for the dog to sniff.

Mack regarded the stranger with his one eye, darted forward for a quick sniff of the hand, then stepped backwards.

'Come on, Mack.' Natalie was embarrassed by his lack of welcome.

'He's wary,' said Sullivan. 'Probably wondering if I had something to do with your dad disappearing. Best if I play it cool and let him get used to me.'

The living room was filled with stuff from the house Natalie grew up in. Frank had taken his share of furniture from the property split and arranged the pieces in his divorced man's apartment to form a replica of her childhood home. The milk-coffee lounge suite, teak wall units, the marble-topped side table with its tizzy gold base, the framed prints positioned exactly as they had been years ago in the family home.

'Feel free to use everything here,' said Natalie. 'The telly and sound system are pretty straightforward.'

'Thanks. It's a really comfortable place,' said Sullivan. 'I'm very grateful.'

Nat avoided meeting Sullivan's gaze, which she knew would be dripping with a gratitude that would make her uncomfortable. Who was this man? Would he try to kill himself again? Might he self-immolate in her dad's lounge room? Was it painfully undignified for him to be here as a basketcase, dumped on his ex-wife's friend?

For the sake of Sullivan's dignity, she decided to play this encounter in a business-like way, moving briskly around the apartment, flicking doors open and shut like a hyperactive real-estate agent.

'So – uh – bathroom in here. Laundry. Kitchen. Oh yeah, the pantry.'

The shelves were full of tins, bags of rice, jars of olives, mustard, honey, six packets of a hardcore bran cereal.

'Please use all this stuff,' she said. 'No point wasting it.'

'Okay, thanks. I'm not too proud to eat charity sardines.'

Natalie tapped the freezer door. 'There are parcels of chicken necks and roo meat in here for Mack. Oh, yeah, I whacked some milk in the fridge so you've got something for the morning.'

'Great. Thanks,' said Sullivan. 'It's very thoughtful to buy fresh milk for a man straight out of hospital.'

Again, to avoid facing the full blast of his gratitude, Natalie resumed the brisk tour of the place.

'Okay, through here is the laughably small second bedroom,' she said, leading Sullivan to a boxy room where Frank had kept a desk, filing cabinet and rowing machine, now coated with dust.

She flung open the linen cupboard in the hallway. 'Help yourself to towels.'

She noticed Sullivan pause before giving a grim little nod.

'A dead person's towels – does that creep you out?' she ventured.

'No, no, that'd be . . .'

'I get that it could feel creepy,' she went on. 'You hop out of the shower and feel like you're wiping deadness over your skin.'

As Natalie and Sullivan both stared at the towels, she felt the urge to laugh. Rational human beings with such primitive thoughts sprouting in their minds.

'I could bring you some towels from my place,' Natalie offered.

'Oh Christ, no. You can't give in to voodoo. I'll handle it.'

Sullivan pulled a green towel from the cupboard and held it at arm's length as if it were a dangerous animal. Then he took a deep breath and buried his head in it, smearing the towel over his face and neck. When his face emerged from the towel, smiling, Natalie laughed.

'Main bedroom's in here.' Natalie marched into the bedroom and slid back the wardrobe doors. 'Plenty of wardrobe space.'

'Thanks. Not that I need any. I deposited the last of my clothes in a charity bin.'

'Oh. Right.' Natalie felt bad for drawing attention to the fact that he was empty-handed. 'Well, please take any of my father's clothes you want.'

'Oh . . . that wouldn't seem right,' said Sullivan.

'Look, no really – yes, please do. I was planning to haul everything to the Salvos anyway. If you take what fits and give away the rest, it would save me doing the sorting.'

'Well, if it would be useful to you . . .'

'It would,' said Natalie.

'I'll buy my own undies,' Sullivan said. 'Wouldn't feel right to wear your dad's undies.'

'I guess not.'

They smiled at each other. Natalie resisted the urge to ask him a thousand nosey questions by checking her watch.

'I'd better hurry,' she said. 'Have to pick up my son. There's a note on the fridge with my contact details. Oh – Astrid said you lost your mobile.'

'Yeah, I'll get another one soon,' Sullivan assured her.

'The landline's still connected for now. Also, Astrid said this belongs to you.'

Natalie handed Sullivan an envelope plump with cash. He'd withdrawn the balance of his bank account (four hundred and fifty bucks) on the day before the rooftop episode. He'd put the cash under Astrid's front door, meant as partial recompense for the money she had given him over the years.

Natalie found herself babbling. 'Will that money be enough for – well, I'm not sure what plans you have or . . .'

'I've got a few ideas, a few things in the works,' said Sullivan.

She saw the coating of sweat on his face, the skin doughy and almost grey. It felt wrong to look at it. She crouched to give the dog a farewell cuddle. 'Relax, Mack. Sullivan is not going to hurt you.'

'Thank you, Natalie. Thanks so much for this.'

'You don't have to keep saying thank you. You're helping me out by looking after Mack.'

'I promise you I won't top myself in your dad's flat.'

He widened his eyes in a jokey way as he said it, making Natalie laugh nervously. Then she stopped herself and held his gaze directly for the first time. 'Call me if you need to ask anything or if you – y'know . . .'

If y'know what? What did Natalie think she could offer the man? *If you feel like killing yourself again, call me and I'll give you a reason to live, even though I barely know you and am hardly a font of life-affirming wisdom myself?* Ridiculous.

Natalie did an odd truncated wave, an attempt at jaunty, then scooted out the door before she said anything else inadequate.

*

The instant Sullivan was alone in the flat, the energy leached out of his body and he flopped out on the brown sofa. Here he was in a place he'd been many times before – bludging off some good-hearted person, making feeble promises, bleating 'sorry' and 'thank you', bullshitting about having 'plans'.

The twenty-three storey jump had been designed to put an end to such shit coming out of his mouth. He did not have 'a few ideas'. He had one idea: the kidney thing. And even then, he was kidding himself. He'd read through the pamphlets. It was a daunting process. And there was no way they'd want his kidney.

Sullivan thought about Natalie, that lovely woman with her hips and her thoughtfulness about milk. That depressed him and the lethargy grew heavier until it became a leaden mass immobilising him on the sofa.

The dog padded out from the spare room but wouldn't venture any closer than the hallway. Mack eyed Sullivan with the deepest suspicion. Where was Frank? And who was this stranger lolling on the furniture? Sullivan was supposed to earn his accommodation here by being the dog minder but the dog was clearly unconvinced.

Frank had impressive shelves of DVDs – a few interesting ones from what Sullivan could see while flaked on the sofa. He ran his eye along the spines of the movies, doubting he could muster the decisiveness to choose one, until he reached what Frank had used as a book-end – a bottle of Glenfiddich, two-thirds full.

The imagined taste of the scotch filled Sullivan's mouth before he'd even formed a single thought about it. His whole body was aching. A nip would ease the tight braid of muscle along his shoulders. He'd obviously injured his neck and shoulders in the fall. And a drink would take the edge off the pain of those injuries.

Before he finished that line of thought, he was up off the couch, with the bottle in his hand. He glugged scotch into one of Frank's crystal glasses and then poured it down his throat. The alcohol fizzed through his brain cells mighty fast. Faster than usual? Hard to be certain. It certainly felt good, though, and he reached for the bottle again.

A shudder went through Sullivan, followed by a prickle of sweat, then a surge of nausea. He lurched across the hallway into the bathroom to throw up. He vomited up hospital roast beef and hospital custard and hospital tea.

Sullivan shivered on the bathroom floor, arms flopped on the toilet seat, legs bent under him on the cold tiles. Maybe alcohol and concussion were not a good mix.

The dog peered through the wedge of doorway, head tilted up to take in the unfamiliar smells. Sullivan was aware of Mack eyeballing him, judging him. When he croaked, 'Hey, Mack,' the dog retreated out of sight.

After several minutes, Sullivan was sure the urge to vomit had receded so there was no reason to stay on the floor cradling the toilet. But he was having trouble thinking of a reason why he should ever get up.

A large photo frame with a collage of family snapshots hung on the bathroom wall, in a spot where Frank would have been able to see it when he sat on the toilet. There were photos of Natalie as a child and a slightly younger fair-haired boy. Natalie was adorable as a little girl, earnest as an older girl, then cringing from the camera as a teenager.

Sullivan pictured Frank perched on the loo, looking at those pictures, proud of the two human beings he had created. Sullivan envied that. When he'd found out he had unviable sperm and couldn't father a child, he'd mostly felt bad for Astrid, guilty for wasting so many of her baby-making years with his hopeless-joke sperm – the situation aggravated by the fact that he hadn't been much chop as a partner in any other way either.

Now looking at luminous little Natalie and her brother, Sullivan felt a pang of sadness that he would never make a human being. It must be a spectacular experience, however terrifying. Then again, Sullivan wouldn't wish himself as a parent on any kid.

That thought, on top of the post-vomit queasiness, sent the familiar shame mechanism whirring in his belly.

He lay right down, with his face on the bathroom floor, hoping the chill of the tiles would shock him out of the miserable spiral. From down there, he could see there was a newspaper clipping in the top right-hand corner of Frank's photo collage.

Sullivan had to get up to read the yellowed fragment of newsprint. He could see enough to know that Frank Dennis had rescued a child from drowning at McMasters Beach.

Frank was a hero. He'd thrown his body into the surf and because of him, a kid, a stranger, was alive. It was such a clear worthy act you could pin on the back of your bathroom door for the rest of your life. Sullivan wished he could save a drowning child. But then he felt bad that this involved wishing a child to drown. And he wasn't that strong a swimmer anyway. Then again, if a child were ill with renal failure, he could possibly be of some use to them.

He pulled the kidney donation pamphlet out of his pocket. *How Do I Become A Donor?* Step one was *See Your GP*.

Without allowing himself time to think about it, Sullivan walked back into the living room, found a phone book, rang a medical centre and made an appointment to see a GP the next morning.

When Sully put the receiver down, he realised the phone lived on the same shelf of the wall unit as a bottle of Maker's Mark. The flat was booby-trapped to catch out persons of weak character. The bourbon bottle was furred with dust, seldom used. So obviously Frank himself had had some strength of character. That was why he could leave bottles of hard liquor lying about his living room.

Sullivan imagined the booze fizzing in his head again and it was an enticing thought, even so soon after vomiting. But then he pictured a stream of bourbon sliding down his gullet, soaking into his kidneys, making them soggy and unusable. Quickly, before he could change his mind, Sully tipped the Glenfiddich and the Maker's Mark down the kitchen sink. From now on, for the sake of his kidneys, he would have to go teetotal.

He fed Mack chicken necks and a scoop of dry food, according to Natalie's instructions, then left the dog in the courtyard to roam around the patch of grass and rectangles of low shrubs and make the most of the warm summer evening.

He found a tin of red kidney beans in the pantry and it gave him childish pleasure to contemplate a meaningful link between the human organ and its namesake bean. He made himself a bowl of food – mixing the red kidney beans with tuna and corn kernels. As Sullivan bit through the smooth skin into the starchy centre of each bean, it was satisfying to imagine them nourishing the two kidneys inside him.

He was mindful to leave a few bits of tuna and put the bowl on the floor for Mack. The dog came inside and ventured close to lick the bowl clean but then did his odd backward walking to reinstate the distance between himself and the stranger.

In the laundry, Sullivan found a hamper of Frank's unwashed clothes. He carried the hamper into the spare bedroom, which seemed to be the dog's refuge of choice, and tipped the clothes out to form a mound on the carpet. Within a few minutes, Mack slunk in there and burrowed his body a little way into the clothes, like a nest. Finally, the animal could relax.

When Sullivan lay down on Frank's bed for the night, Natalie's lovely hips swung into his mind but he didn't allow himself to pursue them. He wasn't worthy of fantasising about a woman like that. Instead, he focused on the kidney donation. He just concentrated all his attention on his kidney, nestled in his torso below his ribcage – he didn't know exactly where – until he could feel it tingling inside him.

Sullivan hadn't slept decently for so many years, he'd lost all measure of a solid night's rest. He spent the night dozing as usual, never losing himself utterly to deep sleep. At some point, Sully was aware of a damp nudge against his arm and realised the dog was sniffing him.

'Hello Mack,' he muttered and stroked the dog's ear.

Mack then flopped onto the carpet beside Sullivan in one crumpling action of his body, all the joints releasing in one go, with a relieved exhalation of breath.

In the morning, Sullivan flicked through the wardrobe and found a pair of jeans and a maroon button-up shirt that fit him. The dog stared at him, standing there in Frank's clothes.

'I'm sorry if this freaks you out, Mack. I don't have anything else.'

7

Tim stayed at work until almost midnight then jumped in the car and punched up the volume on the stereo. He drove across the Harbour Bridge, looped around North Sydney, back via the Harbour Tunnel, through the CBD and back across the harbour, six times over, hardly hearing the repeated beeps of the electronic tag through the blast of the music.

He'd made a playlist of the bands he used to see with Pete and Sully. The Mighty Reapers, the Backsliders, Screaming Jets, the Hippos, Jackie Orszaczky, as well as the big acts like Midnight Oil, AC/DC and Chisel. In the five weeks since Pete died, Tim had filled his head with that playlist at every opportunity.

The three of them – Tim, Pete, Sully – were best mates all through school. Tim was a competitive guy and he'd been drawn into plenty of swaggering male bluster at high school but it was never like that with Pete and Sully. Their bond had been more authentic than any friendship he'd ever found since. It was trickier to form friendships as an adult, with everyone pressured for time and the relationships always hedged around with issues of money and status.

Tim still sometimes scrolled through his phone to Pete's number before remembering he was gone. Okay, it wasn't as if they'd been hanging out together every week in recent years but the bond was always there, a touchstone for what friendship could mean, an archive

of the people they used to be, their authentic selves. Well, that was
how it was until Pete died and Sully wrecked what was left of their
friendship.

It was three days since Tim had heard about Sullivan's suicide
attempt, and he was trying not to worry about him. The one time he'd
reneged on his vow and dialled Sullivan's mobile, he heard the 'this
number is not connected' message. Just as fucking well. As far as Tim
was concerned, they were no longer connected.

Tim had paid extra for a top sound system in this car and at this
moment, halfway across the bridge, it was worth it. The windscreen,
the dashboard, the seat, everything was pulsing with the beat of the
music and that felt good. Or at least it felt strong and intense.

Tim remembered how intensely he used to experience things and
realised how much he'd let things shrivel, what a meagre amount of
emotional sustenance he expected to suck from his life, his marriage
being the prime example.

At the beginning it had been good between Juliet and him. Yes,
they had rushed into marriage too young – him twenty-four, her
twenty-two. Juliet had assumed the vomiting and tiredness were
thanks to the rotavirus going round her office, not realising she was
pregnant until she was eleven weeks gone. That only gave them a week
to make the abortion decision. They figured a baby would be fun.
None of their friends was anywhere near having kids and during the
pregnancy, they both relished feeling different and special. A curiosity
with added drama once they discovered it was twins.

When Pia and Justin ended up in the NICU for weeks, Tim and
Juliet had been so close, sitting together by the humidicribs, breathing in tandem as they willed their tiny, wrinkly offspring to breathe.
Or they'd operate as a tag-team, allowing each other to sleep, sharing the load with truly loving collaboration. You wouldn't wish to see
your babies gasping for breath in a humidicrib but to have that level of
closeness with your partner – Tim would like to have that again.

When they brought the kids home, it was overwhelming but they were in it together. They really had loved each other intensely. He was sure he remembered that.

Tim finished a final lap of the bridge and drove home. By the time he parked the car and crept inside Juliet was asleep or pretending to be.

The next morning, it was Tim's turn to pretend to be asleep. While his wife dressed to go running yet again, he kept his head bundled in the doona so she couldn't see him awake. He didn't feel up to fielding any barbs from her this morning.

Even now, hiding from Juliet, Tim craved some way to connect with her again. It struck him that her running gear was like a snake-skin on her sinuous body, matt black with red markings. Tim yearned for her to slide up onto the bed and wrap her snake body around him. At first it would be a firm embrace, then more forceful, until she was coiled around him like a boa constrictor squeezing a little more tightly every time he exhaled. Through her python skin, she would monitor his slowing heartbeat as she pressed the air out of his chest. When his heart stopped entirely, she would disconnect her jaws, open her mouth to one hundred and fifty degrees and swallow his still-warm body, in languid, patient gulps, consuming him whole. Then she would lie on the bed with him inside her like a huge pregnant belly and she would slowly digest him over weeks – no, months – until all of him had been broken down and absorbed into her tissues.

Tim realised that this wasn't the healthiest way for two people to connect.

Sullivan watched the transplant coordinator walk through the renal unit and felt her gaze land briefly on him. He must've looked familiar to her but Diane Milton couldn't place him now that he was wearing Frank's maroon shirt and jeans instead of a hospital gown.

Sullivan stood up and stepped into her path. 'Ms Milton. Hello.'

'Oh. Hello. Mr —'

'Moss. Man with spare kidney. You gave me pamphlets.'

'Yes. I remember.'

'I've just been to a GP and I'm in possession of a referral to a renal specialist. Now wondering what else I need to be doing.'

'Right. Well, we'd normally ask you to make an appointment.'

'Of course. Can I make an appointment now?'

Sullivan smiled, eager to appear compliant. Diane frowned at him but then said, 'Look, I've got a few minutes before – how about you come into my office.'

Before Sullivan had even got his bum onto the chair in Diane's office, he started talking, hoping to leapfrog over awkward preliminary questions. 'Please know I'm very committed to this idea. When I fronted up the other day, you thought I was an ambulant nut-bar.'

Diane was unfazed. 'When we first met you did seem unsettled, in the throes of some kind of crisis so I assumed —'

'You assumed you'd never see me again.'

Diane shrugged and nodded.

'And now you're thinking – why waste my time when this guy will obviously never follow through with the donor program.'

'Mr Moss, I learned long ago not to forecast how things will play out. It works better just to follow the steps of the process. The test results and the – well, the unpredictable factors – I let those things run their course and hope for the best outcome.'

Sullivan liked the way she spoke, frank, measured and solid. He was in safe hands. 'A process with steps sounds good.'

'Well,' said Diane, 'there are quite a number of steps.' Sullivan could hear she was using the rhythm of her words to impress upon him the steady pace of that process. 'We need to fill out some forms. The renal specialist will order some tests then we'll follow up on those.'

'I've been reading material online about living donors,' Sullivan jumped in. 'Especially when the donor isn't related to the recipient ... giving a kidney to a friend or whatever. You have those cases here, right?'

'We do. But donating to a stranger, altruistic donation, we

consider in its own special category. For this scenario, the case must be approved by our transplant committee and we require at least two consultations with a psychiatrist.'

'Oh . . . okay,' said Sullivan.

'And we need you to have the sessions several months apart.'

'Several months!' he said. 'I was hoping to do this faster. I'm not known for my patience. I'm powered by a dynamite combo of procrastination and impulsiveness.'

Sullivan tucked in his chin so he was looking up at Diane through the hair flopped across his blue eyes. This was a practised strategy: admit to an exaggerated jokey version of his real fault in order to cauterise disapproval. Diane stared back at him, unwavering and uncharmed. Clearly she was not a woman to be fooled by his tactics and that was surely a good thing.

She waited until Sullivan's boyish grin faded and he was facing her squarely, then she continued. 'You can choose your own psychiatrist. Or if you'd prefer, we have a list of psychiatrists who've worked regularly with this unit.'

Sullivan glanced at the page of names she offered him. 'Uh . . . yeah – look, there may be a money issue.'

Diane circled one of the names on the list. 'I know this doctor will waive his fees for someone considering altruistic donation.'

'Right. Great,' said Sullivan, taking the piece of paper. 'So just to reiterate, this process – me giving someone my kidney – could take months?'

'Nine months to a year,' she confirmed. 'And that's if you stick with it that far. Does that —'

'No, no, no,' interrupted Sullivan. 'I'm committed to this. Just want to be clear about what's involved.'

The fact that she clearly thought he wouldn't stick with it spurred Sullivan on. She wasn't hostile, just sceptical, and he had to respect that.

He liked the idea of Diane Milton sitting solidly in her office, with her sturdy bosom and her no-nonsense slate-grey hair and her measured process. He would show her. He would surprise Diane with his resolve.

Sullivan went straight downstairs to the hospital cafeteria. He stared at the food in the display cabinet, adjusting his neurones to this new timeframe. How would he make it through a whole year? He chose an apple over a chocolate croissant and felt good about that decision.

If this was going to take longer than envisaged, he would need a source of income. Sullivan had never been interested in money and was certainly not greedy for it. Of course obtaining some cash had always been necessary. In his recent downhill period, he had kept the focal length very short – enough money to survive and to buy something to drink for a couple of days at a time. Now he needed a sufficient income to support himself and his kidney for months, maybe a year.

He decided against signing on for the dole again. There had been some unpleasantness with Centrelink. But more importantly, 'dole recipient' wouldn't look good on his application to be a kidney donor. He must look like an upstanding citizen who was making a sober decision to hand over his upstanding kidney. That meant getting a job.

He spotted a freebie newspaper on one of the cafeteria tables and flicked to the jobs section at the back.

Forklift driver. Childcare worker with a Certificate III. Metal fabricator. A CNC operator, whatever that was. Most jobs required a special licence or accreditation or three years' experience (even to work as a sandwich-hand apparently). Every other job necessitated extreme youth. Sullivan had not been a 'junior' for a long time.

He'd done plenty of bar work but he figured working around alcohol should be avoided if he had any chance of sticking with the teetotal thing. He'd worked in a call centre once, flogging wine, like a lot of unemployed actors, but that place wouldn't have him back. Was there any job he was qualified to apply for? How did he get to the age of thirty-nine with so few employable skills?

Sullivan was one of the smart kids at school. When Tim, Sully and Pete were best mates in high school, Tim was known as the maths brainiac, Sullivan staked out the territory as 'good with words' and Pete seemed to be effortlessly talented at most things. But he was such a decent, humble guy that no one hated him for it.

Sully skated through school on raw intelligence and luck but university didn't go so well. He started out doing a psychology major but then baulked at the requisite statistics subjects. Tim tried to help him with the stats work but that many numbers made Sully's brain hurt. He enrolled then withdrew from more courses than he ever passed – history, anthropology, political science, plus a few stray experiments with marketing and linguistics.

Sully told his friends he was only enrolled at uni as a means to focus on student theatre and playing in bands but the truth was he didn't do much of that either. A mate would be going on a trip to some intriguing country so Sully would quit the band/play/student newspaper he had committed to, empty his bank account and head off travelling.

Surviving on bar jobs, he travelled and messed around at uni until he was twenty-four and even then, when he wandered off the campus for good, he had no degree. By that time, most of his friends were beavering away at whatever career they were pursuing. Tim was a hot trader at the bank, Pete a medical intern.

In his twenties, Sullivan was trying – sort of – to be an actor. He was seen for some auditions (he had an appealing head shot) and did the bittiest of bit parts on TV. No one would accuse him of being dedicated to his craft. He never put any effort into studying or improving his acting. Mates would ask him to be in a co-op theatre production or a no-budget film because he was fun to have around. But then they'd be disappointed by how unreliable he was. After a while, people stopped asking.

By his late twenties, he was putting on weight. It was the beer mostly. He was too pudgy in the face to be considered for hot-guy roles any more but not fat enough to be cast as the 'fat guy'. He wasn't ginger or funny-looking or menacing or any specialist physical type that might have got him cast as a henchman or a butt of jokes. He was just an overweight, unfit, formerly good-looking, not-very-good actor.

He also kidded himself he was pursuing music. Some musician mates asked him to join their band, Doctor Smith and the Open Wound, as keyboard player. There was something about Sully in those days that made people think he was this talented guy. In reality, he was no good at keyboards and could only manage a basic sequence of chords.

When Doctor Smith and the Open Wound started being paid for gigs, the bass player resented sharing the small gig fee with Sullivan because he never showed up for rehearsal and couldn't play for shit. When the band broke up, the other musicians quietly re-formed as Bonesaw without Sully. He didn't blame them. He genuinely wished them well.

Sullivan let the acting notion die, formally, a few months after he'd filmed a guest role in a hospital TV series. He was working in a pub when his episode came on the TV set mounted on the wall across from the bar. Unfortunately for Sullivan, he was sober – not long out of bed – as he watched his performance. Sober enough to realise that even as Drunk Guy he was unconvincing.

He strolled into his acting agent's office and said, 'Please don't go to any trouble on my account any more.' The women in the agency were really sweet about it. They liked Sully. People generally did.

A couple of years later, and with Astrid's fervent support, he decided photography was the go. She lent him the money to buy an expensive camera. Sully's plan was to do the head shots for his actor friends and take photos at gigs that his musician mates could use for promos. Trouble was, his photos weren't much good. When the camera got nicked from the back seat of the car, Sullivan didn't bother replacing it.

The truth was, Sullivan was never that passionate about being an actor or a musician or an anything. Other people assumed he was and so they cut him the slack to 'pursue his dream' while in fact he was simply being slack. He enjoyed being around the people in the music and theatre and indie film worlds. They were all young with heaps of time to find their way. There was a lot of rhetoric about 'operating outside the mainstream' and being unsuccessful could be regarded as a badge of honour.

Sullivan sailed along on that windy talk and used it to avoid being a grown-up until well into his thirties. Then suddenly – it felt sudden to him – everyone had moved on. Most people had either made it or shifted sideways into related employment or taken other kinds of real jobs. They were living solid adult lives, most of them anyway.

Sullivan swerved into a period of uncharacteristic anger. He felt ripped off by the lie that there was all the time in the world. The truth was there had never been a lot of time. One minute you were twenty-three, the next minute you were thirty-two and fucked. It turned out there had always been a tiny window to construct a functional life and Sully had missed it.

It was around this time that the drinking got out of hand. Frontiers like 'no major daytime drinking' and 'no drinking alone' were crossed so often the lines were eventually rubbed out.

In the hospital cafeteria, Sullivan gnawed the apple right down to the core, fighting off a formidable urge to down a beer.

Sully looked at the empty glass with the lacy dried remains of beer coating the inside and could hardly remember drinking it. No, that was a cop-out. If he chose to, he could remember walking round the corner from the hospital to this pub, fishing out the coins to pay and then drinking it. One beer had seemed like a reasonable consolation on a hot day.

Sullivan drank two more, letting his gaze wander vaguely across the bank of TV screens showing cricket and horseracing. There was an elusive balance – a certain amount of alcohol, some visual distraction, no demands – where the mind could fall into a trance, a faintly miserable stupor but not spiked with any specific disturbing thoughts.

When Sully first walked into the pub, it was almost empty – just a handful of single blokes nursing beers, scanning form guides, watching the TV. This was a familiar sight. These were the people who were free to sit in a pub at four-thirty on a Tuesday afternoon.

It was only when the place started to fill up with clusters of after-work drinkers that Sullivan realised it was six-thirty. He'd been sitting there for two hours. There was something cheering about the lively chatter of the strangers around him. Maybe he should stay and settle in for a night of it. But then – shit . . . Mack.

Sully slid off the stool and headed out into the street. He'd planned to be away from the flat for only an hour but had forgotten about the dog who was locked inside without food.

By the time Sullivan made it back to Frank's there was an unmistakably desperate look on Mack's face. The dog shot out into the yard and cocked his leg, releasing a stream of piss that went on for a considerable time, his jaw slack and his one eye glazed over.

'I bet that's a relief, mate,' said Sully.

He took the food bowl outside and as he watched Mack wolf down the chicken and kibble, felt awful. It wasn't as if the dog had been about to die but the point was Sullivan had forgotten he existed. He'd forgotten that a living creature depended on him for its survival.

'Sorry, Mack,' said Sullivan and the dog, now with an empty bladder and full belly, trotted over for a pat.

8

The best moment in Natalie's day was three o'clock pick-up time at the school gate. With her eight-year-old son Louis, she would walk the fifteen minutes from school to the house – sometimes just the two of them, sometimes with one of Louis' friends. Louis would talk all the way home and Natalie inhaled every word, as the excited, outraged or amused thoughts tumbled out of him.

Natalie paid a price for the privilege of these afternoons with Louis – they were only possible because of the unwieldy construction of her life.

As producer of a breakfast radio show, she needed to be at the studio by four-thirty a.m. Natalie had trained her body to sleep in two segments. After work, she napped from midday until two p.m., waking in time for the school pick-up. Then she went back to bed from ten p.m. until three-thirty a.m. The split-shift sleeping wasn't so bad. When she'd first returned from Kuala Lumpur in need of an income, she was lucky to land a great job like this on the ABC's Sydney station. The weird hours were a plus since she was more available to Louis than a regular job would allow. She owed it to him – since her son's life had been disrupted and moved so far away from his father.

Yes, she could handle the sleep stuff. The truly costly compromise was Natalie's decision to live with her mother, Judy. Someone needed to be at home with Louis when Natalie left the house before dawn and someone needed to drop him at school. The only way to manage that was by moving in to her mother's house. What was supposed to be a temporary arrangement had been going on for almost two years.

On the walk home today, Louis was more subdued than usual. Natalie could feel him sneaking looks at her every few minutes. He had been checking on her like this all week, since Frank died.

Frank had done a good job of being fatherly to Louis, showing up at every soccer game and school concert, organising movie outings, happy to discuss Louis' obsessions with him at earnest length (recently it was jungle survival techniques).

Louis' grief over losing Frank was intense, straightforward and effusive. He sobbed, demanded explanations, spoke in great rolling waves about what a wonderful man his grandfather was until the tears would overtake him again. Natalie had been ready for this response, however painful it was to watch. She had not been ready for Louis' anxiety about her.

The night after Frank died, Louis woke up, padded along the hallway to Natalie's room and found her having a weep, snotty and gulping for breath. Louis had never seen his mother cry like this. Now he'd taken on the duty of watching over her. Natalie felt obliged to be robust around him so this duty wouldn't weigh too heavily on his flimsy shoulders.

When they reached the house, Louis galloped up the steps to open the front door with his own key. He felt more at home in Judy's place than Natalie ever would. At least it was a nicer house, full of nicer things than Natalie could have afforded.

She made tea while Louis prepared himself an after-school snack – a dinner plate arranged with cheese slices, a small mound of sultanas, two shortbread biscuits and a whole red capsicum, which he chomped through like an apple.

'Do you want to help me with the photos?' Natalie asked. 'You don't have to if you don't want to.'

'I want to definitely,' he said.

Natalie was choosing and scanning a sequence of photographs for Frank's funeral tomorrow. She spread the snapshots out on the dining room table. Meanwhile Louis went to the stationery stash in his desk to fetch a packet of tiny Post-its.

'We can use these to write numbers on the photos in the right order,' he explained. 'Then we can swap the Post-its around if we change our minds.'

'Good plan.'

Louis loved stationery. Sometimes, on a Sunday, when being in this house with Judy would press so heavily on Natalie that her lungs could barely inflate, she would suggest they head out to Officeworks. Louis was always up for a trip to Officeworks. The two of them would take their time, wheeling a trolley along the aisles, Louis enthusing over the computer and electronic stuff but saving his most reverent attention for the shelves of file-card systems, clips and pens.

Louis enjoyed laying out his grandfather's life as a photographic storyboard. Frank as a little kid on a bike. As a teenager in cricket whites. In mining gear during the years he worked in Mount Isa to save money for university. At some uni pub, holding up a huge tankard of beer at a table of equally beaming young men. As a scrubbed, proud newspaper cadet holding up the edition in which his first piece was printed. On a beach with his fiancée Judy – Frank looking chuffed, Judy posed and conscious of how she looked in her costume. Formal wedding portraits. Snaps holding his two children and then cradling Louis himself as a small baby. Frank's happiness radiated out from those images. There was a range of photos with colleagues at the newspaper where he worked as a journo and then as a sub-editor until he was retrenched.

None of the pictures triggered any fresh distress in Louis until the last few – shots of Frank with his dog Mack.

'Poor Mack,' murmured Louis, his throat tight. 'Wish he could come and live with us. My stupid dumb stupid asthma.'

'You can't help being allergic to him,' said Natalie. They'd been over this several times already.

'Who's going to look after him?'

'I'll find someone fantastic. And for now there's that guy Sullivan. Mack really likes him.'

From the next room, they heard the bong of an incoming Skype call and Louis skated across the hallway floor on his socked feet to reach the computer. He had messaged his father two days previously, requesting a chat. Brendan was finally responding to the call.

Natalie stayed in the dining room and tried to concentrate on the photos. She wasn't close enough to hear what Louis was saying but she could discern the rhythm of his breathing.

Louis' asthma had improved a little once they left the polluted air of Kuala Lumpur but he still used Flixotide every day and a Ventolin puffer when he needed it. There was a portion of Natalie's brain always on alert for any wheeze or laboured breath.

She was also distracted by the sound of Brendan's voice punctuating the flurries of talk from Louis. The voice of a man she had thought she would be with for the rest of her life.

Natalie and Brendan had been together only a few months when he was offered a job in Kuala Lumpur. Pushed to make a decision about the seriousness of their relationship, they got married.

At the time, Natalie was working as a producer on the drive-time show at the Sydney ABC station. She'd started doing regular segments chatting on-air with the presenter and had talked her way into one week as summer fill-in presenter of the morning program. She was well-placed, doing nicely for twenty-six. It seemed a reasonable choice to give up that perch in Sydney temporarily to head off for an adventure in Kuala Lumpur and a commitment to Brendan.

Natalie had wrongly assumed she could get radio work in KL. She ended up teaching English language classes, doing scraps of freelance journalism, having a baby and then two miscarriages. She travelled around the region at first but then increasingly less. She enjoyed being a mother. She avoided tracking the fact that she and Brendan were having less sex and fewer conversations of any significance. She tried not to think about whether she was lonely, bored and had made the wrong decision.

Then, when Louis was five, Brendan announced he was in love with someone else who was already pregnant to him. Some months after that, Natalie flew back to Sydney with Louis.

Father and son skyped once a week but in truth Brendan wasn't that engaged with Louis. He was sweet with him, but like an affectionate uncle. This child's wellbeing wasn't a primal thing for him as it was for Natalie.

Louis finished the Skype session, came back into the dining room and was helping make the final selection of photos when Natalie's mother arrived home.

'Hi, Nana! We're in here,' Louis called out.

Judy came to the doorway of the dining room. She was sixty-one, short but always in high heels and resolutely trim, having maintained an austere diet her entire post-puberty life. Her hair was dyed a non-colour of ashy-blonde grey, cut into a jaw-length bob.

She ran the human resources department for a chain of home-ware stores. This involved managing a cohort of young and often scatty employees. For someone with as low an opinion of human behaviour as Judy, this job suited her perfectly. Natalie always set aside a measure of sympathy for the people forced to work with her mother.

While Judy cast her eyes over the photos laid out on the table, Natalie held her breath. She could hear the disparaging thoughts clunking around in her mother's brain – Judy was doubtless finding fault with Natalie's funeral arrangements or taking the opportunity to restate what an idiotic disappointment of a husband Frank Dennis had been.

In fact, Judy controlled her tongue surprisingly well and simply indulged herself with: 'That dog.' She flicked her fingers at the photos of Mack.

Judy would never have a dog in the house. She considered pet-owning a dirty and perverse choice, akin to inviting livestock to live inside one's home.

'Why do some people have this infantile need to believe they have a meaningful relationship with a dog?' Judy wondered.

Louis didn't understand 'infantile' but he grasped Judy's tone and took her on. 'I saw a history show on Discovery Channel about how dogs were really important for humans – the prehistoric humans. Dogs helped them to hunt and be organised and other stuff.'

That shut Judy up. She couldn't contradict him now without being seen to discourage Louis' laudable interest in prehistory. Did Louis knowingly snooker his grandmother or was it just an accident? Either way, Louis was better at handling Judy than Natalie would ever be.

Judy waited until Louis had gone to bed to reassert herself. As Natalie was cleaning up the kitchen, she felt her mother's eyes on her.

'Do you think it's a sensible idea to rope Louis into this funeral quite so much?' asked Judy. 'I'm not convinced children should go to funerals at all, let alone help to stage-manage them. I came home to the sight of your eight-year-old sifting through photos of his barely cold grandfather for a crematorium slideshow. The child was talking about coffins and funeral music at the dinner table.'

'Well, I think —'

'It's surely damaging from a psychological point of view. It's morbid. It's a mistake.'

'I'm being careful, keeping an eye on how Louis is coping with —'

'You have to keep an eye on how this is affecting him.'

'I am. But so far I think the ritual is helping him handle it. He was very close to his grandfather and it's good for him to feel like he's honouring Grandpa and not being shut out of some grown-up process.'

'Well, Louis certainly relied on Frank as his father figure once you dragged him away from his real father – whatever Brendan's shortcomings.'

Natalie took a steadying breath. If she bit back on that one, she would invite a familiar spiel from Judy about the foolishness of following Brendan to Kuala Lumpur in the first place and the stupidity of allowing herself to be impregnated by a man anyone could tell was an unfaithful, emotionally stunted bastard who'd never really loved her.

Instead, Natalie said, 'Of course I'm worried the funeral might be a distressing experience for Louis and if I think he's —'

'Oh, he has to be there,' said Judy executing one of her trademark changes of tack. 'There are good reasons these rituals have existed for thousands of years. Don't imagine shielding your child from the reality of death is doing him any favours. Really, Natalie, you'd be a fool to cottonwool Louis through this. It's like the asthma business. You've let him get dependent on that asthma huffer and that's doing him no favours.'

This was often how their exchanges would run: Judy would initially take up a contrary position, painting Natalie's opinion/decision/taste as ridiculous. If Nat unpacked the reasons for her choice, Judy would loop back to co-opt Natalie's position as her own, then incorporate other evidence of her daughter's mistakes to prove her thorough-going foolishness. Natalie cursed herself for allowing Judy to draw her into this infuriating circuit.

Tonight, luckily, Nat had to finish writing Frank's eulogy so there was an excuse to retreat to her bedroom early. She sat up in bed with the laptop resting on a pillow and read over the draft of the speech. She stressed the achievements and joys of Frank's life. She didn't point out his professional blows, sense of failure, wretched marriage with Judy, stilted relationship with his son Nick, the shrivelled shape of his final years.

From what Natalie could observe, by middle age, every person's life had rolled some distance downhill, even if it was a very gentle slope, coming to rest at a place of disappointment. Some spheres of an individual's life might have gone spectacularly well but there would always be an obstinate slab of disappointment in another department – a stalled career, inability to have kids, a dismal marriage, whatever.

By the age of thirty-five Natalie had already made so many bad choices – all her major boyfriends, her husband, the move overseas, her current situation. She'd rolled downhill and got herself wedged in a disappointing corner. She wished she had talked to Frank about whether the phenomenon felt that way to him and if it had, whether he'd found some consolation.

Natalie amused herself by writing an extra paragraph in the eulogy.

Frank found comfort in an unlikely sexual liaison with his Croatian neighbour Gordana Dadic. (Pause to seek Gordana out in the chapel and acknowledge her with a smile.) *Thank you, Gordana, for the unexpected delight you brought Dad in his final months.*

She hit delete.

Natalie would've enjoyed telling Frank the story: two women moving a dead man, swinging in a fitted sheet, to avoid scandal and distress. Her dad had always appreciated a weird story.

9

Sullivan caught a train and bus to the Northern Suburbs Crematorium then walked up the tree-lined avenue to the chapel assigned to Frank Dennis's memorial service. Sully had avoided funerals his entire life but he had travelled to this place once before, for his mother's service.

He kept what he judged was a respectful distance from the mourners gathering outside. He wondered if he should be wearing a suit jacket but then saw the men in suits sweating uncomfortably in the summer heat and figured he was better off as he was.

Sully wandered round the corner into the gardens, which struck him as lovely in a way he hadn't appreciated before. Something about the combination of its formality – conifers pruned into neat shapes and precise Italian-style plantings – with the natural jumble of foliage and flowers spilling over the low stone walls was deeply calming. He envied the crematorium gardeners. That must be a fulfilling job – maintaining a beautiful consoling garden for grieving people. Sullivan regretted that he had neither the skill nor the patience for gardening.

He was considering slipping inside the chapel in an unobtrusive way when he spotted his ex-wife getting out of a Subaru in the car park. He ducked behind a person-shaped conifer.

It hadn't occurred to him that Astrid would be there but it should have. She was Natalie's friend and the sort of robustly kind person who attended the funeral of a friend's parent.

From behind the conifer, Sullivan watched his ex-wife help her current husband out of the passenger side. Grahame Linney was a children's fantasy author, successful enough to make a living. Bookshops devoted a substantial chunk of shelf space to his various fantasy series, with their eyeball-assaulting iridescent covers.

Astrid was a school librarian and had met Grahame Linney two years ago at a writers' festival when she queued up to have library books signed. They married three months later, the day after her divorce from Sullivan was finalised. Astrid had always been a decisive person.

Astrid helped Grahame swing out of the car seat and steady himself with a cane. He was considerably older than her – the guy was fifty-four – and not long before their book-signing/romantic encounter, he had been diagnosed with late-onset multiple sclerosis.

As Grahame moved slowly out of the car park, Sullivan noticed the way Astrid reined in her natural stride to match her husband's pace. The guy was lucky to have Astrid for many reasons, including the fact that her sturdy legs and strong shoulders would come in handy in the years ahead.

Closer to the chapel, Astrid dropped her sunglasses and when she bent to pick them up, Sullivan found himself imagining her body inside her clothes. He had been allowed intimate access to that body for some years and his hands could remember the texture of her skin, the shape of her thighs, the lovely soft spongy weight of her breasts. And now her bits and all that gorgeous skin would forever be inside clothes and inaccessible to him.

At university, Astrid wasn't considered pretty – she had an emphatic nose and little pouchy bags under her eyes, especially when tired – plus she was too tall and strapping to be one of the delicate creatures so many guys seemed to favour. But for Sullivan she stood out straight away, with her milky skin (she resolutely avoided sun), green eyes, thick coil of dusty-blonde hair and assertive manner.

After a gap year teaching English in Korea, Astrid arrived at university as a nineteen-year-old virgin and determined to remedy that. At her first orientation week bar session, she selected twenty-year-old Sullivan and escorted him back to her share house to participate in her deflowering.

Astrid had done her reading – she was a big believer in research – and had a mental list of sexual positions and activities she was keen to try. She was energetic and responsive and there were no complaints from Sullivan.

Astrid had sex with him on a number of occasions before explaining with no-nonsense briskness that she needed to move on to other young men because her sexual self-education required a certain amount of diversity. Sullivan understood this policy and was hardly a candidate for monogamy anyway.

Over the years Sullivan would run into Astrid when their social circles intersected and he never stopped liking her. He respected the fact that she was unapologetically unfashionable in all her choices. Her clothing was dowdy to an almost perverse degree and her attitude was scathing about anything she considered pretentious. She held many firm, well-meaning opinions about how her friends should run their lives.

Astrid hit another self-designated milestone – turning thirty – the week before she and Sullivan happened to attend the same party. That night, she selected him to be her baby-making partner. At the time, aged thirty-one, Sullivan still looked reasonable and Astrid could imagine he was just a late bloomer, vibrating with potential, sure to blossom with the right care. Astrid's judgement was distorted by her doubt-free turn of mind and general determination – she regarded him as solid genetic stock allowed to go to seed, a bargain in slightly battered packaging that she was canny enough to spot.

She took Sullivan on as a renovation project – bossing him, attempting to give him focus. She failed at that. She also failed at her other project: using Sullivan as a sire. Neither failure was Astrid's fault. He was the one with the defective character and the dud sperm.

Sullivan had loved Astrid. But probably no more than he'd loved quite a few other women.

When Astrid went inside the chapel, Sullivan stepped out from behind the conifer just as Natalie was approaching the garden. The instant she saw him, she jerked with fright.

'Sullivan,' said Natalie. 'Hello. Sorry if I looked like a startled rabbit. I saw that shirt out of the corner of my eye and I felt – well, my stomach lurched a bit.'

Sullivan was wearing charcoal suit pants and a teal shirt he'd borrowed from Frank's wardrobe.

'Ah. Sorry. I didn't think . . .'

'Don't worry. It's okay. It's good,' she said, smiling. 'And kind of you to come.'

Natalie had come round to the flat two days before, searching for family photos. They'd chatted briefly and she mentioned the funeral, careful to make clear he was not obliged to come. But Sullivan did feel obliged to pay his respects to Frank Dennis, under the circumstances.

'How's Mack going?' she asked.

'Great. He still searches the flat for your dad but generally he's in good form.'

Just then a severe-looking woman and a boy came over to join Natalie. Sullivan recognised Louis from the photos around Frank's place. Natalie introduced her son and her mother.

Sullivan felt Judy's eyes like uncharitable scanners tracking him up and down.

'Oh, so this is the one living in your father's flat,' she said. 'Wearing your father's clothes too. It's efficient, I suppose – a bit like those scavenger birds that go in after something has died in the wild.'

The open rudeness took Sullivan's breath away. At the same time, he was impressed. Judy herself had used an analogy from the animal kingdom and now Sullivan was recalling wildlife documentaries (a hangover favourite). He'd always been mesmerised by footage of skilful predators in action on the savannah or the efficiency of venomous creatures in the jungle. A person like Judy – someone who truly did not care if people disliked her – had the impressiveness of nature's ruthless predators. Then he noticed Natalie wince apologetically in his direction, so pained by her mother's offensiveness that Sullivan felt bad for her.

'For God's sake, Natalie, what are you wearing?' Judy took a step back and scrutinised Natalie's outfit. 'You look Amish on your bottom half and like something out of a French bordello on your top half.'

Natalie was wearing an ankle-length, tiered white cotton skirt, conceivably seen as Amish. Her silk top had a lush retro floral pattern, which presumably made Judy think of a bordello. Sullivan thought Natalie looked great.

'I like Mum's funeral clothes,' said Louis. 'She went shopping for an outfit Grandpa Frank would've liked.'

Louis held his grandmother's gaze to reinforce his defence of the wardrobe choice. Judy jiggled her head in a gesture that conveyed, 'I'll let it drop but I'm still right.'

Louis' sticking up for his mother was remarkable. Sullivan wouldn't have had the guts to challenge a scary creature like Judy when he was eight. Not even now.

The awkward silence was broken when Natalie spotted an escape route. 'Oh look, there's Uncle Nick,' she said.

'Thank Christ. Nick!' called out Judy, and barged past Sullivan to greet her son.

Natalie flicked an apologetic smile to Sullivan and hustled Louis over to join his uncle.

Inside the crematorium chapel, Sullivan chose a seat in the back row. He tried not to register the huge amount of sorrow that must have permeated this place year after year. The walls, the chairs, the air he was breathing – everything was coated in the residue of all that sadness. Sullivan had never felt at ease in the presence of other people's pain. He was good company when someone was happy or bored or off their face but sitting with a person in pain, Sully knew he had no aptitude for that.

A bright smudge of orange two rows in front alerted him to Gordana's presence. Next to her, he could see the blockish shape of her husband, Mirko, in his security guard uniform. Sullivan had introduced himself in the foyer that morning as Mirko was arriving home from overnight shift. What kind neighbours Gordana and her husband must be to come to Frank's funeral.

Frank had been an atheist so it was an entirely secular ceremony. After the funeral celebrant spoke, there was a presentation of family photos, during which Louis played a piece on the cello. The way Louis scrunched his mouth in concentration as he sawed away at the cello made Sullivan like him even more than when he'd seen him stand up to his grandmother.

Natalie delivered the eulogy. Sullivan wished someone would speak with a small portion of such love and respect at his funeral but didn't kid himself that would ever happen. He decided to tune out the content of the eulogy, closing his eyes to focus on the warm, deep tones of Natalie's voice. He wished he could describe her voice using precise language, like the subtle flavour notes on a wine bottle. A person who had drunk wine with an attentive palate would be able to do that.

The last part of the service was a small ritual in which family and anyone else who wished could walk up, take a rose from a basket and place it on the coffin as a final farewell. Sullivan didn't even consider going up, since he'd never met Frank Dennis and wearing the deceased's clothes in such a moment might seem disrespectful.

Natalie held Louis' hand as they both picked up a rose. Approaching the coffin, Louis started to cry, suddenly looking like a very little kid. Sullivan couldn't see Natalie's face but he saw her scoop Louis in to her side and hold him firmly, virtually holding him upright. She really was a magnificent woman.

Watching Natalie way up the front, Sully realised that the colours in her silk shirt were the colours Frank favoured in his wardrobe – wine colours and deep blues. He imagined Natalie going shopping, seeing the shirt on a hanger, choosing it, missing her dad.

Sullivan had not been so thoughtful when he was the child of a recently deceased parent. He had attended his mother's funeral but so hung-over it was a blur. He'd scooted away as soon as the ceremony was over, not wishing to be looked at and judged by his mother's friends.

He'd been well aware of the day of Pete's funeral because Tim had called him all morning, every five minutes. Sullivan let the calls go to voicemail and got hammered on tequila.

Tim's messages were all pretty similar: 'Get up, you lazy fuck. Today is the funeral of our good friend Pete – *your* good friend – and you should be there.'

Sully never made it to the funeral but did make an attempt to show up at the wake. On a gust of guilt, he had stumbled to Pete's house in Redfern where the event was due to be held. He was accompanied on this mission by Travis, a stringy guy with a spider-web tattoo on his neck – more of an acquaintance than a friend – who had been listening to Sully's maudlin ravings at a pub.

Sitting here now, Sullivan didn't want to revisit the details of his misadventures at the wake. Suffice it to say, it had not gone well. When the mourners arrived at the house, they had found Sullivan Moss passed out naked on the floor of the upstairs bathroom. Three thousand dollars' worth of cash, laptops and other valuables had been stolen by Sully's companion Travis.

As Sullivan was bundled out of Pete's house into a taxi, Tim's final words to him were: 'Consider our friendship over.'

Maybe sitting in this chapel now was an attempt to atone for that. Not that coming to the funeral of a man he'd never met could make any dent in the monolith of shame he had built with his every act of neglect, every phone call dodged, every item stolen, every day Pete lay in hospital hoping Sully would visit.

Thinking on that created pangs of guilt, which must surely lead to the secretion of stress hormones not conducive to renal health. He mustn't ponder all that negative history stuff. Nor should he think too much about Natalie and her lovingly chosen silk shirt, her grandmother-defying son, her melodious voice. None of the above.

His only role in life now was as a life-support system for a donor kidney. His purpose was to become healthy and to support himself during the year it might take to get through the program. Nothing else.

10

Natalie waited outside until Sullivan buzzed her into Frank's building, even though she had her own key. This was to protect his privacy but was also a layer of protection for herself. She didn't fancy walking into the flat to see the man hanging from a doorframe or slumped in blood-stained bathwater.

When she reached the landing between Frank's front door and Gordana's, Nat was hit by the memory of what she'd done in that place. She felt it in her body – the weight of her father's body in the sheet, the thud of his hip against the doorframe jarring up her arms, the unfamiliar surge of power in her chest to discover she was capable of doing something like that.

When Sullivan opened the door, Natalie gasped and had to feign a coughing fit to cover herself. He had completely shaved his head. All the floppy boyish hair was gone and his scalp was surprisingly white, with the dark roots forming a shadowy cap across his skull. The bruising from his fall was fully revealed – a yellow and purple stain spreading round the side of his head. His shaved head was a shock – so raw and brutal – and he looked older, like a slightly scary man rather than the hard-living teenager he'd appeared to be before. But then she heard Sullivan's gentle voice – 'Hi, Natalie. How are you?' – and the intimidating effect of the fiercely bald head diminished.

'Did you – is the hair thing because – uh . . .' she said.

'It's full on, isn't it!' Sullivan grinned and Natalie noticed that his newly pale head made his eyes appear more intensely blue. 'It seemed like a good idea. Do you fancy a cup of tea? I just boiled the kettle.'

'No thanks,' she said automatically but then changed tack. 'Oh, actually, I've got time. That'd be nice.' Bringing supplies for Mack had been a flimsy excuse to check up on Sullivan and she should make the most of it.

Natalie was touched that he'd showed up at Frank's funeral and grateful that he was so lovely with Mack. She felt an upswelling of tenderness for Sullivan Moss, then reminded herself that she had a lot of high-octane emotions going through her during this period of grief and must be careful not to ascribe intense feelings to the wrong source.

Sullivan made the tea. He had been sober for ten days now but the Thirst was still ferocious. Night-time was the worst because his patchy sleeping pattern had degenerated into powerful insomnia. This was apparently a common symptom for alcoholics trying to dry out. He'd looked it up online.

Last night, he'd given up trying to sleep. While prowling the flat at two a.m., he'd discovered clippers in the bottom drawer of Frank's bathroom vanity and the idea of shaving his head suddenly seemed right. In fact, essential.

The electric clippers had buzzed across Sullivan's skull, shearing the hair off to fall on the bathroom floor in satisfying chunks. He stopped after the first few sweeps of the clippers to enjoy the sight of the dramatic strip ploughed through his thick hair, as if a powerful harvester had cut a swathe through a cornfield. Clipping the bits at the back was awkward but he persevered until the job was done.

Mack, not keen on the noise of the clippers, observed the head-shaving from the bathroom doorway but he padded in to sniff the fallen locks of hair as Sullivan swept them up. Then the two of them retired to the lounge room to watch movies.

Earlier in his life, Sullivan had read a huge amount but these days he couldn't concentrate enough to read a whole book of anything. So, instead of making a selection from Frank's books, he was working through the DVD shelves. *A Man for All Seasons*, *12 Angry Men*, *Born Yesterday*, *They Shoot Horses, Don't They?*, *O Lucky Man!*, *Mr Smith Goes to Washington*.

For his first shaven-headed movie-viewing, he'd chosen a Ben Kingsley film festival to honour baldness. Mack arranged himself at Sullivan's feet and quickly fell asleep. Sullivan ran his hand repeatedly over his shorn head as he watched *Sexy Beast*, *Searching for Bobby Fischer* and finally dozed off halfway through *Gandhi*.

For the past week, Sully had been clinging to a self-devised daily schedule as if he were gripping onto the railing of a lurching boat. First thing each morning, take Mack to the park, then spoon down some of the bran cereal he'd found in the pantry, then tidy the flat. He kept the flat neater than any place he'd ever lived, out of respect for Frank.

The main task of each day was to head down to the employment centre to check for any new jobs on the board. He'd done a couple of interviews but no result so far.

Next, there was a section of his day given over to assorted errands, including the purchase of a cheap mobile phone and the first appointment with the renal specialist.

This morning Sully had stopped by a fruit and vegetable shop to stock up on nutrient-rich fresh food for his kidney. He had tried jogging back from the vegie shop to the flat but within two hundred metres, he thought he was going to have a heart attack. He told himself he should stop running to avoid bashing the strawberries around in the shopping bag. But that excuse crumbled in his mind and he accepted that he was simply an unfit man heaving for breath in a park.

'I must be dogged about this,' Sullivan had said aloud. By 'this' he meant all of it – not just exercise but the whole enterprise he had undertaken. He hoped saying the words aloud would solidify the idea and help him be a dogged person. He set off again, holding the strawberries against the cushion of his belly, and adopted a hearty stride that surely counted as some form of cardiovascular work-out.

Much of the time, Sullivan was aware of the Thirst skulking on the periphery of his thoughts or crawling across his skin in the form of strange itches. On occasion, the itch was so insistent, he had to rub his back up and down on a tree or brick wall for relief.

When Sullivan brought the tea out to Natalie in the lounge room, that itchy feeling scurried across his shoulders and he had an urge to scratch himself on the door jamb. He resisted the urge so Natalie wouldn't think he was any weirder than she already must.

'You and Mack seem to be going great guns,' said Natalie.

The dog parked himself at Sullivan's feet, chin propped on his knee.

'Ah, well, he's a star, this dog,' said Sully. 'When we go to the park, everyone knows him. They ask me about Frank.'

'I'm sorry if it's awkward for you – having to explain he died.'

'Your dad was a well-respected gent in the parks of Glebe. One lady pressed me up against a fence and raved about what an excellent listener Frank was, how he used to ask people about themselves, really interested in their lives.'

'Yeah,' said Natalie, 'Dad was an old journo. Always interviewing people.'

'Ah. I see.'

'He used to interview my school-friends when they came round to our house. Which is embarrassing when you're a teenager.'

'I bet.' Sullivan smiled. 'Oh and hey – Gordana, the lady across the hall, she never stops singing Frank's praises.'

Natalie jerked an odd smile then quickly changed the subject. 'Listen, I meant to ask you . . . my son, Louis —'

'He played the cello beautifully at the funeral.'

'Yes. He did,' said Natalie. 'He really loves spending time with Mack.'

'He can come and hang out with Mack anytime,' Sullivan offered.

'Thanks. But the trouble is, Louis has asthma. He has a bad allergic reaction in this flat. My dad used to bring the dog to Louis' soccer training, so he could —'

'I could bring Mack to soccer training,' Sullivan jumped in a bit too quickly.

'Oh . . .' Natalie was caught off guard. 'Thanks but . . . all I was going to suggest was that I could borrow Mack for an hour and then drop him back here afterwards.'

'Right. Makes sense. Of course.'

'I mean, thanks for offering. That's lovely. But you shouldn't have to drag yourself over to Annandale and back again.'

Sullivan could see she was uncomfortable, fobbing him off. Why would she want a guy like him hanging around her kid at soccer practice? Of course she wouldn't.

'Ooh,' said Nat, jumping to her feet as if she wanted to leap away from this awkward moment. 'I forgot to put Mack's chicken wings in the fridge.'

Natalie took the shopping bag to the kitchen and put the chewbones on the bench. As she opened the fridge to put away the chicken wings, Sully remembered what was in there. On the central shelf was a large plastic screw-top jar filled with a litre or more of yellow liquid. He looked at her looking at the jar.

Sullivan could tell Natalie was wondering. 'It's urine,' he said. At the request of the renal specialist, he was undergoing a test involving a twenty-four-hour urine collection.

'The contents of the fridge are none of my business.' She closed the door.

'It's *my* urine.' Did that sound any better than if it were someone else's urine? Maybe. Sullivan continued, 'Don't know why I felt the need to put it in the fridge. I know it doesn't go off or curdle or anything.'

Sullivan felt his spirits sink and it took him a moment to identify the reason: a woman who has seen such a huge quantity of a man's urine in a jar would never consider having sex with him. And at that moment he realised that in a tiny back pocket of his brain, he must have been harbouring a hope that sex with Natalie might be possible, however absurdly remote a possibility. Now she'd seen the piss jar, sex must be filed under impossible.

'It's for a medical test,' Sullivan explained. 'It's one of the ways they test kidney function.'

'Are you ill?'

'No. Well, presumably I'm mentally ill, given – y'know . . .' he said. 'But not physically ill.' He found he couldn't stand the idea that Natalie would think he was physically ill and would therefore have more grounds to pity him. So apparently he still had some shreds of pride remaining. He'd baulked at telling her the real reason for the urine jar, not sure how his plan would land in a normal person's head. But he had no choice but to explain.

'I'm having tests done to see if I can be a living kidney donor.'

'Oh. Do you have a relative who needs a transplant?'

'No. I'm what they call a non-directed donor. My kidney will go to a stranger.'

He heard himself explain, curious to know how the words would feel in his mouth. She was the first person he'd told apart from the necessary medical folk.

Natalie nodded slowly. 'Wow. That's really – uh . . .'

'Over the top? Absurd?'

'No, I was going to say it's really selfless.'

'Nah, well, it's not selfless. It's a way to trick myself into thinking I have some useful purpose on the planet, even if only for my trans-plantable tissues.'

'I get what you're saying.'

'So don't say selfless, because it's not,' said Sullivan, firming this up in his own mind as he expressed it to her.

'Okay. May I say it's "interesting"?' she asked.

'Yes, you may.'

Sullivan took the cellophane wrapping off the giant pork knuckle Natalie had brought and tossed it onto the patch of grass in the court-yard. He and Natalie stood watching Mack gnaw at the bone. Sullivan explained how the living donor program worked to the extent that he understood it.

'Right. Wow,' said Natalie. 'I've ticked the box on my driver's licence to be an organ donor if I end up brain-dead. And I give blood.'

'Good on you. That's great.'

'But I don't think I would consider giving a kidney to a stranger or even a friend because – well . . . I have to keep my kidneys in case Louis ever needs one.'

'Fair enough,' said Sullivan. 'I reckon that's the appropriate posi-tion for a parent.'

'I guess it is. I've never thought about it . . . but in fact my body is an emergency greenhouse. I'm a walking organ farm for my child.'

Sully smiled – he liked that notion – but Natalie herself looked flustered.

'Well, good luck with it, Sullivan,' she said. 'It's a generous thing to do.'

As Natalie walked out into the street, she was feeling bad about reject-ing Sullivan's offer to bring the dog to Louis' soccer training. Was she that kind of over-protective parent? Then again, she really didn't know this guy at all and if he showed up at soccer with Mack, Louis would automatically trust him. Who knew what influence an unstable guy like Sullivan would be on an eight-year-old boy's world view. Then Natalie listened to her own narrow-minded thought process and berated herself for being so eager to edit life for her son.

She was thrown off-balance by the sudden intense turn the visit had taken. When a man had tried to kill himself and followed that up with a plan to donate an organ, it seemed to create a shortcut, jumping over the ordinary verbal clutter and polite waiting periods between people to reach a profound place more rapidly.

She wondered how Sullivan's donation goal fitted with his suicide goal. After the surgery, would he then kill himself? Should she have quizzed him about that?

No, it was none of her business. Or maybe it was her business, since they'd entered into this arrangement. But she should avoid investing too much energy in worrying about Sullivan Moss. She was only just managing her own emotional equilibrium as it was.

11

The psychiatrist's office was inside a Victorian terrace house on a suburban street. The waiting area was set up as if it were a cosy lounge room in a house where people really lived. Sullivan wondered if this was to make mentally unstable clients feel as if they were just popping in for a chat with a wise friend who lived in a nicely restored period home rather than paying substantial money to a stranger to pick over their shortcomings and pathetic fears.

'Sit down,' said the smiley receptionist as she watered a maiden-hair fern in an antique pot. 'Anthony won't be long.'

Sullivan perched his bum on the edge of a velvety armchair. He considered explaining to the receptionist that he was only here as a potential organ donor rather than as a troubled soul. But that would sound pompous. And anyway, he was a troubled soul. Probably more troubled than the majority of the neurotic but functional individuals who visited this practice.

Inside Anthony's office, there were more homely touches and softly upholstered furniture. There was something softly upholstered about Anthony himself. He was in his late forties with a studied serenity. Sully had an urge to shove the guy off his armchair to see what would happen.

Instead, Sullivan got straight down to business. 'I assume Diane Milton from the renal unit told you I tried to kill myself. So let's deal with that first off.'

'We can,' said Anthony in his velvety voice.

'Ah,' sighed Sullivan as the realisation landed. 'Diane didn't tell you.'

'No.'

'Fuck. Okay. Fuck.'

Sullivan was flustered and seeing Anthony write notes in his folder only made him more so. If he said 'fuck' too many times, would that rule him out?

Anthony let a significant pause go by before he spoke. 'Shall we talk about why you wanted to kill yourself?'

'I'd rather not. I'm only here about the kidney.'

'Okay.'

Sullivan's legs started twitching. This had happened at various moments in his life. His legs would become restless because they could sense impending trouble and wanted to run him out of whatever scenario he was about to stuff up.

Sullivan's voice was also shaky, betraying how flustered he was. 'So what do we – what's the – uh . . .'

'Sullivan, can I just ask this: do you think donating a kidney will change whatever it was that made you want to kill yourself?'

'Does it have to? It could change something for the person who gets the kidney.'

'Well, that's true. But right now, I'm —'

'Why is my desire to donate a kidney any more a symptom of pathology than other people's choices to make money or chase fame or have kids or – or any of the things that people – it's not. It's no different. And at least it gives some benefit to someone.' Sullivan could hear himself – too loud, a bit shrill, almost petulant – but he couldn't stop his voice coming out that way.

'I agree,' said Anthony. 'But my task is to assess the effect on your wellbeing.'

'You have to make sure I'm not too mentally ill to donate. But why? If a person is a nasty piece of work, fine, you'll have their kidney.

If the person is a useless waste of space, also fine. But if a person *knows* he's a waste of space sufficiently to feel it's best to remove himself from the planet, he's mentally ill, and therefore it's not okay for him to offer something he can offer – for example, a kidney?'

'I appreciate what you're saying, but I think —'

'But odds are you're never going to think I'm fit to – fuck . . .'

'We haven't even started yet, Sullivan. Why don't we just —'

Sullivan's legs couldn't remain still a second longer and he stood up. 'Nah. Sorry. Nah. This is a waste of time. This is never gonna – oh . . .'

Sullivan walked out of the office into the charming Victorian vestibule and headed for the street. Why was it necessary to stir up the sludge from the bottom of his psyche? Pushing his face into that sludge would do no one any good. He'd always thought insight was overrated as a therapeutic tool. You could understand how and why you were screwed up but that didn't mean you could do anything about it. Why couldn't they just attest he was a legally sane individual, offering his kidney without coercion, and leave it at that? Fuck this. He should forget the whole business.

But then he stopped. Maybe Anthony wasn't fussed about Sullivan's psychological sludge. This psych assessment was just a formality to establish he was fit to donate an organ, much like an accused murderer must be declared fit to stand trial. If Sully walked out now, it was probably all over. And then what would he have? What would he do?

He forced his legs to turn and walk back into Anthony's office.

'Sorry. That was – well, I was rude and petulant.'

'Don't worry, Sullivan,' said Anthony calmly.

'My mother always used to say at parent–teacher night, "Sullivan drops his bundle too quickly." Which is true. So write that in your notes. Anyway, look, I'm sorry. Is there any chance we can start again?'

'Of course,' said Anthony as if he'd never doubted Sullivan would walk back in just like this.

Sullivan used the rest of the fifty-five minutes to deliver his life history to Anthony, including the ugly bits. It was important to be as candid as possible. In Sully's mind it was the equivalent of a Catholic giving a full and genuine confession on their deathbed in order to get into heaven. There was no point offering up a kidney tainted by unconfessed sins. The purity of the offering he made Anthony would ensure the purity of his donation.

For his part, Anthony took a bucketload of notes and listened. They made an appointment for two weeks' time.

Baked goods kept arriving at the radio station, addressed to the breakfast program. There was always a handwritten note identifying the gift. Today it was a box of 'walnut half-moon biscuits', last week a 'sour cherry cake' and 'sweet bread with apple and poppy seeds'.

Heather assumed the home-made Croatian treats were coming from one of her fans and Natalie let her go on assuming that. The first cake had arrived the day after Frank's funeral with an extra note included: *Thank you, Natalie. G.*

Natalie couldn't eat Gordana's cakes. Guilt and discomfort converted each bite she took into chaff, sucking all the moisture out of her mouth, making it difficult to swallow, even though the cakes were in fact moist and tasty. Her mind was immediately spun back to that moment when she'd helped move Frank's body. There was also the question of motivation: were the baked offerings intended as a show of gratitude, bribery, payment for her silence or an intimidation tactic? Were those cakes and biscuits really saying, 'Don't tell anyone about the body in my bed or who knows what will be in the next batch of goodies'? Natalie suspected that was crazy thinking but still, what *should* she think?

She couldn't take cakes home because Judy would bang on about white flour and use the opportunity to criticise the size of Natalie's thighs. Nat was tempted to take one cake home so she could say, 'Oh Mum, do you want to eat a slice of cake baked by a woman out of gratitude for my silence in not revealing that she and I smuggled your ex-husband's dead body out of her bed in which this woman had been regularly shagging him?'

That would be enjoyable but not worth the earbashings that would follow.

Natalie usually handed Gordana's baked goods around the radio station. Today she decided to swing by the office of the station manager, Neil. She stood in his doorway and flipped open the box to show him the biscuits.

'Do you want to take these home?' she asked.

'No thanks, Nat. I'm gluten-free at the present because of my guts,' said Neil. 'In fact shield my eyes from those delectable treats if you don't mind.'

She made a show of slamming the lid down to rescue him from temptation.

Natalie had worked with Neil in her first radio job. During the years Nat was overseas, Neil had been producing radio around the country, eventually landing the spot as manager in Sydney.

When Natalie first returned to Australia, there'd been a spate of pregnancies among the Sydney staff that meant Neil had found himself suddenly short of experienced producers. By stepping in as a casual, Natalie had solved a problem for Neil as much as he solved her coming-home-without-a-job predicament.

'Nat, you're so good, it'd help me out. Saving my skin in fact.'

When Natalie stepped up to be the senior breakfast producer, she agreed to continue as a long-term casual, rather than apply for other jobs, on the understanding that Neil would keep an eye out for an on-air chance for her, maybe a week as a fill-in presenter somewhere. She'd been working on this basis for a year, still hoping to get on-air experience during the next summer period.

She'd always been fond of Neil. He was bony, ruddy, with pale ginger stubble and a huge Adam's apple that was a distraction when he was talking. There were often a few scabs along his receding hairline where skin cancers had been burned off. Approaching middle age – he was forty-two – he still looked like a farmer who'd just wandered straight from an agricultural show to the radio station.

'Oh, Neil, I hear Roger's taking a slab of leave next month,' she said, keeping her tone light. 'Have you already picked fill-in presenters? Any chance I could get a look-in?'

'Yeah, I have to sort something about that,' Neil muttered. 'You know you're on my radar, Nat. Leave it with me.'

Natalie nodded and smiled, not wanting to be a nuisance or appear pushy. A fill-in gig in Sydney was a big ask. She whisked the box of goodies up into the air with a jokey flourish as she left Neil's office.

In the end, she decided to give today's biscuits to Astrid. Natalie had the afternoon free for coffee with Astrid because Louis was going round to a friend's place after school before moving on to a bowling birthday party in the evening.

Louis had a more vibrant social life than Natalie. Not that it would be hard.

Walking from the studio to the car park, Natalie conducted a social audit on herself. Her social activity had atrophied to a sad withered thing – the odd work-related event, tea or wine with other parents when picking up kids, a chat on the sidelines at soccer.

She didn't even know who counted as her best friends any more. She'd become close to two other expats in Kuala Lumpur – both great women – but they had moved to Berlin and New York respectively. Her Sydney friendships had become diluted since she moved overseas. Those six years she was away proved to be crucial ones for the laying down of social networks. They were the years – late twenties, early thirties – in which people formed couples, defined their allegiances and created cosy social habits.

There was the difficulty of her strange work and sleep hours. Plus the awkwardness of living in her mother's house. Cooking a meal for friends at home, with Judy lurking, was not an attractive prospect.

And there was the problem of being single with a kid. Couple friends found it unwieldy to include a single woman in social activities. And Nat wasn't interested in being a woman in a hunting pack with other single women.

Well, Natalie *hoped* her dismal social life was caused by circumstances rather than by some failure of her personality. She'd always enjoyed the rhythms and humour and consolations of friendship. She'd enjoyed being a good friend to people, had taken pride in it. Her current isolated state was unwelcome and didn't fit with her self-image. It was yet another distorted characteristic of this life she'd somehow ended up with.

As she waited to cross the street, Natalie could see Astrid through the window of the cafe. Her neck was shunted forward, eyes fixed on her laptop. Astrid was always steering extra projects – a primary-school debating competition, volunteer literacy tutoring – on top of her school job and the considerable load she'd taken on with running Grahame's life.

'Hello, missus,' said Natalie, leaning across the table to kiss Astrid hello.

Astrid was wearing an alarming sack of a dress covered in bright blotches that dribbled colour down the fabric, as if it had come from a paintball range. She would have chosen it because the colours brought her pleasure, without caring how it looked to anyone else. Natalie admired that about Astrid.

They'd met during Natalie's first week back in Australia as she waited at the motor registry, hoping to sort out her driver's licence after six years overseas. Astrid was there to fix some problem with Grahame's disabled parking permit.

The two women had been sitting on adjoining plastic chairs, both reading novels. Natalie craned her neck to sneak a look at the other woman's book.

Astrid was more direct. 'What are you reading?'

They talked about books. They talked about why they were there.

Natalie found herself speaking candidly to this stranger about her marriage breakdown and return to Australia. Astrid offered up bits of her own story with equal candour.

When Astrid was finally called up to the counter forty minutes later, Natalie felt sorry to end the connection. Then, to her surprise, Astrid dashed back towards her, tearing a piece off a disabled parking form so they could swap email addresses.

Natalie would never have been so decisive and confident about befriending a stranger but she was glad Astrid was. It was a delightful surprise to be *picked* by someone. A straightforward transaction, like playground friendships in kindergarten before things became more complicated.

Now in the cafe, as Natalie sat down, Astrid was peering at her across the table. 'Natalie. How long since you had sex? It'll grow shut.'

Natalie pulled a face and laughed.

Astrid had some of Judy's outspokenness but there was a crucial difference. When Judy spoke her mind, the content of that mind was uncharitable, with a spiteful agenda: wanting everyone else to be as miserable as she was. Astrid's basic makeup was kind, with an agenda to fix everyone.

Natalie was quick to change the subject by asking, 'How's Grahame?'

Astrid was always happy to talk about her husband, his latest work, his brilliance, which was still revealing itself to her week by week. Natalie envied her having a partner she could admire so passionately.

Astrid fired off questions about Natalie's work situation. 'Has your boss said he'll give you a fill-in spot over the summer?'

'Hasn't decided yet. Not sure I'm ready for it anyway. I haven't done anything on-air for several years.'

Astrid frowned, genuinely puzzled. She often assured Nat that she was *aware* of the irrational self-doubt driving many people, even if she didn't share such feelings herself. Despite Astrid's awareness, she was still baffled by the behaviour of people she cared about and the behaviour of characters in the many novels she read. Every individual she encountered – real or fictional – simply needed to follow the advice Astrid was happy to offer and many problems would be swiftly sorted out.

Today, Natalie wasn't feeling sturdy enough to withstand the beam of Astrid's analysis. Luckily, she could use Gordana's biscuits to divert attention.

'Ooh, I brought you these. Home-made,' she said, handing the box to Astrid.

'Home-made by you?'

'No, no, you know I wouldn't dare cook decadent stuff like this in Judy's kitchen. A neighbour of Dad's made them.'

'Thanks. I'll take them into the staffroom tomorrow. They look yummy,' said Astrid, peeking inside the box before tucking it next to her work folders. Then she reached across the table to grip Natalie's hand. 'How have you been since the funeral?'

'Oh, you know . . .'

Natalie occasionally burst into tears in shops or in the car, missing her dad. She expected that and it wasn't entirely unwelcome. It was satisfying to feel something so strong but explicable. That was better than the general discontent and impotence that often dragged through her. More troubling were the little spikes of panic in her belly when she remembered moving her father's body.

Sometimes when Nat recalled that day, she didn't recognise herself. It was like seeing her own face pixelated the way they do in TV current-affairs shows. Her face could remain an unrecognisable blur for some minutes until the pixels settled back into a clear picture of herself again.

She considered confiding in Astrid. She mentally rehearsed the way she would explain how destabilising the experience was, that it was simultaneously a source of shame, anxiety and an odd sense of power. But Astrid was not the person to tell.

Natalie steered the conversation entirely away from herself.

'I dropped in on Sullivan at the flat last week.'

'Is that working out? I hope I haven't foisted the Sullivan Moss problem on to you.'

'No, no, thank you for suggesting it. He seems to be taking good care of Dad's place and he's fantastic with Mack.'

Astrid nodded slowly. 'And how is he – Sullivan?'

'Well, seems okay but I don't know him so . . .'

'I care about him, Nat.'

'I know that.'

'I want him to get his life together, if that's at all possible. Sullivan is not a malicious person.'

'No, well, he doesn't seem malicious.'

'I remember why I married the man, even if it seems unthinkable now.'

'Of course. We all —'

Astrid ploughed on, keen to put her assessment on the record. 'Sullivan does have a kind heart. Mind you, I don't think kindness is worth much when it isn't supported by self-discipline – the sort of discipline Grahame has.'

Natalie noted the devoted smile at the mention of Grahame's name but then wondered if the smile was actually about Sullivan.

'He was a good lover too,' Astrid went on. 'Which, as you know, I consider an important part of a happy life. And I have to say he could make me laugh.'

Laughter was not an automatic thing for Astrid who was often bewildered when people around her giggled at some flimsily amusing moment.

'I avoid bringing Sullivan up in conversation with Grahame,' said Astrid. 'He gets so cross on my behalf. My new husband is more aggrieved about the way my first husband treated me than I am.'

Natalie knew Sullivan Moss had hurt Astrid deeply, taking advantage of her good impulses repeatedly, wasting her money. But all of that was nothing compared to the pain of the infidelity.

Astrid had explained it to her once. 'Sullivan had the self-control of a toddler when it came to a sexual opportunity. He could be enthusiastic about the person right in front of him but he couldn't hold other things of value in his head at the same time. The thought *Here's a woman who wants to have sex with me* obliterated any thought about me, the future, the stupidity of what he was about to do.'

Twice she had caught him having an affair and allowed his remorse to win her over. The third woman she found out about was a teacher she worked with. That was the end for Astrid. Natalie recalled the end of her own marriage, the pain of being cuckolded, how much she'd hated Brendan for making her feel duped, stupid, unattractive.

Astrid now shook off any vulnerability she might be feeling about Sullivan Moss and adopted her bracing welfare tone. 'You know Natalie, the real mistake I made was not realising the man was irreparably damaged and I couldn't help him. Did you know his father died when he was a kid?'

'No. A kid? How old?'

'Sullivan was seven, poor little soul. The father was an alcoholic. One day he left a map to show where he'd parked the car then climbed down an embankment to put his head on the railway tracks.'

'Fucking hell,' said Natalie. 'Was Sullivan told about it?'

'One of the aunts told him a week later.'

Natalie took a deep breath, picturing Louis as the kid being told that his dad had been pulverised by a train.

'Sullivan's mother indulged him after he lost his father,' said Astrid. 'She made too many allowances for him, so he never grew up properly.'

Natalie felt a pang of anxiety. Was she indulging Louis because of his absent father, thereby stunting his emotional maturity so he'd end up a wretched drunk man jumping off a building? Was Astrid having an oblique go at her about her parenting? No. If she wanted to criticise Natalie, she'd do it directly. One of the good things about Astrid was that you never had to worry about covert attacks. She operated without subtext and never went in for sly tactics.

Even so, Natalie decided to steer the conversation away from over-indulgent mothering and said, 'Sullivan's planning to donate a kidney.'

'What?'

Natalie explained how altruistic donation worked.

'This is a crazy idea,' Astrid said. 'It's typical: a childish notion about being a noble person or some equivalent nonsense Sullivan's got into his head. He'll never see it through if it requires any level of persistence. Why does he have to do something so ridiculous and show-offy? Why can't he just be a reasonable productive person like the rest of us?'

Natalie shrugged. She was hardly in a position to explain Sullivan Moss's life choices.

'And after he donates his kidney – which, by the way, won't happen because he won't manage to stick with any kind of – but assuming he did give someone his kidney, is he planning to kill himself afterwards?'

'He didn't say.'

12

Gliding down in the express lift, Tim looked through the transparent wall and spotted a man waiting on the forecourt. The guy had the body shape and slack posture of Sullivan Moss but the clothes were wrong. And anyway, it couldn't be Sully because this man's face wasn't half-covered by a hank of dark hair.

As Tim stepped out of the lift and moved closer, he realised it *was* Sully, but virtually bald, with a few millimetres of stubble on his head. Astrid had mentioned some crazy kidney plan but now Tim wondered if the guy was in fact ill, having chemo.

Sully's head was tilted way back, staring up the length of the massive bank tower. Was he assessing it as a suicide spot? This was a friend who had recently tried – or at least contemplated – topping himself. Would Sullivan now be profoundly different in some way Tim would have to deal with? Tim felt a voodoo shiver at the thought of it but then quickly shook that off and strode across the granite forecourt towards him.

Every time Sullivan had been to the bank headquarters where Tim worked, he was enfeebled by the monumental size of the joint. Not just the thirty-five storey height but its vast concourse, colossal maw of an entrance, two rows of steel and glass lifts like creepy alien pods, every space defined by *Land of the Giants* granite blocks. Sullivan always pictured himself as a tiny plastic figure in an architectural model – a plastic figure whose only purpose was to indicate the impressive scale of the atrium.

Sullivan had been living in Frank's flat for three weeks when Tim had sent him an email, arranging to meet outside the bank building at seven. Sully had no idea why.

'Did you let a rat chew your hair off, you dozy fuck?' said Tim by way of greeting.

'Ha. No. Did it myself with clippers,' said Sullivan.

'Looks like you did it with cheesy toenail scissors.'

'Cheaper than getting a haircut.'

Tim snorted a laugh and for a moment Sully thought he'd got away with it – they could be back in their old routine, without the Pete stuff wrecking things forever. But then Tim took a step back and stared at him.

'Can't believe I'm standing here looking at your ugly face. I was never going to have anything to do with you again after your scumbag performance.'

'Don't blame you,' said Sullivan. 'A perfectly reasonable decision.'

'Did you know the police recovered most of the items your associate stole from Pete's house?'

'I didn't know that. That's good.'

'Better we don't ever talk about it. Otherwise I won't be able to stomach you.'

Sullivan nodded, feeling Tim's anger radiating at him. He wondered if he should make some excuse and flee.

'I'm only seeing you now because I promised Astrid I would,' said Tim. 'She reckons you're auctioning off your internal organs. She wanted me to talk to you. I told her it must be a joke.'

'Not a joke. I've done the first few steps in the donor program. There's no guarantee I'll get all the way through to surgery.'

'Fuck me dead! You're serious,' said Tim.

Sullivan nodded.

'Have you told the transplant docs that your kidney's been marinating in vodka for years?'

Sullivan chuckled politely. 'I've been scrupulously honest. You'd be amazed.'

'I assume they said no to using your liver. Your liver'd make some poor bastard sicker than he was to start with.'

Tim went on in a similar vein for some time. Sullivan responded to each volley by laughing or smiling stoically. He had been copping Tim's mock abuse since they were both ten years old. He knew Tim was a good guy, a loyal friend. He knew it was only jokey bluster. But sometimes it felt as if Tim were landing a series of punches at one spot on your arm – small playful punches but so many that the arm would end up bruised. Then Tim would punch the spot one time too many so you'd flinch and pull away. If Sully ever called him on it, Tim would splutter, 'Mate, just joking around.'

That's what happened as they stood there on the granite steps. Tim saw the bruised expression on Sullivan's face and said, 'Hey, Sully. You know I'm only taking the piss, mate. Get it? A kidney joke. So. Let me buy you and your kidneys a cold beverage.'

Tim led the way around the corner to a stylish upstairs bar. Being Friday evening in the CBD, the place was full of bankers, lawyers, marketers and other slick types, mostly in their late twenties. A meat market for young professionals. Even this early, the air was crackling with sexual hope as suited young men assessed their chances with the smaller number of expensively dressed women. Later in the night, when the pairing-off would grow more desperate, the air would be thick with it. As Sullivan observed the posturing of the young men, he knew he could no longer compete in that event, given his questionable appearance and lack of credentials.

Sullivan and Tim sat up at the bar, in a corner away from the mating action. Predictably, Tim made a palaver about Sully ordering lime and soda instead of alcohol. Tim knocked back his first two vodkas and tonic mighty fast. Sullivan figured that's what he used to look like when drinking, eager to achieve that loose pissed sensation as soon as possible.

Sullivan yearned for that lovely sensation right now. He was three weeks dry and this was the first time he'd ventured into licensed premises.

He steeled himself with this thought: being a non-drinker because he was a potential kidney donor gave him an identity in this bar, even if the identity existed only in his own mind. Without that, how would he be measured in this roomful of successful young men? How would he be weighed alongside his wealthy, fit, loyal, responsible, father-of-two friend Tim? How would he be regarded by the gorgeous young women in their tight corporate outfits? He would be a loser, laughable, pitiable or even disgusting. At least as a man eschewing alcohol for a noble cause, he did not have to regard himself as that loser. And that gave him just enough motivation to hold off the urge to drink.

'What's with the clothes?' asked Tim, waving his hand at the charcoal suit pants and blue shirt Sullivan was wearing. 'Do they issue you with those when they release you from the psych ward?'

Sullivan explained the Frank situation – the flat, the clothes, the dog. He tried to describe what a top gent Frank must've been, keen for Tim to understand.

But Tim wasn't really listening, so wasn't aware he was interrupting Sully's earnest testimony about Frank. 'Sully, mate, are you really going to do this kidney thing?'

'I'm going to try.'

'What if something goes wrong with the one kidney you have left? I mean, you know I think you're a gutless tool not worth my fucking time.'

'I'm well aware of that,' said Sullivan.

Tim jabbed the air with his glass on key words. 'But I cannot sit here and let someone who used to be a good mate do something risky with his health.'

'It's not really that risky.'

'What if I give you money not to do it?' said Tim.

'What? It's not like anyone is paying me to do it.'

'Okay, okay, okay. How are you gonna live while you go through all the medical shit and afterwards when you're recovering from the operation? Do you want me to give you some money to live on while you're . . . y'know?'

'You mean, you'd sponsor me to donate my kidney?' asked Sullivan.

'A kidney-a-thon. Why the fuck not?'

'Tim, this is not like the forty-hour famine we did in Year 8. Anyway, I've got a good job prospect next week.'

Tim puffed out a breath, scornful. 'Oh yeah, what are the chances you'll —'

'Mate, thanks for the offer but —'

'Are you telling me you won't need money if you go ahead with it?'

'Make up your mind, Tim. One minute you want to pay me *not* to donate a kidney and now you want to pay me to do it!'

'Don't take my money then, you self-righteous dick.'

'Sling some cash to renal research or something,' suggested Sullivan.

'I will,' said Tim and flicked his hand to the barman for another vodka.

By the time Tim had finished his third vodka, Sullivan realised it was well past eight o'clock.

'Should you ring Juliet? Tell her where you are?'

Tim shook his head. 'She hates me. She'll be glad not to have me in the house for a few more hours.'

Tim related the state of his marriage to Sullivan in ugly detail. Sully listened and made appropriate noises of dismay or sympathy.

When Tim had spilled his guts sufficiently, he gripped Sullivan's arm. 'Jesus, Sully, d'you realise you're the only person I can be honest with about this stuff? There's no one else I can talk to like this.'

Sullivan wondered if that was because Tim could admit any kind of personal failure to him and still feel comfortably superior. No, that was unfair. Tim was a genuinely sentimental guy, especially when pissed, especially about old friends. Whenever he was caught up on some emotional topic, Tim would lean sideways as if buffeted by gusts of strong feeling.

Tim was hit by one of those gusts of nostalgic longing when he saw a freebie music newspaper on a side table in the bar. He grabbed the paper and slapped his fingers against the pages of gig listings.

'Remember how much we used to go to live music? We used to go all the fucking time. Remember? When was the last time you went to a gig?'

'Ooh, it'd be yonks ago,' said Sullivan.

'I don't recognise most of these band names. Shows how long since I went to music. It was so fucking good, wasn't it. Why did we stop going to gigs?'

'Well, I guess, you were busy with work and the twins and I was —'

'We should go. Now,' announced Tim.

'Okay.'

They picked a gig out of the listings – they didn't know the band but Sullivan knew where the venue was.

On the way there, they stopped to eat kebabs. As Tim stood on the footpath eating, he left a phone message for Juliet. His tone was abrasive, defiant, as if Juliet had expressly forbidden him to go. 'I'm going to a gig to listen to some live fucking music for the first time in a million years.' He didn't mention that he was going with Sullivan because that detail would be way too inflammatory.

A few years back, Juliet had decided to open a small chic bar in Surry Hills. She had a good eye for design and this would be her chance to create an elegant drinking establishment like the private clubs she'd seen in London. Astrid had urged Tim to urge Juliet to give Sullivan a job as a barman.

'I'll grant you Sullivan's a hopeless idiot,' Tim had argued. 'But bars are his natural habitat. He's got that laid-back charm thing. He relaxes people. This is the one thing he's built to do.'

The night before Juliet's bar was due to open, Sullivan slept on a camping mat in the stock room. This had been the week Astrid discovered the most galling of his infidelities and she had, quite reasonably, kicked him out of the house. Until he talked his way back in or found somewhere else to live, there was no harm in his kipping on the floor of his new workplace.

At three a.m., the smoke alarm woke Sullivan up. He'd tried to cook frozen hash browns in a wok on a hotplate but then forgot about them and fell asleep. The plastic handles of the wok had melted and set fire to the kitchenette.

Sullivan scrambled safely out into the rear lane and the fire brigade arrived quickly. But the smoke and water damage was bad enough to destroy Juliet's lovely elegant interior. She was so disheartened she abandoned the project and let the lease go. The place was taken over by a series of restaurants that only lasted a few months apiece. Sullivan's hash browns had left some curse wafting over the site.

Since the bar fire, Sullivan had done his best to avoid direct contact with Juliet. Tim suggested that was the best course of action and cowardice meant Sullivan was happy to comply.

The music venue, the Hammond Room, was narrow, dimly lit, warm from the press of bodies, its blood red walls pulsing with sound. Sullivan felt as if he were sliding inside an abdominal cavity but in a way that felt invigorating.

They bought drinks at the bar – soda for Sullivan, beer for Tim – then zigzagged their way closer to the stage and found a spot against the side wall. The band was playing blues at the rock end of the spectrum – some classics, some originals. The lead guitarist was an inventive player with husky, emotive vocals. The bass player wasn't one of those lethargic dudes plunking out a minimal bass line. This guy was dynamic, hands flying over the bass, occasionally leaning forward to the mike to do backup vocals. The drummer did the patter between songs, witty and likeable, and then banged the bejesus out of his drum kit with precision and power. For a three-piece, they managed to create a full, layered, driving sound.

Tim was right. Sully had forgotten how much he loved live music. He closed his eyes, let the drums thump in his ribcage, let the guitar twang through his sinews, let his blood swoop up and down with the vocals.

It occurred to him that he'd never really heard live music when sober. It turned out it was still good, maybe even better. Crisper, less muddy in his ears, but it still plunged straight to primeval receptors in his brain in a very satisfying fashion. Sullivan glanced across at Tim and saw he was loving it too.

A keyboard player jumped on stage to do a guest spot on 'Got My Mojo Working' and a few other numbers. He was a flamboyant performer and a blisteringly good musician, reminding Sullivan what a low-grade musician he himself had been in every way. If Sullivan could have ripped through a brilliant keyboard solo like this guy, he would have earned his berth on the planet.

Sully decided to give the self-flagellation a rest and try to enjoy the night. It gave him pleasure to see how a group of strangers in the bar moved to the music together, the same beat travelling through each body, so the whole crowd was one organism. Maybe it was merely an illusion of togetherness. No, the togetherness was real but it was only for a moment and would dissolve the second the music stopped.

Tim splashed his face with water at the basins, then stared at himself in the mirror as the water dripped off. Sullivan was washing his hands at the next basin. Pete should've been in the third mirror along. Tim felt the absence as a painful constriction of his throat.

He made eye contact with Sully in the mirror. 'Hey dickhead, if you really do this kidney thing, will it affect the way you piss?'

'No. I'll still have one kidney to do the job for me,' said Sullivan.

'You're less funny sober,' Tim pointed out.

'I know. Sorry.'

They took another beer and another soda into the side alley to inhale some fresh air.

'We talked a truckload of shit at uni, didn't we,' said Tim. 'We said you were going to be a journo or an actor or a musician. Something colourful and creative. Now look at you.'

Sullivan bowed. 'Only good for spare parts.'

'Exactly.'

'We were right when we predicted Pete would be a medical saint, saving the lives of the poor and powerless,' Sullivan pointed out.

'True. But I was only supposed to stay in the grubby banking sector for three, four years max.'

After uni, Tim's plan had been to use his finance brain to make a quick fat fortune with which to start a record label and launch new bands. He used to set exit targets and ask Pete to be the Keeper of the Pledge. 'I vow that I, Timothy Karl Wozniak, will be out of the money market by my twenty-sixth birthday.'

As the years went on, he added forfeits. 'Pete, if I'm not out of the market by my thirtieth birthday, I'll take you to dinner at the most expensive restaurant in Sydney.' Pete and Vincent scored a number of three-hat fine dining experiences.

By thirty-five, Tim had stopped setting the deadlines and had given up using Pete as a repository of his conscience. Now he cringed, not sure if he was more embarrassed by the naive twenty-one-year-old who made those pledges or the thirty-nine-year-old who'd let them crumble.

'Ah, mate,' said Sully as he sipped his soda water, 'things don't always pan out the way we'd hoped.'

'Yeah, well, I'm still there in the banking tower of evil, busy as a bee helping to destroy the world.'

To begin with, Tim had seen his job as value-neutral. He moved money from one place to another, like a board game for which he had a special talent. Sure, he didn't create anything of value and didn't use his considerable brainpower to better anything. But Tim used to believe his job wasn't actively immoral. He didn't kid himself about that any more.

'People are right to hate bankers,' he observed.

'If it's any consolation, we all do,' Sully replied cheerfully.

'At least Pete did what he said he was going to do.'

Sully smiled. 'He was such a considerate man, he even did his coming out in a considerate way.'

In high school, Tim and Sullivan had always been baffled that Pete never responded to the many girls who hurled themselves at him. Pete had one sweet girlfriend in the first year at uni. Then halfway through the second year, he announced he was gay. His main focus was on not making Tim and Sully feel uncomfortable about it or feel they'd been deceived.

Tim did his Pete voice: 'Don't worry. I don't find either of you guys attractive. I haven't been secretly wanking over you.'

Sullivan laughed. 'You were offended!'

'I was not,' Tim insisted. But in fact he had been a bit hurt that his freshly outed friend found him resistible.

When Pete met Vincent and fell in love, Tim had found himself slightly jealous, never having seen Pete's face light up like that before. But he let the jealousy drop when it was clear that Vincent would be a long-term and positive fixture. Tim ended up becoming friends with Vincent – not quite independently of the Pete connection but almost.

'How is Vincent doing?' asked Sullivan.

'I've only seen him once since the funeral,' explained Tim. 'We talk on the phone every week though. We're playing squash next Wednesday. It's going to take him a while.'

When the band finished at midnight, Tim was too drunk to navigate the city safely. Sullivan hailed a cab and told the driver Tim's address.

'It was good, mate. It was good,' was all Tim could say before Sullivan shut the cab door.

Sully decided to walk back to Glebe. His old mate Tim was a good man in many ways. Loyal. Brave enough to visit a dying friend in hospital every single day and brave enough to ring the bereaved partner and offer him open-hearted support.

If Sullivan thought too much about Pete, his body sagged into a defeated posture. So he forced himself to walk with his head up, shoulders back, spine elongated. He relished the chill of the night air on his face and the not unpleasant ache in his calves from all the walking he'd been doing with Mack.

Juliet lay in bed listening to Tim stumble in the front door sometime after midnight. He was obviously quite pissed, but engaged in that farcical business of trying not to appear so, steadying himself against doorframes as if he had just happened to choose that moment to pause and look around. He still dropped his keys too heavily on the hall table like a drunk person. He still bumped into the bookcase like a drunk person.

It was the pretence of it that annoyed Juliet. If Tim just let himself stumble around, honestly acknowledging how sozzled he was, she could respect that. But this self-delusion was pathetic and a further reason to scorn the husband to whom she was lashed like a hostage who'd given up all hope of rescue.

Juliet blamed Tim for the original dumb decision to go ahead with a pregnancy when she was so young it had stymied her life choices. But in those moments when she allowed a glimmer of mercy towards Tim, she acknowledged she'd also thought having a baby would be an adventure. And to be honest, pregnancy had given her an excuse to step back from what was turning out to be a lousy career.

Before the twins, Juliet had a series of shiny non-jobs – assistant to wankers in glamorous-looking businesses or working as an event coordinator – one of those things that sounded exciting but in fact involved booking portaloos and putting stickers on hundreds of place-cards.

But she and the other young women with event-management quali-
fications performed this drudgery wearing high heels and said they
were in 'public relations'.

Even if she and Tim had made the let's-have-the-babies decision
more or less together, Juliet later discovered, when she first emerged
from the sleepless, milky daze of the twins, that she was effectively on
her own. Tim was so busy at the bank, working long hours. Even at
home he was forever in his study following the markets. There was a
market open somewhere in the world twenty-four hours a day, so she
never really had him to herself. Tim would occasionally have a sooky
moment when he'd want togetherness, nuzzling up to her like a dog.
But a lot of the time she was very lonely.

So Juliet had looked around – what to do with herself now? She
decided against more kids – she hadn't enjoyed the process enough to
push out another one. She tried a few different part-time courses but
she'd never been one for studying.

She took a job for a while in a friend's boutique, selling strange
shredded silk garments, but the rich females who came into the
shop gave her the shits. And then when she brought home the modest pay packet from this irritating job, the amount seemed comical
and pathetic alongside the thumping great wads of money Tim was
earning by then. There was no need for Juliet to earn a single dollar
and it felt undignified to persist with a dull job for the sake of a pal-
try income. She could hardly complain that her work choices were
buggered because her husband earned so much – that would sound
obscene. But then the fact she was disqualified from complaining only
made her more furious.

Juliet envied people who found something they were good at and
did it. Their bright faces as they prattled on about their latest project
felt like a slap in her face, a reproach. Whenever she tried some new
course or job or business prospect, Tim would eagerly chirrup, 'How
was it?' He wanted her to get into something so he wouldn't have to
feel responsible for her happiness. Well, she wasn't going to enjoy

something just to make him more comfy. She had small moments of clarity when she knew this was self-defeating but how did that realisation help? She still couldn't see how to rearrange the components of her life that would make her any happier. She knew her own limits.

Juliet heard Tim walk up the hall in his socked feet and lean in the bedroom doorway. She knew he was hoping she was awake, hoping they could talk or have sex or both. He'd most likely got pissed because he was missing Pete so badly. Tim believed he had some exclusive hold on that grief, but he didn't. Juliet missed Pete too. She pretended to be asleep.

13

At six forty-five a.m. Sullivan was waiting at the job site when a truck pulled up, the back tray filled with rolls of heavy-duty black plastic sheeting.

A Colombian guy in his mid-forties hopped out of the driver's seat. He looked fit, solidly built, his work gear ironed, his manner politely formal.

'Good morning. I'm Jose Luis Rojas. Are you Mr Moss?'

'Yep. Yep. Please call me Sullivan. The guy at the office just said to show up here.'

Jose Luis nodded. 'Let's see how we go today. These are the guys you'll be working with.'

'Yep. I've already met Daramy and Rickie.'

Sullivan smiled at the two Cambodian men who were part of Jose Luis' regular crew. They were leaning against the cyclone wire fence, waiting for the boss to unlock the gate to the worksite, fiddling with their phones and murmuring to each other in Khmer.

Sully had gone for asbestos removal because he figured it was a job that people with other options would not choose, given the perceived health danger. Surely even Sullivan Moss could find work in that industry.

To be permitted on this job site he'd been required to attend a two-day TAFE course in the removal of bonded or non-friable asbestos. There were about twenty guys in the class, including half a dozen Khmer-speakers. Sully was intrigued to learn of the high percentage of Cambodians in the Sydney asbestos trade. A couple of Cambodians had established businesses some years back and drawn new arrivals in to work for them ever since. The Anglo guys in the tech course all seemed to be damaged in some way – ex-cons or shearers with broken bodies or sweet dumb lumps of boys sent there by their mothers.

Sullivan was surprised at how much he enjoyed doing the course. There was a bit of theory, practical exercises and a small written exam. He'd forgotten the pleasure to be had in learning about something and then scoring good marks in a test.

Sully had felt unusually confident on the afternoon he earned his TAFE certificate but standing here now on the footpath, he was nervy. He could see Jose Luis scrutinising him, assessing the likely value of this new worker sent from the employment office. Here was a soft, fat, sagging man, scuffing his runners along a hunk of broken concrete. Not a promising sight.

'Hey, boss,' grinned Rickie. 'We'll unload the truck, yeah?'

'Thank you, Rickie. Yes. And then I can explain the job to everyone,' replied Jose Luis in the deliberate English of a man picking his way around his own strong accent.

It was a simple job: removing the old fibro panels from a large extension at the rear of a house. Rickie and Daramy showed Sullivan how to prepare the site – laying the two-hundred-micron plastic sheeting and taping it down. They found a blue protective suit big enough for someone tall and helped him secure the extremities with duct tape, ankles to boots and sleeves to gloves.

When Sullivan was adjusting his respirator to fit, Jose Luis came over to explain earnestly, 'I know it's a hassle, mate, but I always want my guys in the full gear. Lot of cowboys in this business but not me. I do things properly. Safely.'

'Yep. Good. Excellent,' said Sullivan.

Sullivan tried to be methodical about the procedures he'd been taught at TAFE but he was frustrated by his own clumsiness, not used to handling a screwdriver and a nail punch, hesitant and constantly relying on Daramy to give him instructions. On the positive side, he avoided any glaring mistakes in procedure and worked hard, doggedly carting the plastic-wrapped parcels of fibro to load into the truck.

From the study Sully had done – in class and on the net – it was clear the job would put him in no more danger from asbestos than he'd ever been. He'd played on building sites as a kid, breaking apart fibro off-cuts and burning them in bonfires. He'd ripped up old carpet with hessian underlay, which he had now learned was recycled from the bags used in the fibro factory, full of blue asbestos, the deadliest kind. He probably already had a lungful of asbestos fibres. Doing this work – suited up, respirator on, spraying down the fibro sheets with water, using a special vacuum cleaner to suck up any fibres that might be released and following decontamination protocols – he wasn't really increasing his personal risk. Anyway, long-term health was not on Sullivan's list of priorities now. Asbestos would not damage his kidneys before he had a chance to donate one.

No, danger wasn't the issue with this job. It was the physical discomfort. The protective suit was like a person-bag made of Chux Superwipe but more tightly woven so it didn't allow the tiny asbestos fibres to penetrate. This also meant that the fabric didn't breathe at all, especially once the thing was taped up, zipped to the chin and snugly elasticised around the face. After only a few minutes of work, Sully was stinking hot inside, encased in his own personal tropical climate, and he was sweating litres. The respirator added another layer of unpleasantness, hot and chafing against his face.

Every time you wanted to take a leak or drink something, you had to decontaminate, rip off duct tape, peel off the sweaty suit. Then afterwards, you'd chuck out that suit, grab a fresh one and do the taping-up all over again.

By the lunch break at twelve-thirty, half the panels were down and packed. Rickie, Daramy and Sullivan vacuumed off each other's blue suits and chucked them in the hazard bags.

Sully was exhausted and dizzy – dehydration, probably – and stumbled across the nature strip to grab one of the water bottles Jose Luis provided. He guzzled water, flapping his sweat-soaked T-shirt to cool himself.

It was a shit job, no denying that. Sullivan was amazed he'd lasted until lunchtime. It was largely thanks to the help from his Cambodian co-workers. Rickie was young, cheeky, a bit of a joker. Daramy was quiet, dignified, patient. Both good guys. They'd even shared their lunch with Sully when it was clear he didn't have the energy to walk the three kilometres to the nearest takeaway food place.

Rickie and Daramy made phone calls and chatted to each other as they ate. Sullivan noticed that they spoke to him in English at regular volume but spoke their own language at low volume, barely audible, some mysterious pitch that only other Cambodians would properly hear.

All morning Sullivan had been aware of the boss observing him. Jose Luis went about the job of supervising the site in a straightforward, energetic way, but his face was knotted up with all the things he had to worry about. He spent the lunch break making a dozen phone calls and slogging through paperwork on the bonnet of his truck.

At three, the end of the work day, Sullivan found himself working alongside the boss as they packed up.

Sully tried a low-key, chatty question. 'How long have you been in this business, Jose Luis?'

'Fourteen years. Eight years since I started my own company.'

Sullivan made an I'm-impressed noise.

Jose Luis responded with a slightly spiky tone, as if answering some criticism or accusation from Sullivan. 'I keep the business small. I don't do the friable asbestos work.'

'Right. Why is that? Because the friable stuff is —'

'You need a lot more set-up capital for that stuff.'

'Right, right,' said Sullivan. 'That's a much bigger operation.'

'Yes. I stick to the medium-sized non-friable jobs. As long as I work hard, I follow the regulations and I have three or four good guys, it's a solid business.'

Sullivan realised that he'd been wrong to think Jose Luis was spiky. The guy was proud of his business, a little bit defensive, but not prickly.

'See you back here tomorrow?' said Jose Luis when they finished the pack-up.

Sullivan definitely heard the question mark. The boss obviously didn't expect him to show up again – based on long experience, presumably. But what Jose Luis did not appreciate was Sullivan's lack of options, nor was he aware of the quest that was guiding Sully's choices over the next nine months.

'Yeah. See you at seven,' Sullivan replied, with a tiny defiant edge in his voice.

By the time he made the long train trip home and slumped on the couch, Sully's good intentions to show up at work the next day leaked out of his aching body. He was supposed to go back to that job tomorrow and the day after and many days afterwards. He'd forgotten that part about having a job. It was a shit part.

Mack was happily licking the dried perspiration off Sullivan's forearms.

'Did you miss me, Mack? I reckon you had a better day than me, mate.'

Sullivan hauled himself up, deciding he should walk the dog before having the longest shower in human history. They'd take a stroll to buy vegies at that small supermarket where he could tie Mack up outside.

Assaulted by the harsh fluorescent lights inside the supermarket, Sully noticed the aisles were full of happy couples discussing biscuit choices and suddenly felt his loneliness weighing heavily on him. He should buy a treat to console his lonely self. And he deserved a reward for being brave enough to work with asbestos for a whole day.

He put bags of salted cashews and tortilla chips in his basket. After all, it would only be wise to replenish salt after all that perspiration. He also had a yen for something custardy – always a comfort food – so selected a twin-pack of custard tarts. Then while he stood at the fridge cabinet, the smoked cheddar presented itself as an obvious choice. Prowling the aisles for a tasty pickle product to go with the cheese, his eye fell on bottles of Tabasco, which sent his mind turning to Bloody Marys.

Would it be that big a deal? He could buy a very small amount of vodka so there would be built-in portion control. He had been scrupulously teetotal for something like four weeks now and a small amount of alcohol would be a harmless reward for that and all his other efforts. To be eligible as a donor he needed to improve his liver function tests, but there was enough time between his medical appointments, so two or three standard drinks would not mess with the results.

Sullivan added a carton of tomato juice and a bottle of Worcestershire sauce to his supermarket purchases, then went a few doors down to the bottle shop and bought 200 ml of Smirnoff. Wanting to avoid associations between drinking and being in Frank's flat, he walked to the park with his treats.

Sully took a few swigs from the tomato juice carton, then topped it up with Tabasco, Worcestershire sauce and vodka. This way he was ingesting vitamins, lycopene and other good stuff in the juice.

The alcohol rushed through his bloodstream like an old friend running into his embrace. He felt good. Stronger. Probably if you drank after a day of physical labour, your body could handle it, maybe even needed it. So this was different to his old drinking habits (boozing to get blotto after a day of lying around on a couch). This was entirely different.

By the time he finished the hipflask, he'd also chomped his way through a large bag of tortilla chips and the cashews. All that salt made him thirsty. A hipflask really wasn't much. He could surely have another one without doing meaningful damage.

Back in the bottle shop, he was proud of himself for again selecting a small 200 ml bottle from the shelf. Fortunately they also sold small tins of tomato juice he could use as the mixer for the second hipflask.

When Sullivan bought his third hipflask of vodka, he drank it neat because there was already too much tomato juice sloshing around in his belly. He felt a twinge of regret about the quantity but once he'd broken his sobriety, what difference did it make if he had two drinks or ten? The damage was done.

By the end of the third 200 ml, he felt decidedly pissed. Was he no longer piss-fit? Whatever. He wolfed down the tarts, dropping globs of custard on his shirt and onto the park bench when the pastry lost its structural integrity. He ate the smoked cheese straight from the packaging, biting into the block and breaking off a few pieces for Mack, who loved cheese.

Stroking that beautiful, loyal, champion dog, Sully pondered his good fortune to be living in Frank Dennis's flat, which reminded him he should thank Astrid.

He thought he remembered her mobile number but the first two numbers he called, confused strangers answered. He tried one more combination of digits.

'Hello?' said Astrid in that tentative voice people used when they didn't recognise the number.

'Hi. It's Sullivan,' he said, then went on without pausing for breath so she couldn't hang up on him. 'I wanted to thank you for organising for me to live in Frank's flat.'

'Right. I hope it's working out. You won't muck Natalie around, I hope.'

'I won't. And I really appreciate that you showed me that kindness.'

'Are you drunk, Sullivan?'

'Yes. Yes I am a little bit drunk,' he said, pompously. 'But it's the first time in ages.'

'Drunk,' she said flatly.

With the thump of that one word from her, Sullivan felt his good buzz vanish. Astrid had the ability to make him feel impotent and disappointing and sometimes disgusting. She didn't do it all the time but she could do it quickly when she wanted to. He suddenly saw himself sitting in a park at night, eating a block of cheese, with custard all over his shirt and three empty Smirnoff hipflasks in a nearby rubbish bin.

'Listen, Astrid, that's – look, fair enough – I only wanted to —'

'Natalie told me about the kidney donation idea. You're not really going to do that, are you?'

'I'm on the program. Don't know if I'll end up – y'know . . .'

'You know you won't follow through with it. So don't waste the time of the hospital staff, who've got better things to do than get the run-around from you.'

'Jesus, Astrid, you can be tough.'

'Sullivan, just look after Frank's dog and yourself. That's enough for you.'

'If someone could give up an organ and it would cure Grahame's MS, would you want that?'

'What? What? You can't – you know nothing about our situation. Do not say anything about Grahame.'

'Sorry. I'll shut up. It's just – oh fuck . . . why do you have to turn this into something bad? I can hear you judging me. I can it hear down the phone line. I can hear it in your breathing. Please just listen to what I'm . . . Why can't you just let me —'

'I'm going now, Sullivan. I don't want to speak to you, drunk or sober,' she said and hung up.

An hour later, Sullivan collapsed on the bed regretting the call. He needed an alcohol-sensitive lock on his phone, like the breathalyser ones they put on car ignitions. Given that such a device did not exist, he should avoid drinking at all, so there would be less risk of dumb phone calls that upset good people.

*

The next morning, Sullivan scraped together just enough energy to haul himself out of bed for his second day on the job. The motivational trick was imagining Astrid, Jose Luis, Anthony, Natalie and Diane Milton could all somehow witness this display of his diligence, and so would realise he wasn't as hopeless a character as they believed.

On the job site, his head was pounding from a hangover, his gut squelching its way through the ill-advised mix of tortilla chips, custard, Tabasco and cheese. On the positive side, he was managing to work more competently. But as the yard heated up – it was a much hotter day – Sully could feel all the moisture being sucked out of him, turning him into a strip of beef jerky inside the blue suit.

A hangover made working in the protective gear go from vile to unutterably vile – zipped up inside a non-breathing sack and a stifling face mask with your own foul body odours and secretions, rendered even more pungent when they were cooked up like some disgusting soup.

During the lunch break, Sullivan stripped down to his sweat-soaked singlet and shorts and sprawled on the nature strip. He drank huge amounts of water but no amount of fluid could replenish his desiccated tissues. How did the Cambodian guys do this? How did anyone do this? Sully had given it a red-hot go but clearly he wasn't built for the job. Presumably work that involved dehydration was not conducive to renal health. He should quit and have a go at scrounging some money out of Centrelink. Better to cut his losses with this job and scoot. He just needed some excuse or lie to offer the boss so he could extricate himself without too much ill-feeling.

Sullivan got to his feet, mind spinning with plausible lies, and walked towards Jose Luis who was talking on the phone, scribbling in a notebook.

Before Sully had a chance to utter any bullshit, Jose Luis turned to Daramy and asked, 'You two okay to finish off here this afternoon?'

'No problem, boss.'

'Good. Sullivan, can you come here?'

'Yeah listen, Jose Luis . . .'

'I need you to come with me. An urgent job. Grab yourself some gear,' said the boss, swinging open the passenger door of his truck.

Jose Luis landed a couple of council jobs a month – cleaning up small illegal asbestos dumps, chucked on the roadside by some dodgy builder or home renovator who didn't want to pay the special tip fees for asbestos waste.

This particular dump was considered urgent because it was outside a primary school. The stuff needed to be gone before the kids swarmed out of the school buildings at three.

Jose Luis and Sullivan parked the truck near the rubbish, suited up and established barriers around the pile of corrugated asbestos roofing. The two men fell into a productive working rhythm – lifting the broken roofing pieces together and laying them on plastic. Sully admired Jose Luis' dexterity with the duct tape to seal the double-wrapped packets of the evil stuff. Sure, it was a money-making business for the guy but there was skill in it and, this afternoon at least, urgency and purpose.

They worked quickly, wanting to finish before the three-o'clock school bell. It would freak out the kids if they saw men in hazmat gear on the street outside their playground.

The mess was cleaned up, the truck loaded and ready to leave, as the first flock of kids streamed out of the classrooms into the yard, chattering to each other, carting their enormous bright backpacks on their tiny backs. Sullivan found himself smiling.

Driving away in Jose Luis' truck, Sullivan swivelled his neck back and forth so the dashboard vents could blast him with chilled air. He was just as hot and sweaty as he'd been earlier in the day but now he refigured the sensation in his mind: imagining that he had sweated away all the booze from the night before, detoxifying, cleaning himself out. Maybe it could be seen as a spiritual cleansing, like a Native American sweat lodge. The pomposity of that notion made Sullivan laugh aloud.

'What?' asked Jose Luis, wondering why his employee was chuckling.

'This is good work you do. On the side of the angels.'

Jose Luis looked surprised, then frowned, then nodded. He offered to drop Sullivan at a railway station.

That night, Sully looked at photos of asbestos on the net. The magnified images were quite beautiful in their wicked spiky way, bouquets of translucent crystals, designed for some florid fantasy TV series.

He pictured the tiny treacherous fibres lodging in a person's lung tissues, multiplying, hardening, suffocating, then killing them. He could help prevent that happening to those little kids who played in the school yard. Sullivan Moss had the ability to remove some of this malignant substance from their environment. That work wasn't quite the same as rescuing a child from drowning but you could put it in the same rough category.

Sullivan had scheduled more appointments with the psychiatrist than would normally be required for his assessment as a potential donor.

'Given your situation,' said Anthony, 'I'm happy to do extra sessions if that suits you.'

That did suit Sullivan. Anything that felt like a step in the process helped him to stay on the path. Some of the cognitive behaviour therapy and visualisation techniques the shrink used were intriguing. And Sullivan found he enjoyed talking about himself with Anthony, as if they were discussing a guy they knew who'd lost his way but towards whom they both felt kindly. He also suspected his case carried a curiosity factor for Anthony and Sully always did his best to be entertaining.

At the beginning of the head-shrinkery, Sullivan refused to discuss his intentions after the donation – that is, whether he still planned to commit suicide. 'I'm keeping my eyes focused on getting ready to donate the kidney, not thinking beyond that.'

When Anthony pressed him on the suicide question at the next session, Sullivan proffered an answer he had prepared between appointments. 'Don't worry. I'm not thinking in terms of suicide any more. That's off the table now.'

He suspected that Anthony suspected this was a pacifying strategy but for whatever reason, he didn't call Sully on it.

Sullivan then asked Anthony straight out, 'In your opinion, am I wasting everybody's time? I mean, do you reckon I'll be cleared by the transplant committee in the end?'

'Well, in your case, there are a number of particular obstacles to overcome.'

'You mean my psychological instability.'

'And physical factors like your poor liver function. I imagine the committee will be concerned by your precarious financial situation and other issues.'

'So you're saying you don't hold out much hope for me.'

'That's not what I'm saying at all,' said Anthony. 'So far you've complied with every request, you've found employment and you're working to improve your health. Sullivan, you're an intelligent man and I believe you have considerable capacity for insight. Especially if you stay sober. Let's just see how we go.'

14

Sully drifted back to consciousness as if floating up to the surface of a rock pool on a warm day. The sensation was so unfamiliar that it took him a few seconds to identify it. This was what it felt like to wake up truly restored, having gone to bed sober but fatigued from physical labour, having slept solidly for eight hours, delicious sleep uninterrupted by endlessly looping thoughts or headaches or bathroom visits or nameless dread.

Mack was beside the bed, staring at Sully, patient. Sullivan reached out to scratch behind the dog's ears. 'Morning, Mack. Hope you slept as sweetly as I did, mate.'

Sullivan rolled his shoulders and noticed the existence – or maybe the reactivation – of a few muscles there. He'd been working for Jose Luis for three weeks now. It wasn't heavy work but it was constant, and more physical labour than Sullivan had ever done. There was definitely an increase in strength in his arms, back and legs.

Sullivan was about to swing himself out of bed, utilising some of this well-rested energy, but then remembered it was Sunday. There was no imperative to get up – not an ideal scenario for Sullivan Moss.

Weekdays were easier to manage. Sullivan had found a pinboard, file-cards and marker pens in Frank's spare room. He'd propped the pinboard on the kitchen bench and written up his work shifts and appointments on file-cards in block letters – the dates he was due to see Anthony the shrink, Dr Rupert the renal physician, Diane Milton or to have blood tests. In moments when motivation failed him, when it was hard to haul himself out of bed or stay away from the bottle shop, Sully would fix his gaze on the appointment board, like a coat-hook to hang his brain onto. He just had to plod onwards to the next appointment.

That still left the problem of weekends.

In the past, Sullivan could fill his waking hours with television but now he'd imposed restrictions on his viewing time. Being flaked out in front of the telly was a dangerous position. A guy like him could easily slide from that position into unhealthy thoughts. The same went for allowing the internet to soak up the hours.

Socialising wasn't an option. His old friends fell into two cat-egories – individuals who had endured a gutful of Sullivan Moss or individuals who might tempt him to drink. Tim occupied both categories.

So at eight-ten on a Sunday morning, the day stretched ahead for many hours before it would be reasonable to go back to bed. Days were mighty long when you were sober and alone. But Sullivan knew the dangers of inertia so he forced his feet to the floor.

If he was casting about for a purposeful activity, there was always one sure-fire option: make Mack happy by taking him for a walk. Sullivan and the dog set out on an extra long stroll, winding through the streets, into Jubilee Park and along the harbour's edge. Sully was content to linger in the sunshine in the leash-off area so Mack could explore or socialise with other dogs according to his fancy.

On the way back to the flat, Sullivan shopped for nourishing foodstuffs including lentils in three different colours. He planned to do some cooking, then he would allow himself a movie. It was starting to look as if he could coast safely through this Sunday, until the rou-tine of the week would hold him in place.

Sullivan fired up Frank's elderly computer to search for lentil reci-pes and saw that Tim had emailed some photos. Photos of Sullivan,

Pete and Tim – at a party in Year 10, a gig at the Bridge Hotel in 1992 and at Tim's wedding – all three of them laughing or pulling stupid faces.

Sully, Tim and Pete had ended up at the same small school in the last years of primary and as the three smart boys in the class, they fell into a friendship group. When it was time to confront their first weeks at the local high school with its slightly rough reputation, they were protected by the invisible armour of that primary-school friendship. Eventually each found his own place in the high-school ecosystem. Tim was loud and sporty, with lots of mates. Sullivan sustained a level of popularity by making people laugh and never challenging anyone else's status. Pete managed to be loved by the girls and still respected by the guys.

As adolescence progressed, they seemed an unlikely social trio. Music was one thing holding them together. They swapped mixtapes, tried to sneak into band venues together, packed tents into Tim's sister's Toyota to camp at music festivals. It was reassuring to have a friendship bond that existed separately to the surface posturing and judgement in the world of young men.

As Sullivan stared at those photos now, he missed Pete so badly he had to turn the computer off and shut the bedroom door to neutralise the power of those images. Tim must be indulging in one of his nostalgic moods. Understandable. But why send the photos to Sullivan? If the plan was to prod him into shame and self-loathing, it was working.

Sully gave up on the cooking idea and wandered into the lounge room. He lay on the floor with Mack sprawled beside him and remembered the last time he saw his now dead friend. Five months ago, in October last year.

Pete had texted, suggesting they meet for coffee in Newtown. Sullivan suspected this might be an intervention, instigated by exasperated friends sending Pete as their envoy to talk sternly to Sully.

By the time Sully got to the cafe in King Street he was late, but only ten minutes late. Maybe fifteen. Pete was waiting at a table by the large window open onto King Street.

'There is no doubt you are devilishly handsome, sir,' Sullivan said loudly enough to embarrass Pete in front of the other cafe patrons. This was something of a greeting tradition. Pete did indeed look handsome, sitting there wearing Vincent's brown leather jacket. Sully hadn't seen him for a while and he looked thinner in the face, which accentuated his strong jaw. Pete's slimness felt like a reproach, since Sully was turning into more of a lard-arse with every wine-guzzling, kebab-eating day.

The two friends hugged, made great-to-see-you noises and sat down. Pete was already drinking fresh mint tea. Sully ordered a cappuccino. (He liked the milky foam and the sprinkle of cocoa, even if it was considered an immature beverage choice by some.)

Sully decided to head off any well-meaning questions from Pete by saying, 'Hey, get a firm grip on the hand-rail, keep some oxygen and smelling salts handy: there's a job possibility for me floating around. In fact the guy might call me this arvo.' Which wasn't entirely untrue.

'That's great, Sully. About time you pulled your finger out.'

They chatted about a range of subjects, including people they knew, TV shows they liked and world events they fretted about. Usually Pete was full of news about some upcoming medical project in central Australia but today he seemed more keen to listen than talk.

Sully launched into a story about how he'd come to be chucked out of his most recent share house. It was a long tale about a hirsute flatmate wanting to shave his tufty back before a big date and Sullivan helping out by secretly borrowing a third flatmate's electric shaver in what he described as 'a covert operation'.

As Sully acted out the story, playing all the parts, juicing up the facts a little for entertainment value, he was glad to see Pete laughing. That was the object of the exercise. Sullivan felt the price he paid for being carried by his friends in so many ways was to be good company. Tim had a high-pressure job and a difficult family. Pete worked punishing hours in often grim scenarios. Sully saw his role as offering respite from the stress in their lives by being easy, undemanding, sometimes amusing company.

When Sullivan finished the story, Pete was smiling at him in an affectionate but oddly intense way.

'Listen, there's something I want to tell you,' he said. 'You remember when I had the mole cut out of my shoulder?'

'Years ago.'

'Yeah. I'm not sure if I ever told you the mole was a melanoma.'

Sully nodded warily, knowing enough to realise this conversation was taking a bad turn, when a shriek from the street outside cut through the burble of music and chat in the cafe.

Repeated shrieks came from a woman in her sixties with caked blue eye-shadow and eyebrows drawn on like black slugs. She was trying to extricate her shopping buggy from where it was wedged in the frame of a garbage bin on the street outside the cafe. In the process, she must've gouged her arm on the metal post. It wasn't bad but the blood from that small wound was making the woman, most likely mentally ill, hugely distressed.

Passers-by were wary of her. A couple of people approached to help but quickly backed away, repelled by her flailing hands and high-pitched squawking. Sullivan didn't blame them. People weren't sure what to do, worried they'd make the situation worse.

When it was clear no one closer was going to help, Pete stepped over the window ledge onto the footpath. He moved straight to the woman and took charge of the situation with confidence. The woman's shrieks, relentless like a car alarm, were doing Sullivan's head in but Pete didn't seem troubled by the noise or the blood. Another passer-by called an ambulance while Pete checked the woman's injury, murmuring reassurances, almost chanting to the poor lady.

Sullivan stayed where he was inside the cafe. It was better if he didn't get in the way. Pete was used to this kind of stuff because he was a doctor.

Pete took off the leather jacket and put it down on the footpath to coax the woman to sit. That was when Sully realised how gaunt his friend was. The flesh had melted off his skeleton leaving his ribs displayed like fence railings, shoulder blades protruding through the T-shirt material.

Sullivan couldn't handle listening to the squawking woman a second longer. He couldn't handle staying there to hear Pete say some terrible fact directly to him. He needed to find a way to escape.

Just then Pete looked up, smiled at Sully, and grimaced: *What a mess*. He was squatting on the footpath, holding the woman upright while they waited for an ambulance to come. Sully held his phone to his ear, pointing at it to indicate he had an important call and had to go.

Pete signalled back, waving goodbye and giving him a thumbs-up, assuming Sully was on the phone to the guy about the job.

Sullivan pretended to be listening to a call. He mouthed to Pete, 'I'll call you,' before scooting out the back of the cafe into the rear laneway.

A couple of months later Pete was dead without Sully ever having called.

Sullivan had made some effort not to revisit that scene in his head. Now, thanks to Tim's photos, he was lying on the floor of a dead man's lounge room, loathing himself.

What was he even doing here anyway? He didn't want to be here, lumped with these duties he wasn't really up to. He could walk out of this flat right now. No one would be surprised if he did something erratic. If he sent Natalie a text, she could surely find someone else for the dog. It would be easy to leave a phone message for Diane Milton. 'Sorry. Giving up the kidney donation thing.' Diane must be used to donors piking – she'd said as much. Jose Luis wouldn't miss him – he had other guys.

Sully could catch a bus up the coast to some pretty spot. Maybe camp out like the summer he spent in a tent in bushland at Crescent Head. Yes, it wouldn't be too difficult to slide out from the obligations he'd accumulated in recent weeks, find a beach somewhere and disappear. Why not do that? He should do that. His legs were twitching on the carpet, urging him to leap up and escape.

There were three sharp knocks on the door, which made Sullivan jerk with fright. He got to his feet and opened the door to find Gordana standing there. They had spoken a few times – on the entrance stairs and in the rubbish area – usually about Frank. She had obviously been very fond of Frank in her brusque unsmiling way.

'I need your help,' she said.

'Oh. Hi, Gordana.'

She didn't seem to notice that Sully was jittery and upset. 'Please leave the dog inside Frank's unit,' she said.

Sullivan left Mack in the flat and followed Gordana to the street.

She had purchased some furniture from a pine warehouse but the delivery guy was refusing to carry it beyond the building entrance. Sullivan saw a wooden dresser sitting on the pavement next to the truck. The thing was enormous, with a coating of yellow lacquer the colour of earwax.

'If you won't help me,' Gordana snapped at the delivery guy, 'my neighbour will help me.'

Gordana signed the receipt, almost tearing the paper with angry slashes of the biro. She must have recently refreshed her tangerine hair colour because it was especially bright, pulsing against Sullivan's eyeballs in the glare of the afternoon light. Then he realised the delivery guy was trying to make eye contact with him, smirking, conspiratorial, flicking his head towards Gordana as if to say, 'She's a weirdo.'

Sullivan felt protective, hating to think this guy was laughing at Gordana.

'If you're not going to help, you might as well head off now, mate,' said Sullivan, wanting the man to take his smirk away as soon as possible.

Sully helped Gordana carry the dresser inside her flat. It was heavy, an awkward manoeuvre, with Gordana making sharp warning grunts whenever the corners threatened to dent the walls.

The flat felt familiar because it was the mirror-image of Frank's. Gordana's was filled with way more stuff, too much furniture for the modest size of the room, the shelving covered in ornaments, framed photos of people, miniature vases of dried flowers, ethnic-looking craft items, all neatly lined up, even along the narrow top of the TV monitor. Sullivan imagined Mirko having to move gingerly, squeezing his big blockish body to sit somewhere between all the knick-knacks.

Sullivan helped Gordana position the dresser in front of another bookshelf in the lounge room.

'Do you want me to help shift the furniture?' asked Sullivan.

'No. I can do it later. But while you're here, you can help me with another task.'

'Oh. If I can. I mean, if it's something I can do.'

Gordana ducked into the kitchen. 'One moment.'

Sullivan had a sticky-beak into the backyard. Frank's yard had a square of lawn and U-shaped garden beds with enough space for a small outdoor setting. Gordana and Mirko's equivalent area was all paved, almost completely filled with potted plants, wrought-iron stands covered in yoghurt tubs planted with herbs, trellises growing vegies and two small frilly wrought-iron chairs that wouldn't have been wide enough for even one of Mirko's hefty arse cheeks.

Sullivan could hear a radio going in the small second bedroom. That room appeared to be set up as Gordana's workspace, with an ironing board and a row of laundry baskets on a trestle table. She ironed for people as well as working several shifts a week in a drycleaners.

Gordana reappeared with a hardware shop bag. 'I want to put this blind over the bedroom window. So it can be very dark when Mirko needs to sleep in the day.'

'Oh right, when he's been on night shift.'

'I have tools.' Gordana brandished a cordless drill. 'And I know how to do it. I need another person to hold the end while I drill.'

So Sullivan held the blind while Gordana measured and drilled holes for the brackets. Why Mirko couldn't help with this when he came home was never explained.

While Sullivan stood on the bed with his arms up, Gordana kept glancing at the tiny round Band-Aid and the bruise on the inside of his elbow.

'Is this from a medical test?' she asked eventually. 'Are you sick?'

Sullivan explained the kidney donation and the need to have blood taken from time to time. Gordana's face contracted into a tight squint as Sullivan spoke.

'Oh no,' she said. 'You won't for sure do this, will you?'

'Well, no, exactly. I might not get through the selection. I have to be approved by a special committee.'

'No. I don't mean . . . I mean you should not do this.'

'Oh.'

'A person must never do this to their own body. This is – oh . . .'

Gordana strode back into the living room and snatched a Croatian–English dictionary from a shelf. She beckoned Sullivan over and scrubbed her finger underneath one word: *povreda*, meaning 'violation'.

'Oh right. I get what you're saying,' said Sullivan. Maybe he should describe to Gordana how he had been violating his body in a multitude of pointless ways for the last twenty years, or the fact that he had planned to violate his entire body pretty thoroughly with the help of a twenty-three-storey building.

Gordana was staring at Sullivan, gazing with such intense pity it made him squirm.

He tried a perky grin. 'Anyway, I've got lentils so – uh . . .'

Gordana frowned at him. He realised 'I've got lentils' might sound to a non-native speaker like admission of a disease.

'I have to cook my lentils now,' said Sullivan, to clarify things, and made a quick escape.

An hour later he was stirring dhal when there was that distinctive knock on the door.

'It's me, Gordana,' she called out. 'Please keep the dog away from the door.'

Sullivan put Mack in the second bedroom and then opened the door to see Gordana holding out a plate piled with crescent-shaped biscuits, sprinkled with icing sugar, still warm from the oven.

'These are for you,' she said. 'Walnut half-moon biscuits. For helping with the furniture and the blind.'

'Wow. You didn't have to do that.'

'I want to thank you,' she insisted in her thudding monotone.

'Great. Well, great. You made them? They smell delicious. They look delicious. I'll hop into those later.'

Gordana nodded and then announced, 'I will not ever have sex with you.'

Sullivan stood, holding the door open with one hand and the plate of snowy biscuits in the other. He was frozen for several long seconds, then attempted a response that would convey acceptance of this declaration but with a tinge of disappointment so Gordana wouldn't feel unattractive, all of this hopefully communicated without any lascivious edge. This response came out as a nondescript 'oh' and he had no idea how Gordana would interpret it.

She nodded, apparently satisfied that she'd made her position clear, and indicated that she was leaving.

'Thanks for the lovely biscuits,' Sullivan called after her.

Late on Sunday afternoon, Natalie phoned Sullivan to check it was okay to fetch some of Frank's papers from the second bedroom.

Sullivan buzzed her through the main entrance. Natalie was thrown off-balance again by being in that hallway. This time, it wasn't the memory of moving her father's body. This time, her imagination flashed on Frank hurrying across that hallway on his way to a tryst with Gordana. Nat imagined he would have walked with that bouncy step he adopted when he was looking forward to something. She wasn't sure how to feel about that. Glad to know her dad had enjoyed those moments of happiness? Creeped out? Annoyed he'd never told her, even though they'd always been close?

Maybe there was a tiny amount of envy about his secret amorous arrangement. Frank and his neighbour enjoyed the frisson of naughty fun with no complications, the ego boost of being found attractive by someone, the straightforward physical pleasure. Natalie wouldn't mind a bit of that. But of course it was never straightforward and without complications. How on earth had Frank and Gordana seduced each other? Was it simply about convenient geography or did Frank have a penchant for strange dour women with garish hair?

And now Natalie had been thrust into a kind of twisted intimacy with Gordana through their joint criminal act.

Natalie was stalled in the hallway, trying to clarify her thoughts, just as Gordana emerged from her place with an armload of ironed business shirts.

'Natalie. Hello.'

'Gordana! Hi.'

Gordana was staring at her, direct and unblinking. 'Did you receive the —'

'Yes! Yes, yes. Thank you for all the yummy cakes and biscuits and . . . Delightful. But no need to send any more,' Natalie blurted. The baked goods had been arriving at the radio station at least twice a week for the last six weeks.

'I wanted to thank you.'

Natalie found herself babbling. 'I know! Very kind of you. Thanks received. Message received. But please don't send any more – not that they weren't delicious. But you don't need to – I am not going to say anything or create any – Look, just no more cakes, is that okay?'

Gordana responded with one brisk nod and headed out into the street. Natalie wanted to wait a moment on the landing, to settle herself before knocking on Frank's apartment door. But Sullivan had already opened the door and Mack loped out to greet her.

'Hello, Mack. Hello, my beautiful.'

Sullivan held the door open. 'Hi, Natalie.'

His hair had started to grow back so he looked more normal. His skin looked appreciably better, less cadaverous. He was smiling broadly.

Sullivan called out to Natalie from the kitchen. 'Tea? Cranberry juice? It's excellent for urinary tract health.'

'I'll go a cranberry juice,' Natalie called back.

When Sullivan brought the juice to her, she was kneeling on the floor of Frank's small second bedroom, flipping through the filing cabinet with one hand and scratching Mack's belly with the other.

'I need to talk to you about the plans for this flat,' she said. 'I was thinking —'

Natalie broke off with an odd gulp of breath when Sullivan offered her a couple of the half-moon biscuits on a plate.

'They're really good. Gordana from across the hall made them,' he explained.

Natalie shook her head. 'No thanks.'

She seemed awkward, upset even, avoiding Sullivan's gaze. She must want him to leave but was too kind to say it directly.

Sullivan should put her out of her misery. 'Do you want me to move out?'

'What? No, no.'

Natalie still seemed flustered. He tried to sound relaxed about vacating the place, to make it easier for her.

'It's cool. I mean, you probably want to put this place on the market and you don't want me dug in here like a tick.'

'No, it's not like that at all. The opposite. My brother and I haven't decided if we should sell or lease it out. So until we sort out Dad's estate, it's really helpful if you stay on. If that suits you.'

'Yeah, of course. It's perfect for me. But only if I can pay you some rent.'

'Oh no, don't worry. You're looking after Mack for me.'

'I have a job now, so I'd feel happier if I paid something,' Sullivan insisted.

He didn't want to taint the purity of his kidney project with any trace of bludging or advantage-taking. They agreed on a small rent – a quarter of market value was the most Natalie would accept.

'Astrid mentioned you had a job. That's good news,' she said.

'I've been lucky. I'm working for a great guy.'

'Isn't removing asbestos dangerous?'

'Not if you do it properly,' Sullivan assured her. 'And a job dealing with toxic material – well, many who've known me would say it's the field that best suits my aptitude and experience.'

Sullivan and Natalie exchanged a smile.

'Oh . . . next Wednesday, soccer training,' Natalie began.

'Yep. Mack's raring to go,' said Sullivan. 'Louis must be busting to see him.'

'He is. But I don't want to disrupt the routine you and Mack have going. What time do you usually walk him?'

'We're flexible. I mean, I'd be happy to time it so we arrive at the park in time for training.'

'Look actually, it'd be . . . if you really don't mind, it'd be —'

'I don't mind at all if that's helpful for you,' Sullivan jumped in and then worried that he might have sounded overeager.

'It's not ideal for Louis if I get a lot of dog hair in my car,' she explained.

'Dog hair and asthma. I get it.'

'Yes, so if you could bring Mack down some weeks, that'd really be a help.'

By the time Natalie left, it was late enough that Sullivan could eat an early dinner and watch a movie. That way he could traverse those last dangerous Sunday hours until bedtime, when sleep would sweep him to Monday and his routine would be there to hold him in check.

*

The following Wednesday, after work, Sullivan walked Mack to the soccer training ground – a small oval on the harbour, across the water from Anzac Bridge. Swarms of little kids occupied sections of the field, running between plastic cones or practising goal kicks.

Natalie, on duty in the canteen, waved hello. Before Sullivan could go over to her, Louis came sprinting across the grass and threw his arms around the dog.

Sullivan left boy and dog to play-fight uninterrupted for a while.

'Hi, Louis. I'm Sullivan, the guy minding your grandpa's place.'

'Hi.' Louis plonked himself down on the grass next to the dog. 'Thanks for bringing Mack. I can pat him, especially when we're outside. I just can't live in the same house as him.'

'Because of your asthma.'

Louis nodded. Sullivan left a pause. The kid must get sick of adults talking about his asthma.

Louis sighed. 'I really want to get a dog one day.'

'Maybe you could get some kind of oodle dog that wouldn't make you wheeze,' Sullivan suggested.

Louis said a polite 'Yeah' but Sullivan could hear that oodle dogs were not an exciting prospect for him.

'But you want a dog more like Mack. A *dog* dog.'

'Yeah,' said Louis emphatically.

'In Mexico, they have these ancient hairless ones. Well, obviously the actual dogs living there now aren't ancient but the breed started a long time ago. The Aztecs thought they were sacred. Xoloitzcuintli.'

Louis giggled. 'What?'

'I know. The name is hectic. Show-low-*its*-queen-*tli*. They're usually black, no hair, pointy ears, muscular bodies and tight little bellies. They don't shed hair because they don't have any but they're still proper dogs like Mack.'

'They sound excellent.'

'Smart too. Do an image search when you get home,' said Sullivan. 'The name is spelled all Aztecy.'

Sullivan wrote *Xoloitzcuintli* on a scrap of paper for him and Louis exclaimed, 'It starts with an X!'

'Which is always cool.'

'The Aztecs used to do human sacrifices. They cut out people's hearts when they were still alive.'

'So I believe,' said Sullivan.

It was coming up for Louis' turn on the goal-shooting drill so he straightened his shin guards and yanked up his football socks. 'Will you and Mack still be here for a while?'

'Oh yeah. We'll be here until practice is over.'

Louis ran back onto the field to do the drill.

Sullivan hitched up the pair of Frank's jeans he was wearing. They were so baggy in the waist, he must've lost a fair bit of weight. He would buy a belt.

15

Jose Luis' work crew was starting a new job – stripping fibro cladding off a garage behind a church. They would spend most of today, Friday, setting up the site and then complete the task on Monday and Tuesday. The weather was starting to cool a little, which made working in the blue protective suits slightly more bearable.

After almost two months of doing this work five days a week, Sullivan knew what to expect. He could count on the methodical stages of the job to keep him on track, a reliable rhythm that swung him through to the end of each day, even if it was one of the days he felt pissed off and yearning for a drink.

Sully liked being good enough at something. He enjoyed solving problems, figuring out how to get the job done with minimal release of asbestos fibres. He liked Daramy and Rickie, and the Cambodian food they brought for lunch was always delicious. He respected Jose Luis and the fair, careful way he ran the operation. In recent weeks, once Sully had proved himself, his boss had become quite friendly.

As a bonus, Sullivan enjoyed having someone to talk to about Colombia, a favourite from his travelling days. Once Jose Luis realised that Sully held genuine fascination and regard for his home country, he was relieved.

'Usually when I say "I'm Colombian", people ask me a lot of questions about Pablo Escobar and drug mules or they ask to buy cocaine. Big joke.'

Today, as they prepped the site and suited up, Sullivan was aware of a neighbour from a house adjoining the church grounds. The man in his late sixties was making scouting missions into his yard, keeping up surveillance, scowling as if he could make them disappear with the power of his disapproving gaze.

Jose Luis had leafletted the surrounding properties, informing residents of the job in their street. But once people saw the signage – *Danger. Asbestos Removal In Progress* – it could generate a degree of panic.

Sullivan admired the way Jose Luis dealt with disgruntled neighbours. He would courteously explain the safety procedures, countering suspicious questions about his accent, enduring the reality that he was unlikely to convince the person of anything.

After each of these encounters, Jose Luis would be cranky, with that spike of defensive pride Sullivan had seen on their first meeting. He would slam the tools around, declaring to no one in particular, 'Perhaps these people would like to know that I am an honourable man – trying to comply with the regulations and get some necessary work done. But still I have to be polite to these ignorant people. These offensive people.'

It was when Jose Luis' work crew was taking a lunch break, sitting on the stone wall beside the church, that the neighbour made his move, walking up the path to his front gate. The self-important way he held his neck was enough to give an idea of the outraged speech ready to come out of his mouth.

Jose Luis couldn't see the guy approaching because he was on the phone, leaning over the bonnet of the truck, entangled in a difficult negotiation. Struggling to keep his cool, he kept repeating, 'That's not what we agreed. No. That wasn't the agreement.'

If the pissed-off neighbour tapped Jose Luis on the shoulder in his current mood, it could turn nasty. To avoid an inflammatory moment, Sully grabbed one of the leaflets and decided to head the man off before he reached Jose Luis.

As Sullivan walked across the grass, he felt like a piss-weak gladiator stepping into the arena to face a wild beast shipped from Africa. Obviously this man wasn't a beast who could tear Sullivan's arms from their sockets and shred the flesh from his ribs. Still, the guy reminded Sully of Pete's father, a dark-tempered policeman who had always made Sullivan feel feeble, caught-out and about to be dismembered.

'Hello, sir,' said Sullivan. Something about the guy's stiff posture made him opt for 'sir' over 'mate'. 'Did you receive one of these information leaflets in your letterbox?'

The gentleman snorted. 'Do you think I'm some kind of idiot? I know what happens when you muck around with asbestos. I know demolition guys are ratbags.'

He had no intention of loosening his grip on righteous anger. Sullivan would just have to stand there and let the man's fury blast at his face. It wasn't pleasant but it wasn't going to kill him.

'Let me assure you, sir, that our supervisor follows the regulations to every detail. Jose Luis is busy right now but . . . look, I could explain the safety protocols to you if that would —'

'You don't need to explain any damn thing to me, sunshine. I was in the building trade.' The angry man was craning his neck now, squinting at Daramy and Rickie. 'You trying to tell me those jokers have their tickets for working on a site like this?'

'Yep. They do.'

The guy grunted, unconvinced. Sullivan tried a different tack, meeting the man's gaze directly. 'You were a builder?'

'Forty-five years.'

'Forty-five years. Wow. Did you build the extension on the back of your place?'

The gentleman nodded, thrown off-balance by Sully's chatty tone.

'Nice work,' Sully went on. 'I noticed the roofline you went for on that back section – the way it slopes down and then up again.'

'Butterfly roof.'

'Oh, yeah, a butterfly shape. Does that give you a lot of light in the back room?' asked Sullivan.

'Oh yes, it lets in way more light than a traditional skillion roof.'

Sullivan persevered, relentlessly matey, asking questions that flattered the man's pride in his building knowledge. Eventually, the guy was chatting away, offering professional advice about the timber frame of the structure being demolished. By the time Sullivan had finished, the neighbour actually smiled at Jose Luis before heading back inside his house.

Sully walked over to join his workmates, buzzing with pride at this achievement.

'Thank you, Sullivan,' said Jose Luis.

'No worries.'

That afternoon, he and the boss stayed back on their own for the clean-up. While Sully was taking down the warning signs, Jose Luis was on the phone, speaking Spanish.

Then he glanced up and said, 'My wife said you should come for dinner tonight.'

'Oh, that'd be lovely. Are you sure?'

'I'm sure. Let's go.'

Jose Luis was kind enough to make a detour via Glebe so Sullivan could run inside and feed Mack.

'Sorry to leave you on your own tonight, mate,' Sully said to the dog. 'But I've got a social invitation, which as you know is a rare and precious thing for me. We'll go for a walk when I get back, no matter how late. That's a promise.'

Sitting at the round pine table in the Rojas family kitchen, Sullivan realised that until tonight, he'd only seen half or maybe two-thirds of his boss. In the company of his wife and daughter, Jose Luis was a larger spirit, louder, more handsome even. And physically he seemed to take up more space. The business worries that clamped him down during the day were put aside, and with his family around him, he expanded, like bread dough rising. Joyful bread dough.

Jose Luis strode around the kitchen of the small Marrickville house he had renovated himself. He was grinning, scrubbed, wearing a red and blue checked shirt, his wet hair combed back. He and Sullivan had both showered and put on clean clothes.

It was loud in that house. No wonder Jose Luis found the barely audible murmuring of the Cambodian guys unnerving. There was music playing, at high enough volume that conversation almost had to be shouted. Jose Luis' wife, Liliana, a voluptuous forty-year-old woman with a love of black eyeliner, was preparing dinner, clattering the cookware with surprising force. She kept yelling in Spanish through the house to her daughter who yelled back in English. Jose Luis participated in the bellowed exchanges as well as singing along with the choruses of songs and peppering Liliana with questions about the whereabouts of the good drinking glasses. She roused on him for getting in her way, feeling the need to do so quite loudly. It was amazing that it only took three people to make so much noise.

'A drink, Sullivan?' asked Jose Luis. 'You have tried aguardiente before, yes?'

Yes, Sullivan had indeed drunk his fair share of the 'fiery water' from Colombia.

'It's great stuff. But I won't have any, thanks. I'm not drinking alcohol at the moment,' Sully explained.

He noticed Jose Luis and Liliana exchange a look, as if this were an issue they had both wondered about.

'Some unfiery water would be lovely, thanks,' said Sullivan.

After more noisy argy-bargy about glassware, Jose Luis sat at the table with water for Sullivan and an aguardiente for himself. 'I only drink this on Fridays and Saturdays. Never before a work day.'

The strong anise scent of the stuff took Sullivan back to many long nights in Colombia. Fortunately, the memory of the fetid aguardiente hangovers helped him resist the temptation to drink it now.

The daughter, eighteen-year-old Teresa, joined them at the table for chicken soup. She was a younger version of her mother, right down to the black eyeliner and boisterous manner.

'Teresa is now studying at Sydney University to be a dentist,' announced Jose Luis proudly.

'That's fantastic,' said Sullivan. 'You enjoying it?'

Before Teresa could answer, Jose Luis jumped in. 'Not easy to get into dentistry. My daughter's smart but also she worked very hard for the marks to get in.'

Teresa thumped him on the shoulder and rolled her eyes at Sullivan about her father's boasting. 'Yeah, big workload but it's good.'

After the soup, Teresa jumped up from the table, heading out to a party. This sparked another noisy argument among the three of them. The shouting was mostly in Spanish but Teresa put her case in English, so Sullivan caught the gist of it. Jose Luis thought Teresa should stay for the rest of dinner, Liliana disagreed with him but also seemed cross with Teresa about a number of separate matters, and Teresa was determined to go no matter what they said. The upshot of the shouting was that Teresa dashed off to her party and her parents were quite happy about it, as if the argument had been conducted out of duty rather than real concern.

'Great to meet you, Sullivan,' said Teresa as she buckled up her absurdly high wedged shoes. 'I'm sure I'll see you again. Dad loves you.'

Liliana served *carne guisada* for main course and dessert was one of Sullivan's all-time favourites – caramel flan.

'Thank you so much, Liliana. This is all incredibly delicious,' said Sullivan.

'Ah well, I don't have time to cook like this every night,' she replied. 'Just on Fridays, to soak up the aguardiente.'

Sullivan flashed her a smile. 'Jose Luis is a lucky man.'

He found himself flirting with Liliana but in a safe way. Jose Luis and his wife were so connected, touching each other constantly, even holding hands under the table sometimes, that it meant flirtation with anyone else could be flattering, but neutralised and harmless.

After dinner, they moved into the tiny lounge room. Jose Luis took the bottle with him, having drunk a fair bit of it already. Full of good food, pissed on Colombian liquor, stroking the curve of his wife's calf, Jose Luis waxed lyrical about various topics.

He became most soulful when he talked about their decision to emigrate to Australia fifteen years ago. 'It's *because* I love Colombia so much that I must, must, must make a success of our life here. Because Liliana and me, we made a sacrifice – to leave a country we love – so the sacrifice must be worth it.'

'I get that,' said Sullivan. 'Looks like it has been worth it.'

'Yes. But to do this, I have to stay and run the business and I can't spend time visiting my home. The more I love Colombia, the more is the sacrifice of leaving, which means the more is the reason I have to stay here and make a success. Do you get what I'm saying?'

'I think so,' said Sullivan.

When Jose Luis paused for breath in the middle of his rave, Liliana nudged his leg.

'Ask him,' she urged her husband as she stared at Sullivan with a faint smile on her face.

'What?'

'Ask Sullivan what's going on in his life.'

It was obviously something Jose Luis and Liliana had discussed before tonight. She nudged her husband again and he waved her off. 'That's Sullivan's private business.'

Undaunted, Liliana leaned forward. 'We are confused why an educated person is doing this job. You have no wife or girlfriend and you live alone in a dead man's home with the dead man's dog.'

Jose Luis shooshed her. 'Don't interrogate him. Sullivan is a decent person.'

Liliana smiled and Sullivan felt her curiosity was good-hearted rather than suspicious. She said, 'Jose Luis worries about you.'

This ignited another vigorous discussion in Spanish. Sullivan didn't need to understand any of the words to appreciate that Jose Luis was curious but also genuinely worried about him. Sully had not intended to say anything about the kidney donation, not sure an employer would take kindly to the idea. But he hated the idea of Jose Luis worrying about him, so he had to offer some explanation.

Sullivan told the two of them a short version of the mess his life had become and the basics of the donation process. Jose Luis and Liliana listened, big-eyed, quieter than they had been all evening. When Sully finished his explanation, he saw Jose Luis squeeze his wife's arm.

'Ah, you see?' he said and she nodded, as if Sullivan's plan to donate an organ was a possibility they had speculated about on many occasions.

Jose Luis lurched between exclamations of admiration – 'You are a wonderful person!' – and a barrage of questions – 'Why a kidney? Have the doctors said it's for sure?'

Sullivan did his best to deflect the inappropriate praise and answer the questions but the fervour of Jose Luis' response was beginning to make him uncomfortable. Liliana came to Sullivan's rescue.

'Enough, Jose Luis,' she said. 'You know what I think Sullivan needs right now? A haircut.'

Sullivan's hair did indeed look strange, the shaved stubble having grown out into an unfortunate golliwog shape.

'Yeah, I do need a haircut,' he admitted.

'I'll cut it for you,' said Liliana.

'Oh, no . . . you don't need to do that.'

'Liliana is a hairdresser,' said Jose Luis. 'She's very good.'

The two of them were an unstoppable force. Minutes later, Sullivan was in a chair in the kitchen with a barber's cape around his shoulders.

Liliana was firm, almost rough, positioning Sullivan's head and pushing his hair where she thought it should go. It was the first time in a long while that a woman had touched him, not counting medical personnel. He allowed himself to enjoy the feel of her fingers on his scalp and neck. Later, at Frank's place, he had a good look at himself in the bathroom mirror and was pretty happy with the result.

While Liliana snipped and combed, Jose Luis washed the dishes. He kept glancing across at Sullivan, occasionally nodding to himself with an intensity that was a little troubling. Some of it was the aguardiente, of course, but Sullivan also suspected that his boss was now imagining him to be a much better man than he really was.

16

If Natalie added up the minutes she had spent talking to Sullivan Moss on the sidelines at soccer over the last couple of months, it would amount to more total time than she spent in communication with any other human being, not counting Louis and impersonal work talk.

Sullivan and Mack never missed Wednesday training, even in the rain. If a Saturday game was held at a ground within dog-walking distance, he would be there. Three weeks into the season, when a match was scheduled at a more distant field, Louis had asked if they could give Sullivan and Mack a lift in the car. Natalie had agreed to this plan, ensuring she gave the car a good vacuum afterwards to get rid of any dog hair.

Sully introduced himself to the other soccer parents as Natalie's 'tenant and dog-walker'. A few of the parents must have wondered and gossiped to observe Sullivan and Natalie talking together. She decided not to care what version of reality they wished to construct.

Over the weeks, she noticed that Sullivan lost a considerable amount of weight quickly, the way boozers who stop boozing can. Instead of his skin being pallid and puffy, he was now clear-eyed and tanned from working outdoors.

She enjoyed talking to Sullivan Moss, hearing his stories, his thoughts about Jose Luis, his responses to Frank's books he was reading. And she ended up telling him pretty much everything about her life, censoring herself less than she did with anyone else. This was because Sully seemed genuinely interested, and because he didn't seem to judge.

Many people said 'I'm not judgemental', but that was rubbish. Natalie was familiar with the particular expression on the face of a listening friend or acquaintance – the face pinched in concern but with the gleam of a smug smile just below the surface. *Thank goodness my life is not as stuffed up as Natalie's.*

Sullivan listened with an open face, his sympathy seemingly unconditional. He did his best to understand the subtle politics of Natalie's workplace. She found herself revealing her hope of getting an on-air job and her fear she wasn't good enough. Blessedly, Sullivan didn't respond with patronising pep talks about how Natalie should conduct her career, as Astrid did. Nor was there any condemnation of Natalie's choices, like the ones Judy dished out. Sullivan just listened and tried to be clear about the nature of the issue.

He did venture one opinion. 'Objectively, you have a beautiful speaking voice. And personally, I would find your intelligence, sense of humour and responsiveness to people very enjoyable to listen to on the radio.'

Natalie nodded her acknowledgement of this compliment but then rapidly changed the subject. Compliments were hard to hear, like being poked in the most tender part of your anatomy, so you had to tense up or pull away.

In terms of his own life, Sullivan had an air of serene acceptance. He had one goal: the kidney donation. He wasn't thinking about the future or career or relationships or anything. That seemed to make him enviably peaceful.

One Saturday match, mid-season, Sullivan stood beside Natalie on the sideline watching the kids play. It was clear to Nat that Louis was unhappy out there on the field, not concentrating and missing easy shots, which made him cranky with himself.

Natalie called out, 'It's okay, mate. Shake it off.'

'Something up with Louis today?' Sullivan asked.

'He got a disappointing message from his father.'

Brendan had not been responding to messages from his son and just this morning had sent Louis a text, reneging on a promise to visit Sydney, letting the boy down in a way that had become maddeningly typical.

After the game, Louis flopped on a sideline bench, exhausted and crying. Natalie sat with her arm round him, feeling his shoulders jerk as the sobs went through him. It was always difficult seeing her child unhappy, knowing she was helpless to fix it. She offered reassurance but mostly she just waited him out, staying close until his distress was expressed or expelled or whatever the process was.

Sullivan Moss hovered near the end of the bench, holding the dog on the lead. He looked uneasy, his legs jittery, bouncing on his toes like a runner at starting blocks, ready to sprint in the opposite direction.

'Listen, guys, I should make myself scarce,' he said. 'See you at training.'

But before Sully could escape, Louis reached for Mack and the dog loped across to offer himself for a pat. So Sullivan was obliged to hang about for as long as the dog-patting went on.

'Mum says we can go to Officeworks to cheer me up,' Louis explained. 'Hey Mum, can Sullivan come with us?'

'Oh. Umm . . . I suppose so.' Natalie didn't want Sully to be ambushed by Louis into joining them on this excursion. The poor man already looked uncomfortable about being roped into the whole crying-child-family-angst scene. 'He might be too busy to come to Officeworks.'

But then Sullivan said, 'I'll come. A man is never too busy to go shopping for stationery.'

In the Officeworks car park, they left Mack in the car with the windows wound halfway down, agreeing on a strict twenty-minute time limit.

Inside, Nat watched her son lead Sullivan down his favourite aisles. Even though Louis' eyes were still puffy from crying, he was laughing, having shaken off his sadness with a speed Natalie envied. As Louis raved about the many uses of giant Post-its, Sullivan listened, making suitably impressed noises. The boy was soaking up his attention, hungry for this kind of fatherly company, even if Sullivan Moss wasn't exactly father-figure material.

Friday afternoon in his office, Tim was in a sullen and restless mood. The columns of figures on the computer screen in front of him seemed so monumentally unimportant, he could barely muster the interest to decipher their meaning. He needed to shift himself out of this grumpy state.

He looked through the glass wall to the outer office. There was no one out there he felt like talking to. He grabbed his mobile.

'Dickhead,' he said when Sullivan picked up the call. 'Wanna see a band tonight?'

'Sure,' said Sully.

Tim was surprised by Sully's sobriety and persistence with his new plan. So many people Tim knew were stuck in some way, their concrete had set hard and there seemed to be no changing it. But here was Sullivan, defying every expectation.

The two of them grabbed some Vietnamese food in Marrickville and then walked to the venue. Early on in the band's set, Tim realised they'd chosen the wrong gig.

'Reggae,' groaned Tim. There'd been three numbers in a row.

'I don't mind a bit of reggae,' said Sullivan.

'Mate, a little bit of reggae goes a long way.'

'Is it because the unremitting beats prod at your brain tissue?'

'Yes, they do,' Tim confirmed. 'But that's not the main thing. It just doesn't have any . . . oh . . . Music has to have sexual energy, right? It's gotta have some sort of . . . oh . . . you know . . .'

'You want music to have some groin,' suggested Sullivan.

'That's it. Yes. Groin.'

'Maybe so. I don't reckon it always has to be overt, hip-grinding, grunting stuff,' Sullivan went on. 'The groin can be subtle. Even a country ballad can *potentially* have groin. For example, Dolly Parton.'

'Dolly has plenty of groin in her own way,' Tim acknowledged. 'But reggae has zero.'

'You bop your head to reggae in a flaccid sort of way. There's no impulse to move the hips, even metaphorically.'

'Exactly my theory.'

'The trouble with your theory,' Sullivan pointed out, 'is that reggae is associated with a pretty sexed-up culture. A lot of babies were conceived, in Jamaica and elsewhere, to a reggae beat.'

Tim just shook his head.

'Reggae makes sense if you're very stoned,' ventured Sullivan.

'Arguably. But we're not stoned.'

They left the band room and moved into the quiet front bar of the pub. Sitting together without music, Sullivan totally sober and Tim still quite sober, it suddenly felt more raw and unpredictable between them.

Tim couldn't fight the urge to ask, 'So why the fuck didn't you visit Pete in hospital?'

He could see Sully was caught off-guard, shuffling beer coasters around on the table for a moment, before attempting an answer. 'I did go to the hospital once. Saw heaps of people buzzing in and out of his room. Nurses and doctors who were qualified to take care of him, or the sort of lovely friends who could be emotionally supportive in the right way. Figured there was nothing I could do for him so I snuck off.'

'Come on, you could've talked some distracting bullshit to him or something.'

'But that wasn't going to save him, was it.'

'No,' Tim conceded. 'We all felt . . . I mean . . . you could've at least —'

'There's no excuse. I couldn't face him. Knowing he was dying.'

'Weak as piss.'

Sullivan sighed. 'Yes. I know that. I'd watch myself sitting on the couch listening to his phone messages but doing nothing, like I was seeing myself on a surveillance camera. The only way not to feel totally shit was to stay drunk.'

'You tried to top yourself because of the Pete thing? Is that why?'

'Well, not only that. All of it. You know. That was just a trigger.'

'I can't imagine wanting to do it,' said Tim. Many people did commit suicide – in every country and in every era of history – but it was not a frame of mind Tim could truly comprehend.

Sullivan shrugged. 'I felt bad and I wanted it to be over. I don't think it's very complicated really.'

It pained Tim that he hadn't been able to save Pete and hadn't been able to save Sully. Now he also found himself feeling strangely offended. He'd like to imagine his friendship might have been enough to hold Sullivan in life. But he knew depression didn't operate that way.

They could hear the band starting a new number, 'The Thrill is Gone'.

'There's a bit of groin there,' said Sully.

'There is. Let's go back in, yeah?'

It was a relief to both of them to end the conversation and let the music fill up the space.

At his next session with Anthony, Sullivan plonked himself into the velvet chair in an unsettled mood. Usually he made it his business to be cheerful, to be Anthony's most enjoyable patient, but today he couldn't hide some frustration.

'You know the renal unit has an anonymity policy, right?'

Anthony nodded.

'If I get through the assessment process and cough up a kidney,

I'm happy to be anonymous. But I would like to know something about the recipient.'

'This is really bothering you?'

'It is.'

'Does it matter who receives your kidney?' Anthony asked.

'I guess not – hang on, is that what I really think? No. I would like to be sure my kidney goes to the right person.'

'What kind of person would be "right"?'

'Someone who's making a contribution to the world,' Sullivan said, then laughed at the pompous tone in his own voice. 'I mean, the person doesn't have to be a groundbreaking scientist or a UN peace negotiator or a world-class bassoonist or anything. Just someone who's . . . I dunno, making a decent go of bringing up their kids or doing a job that adds to the sum total of good things in the world. So that getting my kidney helps them survive to do more of the worthwhile stuff they do.'

'Sure,' said Anthony. 'But who's to say what counts as worthwhile?'

'Oh come on, you know what I mean. Whichever skill or personal quality or achievement makes a positive contribution to the planet and would make a person kidney-worthy.'

'I guess I want to challenge the idea you have about what makes a person kidney-worthy.'

Sullivan bunged on a mock-earnest voice. 'Every life is precious.'

'Are you saying every life isn't precious?'

'I'm saying I'd rather my lovely juicy kidney – which I'm spending time and effort growing to its healthiest state – didn't end up going to a wrong-un.'

'Who counts as a "wrong-un"?' asked Anthony.

'Some deadhead like me who is just as likely to squander my valuable renal gift with booze and poor dietary habits.'

'That's not how you're living your life now, is it?'

Sullivan hooted a laugh. 'I'm a model citizen now because I feed a dog and take old fibro to the tip and change light bulbs for a peculiar Croatian lady.'

'Well, yes. Most people would say —'

'Yeah, yeah.' Sullivan flapped his hand dismissively.

'But let's forget all that for a moment,' Anthony went on. 'Ask yourself, isn't every human being . . . well, I was going to say "precious" but you've just made fun of that word.'

'Sorry, sorry,' Sullivan murmured. 'I guess we have to believe every life is precious in one sense.'

'And every person has value unconditionally and has a right to expect —'

'Steady on, doc,' interrupted Sullivan. 'I could give you a list of not-so-precious individuals.'

'I'm sure you could. But think of it this way, isn't there —' Then Anthony paused and said, 'In fact, I want you to close your eyes for a moment.'

Sully closed his eyes, always up for a new game.

'Take a few slow breaths in and out. Be aware of the coolness of the air going in your nostrils and down into your lungs. Focus on the weight of your body in the chair, your feet on the floor, your hands resting comfortably on the armrest.'

Sullivan breathed and felt himself drift into that lovely tingly state of relaxation.

'Now, I want you to picture the person you were four months ago, standing on the top of that building.'

Sully took a moment to conjure the scene. He was good at the visualisation exercises. Within seconds, he saw himself as he had been that day on the rooftop as vivid as a movie clip and muttered, 'That poor fuck.' He tried to make it sound jokey but couldn't entirely hide the pain in his voice. 'I won't even try to describe the tragic Hawaiian shirt that guy is wearing.'

'There he is,' said Anthony. 'Now picture that man being wheeled into the hospital. He's in renal failure, won't survive long without a transplant. You're the best match for him. How do you feel about giving him your kidney?'

'Jesus . . . Can I check with him if he's —'

'No, you can't apply any measurements or conditions,' Anthony insisted. 'He is who he is. A new kidney is his only chance of life.'

'Right . . . well . . .'

'Really look that guy in the eye. He's a human being who needs something from you. What are you going to say to him?'

The room fell so silent Sullivan could hear the rumble of trucks two blocks away. He was trembling slightly.

'I guess . . .' Sullivan took a shaky breath in. 'I guess he can have my kidney.'

A moment later, Sullivan opened his eyes and laughed. 'I tell you what though, doc, as soon as that loser recovers from surgery, I'm gonna stalk him and make sure he takes decent fucking care of my organ.'

Sullivan went on in that vein, joking so vigorously that he broke whatever spell he'd been under moments before, until their appointment time was up.

17

In Jose Luis and Liliana's kitchen, Sullivan dried the last of the lunch dishes, including the plastic container in which he'd brought one of Gordana's walnut cakes.

Over the last three months, Sully had been a regular guest at their noisy Sunday lunches, along with various Colombian friends, neighbours, Teresa's friends, plus hairdressers Liliana knew and demolition guys Jose Luis used to work with. Most of the demolition guys were deaf so the high volume level of the music, chatter and political arguments didn't bother them. The lunches often stretched on into the night. Sully enjoyed these events but his favourite part was staying back to help Jose Luis and Liliana with the clean-up.

'I'm going to have to find a couple of new workers,' Jose Luis was moaning to Liliana as he swept the floor. 'Soon we will lose Sullivan for the time he needs to recover from . . .'

Jose Luis waved his hand around his own kidney region.

'I don't know for sure I'll get through to donation,' Sullivan pointed out.

'We know you will,' said Liliana.

'And in December Daramy is going to Phnom Penh to visit his parents. A month, maybe two,' said Jose Luis, who then went quiet momentarily. He often talked to Sullivan of his admiration for the Cambodian guys' devotion to their parents, their trips home to visit elderly parents as soon as they could afford it.

Liliana deposited the last of the empty bottles in the recycling with an ear-jangling clatter. Jose Luis lunged over and wrapped himself around her. They clung to each other as standing spoons for a long time, not troubled that Sullivan was right there.

'I would give you my kidney if you needed it,' he said to her.

'I know you would,' she replied calmly.

'Teresa too, of course.'

'Of course.'

'And if my parents needed a kidney I would fly back to Colombia straight away,' he said. 'But I don't think I would give my kidney to a stranger.'

Liliana made an *mmm* sound.

'Does that make me a bad man?'

Liliana shot back her elbow to jab him in the belly. 'No! It makes you a crazy man to talk like that!'

Jose Luis laughed but then slumped into a chair and sighed. 'Sullivan, do you know what does make me a bad man? I don't visit my parents enough. I say, "I would give my parents my kidney," but I don't make the effort to fly over to visit them.'

'Go,' Liliana urged him. 'We can afford it now.'

Jose Luis shook his head and turned to explain to Sullivan, 'I can't leave the business. We have a fifteen-year financial plan. And with Teresa at the uni . . . no. I can't leave the business.'

'Sullivan,' said Liliana, 'tell my husband he's a crazy man.'

'Oh no, leave me out of this,' said Sully, holding up the soggy tea-towel as a shield.

Liliana slapped Jose Luis across the shoulder. 'Teresa will be fine. And you have to stop with this "oh the business!" Go to Colombia if you want to.'

But Jose Luis sighed again, more weighed down with every second he allowed the business, Teresa's university education and his filial duty to collide in his head.

'Your parents are old,' Liliana pointed out. 'What if they lose their marbles or die and you didn't spend time with them? How would you feel then?'

'Liliana! You say that to me just before I need to go to sleep? Are you a witch?'

Liliana laughed and tickled him.

He wrestled her off. 'No, it's not funny. I'll feel bad now and won't sleep. You are a witch.'

Sullivan waited for a gap in their laughter to say, 'I might head off now, guys. Thanks for today. As always.'

After a rib-crushing hug from Liliana, he headed out the front door. Behind him, he could still hear her and Jose Luis.

'I'm sorry.' Liliana was teasing Jose Luis. 'What can I possibly do to help you get to sleep?'

She said something else in Spanish and Jose Luis replied, 'Maybe there is something we can do,' followed by a volley of Spanish.

As Sullivan closed the door and stepped out into the street, he heard Liliana squeal with a gloriously lascivious edge.

He wouldn't be coming for lunch next weekend because he'd agreed to go to a one-day music festival with Natalie and Louis. Sully found himself wishing the week would zip by quickly, the way little kids can wish for time to accelerate.

Natalie worried she was crossing a line with this Sunday outing. It was the first time she and Louis would be going somewhere with Sullivan Moss but without Mack, without the dog as the excuse for being together.

Sullivan and Louis had taken to discussing music and the boy was curious to see some live bands. The festival, put on by the council, was advertised in the local paper. Louis tore out the page and placed it pointedly on Natalie's dressing table one morning. The next day she found it in her tea caddy, after that in the console of the car – anywhere

Louis could think of – until she finally said they could go. Louis insisted they invite Sullivan along because he was 'into music'.

The park was alive with colour on the bright cold Sunday, red pennants hanging from poles and marquees. Around the street edges were stalls selling nubbly hippie clothing and cheap jewellery. There was a sausage sizzle, a taco stand and Turkish women cooking gozleme.

Because they would be outside for hours in the cold, Natalie and Louis were both rugged up, wearing woolly hats, which made the excursion feel more like an adventure.

'Sullivan!' yelled Louis.

Sullivan ran across the grass towards them. 'I stopped at a chemist to buy Louis some earplugs.'

'Will he need those?' asked Natalie. 'It won't be that loud, will it?'

'It'll be loud right up the front. And that's where we need to be.'

'Yes!' whooped Louis, then he and Sully did some sort of ninja move in unison.

There were two tented music stages so one band would be playing while the next musicians were setting up. Nat, Sully and Louis stood right at the front so Louis could see the musos up close and feel the beat in his chest.

There were a couple of folk duos, a swampy blues band, a funky outfit with a wonderful Hammond organ player. Louis declared every act to be his favourite until his ultimate favourite began to perform. They were a big band, uni students, with a horn section and lots of percussion, all good musicians but playing it for comedy too, wearing silly costumes – snorkelling gear, animal suits, sparkly top hats and such. Louis laughed gleefully, adoring them.

All afternoon, he asked Sullivan questions. How does the sound mixing desk work? Who writes the songs? In the solo bit, does the guy just make it up in his head or is it all practised? Sullivan did his best to answer these questions.

Nat wondered if she should have pushed Louis into applying to a kids' orchestra or trying guitar lessons instead of cello. She baulked at the idea of signing him up for a million activities and she disapproved of the way some parents strove to value-add to their children. But had she been remiss, stunting Louis' development?

Her guilty thoughts were interrupted by Sullivan turning to smile at her. 'I've just realised one of the excellent things about having a kid,' he said. 'You get to remember what it's like to see something for the first time. I know that sounds wet.'

'Doesn't matter if it's wet,' she said. 'It's true.'

Natalie looked down at Louis' enraptured face focused on the band. He kept glancing at his mother to make sure she was seeing everything and loving it as much as he was. Now she felt ashamed that it took Sullivan Moss to remind her to enjoy her own child. But a moment later, she yanked her thoughts in the other direction, resenting Sullivan for his facile comment. Sure, he could get a kick out of being here with Louis at his event but he didn't have the responsibility of a kid always and forever. He could enjoy the good bits but with none of the worries or restrictions. Then a moment later, Nat felt mean for thinking so sourly about Sullivan and cross with herself for over-analysing instead of simply enjoying this lovely day they were having.

She made a point of smiling at Sullivan who frowned, confused, but smiled back anyway. It occurred to Natalie that Sully had become a good friend. Sometimes this made her nervous and she would remind herself of various stories Astrid had told her about Sullivan's failings. Then again, the man was making a significant effort to modify his ways.

She and Sullivan Moss happened to have met at a destabilised time for both of them and she wasn't sure what that meant. They never discussed the nature of their relationship. It was an undefined and delicate connection that might disintegrate if they prodded at it.

Natalie then noticed Louis was hopping from foot to foot.

'Louis, do you need to go?'

Louis shook his head, not wanting to miss any of the music.

'You're dancing on hot coals. Go to the loo. You'll only miss a bit.'

Louis shrugged okay, but when they peered round the side of the tent, they saw that the men's facilities consisted of a portaloo trailer with a queue of blokes outside, many of them huge and bearded. A bit daunting.

'Come to the ladies with me. I can stand outside and guard the door,' Nat suggested.

'No way,' said Louis.

'Listen, mate, I'm busting and it's not good for my kidney if I hang on,' said Sullivan. 'Why don't we head over there and line up together?'

Louis was okay to go with Sullivan as protector. Natalie watched the two of them walk across the grass and join the queue. They waved to her and she waved back. Then the two of them started a comic act about the toilets being stinky, holding their noses and staggering from the overwhelming smell. Louis kept breaking out of character because he was laughing uncontrollably.

Natalie's spirits lifted to see Louis having such fun. There was no denying he adored Sullivan Moss. Was Sullivan planning to kill himself after the kidney donation? If so, how would she explain that to an eight-year-old?

When the music was over, the three of them drove to Ashfield to warm up inside one of the Chinese dumpling joints.

'By the way, did I mention that you had a blinder of a game yesterday?' said Sullivan.

'Thanks.' Louis was playing it cool, which made Natalie smile.

'These dumplings are excellent,' she said.

'They are,' agreed Sullivan. 'Hey Louis, if your team makes the grand final, I'll buy dumplings for everyone after the game.'

Sullivan and Louis shook on that promise with their dumpling-sticky hands.

*

'Things are going well for you, don't you think Sullivan?' said Anthony towards the end of a session. They were six months into the psychiatric assessment process.

'I guess so.'

'You're healthy, lean, sober, in stable employment. You've made some new social connections.'

'Well, with Gordana and me it's more of a bartering arrangement,' joked Sully. 'I do household maintenance in exchange for Croatian delicacies and homegrown vegies.'

'Are you saying there's no affection whatsoever between you and your neighbour?'

'No, no, no, there is.'

'There's a genuine friendship with your boss and his family,' Anthony pointed out.

'They're very kind people,' said Sullivan.

'And it's great you've re-established contact with your mate Tim.'

Sullivan shrugged and nodded. Contact with Tim had its boundaries. There were no visits to Tim's home, for example. But it was true they enjoyed going to a gig together every couple of weeks.

'There's Natalie and her son,' said Anthony with that sneaky therapist probing tone.

'Yep.'

'Whenever Natalie's name comes up, you evade the topic or use humour to deflect attention from your feelings.'

'Come on, doc. You know my policy. Natalie's endured her lifetime share of dickhead men. She doesn't need to add me to the list. Anyway, my ineligibility for a romantic relationship has nothing to do with my psychological readiness to donate a kidney, does it?'

'No,' said Anthony. 'My point is, Sullivan, you should allow yourself to take some pleasure in where you've got to. Take some pride in that.'

*

As Sullivan walked away from Anthony's rooms, he did allow himself to feel proud for a moment. He could indeed take some pride and pleasure in the progress he'd made.

He smiled at the irony of it – the shrink from the transplant program pointing that out was now leading Sullivan to wonder if he needed to donate his kidney after all. Perhaps he was capable of living a useful life without doing something that drastic. Having an operation would hurt a lot. No one liked pain. There was not inconsiderable risk with the procedure. And maybe being a kidney donor would muck up some of the good things he'd accumulated in recent months.

In fact, he could pull the plug on the donor process and no one need think less of him. He could tell Natalie and Jose Luis he'd been knocked out on unspecified medical grounds. He could tell Diane Milton his job commitments precluded his becoming a donor. It was possible to lie to everyone in a way that no one would be hurt or offended.

Sullivan stood on the edge of the main road, waiting for the lights to change, as the plan formed in his mind. He noticed a bottle shop on the other side of the street. If he was dumping the donation plan, there was no need to abstain from alcohol. Total abstinence was an extreme and, some might say, a cowardly position to take. He should walk into that bottle shop and buy a really good bottle of shiraz, take it home and savour it in a civilised way.

The trouble was, in the time it took for the lights to change, Sullivan's brain – sober and fresh from a session with the shrink – flashed ahead to the likely consequences. Imagining the outcomes of his choices had never been Sully's strong suit but now there was no avoiding the fuckers.

If he purchased that shiraz, he would mostly likely pour it into a huge glass and kid himself that counted as one drink. The bottle would be quickly empty and some excuse would be concocted to visit the bottle shop again. Thereafter it would be an unedifying downward spiral.

The trailer for the movie of Sullivan Moss's likely future whizzed by on fast forward: out-of-control drinking, missing work, more lying, patchy personal hygiene, work totally abandoned, broken promises, things burning down, people disappointed and on and on until he landed back on the top of a building, standing next to a pile of cigarette butts, trying to dredge up the courage to jump.

Sullivan heard the pinging from the traffic lights to indicate he could cross but he just stood there. He needed the donation goal like a donkey needed a carrot dangling from a pole to keep it plodding forward. In his case it was his own kidney he needed to have hanging from a pole in front of his face.

The lights changed again and by now people were staring at Sullivan frozen on the roadside, breathing hard, almost hyperventilating.

He punched the renal unit number into his phone.

'Diane. It's Sullivan here.'

'Oh hello.'

'Listen to me . . . if I ever come into your office and give you some reason why I have to pull out of the donor program, I'll be lying. So don't believe me and don't let me pull out.'

'Well, Sullivan, I can't be a kidney policewoman.'

'You're right. I can't make you be my kidney policewoman.'

A woman standing next to Sully at the crossing sneaked a look at him, intrigued. Let her eavesdrop. He didn't care.

'Here's an idea,' said Sullivan. 'If I ever do try to bullshit you like that, you'll know I'm bullshitting and I'll know you know. That way I can't kid myself and get away with it. All I'm asking you to do is carry that knowledge. Does that sound okay?'

'Uh . . . yes. I suppose so.'

'Great. See you next week.'

Sullivan was relieved. It was like in movies when a person in danger made a videotape as a form of insurance. *If you're watching this video, it means I'm dead. There are documents in the safe that tell the whole story.* That sort of thing. In Sully's case, lodging his message with Diane Milton was a prophylactic against his own capacity to backslide.

It was finally safe to cross and walk past the bottle shop.

18

Sullivan was ravenous. Physical work created an appetite in him that was of a totally different sort to 'mouth' hunger when he craved salty or syrupy or crunchy things to alleviate boredom. This was true full-body hunger like an animal. He saw himself as a bear, lumbering up to the drinks fridge of the hospital cafeteria, using his paw to pull open the door and grab a carton of milk.

It amused Sully to envisage himself as a foraging bear. Accordingly, he selected a salmon sandwich from the fridge cabinet.

Jose Luis had allowed him to finish work early so he could catch the train to his appointment with Diane Milton. Now there was a twenty-minute window to sit in the hospital cafeteria and satisfy his animal hunger.

Sullivan had showered on the job site and put on fresh clothes. He was keen to present himself to Diane as stable and committed, in case his strange phone call the previous week had put his name on her just-too-crazy list.

He had bought a few items of clothing from a St Vincent de Paul op shop so he had one decent outfit he could wear to appointments. He was aware he'd lost weight and gained muscle but it was still aston-ishing to see how differently clothes fit, now that he had shoulders and no belly. He wondered if the garments he found on the racks and purchased for a few dollars had once been clothes dropped off at

Vinnies by a guy on his way to jump off a building.

Sullivan chose a table and ripped open the milk carton. An elderly bloke he recognised from the renal floor walked up to the fridge cabinet and began perusing the sandwich selection.

Certain faces had become familiar to Sullivan from his visits to the hospital. Patients fronting up three times a week for dialysis would walk past the waiting area and Sully would sneak discreet looks. Might his kidney be put inside one of the bodies that had walked past him?

Diane had made the confidentiality rules very clear. If Sullivan ever made it through to donation, he would never be told who the recipient was. With some disappointment, he had accepted that stricture. Determined not to jeopardise his place in the program, he avoided eye contact with the dialysis patients so that curiosity would not gain control of his mouth.

Sully guzzled half the milk in one go. Tearing open the salmon sandwich packet proved quite difficult, as if he really were a bear who had stumbled into the cafeteria and was clumsily trying to prise off this plastic cover. That idea made him smile just at the moment the dialysis bloke came past his table with a tray in hand. The bloke interpreted Sully's smile as an invitation and did a little eyebrow dance – *shall I sit at your table?*

Sully waved his hand to indicate 'please sit', feeling a little awkward about fraternising with someone he knew was in the market for a kidney.

'Ken,' said the man, offering his hand to shake.

'Sullivan.'

Up close, Sully realised Ken was only in his late fifties. He was Maori or Islander and would once have been a powerfully built, striking man but was now depleted by illness, the potency sucked out of him.

Ken grinned and aimed his finger at Sullivan. 'I've seen you talking to Diane. You're going through the system to be a living donor, right?'

Sullivan nodded, hoping he wouldn't have to say more about it.

'It's a good thing you're doing for your family,' said Ken and Sullivan let him assume the donation was earmarked for a family member.

Ken was a talker. Maybe all those hours to kill in dialysis every week had developed his chatting muscles.

'Stick at it, mate. A lot of the living donors fall by the wayside. When I first started on dialysis – this is years ago now – my wife Leone was all set to donate to me. Turned out she's got a heart problem that rules her out. My daughters wanted to donate. I said, "Steady on. I won't be having any of that." My girls are having babies and need to look after themselves. I said, "Some poor bastard will die and I'll get a kidney that way." But didn't pan out.'

'Right,' said Sullivan, nodding sympathetically.

'But then recently I had a stroke of luck.'

'Oh, is there a chance you might get a kidney?'

'Nup.' Ken tapped his chest. 'Lung cancer.'

'I'm sorry to hear that.' Sullivan was aware that sounded pathetic but it was better than saying nothing.

Ken wheezed a laugh. 'The cancer means I can pull the plug on the whole business of my girls wanting to get tested.'

'Right.'

'They reckon there's most likely a connection between kidney problems and my kind of cancer. I've told the docs they can have my body after I go.' Ken palpated his chest and kidney region as a preview of his own autopsy. 'They can see what the story is in here if that's any help to them.'

For a moment Ken looked profoundly tired but the next moment he laughed again. 'Wanna know the good part about the double whammy?'

Could there be a good part to the lung cancer/renal failure combo? Sullivan wasn't sure he wanted to know any more detail about Ken's diabolically awful situation. But he took his cue from Ken's defiant smile and smiled back. 'Tell me the good part, Ken.'

'Kidney failure is a champion way to go. The docs and nurses reckon it's what they'd choose if they could. So when the lung cancer gets worse, I won't be bothered with pain or gasping for breath or any of that gruesome stuff. I can just stop having dialysis and let myself slip away gently.'

'Right, I can see how that might be a relief to know.'

'Do you mind me talking about this stuff to you? Leone reckons I make people uncomfortable talking about it.'

Leone had a point. Sullivan was so uncomfortable, his legs felt electrically charged against the seat of the chair. But there was Ken sitting across the table with his honest, unguarded face so Sully managed to say, 'It's fine. Go on.'

'Apparently, once you stop dialysis, you eventually get sleepy, maybe a bit disoriented. Worst thing sounds like the itchy skin and muscle twitching you can get.'

'Wouldn't doctors be able to give you stuff to help with that?' asked Sullivan.

'That's exactly right, mate. Plus they reckon massage can help and Leone's a beautician so, y'know, she's good at massage and whatever. The point is, I'll be at home, no hospitals, no pain, Leone and my girls and the babies around me, just fading away.'

Sullivan nodded and met the man's valiant gaze as bravely as he could.

Then Ken shook his head and wheezed a laugh. 'Since my kidneys packed up, I really miss the pissing.'

'Sorry?'

'You know that feeling when you're busting to go – so much your teeth feel all nervy? And then you finally let rip with a strong stream of piss. On and on and it feels good. Satisfying. You know that feeling?'

'Yeah.'

'People don't appreciate it until they lose it.'

'I think I appreciate it a bit,' said Sullivan. 'But I'll pay more attention in the future. Make sure I enjoy it.'

'That's the go,' said Ken. 'Relish it, mate. Relish the pissing. I miss a good vigorous piss.'

Ken looked up towards the entrance. 'Ooh, there she is.'

Leone spotted Ken across the foyer. A tiny, birdy woman with peroxided hair and a radiant smile.

'Leone'll have the shits with me for not waiting for her out front and for earbashing you. Better go. Nice talking to you, Sullivan.'

'You too, Ken.'

As Ken headed off to join Leone, Sullivan bolted up the fire stairs to the renal floor. He wanted to blurt out to Diane Milton: 'Give my kidney to Ken! I don't care if he's dying of lung cancer. Just give him my kidney so he can have a few good long pisses before he goes, and so he can spend more time with Leone and his lovely daughters and their babies!'

But Sully knew that's not how it worked. So he tried to calm down and regain his breath as he walked from the fire stairs down the corridor to the renal unit.

Diane looked concerned when she saw Sullivan in the waiting area, breathless and agitated. 'Are you okay, Sullivan?'

'Yes. Well. Yes and no.'

Diane ushered him into the office with Sullivan yabbering to her. 'Diane, fucking hell . . . Do you want to run outside sometimes, pick out a few healthy passers-by, club them on the head, drag them in here and take one of their kidneys to fix your patients?'

'No, can't say I've ever felt an urge to club anyone or force them into the operating theatre.'

'Course not. No,' said Sullivan, flapping his hand. 'I just mean, when people are sick – so fucking sick – it must be frustrating for you sometimes.'

'Well, yes. Sometimes it can be frustrating.'

'It would shit me to tears,' he said, still prowling her office.

'Sit down, Sullivan.'

'Sorry. Yes.' He sat.

'Good news. The transplant committee has approved you as a non-directed donor.'

'What? I passed all the . . . Anthony signed off on it? Really?'

'Yes, really,' said Diane.

'Wow. Okay. Wow. Thank you, Diane. Thank you for pulling me through this.'

'Well, Sullivan, you're the one who's done all the hard work.'

'No, come on. Couldn't've got here without you. You are a goddess. Allow me to acknowledge that on this historic day. Allow me to offer you my thanks.'

'Okay then,' said Diane with a small smile.

'How soon do we go the knife?'

'We have to find you a match. You understand about the six markers for —'

'Six markers for compatibility. Yes. Bring it on,' said Sullivan.

'So at this stage I can't tell you when we might be ready to proceed.'

'That's okay, Diane. I'm happy to wait until you find the best match. As long as I know it's happening.'

When Sullivan got back down to street level, he was revved up. He wondered if he might feel a backwash of anxiety or regret but no, not so far anyway. He had an urge to tell Natalie straight away.

'Nat. Hi. It's Sullivan,' he said to Natalie's voice message. 'I got through the committee. They reckon my kidney is a goer.'

Part Two

19

Sullivan was stripped to the waist, fully conscious and his pupils dilated with terror, as he was laid back over the stone altar, facing the blistering tropical sun. An Aztec priest in plumed regalia held an obsidian knife above his head then plunged it down into Sullivan's abdomen and reached his hands inside the cavity to rip out a kidney.

Once the kidney was harvested, dripping blood, Sullivan's carcass was hurled off the top of the temple to bounce down the deep steps to the blood-soaked ground far below.

That was Louis' midnight dream.

Woken by his nightmare, Louis padded up the hallway and stood in the doorway of Natalie's bedroom. He nudged her door enough to make belts and handbags hanging on the coat-hooks rattle and wake Natalie up.

'What's up, sweetheart?' Natalie asked. She immediately tuned into her son's breathing but there was no sound of wheezing.

Louis sat on the edge of the bed and described the dream. Natalie reminded him that he was mixing up Sullivan's operation with pictures he'd seen in history books.

'We don't know when Sullivan's going to have his operation. The doctors haven't found the matching person yet. And when it does happen, you know Sullivan'll be fine, don't you?'

'I guess.'

'We can't call him now because he'll be asleep,' said Natalie. 'But why don't we ring tomorrow and he can explain how his operation works.'

He nodded but Natalie could still see the Aztec priest stomping around and brandishing his ceremonial knife in Louis' head. She pulled the doona aside so Louis could climb into bed.

Natalie heard her son's breathing fall into the slower rhythm of sleep within minutes. She didn't go back to sleep at all but lay there for the next three hours. By allowing the probably unwise friendship between Louis and Sullivan Moss to go this far, she had pretty much snookered herself, which led her to question if she was a good mother, which led her to fear she would inevitably make a godawful mess of parenting as she had every other intimate relationship in her life.

At three-fifteen a.m., Natalie clicked the alarm off before it woke Louis, then slid out of bed to dress for work. She knew that in a few hours' time, Judy would find Louis in her bed and that evening, Natalie would be the recipient of a disapproving speech about the foolishness of letting children sleep in a parent's bed no matter how terrifying a dream may have been.

The radio show that morning was hard work – a clunking thing that lurched from one mediocre segment to the next, punctuated by technical stuff-ups. The live cross to Los Angeles was buggered when the correspondent wasn't on the end of the phone line at the agreed time. The transport minister was obfuscating and testy but in a dull rather than an intriguing way. The talkback callers were whiny and/ or long-winded. In off-air moments, Heather was irritable because someone had supposedly fiddled with the levels on her panel. The traffic update computer froze twice.

The tweets and SMSs coming up on Heather and Natalie's screens during the show seemed more negative and pompous than usual, criticising pronunciation and grammar (often inaccurately) or offering suggestions such as, 'Why don't you shut the fuck up?' Then again, there were similar nasty messages every day for every program so maybe they just seemed worse to Natalie because she was exhausted today.

To the majority of listeners, the show would have sounded fine, if not one of the team's stellar efforts. Heather was skilled enough to talk her way smoothly out of trouble. The smart, charming way she navigated tricky stuff was a big part of Natalie's admiration for her.

Heather took the final phone interview – a Christchurch-based earthquake expert Natalie had lined up to provide context for the expected Chilean quakes. As the interview began, Natalie allowed her tired brain to drift off for sixty seconds, maybe ninety. At least it was Friday and she had the weekend to repay some sleep debt.

She glanced up and saw that Heather was giving her the hairy eyeball through the glass. Natalie switched her mind back into focus and could immediately hear that the earthquake guy was a dreadful interview subject. He'd been a relaxed and quite colourful speaker when Natalie spoke to him earlier, but now the man was outstandingly dull and nervous, taking long pauses, breaking off incoherently in mid-sentence, using unfathomable technical vocabulary one moment then explaining simple concepts in a kindergarten teacher voice the next.

After the show, when Heather shoved open the studio door, she shot Natalie another foul look.

'That earthquake guy was so terrible, I could hear people turning off their radios all over Sydney,' she snapped.

'I'm sorry about him.' Natalie kept pace with Heather as she stalked back to the office area. 'But you handled it really well and it still sounded fine.'

'Did anyone pre-interview him?'

'I did. On the phone he was good value. But yes, on-air he wasn't.'

'The man was a geology expert and indeed some of those pauses felt like entire geological periods were grinding past.'

Natalie apologised again but Heather was wound up and enjoying her analogies too much to let it go yet.

'One minute into that interview, I wished the tectonic plates would split apart and swallow me into the earth's core,' she said.

'Look, I know. I'm sorry. He was —'

'You hung me out to dry this morning, Nat.'

Heather's tone was so sharp that it stung like a slap in the face. Natalie worried she might burst into tears in the office and she reminded herself she was tired and should endeavour to slough this off.

Heather slammed her insulated coffee mug down on her desk and plonked herself in the chair. Natalie kept her attention on her computer, checking emails, to hold off any kind of tearful disintegration.

Neil, the station manager, popped his head over the top of a partition. 'Can I talk to you when you've got a sec, Nat?'

'Right now is fine,' Natalie replied, glad to escape Heather's cranky paper shuffling.

Natalie sat down in Neil's office praying this wasn't going to be a rap over the knuckles about today's wobbly show.

'Listen . . .' said Neil absently as he tapped through emails. 'There's this guy we want to try out on-air. Not sure when yet. His name's Andy . . . uh . . . Andy, Andy, Andy,' he repeated as he hunted on his computer screen for some record of the guy's surname.

'Andy Price?' Natalie suggested.

'That's the one.'

Price was a twenty-something guy who'd dabbled in stand-up and written a handful of newspaper opinion pieces. He'd been a semi-regular on a TV panel show, had made it on to the People to Watch list in a Sunday paper, and could lay claim to a large Twitter following. From the little Natalie had seen of him – and there hadn't been much of substance for anyone to see so far – the guy was glib, proudly ignorant, only intermittently amusing, with a cruel vein running through his utterances that could sometimes make Natalie suck air through her teeth.

'We'll probably give him a go for a week over the summer,' Neil explained. 'So I'd like to get him in here as an observer and maybe let him play around in a studio, off-air, to get the feel of it.'

'Right,' murmured Natalie, wondering if it occurred to Neil that this notion might be insulting, indeed infuriating, given the promises he'd made to her.

'I was hoping you could look after this guy, teach him what he needs to know.'

'I see,' said Natalie and then, as jokey as she could make it: 'An alternative plan would be to give an already experienced person like me a week on-air over the summer.'

Neil grinned. 'You know that's still on my radar. Meanwhile, you're so good at handling these newbies and training them up, I'd love to put this guy with a strong producer like you to get him over the line.'

He continued with this kind of flattery for a few minutes and Natalie silently cursed the liability of being competent at something that made someone else's life easier. Neil went on at length about the reasoning behind trying Andy Price but Natalie was only half listening.

Should she leap to her feet right now and protest, make demands, be difficult? *Fuck you, Neil, why should I make your life easier by puppy-training this spiky-haired, social-media-cranking, nasty-minded charlatan if you won't offer me what was pretty much promised?* Then again, now was hardly the best time for a confrontation. And she shouldn't be swearing at Neil of all people. He was a good guy just trying to do his job properly. If she was too piss-weak to push herself with Neil, that must indicate something. And what reason did she have to think she would be any better on-air than a guy like Andy Price? A lot of people must find him amusing or relevant or some bloody thing. Was she kidding herself that she would ever be any good at presenting? She'd missed her chance by stuffing about overseas. Or maybe she never really did have the aptitude for it and that was why Neil was casting about for other options.

In the end, all Natalie said out loud was, 'Sure.'

*

Back at Judy's house, Natalie squeezed out an hour of low-grade sleep and woke up entirely unrefreshed. She hauled herself out of bed to find an annoying email from Brendan. He was being difficult about dates for Louis' school holiday visit to Kuala Lumpur, revealing yet again what small importance he placed on the relationship with his son from his first marriage. Natalie closed the email window with a surly stab at the keyboard.

After the school pick-up, she had to pack Louis an overnight bag and drop him at his friend Gaetano's place for a sleepover. Louis was also grumpy from lack of sleep and the two of them bickered over pyjamas and toothbrushes.

'You're obsessed with toothbrushes. You've got a *problem* with toothbrushes,' said Louis.

'Do not speak to me in that smartarse tone, mister,' Natalie said, once they were in the car. 'If you're this tired and spiky, maybe I should cancel the sleepover with Gaetano.'

She was aware she was off-loading her bad temper about Brendan and Neil and the clunky show and Andy Price onto Louis. Why should her eight-year-old son cop the snarly mood that had been generated by a stand-up comedian of limited talent she'd never even met? It was unfair. By the time she dropped Louis off, she was relieved the poor kid would be far away from her in her current state.

When Judy arrived home, Natalie was ready for the lecture about Louis sleeping in her bed. But in fact her mother decided to attack on another front.

'How much longer is the suicidal hobo going to live in that flat, subsidised by you?' asked Judy.

'Sullivan pays rent and we can't sell yet anyway so in no sense am I subsidising anyone.'

'Does your brother appreciate he's being denied proceeds from his father's estate?'

'Nick is happy with the arrangement, until we finalise the legal stuff and find a home for Mack.'

'Absurd. That ageing one-eyed animal is being provided with a lovely life – his own townhouse and a live-in carer. We're talking about a dog, Natalie, a dog.'

'You're the one talking about a dog,' said Natalie. 'I have to go out.'

Sullivan could see Natalie was frazzled the instant he opened the door. He fought off the urge to embrace her. Mack's tail thumped against Sully's leg at the thrill of seeing her.

'Hi Sullivan, sorry to disturb you.'

'You never disturb me.'

Natalie managed a wan smile. 'I need to get the rest of those papers out of Dad's filing cabinet.'

'No worries. Can I get you a beverage?'

'We should talk about Mack too.' Natalie kneeled down on the floor to rub the dog's belly.

'Right. Sure. Is there a problem?'

'Have they given you a date for the surgery?'

'Not yet.'

'Of course you can stay here until you recover from the operation. But I assume that after the kidney donation, you'll want to move on. Which means I need to think seriously about a new home for Mack.'

Sullivan's stomach turned over at the idea of giving up the dog. He had avoided thinking too much about life after the surgery. The kidney donation was a huge wall he was trudging towards but a wall so high he couldn't see over the top of it.

'I'd like to keep Mack,' Sullivan said, the idea forming as he cast around for a way to dispel the churn in his gut. 'When you sell this place, I'd like to take him with me wherever I end up. If that's okay with you.'

'Oh . . . I'd love you to keep him but I can't give him to you if you're planning to, uh . . .'

'If I'm planning to kill myself after the kidney surgery?'

'Well, I guess that's . . . Are you?'

'That had been my plan,' Sullivan said. 'To the extent that I've had any kind of plan for afterwards.'

'Which is your right, I suppose.'

'Look, maybe I could . . . I mean, what if I did manage to hang around as long as Mack needs a home?' said Sullivan, hesitant to make a promise he may not be able to keep.

'Oh . . . but are you sure?'

'I wouldn't be honest if I said I was entirely sure. But I'm pretty sure I could manage to see Mack through his autumn years. That's . . . no, well, can we say that's a promise?'

Natalie dropped her head, massaging Mack's neck, so Sullivan couldn't read the expression on her face. Did she consider him too unreliable to take on the ownership of an animal?

Sullivan tried a self-deprecating laugh to lighten the mood. 'A commitment to a relatively old dog is a level of commitment I can probably manage.'

Natalie still didn't look up.

'I mean, Nat, if you hate the idea, I completely understand.'

When she looked up, her eyes were watery. 'I like the idea.' Then her face crumpled into full-on crying. 'Sorry. God, look at the way I'm – sorry.'

'No need to apologise,' said Sullivan. His usual self-censorship about touching this woman he yearned to touch was now struggling against the need to comfort a crying person. He leaned down to squeeze her shoulder with a few supportive but hopefully not too intimate pulses of his hand.

Natalie found tissues in her bag, wiped her eyes and laughed. 'Sorry. It's been a shitful day. That's why I'm . . . anyway, I'm glad Mack will have you and I'm glad you're not going to kill yourself straight away.'

'Shall I make tea to celebrate these twin reasons for gladness?'

Sullivan suggested. If he stayed leaning over Natalie for much longer he wouldn't be able to control the urge to fold her into his arms and kiss her neck where her top scooped down at the back.

'I sank into black moods a few times when I was younger,' said Natalie.

She and Sullivan were sitting in the courtyard drinking tea out of translucent flowery china cups – the 'best' china Frank had been awarded in the property split because Judy thought it was dowdy.

'In my twenties, when I was at the centre of one of those dark funks,' Natalie went on, 'I'd negotiate a deal with myself. I'd say, "If I still feel this wretched two months from now, I'm allowed to kill myself."'

Sullivan nodded, weighing up this notion. 'Since you're sitting here, full of life, I take it you never used up your designated time.'

'Something would come along to buoy me up again or distract me at least. I'd only remember the time limit ages afterwards.'

'And now,' said Sullivan, 'I really hope you don't ever feel that bad.'

Natalie shrugged. 'I hit a pretty low point in Kuala Lumpur. Couple of months after Brendan left, a week after I lost my job teaching English. Some man shouted at me in the street, spat at me, accused me of pranging his car. I hadn't.'

'I believe you.'

'I remember lying on the bed that night and doing one of those assessments of your life . . . y'know . . . where you accelerate along a totally bleak track and then crash-land in some dark, dark – I'm sure you know what I mean . . .'

'I think I do.'

'And then I realised: It's different for me now. I can't do one of those if-I-still-feel-this-bad-in-two-months deals with myself because Louis exists. I don't have a notional escape hatch any more. That option is crossed off the list.'

'Isn't that a good thing?

'Maybe it is. At the time, though, I had this terrible resentment. I resented Louis for existing.' Natalie winced and then laughed nervously. 'Awful, isn't it.'

'No. Well, awful for you that you felt that way.'

'I pulled out of it pretty quickly. Rang a colleague and sussed out jobs back in Sydney, got some things sorted. Thus you see the psychologically robust specimen before you now.'

She laughed, a full-bodied laugh that, to Sullivan's ear, accommodated all the things she'd just described rather than dismissing them as nothing.

'I should dig out those papers from Dad's files,' she said but didn't move straight away, just sat finishing the tea.

Sully felt privileged that after she'd confided such things, she was still comfortable enough to sit there finishing the tea. It struck him that he loved her helplessly.

'Hey . . .' said Sullivan. 'Just a thought and feel free to say no without risk of offending me. Would you like to go to some music tonight?'

20

Every Friday night, one of the pubs in Erskineville had a free gig in the upstairs room. A seriously good house band played with whichever guest musicians were passing through town. Sullivan chose this because the venue was civilised, not too crowded and the music not overly loud. If Natalie was in an exhausted and delicate state, he figured this kind of gig was preferable.

Sullivan insisted on buying the first round of drinks – soda for him, cabernet sauvignon for her – but Natalie insisted she pay for her own burger. They found a table at what he judged was the perfect distance from the band and the speakers.

Sullivan and Natalie had grown comfortable with each other in recent months but now, with this date-like scenario, a new self-consciousness hummed between them. Sullivan was torn between his desire to be gallant, to make sure Natalie had a good night, and his caution about seeming pushy.

The band was in good form, luckily. In the first set, they did a few bluesy songs, a surf instrumental, then a string of terrific soul numbers when a female singer jumped up to join them.

Sullivan kept sneaking looks at Natalie to check if she was enjoying it. She was smiling, moving to the music in her chair, way more relaxed and less drawn than when she'd shown up at the door. Sullivan took pleasure in watching Natalie's pleasure in the music. He had to check himself so he wouldn't end up staring at her, gooey-eyed, and freak her out.

When the band took a break, she said, 'This is wonderful, Sullivan. Thanks for thinking of this tonight.'

He did a small humble bow.

'Do you want more wine?' he asked as Natalie finished her second glass.

'Better not. I have to drive.' Then a beat later she said, 'You're not drinking, so I guess you could drive.'

'I could.'

'I'll have another one then,' she said, jumping up to go to the bar. 'Another soda for you?'

During the second set, with the help of the music and Natalie's three glasses of red, Sullivan could feel the awkward politeness between them loosen a little. But he was still taken by surprise when, in the middle of a softer instrumental number, Natalie leaned in close to him, not quite touching, but close enough for a discreet conversation.

'Sullivan, can I tell you something I vowed I wouldn't ever tell a single soul?'

'Sure, but don't feel you have to.'

'Promise you won't think less of me afterwards. Or if you do think less of me, pretend otherwise. Oh, maybe it's better if I don't —'

'Come on, you have to spill the beans after a preamble like that,' he said.

'Fair point. You know Frank died of a heart attack in bed?'

Sullivan nodded, his intoxication at being so close to Natalie sobered by the thought of Frank's death. This wasn't the kind of saucy confession he'd been hoping for.

'The heart attack didn't happen in his own bed.'

'Ah. Whose?'

'Gordana's.'

'What?'

Sullivan's mind scrambled to process this, trying to picture the dignified, slightly melancholy gent he'd seen in photos with Gordana astride him.

'Did you know your dad was . . . ah . . .'

'No. I had no idea until Gordana asked me to help her move his body.'

Natalie described the scene – Mirko's imminent return, Gordana's fitted sheet, her own reasoning in deciding to help fake the place of death. Sullivan listened, keeping his expression interested but neutral so he wouldn't impose his own view on Natalie. But then he realised, from the intent way she was scrutinising his face, that she was in fact hanging out to hear his view. Gauging his response – seeing how this story landed in another person's head – was the whole point of the confession.

'Well,' said Sullivan, laying down each syllable cautiously, 'I can see why you would feel troubled by those events. Especially when you were dealing with your dad's death in such a sudden way. I guess what you did broke a few laws.'

'Definitely.'

'But it was only technically illegal. Only illegal in a pedantic, no-one-would-really-want-to-prosecute-you sense.'

'Moving my father's body must count as immoral and undignified and kind of creepy.'

'Can't agree on those other words. It strikes me as a *kind* thing to do.'

'Kind to Gordana you mean?'

'Yes,' said Sullivan confidently. 'And most likely kind to Mirko too. I mean, none of us can ever know what goes on inside a marriage. But chances are you saved them both a lot of pain.'

'But was it kind to Frank?'

'Mmm . . .' murmured Sullivan, not having considered it from this point of view. 'You didn't hurt him physically or emotionally. You saved his reputation from being posthumously besmirched. So I reckon it was kind to him too, yes. And maybe it makes sense to ask yourself:

what would Frank have wanted you to do in that predicament, if there were any way he could express his wishes?'

'Oh. I think Frank would want me to help Gordana out of a tricky spot.'

'I think so too.'

Natalie nodded slowly, as if she needed a pause to absorb this little moment of absolution. Then she smiled. Sullivan smiled back. Natalie sputtered out a small laugh which gave Sullivan permission to chuckle. A second later, the two of them cracked up laughing.

'Can you believe I did that?' said Natalie.

'I love that you did that.'

'You, me and Gordana – we share this secret now,' Natalie pointed out and that made the two of them crack up laughing some more.

A little later, Natalie suddenly announced, 'I envy you.'

'Me? You envy me? Have we met?'

She laughed but then persevered. 'You're going through such a transformation. I mean, most people aren't in a position to transform their lives dramatically, like you are.'

'It only looks dramatic because I'm working off a very low base,' he argued. 'I reckon your life is pretty good. You don't need transformation the way a fuckwit like me needs it.'

'Maybe . . .' she sighed, then blurted out: 'But you get to go on this grand quest with your kidney! I can't do anything noble like that. I'm all . . . all hemmed in and every single thing I do has to be careful and qualified and . . . oh, I'd like to have a grand quest.'

'Looking after Louis is grand.'

'Hmm . . .'

'It is. The grandness of enduring and nurturing someone and – listen, lady, that's grand.'

'Yeah, yeah. Now you're making me feel guilty for not appreciating how lucky I am.'

'No, that is not what I'm saying.'

'It doesn't feel grand. Let's leave it at that,' she said, then grinned and lifted her glass for him to clink.

They stayed until the band had finished their last set and Natalie had downed two more glasses of red.

As Sullivan drove her home, he was keenly aware of Natalie occupying the passenger seat, her right arm only fifteen centimetres away from his left. He could mentally picture the shape of her from the warmth radiating off her skin, as if his body were a heat-sensitive camera. It took all his powers of self-control not to close the tiny gap between them, press her against him and howl like a feral dog.

He parked Natalie's car outside Judy's neat double-fronted Victorian house and hopped around to open the passenger door with a jokey flourish.

'Ha. Thanks,' said Natalie, the two of them grinning at this show of gallantry.

As she lunged out of the car, the strap of her handbag snagged on the gearstick, then slipped free again, yanking Natalie off-balance. Tipsy – in truth, quite pissed – she stumbled, and Sullivan reached out to prevent her falling.

Pressed so close to each other, Sullivan was conscious that he was much taller than Natalie. He felt strong as he held her steady on the kerb and that gave him enough of a surge of confidence that he leaned forward and kissed her.

He had imagined kissing her many times but the reality was better than the imagining. Her mouth felt so warm in the cool air. Together they found the perfect rhythm and pressure, entirely natural and exhilarating. He wanted to kiss Natalie in a way that would communicate the overwhelming admiration, tenderness and lust he felt for her, if it were possible for one kiss to relay all that.

And then – was it fifteen seconds of kissing? – Natalie broke the clinch and took a half-step away on the footpath. She did a small, breathy, awkward laugh.

'Oh Sullivan . . .'

If Sully had been even a little bit pissed, he would have had the unthinking courage to scoop her back in to him and kiss her more insistently. But sober as he was, he could instantly see all the reasons that was a bad idea. Fucking sobriety.

His moment of hesitation lasted long enough for Natalie to roll her shoulders, shift her weight to the other foot and compose her face, as if she were reassembling her pre-kiss self.

'I don't think . . . Probably not a good idea,' she said.

Sullivan nodded, too gutted to speak.

'Thank you for tonight,' she said before hurrying up the steps and disappearing through the front door.

Natalie didn't even clean her teeth before getting into bed. She scissored her legs to warm up the icy sheets, willing herself to fall asleep without ruminating too much on what had just happened.

She hated to think she'd hurt Sullivan's feelings. It wasn't that she hadn't wanted to kiss him. But she didn't want him to receive the wrong signals. Her life was off-kilter enough already without engaging in a sexual liaison with a suicidal, dry alcoholic, relationship-dud of a man whose life goals only extended as far as organ donation and caring for an old dog. And the truth was, Sullivan Moss was at a fragile point in his life and if she cared about him, the last thing she should do was mislead him or embark on something foolish.

With her cheek lying against the cool dry pillowcase, she was hit by the physical memory of his mouth, the solid warmth of his chest, the feel of his hands on her neck and the small of her back. But then she shoved that memory aside. Yes, yes, she had enjoyed that kiss. But she'd been drinking – more wine than she'd drunk for a long time – and couldn't trust her judgement.

Anyway, Sullivan himself had seemed regretful in the post-kiss moment, as if he thought it had been a mistake. Maybe he'd only kissed her out of politeness – after she'd stumbled drunkenly forward and clung to him. He was a kind man and he may well have kissed her because he thought that's what she wanted. He was probably relieved when she gave him the option to extricate himself.

Earlier in the evening, sitting in that warm, comfy pub, with food and wine inside her, moving to the music, her muscles had felt deliciously loose. It made her realise how tightly she held herself most of the time – a habit that had developed over a period of years, in some slow, unexamined process of constriction. It was as if she couldn't allow herself to relax too much, as if the weak connective tissue holding her life together would cause her to fall apart. Now, lying in bed, she felt the relaxing effects of the wine and the music and the kiss fade away. Her body was tightening again, armouring up to tackle this life she'd wound up having.

For once, Natalie's sleep debt acted as her ally, allowing her to fall into unconsciousness quickly, before she could dwell longer on Sullivan and feel any more uncertain, mean or regretful.

Sullivan walked from Judy's house to Frank's flat. The prospect of going straight to bed and alone seemed too dismal, so he took Mack for a late-night stroll.

It was just as well the kiss hadn't gone any further. He should never have taken advantage of Natalie – especially when she was tipsy and vulnerable after a shitty day. He was not worthy of that woman. Arguably he wasn't worthy of any woman, but certainly not Natalie.

A run of downpours meant soccer training and matches were rained out two weeks in a row so Natalie and Sullivan didn't cross paths. Maybe that was for the best. She must be feeling awkward about the imprudent kiss and relieved that she didn't have to see him. The last thing he would ever want to do would be to make her uncomfortable. It was something of a relief for him too. He could pretend he hadn't mucked things up again.

After that night, Sullivan didn't allow himself to have Natalie in his fantasies. It was too painful to imagine something he couldn't have. He used some of the visualisation techniques Anthony had taught him. That way, if he wasn't vigilant and Natalie did creep into a fantasy scene, he could utilise those techniques to swiftly and firmly write her out of it.

The best he should hope for was that she would let him keep Mack, allow Louis to stay in his life and at very best, would remain his friend. Given where Sullivan had been seven months ago, that would be miracle enough. Anyway, now more than ever, with the kidney donation confirmed if not scheduled, he had to keep his eye on the goal.

21

Juliet was surprised Tim was having a fortieth birthday party at all. For a year he'd been refusing to have any kind of celebration. Then a month ago, he suddenly announced he wanted to throw a party. Which gave Juliet the monumental shits.

If Tim had let her organise his fortieth months ago, she could have made it a proper special occasion. For a start, she could have invited people with advance notice. As it was, with invitations going out only two weeks before, too many potential guests had clashes. The majority of the sorry-already-busy-that-night responses were from the lively people you would most want to have at your party.

With notice, Juliet could have employed the event planner her friend Polly knew to transform one of the old industrial sites on Cockatoo Island into a glam venue. She could have hired the terrific Cuban ensemble she'd seen play at the cancer fundraiser. Cuban music was the thing – Juliet might not be a music person but she knew that much. At the very least, she could have sourced some fantastic catering and high-quality wines for the night. If you can afford it, why not throw an amazing party your friends would always remember? That struck Juliet as one of the worthwhile uses of the money Tim had devoted his life to earning. But three weeks wasn't enough time to organise anything decent.

Tim had argued the last-minute preparation wouldn't be a problem because he knew what he wanted. And that's how Juliet found herself holding her wealthy husband's fortieth in this ridiculous low-grade bar, the Hammond Room.

The place wasn't grungy in a way that might pass as a modish joke. It was simply a shithole. Sticky carpet, disgusting toilets, all the fittings scratched or frayed, the most hideous chairs she'd ever seen, the walls slathered with too much red paint which, along with the dim lighting, did manage, blessedly, to blur the full spectacle of shabbiness.

The venue choice was bound up with some ludicrous fantasy Tim had been gripped by – attempting to recapture the gig-going days of his teens and early twenties.

That fantasy also explained the band he'd insisted on booking to provide the music for the night – a three-piece rocky band, presumably another throwback to Tim's youth.

And God almighty, the food. The best the Hammond Room could provide was a selection of reheated frozen items – mini sausage rolls, fish balls (Lord knows what they contained), chicken satay skewers and those prawn cutlets with the ghastly yellow crumb coating which Juliet hadn't even seen served anywhere since she was twelve. She was embarrassed to offer this putrid food to their friends, even to those finance industry slugs she couldn't bear. Juliet's one small triumph had been to order in some good champagne for the toast.

Guests were polite as they arrived, pretending to be delighted by the novelty of being in a different kind of place. Tim greeted everyone, receiving their gifts with jokey grace before placing them on a table near the entrance.

Many of the early-comers were cronies from years ago, friends Tim had lost contact with. In most cases, he'd lost contact with them for good reason, it seemed to Juliet. But he'd spent hours on Facebook, tracking them down.

Not wanting to appear responsible for the event-planning choices, Juliet avoided doing the hostess welcome thing and hung back in a corner. From there, she could hear the distinctive little tune of each person's predictable chatter as they pecked each other in greeting. The wittering sound of their voices filled her with disgust. There were times Juliet suspected she didn't actually like any of her friends. And it was probable they didn't like her either.

Tim was smiling, expansive, hugging people. He appeared to be really happy and Juliet hated him so fiercely it was like a cramp twisting its way through her whole body. At this moment, it seemed the only thing she could do to release the spasm would be to lurch across, grab a chicken satay stick and stab it into Tim's eye. There would be an instant of resistance as the flimsy wooden point pushed against the cornea. Then it would give way and suddenly pop forward into the jelly of the eyeball. Juliet could remember that sensation from the high-school science class when she'd dissected a cow's eye.

For a moment, she allowed the fantasy to expand until she was poking satay sticks into the eyeballs of a significant number of people in the room. But then she decided that if she slid into an acidic mood and had a lousy time that would be a kind of win to Tim. So fuck him. She would find some way to enjoy this wretched night to which he'd sentenced her.

She would drink more than she usually allowed herself. Since she didn't feel any hosting obligations, there was no need to limit alcohol in order to monitor the event. It was Tim's appalling party, so let him worry about it.

As Juliet made her way to the bar in search of champagne, she spotted Pia and Justin. The twins were ensconced in a booth with a small entourage of their friends Juliet had suggested they invite. They weren't supposed to be served any alcohol but Juliet noticed one of the boys topping up glasses of soft drink with a small bottle of vodka. Juliet decided to let it go. If the twins got a bit tipsy there was a chance it might make them more agreeable.

The band started playing – supposedly an acoustic set to allow for conversation but it was still pretty loud. People didn't seem to mind. Maybe they were glad of an excuse not to have the same tedious catch-up conversations. Some were already dancing or jerking on the spot, in semi-dancing mode.

The volume of the music meant that those who wanted to talk had to move in close, faces leaning in to the scoop of each other's necks. There was something a little bit exciting about the intimacy of that way of speaking, a pleasing flirty edge for people who for the most part didn't get much in the way of flirty moments any more.

Juliet scanned the room for Polly who would surely have some choice comments to make about the event. She noticed a man up against the wall near the band and found herself staring. She stared because he was good-looking and somehow familiar but she couldn't pinpoint him. Not a banker or a parent from the school or a friend from one of their current circles. She focused on the man's eyes and then realised who it was: Sullivan Moss, but looking so changed that in such low lighting she hadn't recognised him.

The floppy hair and many kilos of weight were gone. Muscular definition was visible through his shirt. Still, it wasn't just that. The way he held his body was so different. But the biggest change was in his face. When Juliet first met Sullivan – it must've been sixteen years ago – he'd still had his adolescent face. Then he got fat and puffy and blotchy from drinking. Now with the pudge melted off his face and a good haircut, his strong bone structure and defined adult features were revealed.

Once she absorbed the shock, Juliet's next urge was to grab two satay sticks, one for each of the helpless blue eyes Sullivan had traded on for all those years. This was the moron who started the fire that gutted her beautiful, beautiful bar and then was too cowardly ever to face her again. So no surprise he had also been too cowardly to visit Pete when he was ill – Pete who was a thousand times a better man than Sullivan Moss. Better than any person Juliet had ever met, in fact.

Juliet felt that surge of anger and then, like a sure-fire default setting, the anger was swiftly deposited on Tim's head. He was the one who'd persuaded her to employ Sullivan in the bar. She'd always rather liked Sully but she despised the way Tim allowed him much more leeway than anyone else, especially her. Tim had been Sullivan's enabler, stupid, destructive and patronising. So fucking patronising. Hatred of Tim shot through Juliet's head like a signal flare.

Sullivan had felt a difference the moment he arrived at Tim's party – the way women's eyes fell on him and assessed him. At first he wondered if he was attracting attention because his clothing choice was odd. Eventually Sully realised what was happening. He was now considered attractive and it gave the air around him an entirely different electrical charge.

Tonight was his coming out, his debut in the social world as a sober, employed, tanned, lean, muscled, healthy man. It was like the moment at the end of a makeover reality show when the subject, formerly pitifully unattractive, walks down a sweeping staircase towards gathered family and friends to show off his or her surgically and dentally enhanced self, complete with new outfit and hairdo. Tim's fortieth was Sullivan's grand staircase reveal, even if his makeover had been driven by renal rather than cosmetic goals.

Sullivan smiled to himself at that silly image and found that several women – women he didn't know – returned the smile. In recent years if he ever smiled at women, they scowled at him or nervously assumed he was a sleazy character. But now a random smile was bounced back in a delightful volley.

As a young man, tall and good-looking, Sullivan knew what it felt like to be relatively appealing. Then he'd entered his seedy overweight period when he gave off the stench of loser and most women could detect it. The women who did agree to have sex with him in his thirties (Astrid and a few others) were operating from their own agendas or fetishes about scruffy boyish men. Eventually no women wanted to have sex with him. But now Sullivan felt he was emerging from the dark bunker of the not-hot and back into the sun-drenched meadow of hot people.

During the time Sully had been in the bunker, other men in his age group had started to deteriorate – growing bald, packing on fat, acquiring wrinkles, their faces worn by the strain of high-pressure jobs and little kids. Sullivan's infertile, don't-try, loser lifestyle had quarantined him from the ravages of stress on a man's face but he was still young enough that the recent months of healthy living had pretty much reversed the ravages of his dissolute years. So now, in a roomful of men his age, Sullivan was a fair way up the desirability ladder.

For the past eight months, he'd kept his head down, focused on the quest, wearing Frank's baggy clothes, not socialising. The only people he had engaged with – Jose Luis, Gordana, Diane Milton, Natalie, Louis, dog-walkers, the grumpy Italian guy at the vegie shop – were not likely to reflect back to Sullivan that he'd had a makeover. So the response to his new appearance this night came as a fresh experience.

An hour into the party, Sullivan was cautiously enjoying himself. He enjoyed the music (the same band he'd seen months ago at this venue with Tim). He enjoyed fielding compliments from old acquaintances about how good he looked. He enjoyed answering questions from the women he was meeting.

'How do you know Tim?' they would ask.

'Tim and I were best mates all through school and uni,' Sullivan explained.

'So do you work in the money market too?' they would ask, or some similar question to flush out his occupation.

'No, I'm working in asbestos removal,' he would answer, determined to shed his old ways and offer the truth without embellishment.

He would've thought asbestos removal to be a dull and unsexy job to declare. But women at the party seemed intrigued, full of questions and respect for the community service of the job, casting Sullivan in the desirable role of the hot-looking tradesman taking on a dangerous but valuable task.

Sullivan dodged encounters with his old friends. He didn't want to be the guy they knew. He especially steered clear of the men whose girlfriends he'd slept with, the women whose faces he'd lied to and individuals of either gender whose money he'd borrowed, whose floors he'd vomited on, whose cars he'd crumpled, whose trust he'd betrayed. Luckily, it was crowded and dark enough that most of them didn't recognise him.

If someone from the past did identify him, Sullivan offered a playfully brief recap: 'Dropped out of uni, failed at everything, divorced, no kids, turned into a useless drunk. Now working as a labourer, trying to stay sober.' He would then quickly ask a barrage of questions about their life (a person's children were always reliable topics) to divert attention. He didn't ever mention the kidney plan for fear the conversation would come around to suicide.

Being sober at a party was a new experience for Sullivan. As most of the people around him became more sozzled, he felt increasingly detached from them. One of the many disadvantages of sobriety was this feeling of separation from people frolicking together on planet Pleasantly Pissed while he orbited on Space Shuttle Sober. He didn't feel critical of the drinkers, but more benignly observant, like a wildlife documentary maker. He found himself seeking out eye contact with the obviously pregnant woman drinking soda and smiled at her in a spirit of fellowship.

An hour and a half into the party, a pair of hands reached through the thicket of bodies and grabbed Sullivan's abdomen.

'Sullivan.'

It was Juliet, wearing a low-cut black dress that was so tight it was a wonder you couldn't see the outlines of her internal organs. She was quite pissed, in the kind of fizzy high-spirits that can quickly flip into a shrill outburst.

'Hi, Juliet.' Sullivan wasn't sure if he should go for the hug or the peck on the cheek but before he had to decide, Juliet lunged forward to trickle her hands down his chest and stomach, laughing.

'You look good, Sully. Can't believe I'm saying it. You look hot.'

She grabbed his face and pulled him closer, pressing her mouth against his ear so she could whisper, 'Tim told me about the kidney donation. He said you don't want people talking about it.'

'Oh, yeah, probably better that way.'

Juliet was gripping his arm. 'It's amazing. I mean, Tim would never do anything like that. He thinks if he chucks money at a couple of charities, he's a fucking saint or something. He doesn't even give blood, let alone an organ.'

'Oh well, my situation is pretty different.'

Juliet laughed and ran her hand along Sullivan's arm. 'You might have some other organs people would like to get their hands on.'

'Wow. Okay, Juliet.'

'Don't listen to me. I'm pissed as a newt. What is a newt?'

'It's an amphibian. Looks like a lizard but aquatic,' said Sullivan. 'I don't think newts drink heavily.'

Juliet wasn't listening. She was pressing her body up against Sully's arm and thigh, so much so that he had half a mongrel in his pants. It had been a long time since a woman pressed herself against him like this, and he'd always found Juliet very attractive. But Sullivan gently extricated himself from Juliet's grip/caress before she could say or do anything else she might regret.

'Hey, there's your ex-wife,' whispered Juliet, grabbing Sullivan's jaw and swivelling his head round to face Astrid.

'Yes,' said Sullivan, raising his hand in a salute to Astrid.

'Do you hate each other's guts?' asked Juliet.

'No. Well, Astrid has every right to hate my guts but I feel only goodwill towards her. And remorse for the way I behaved.'

'So you should. You acted like an arsehole. And you wasted her best child-bearing years. Then again, she's better off not having a kid with your flaky genes.'

'Yes. I really should say hello to her properly,' said Sullivan, moving away from Juliet and towards his former wife.

Astrid was wearing a peculiar dress with puffed sections on the bodice made out of stiff fabric so she appeared to have vestigial limbs sprouting from her body at several points.

'You look lovely,' said Sullivan and he meant it. He'd always seen Astrid as beautiful no matter what strange garment she might be wearing.

'You look different,' she said.

'Well, yeah, cut my hair and —'

'Much better. You look much better. I'm glad.'

Sullivan could feel her eyes boring into him, assessing. To distract her from scrutinising him, he asked, 'Is Grahame here with you?'

'No. He hardly knows any of these people and crowded rooms can be too hot for him.'

'Right. I've heard about the MS temperature thing. How is Grahame doing?'

Astrid interrupted. 'Are you sticking with this scheme you've concocted to donate a kidney?'

'Oh . . . well. Ha . . . y'know . . .' He did not want to discuss it with her.

Astrid suddenly craned around him. 'Is that Vincent? It is. I wasn't sure he'd come.'

Pete's widowed partner Vincent was the person Sullivan least wanted to face. Coming to this party was beginning to feel like a big mistake. He'd put himself in the way of Juliet's drunkenly flirtatious hands, Astrid's gaze and now Vincent's judgement.

Sully shrunk back behind a cluster of people, out of Vincent's eye-line.

'You should speak to him. You owe him that,' Astrid said.

'Oh no, he shouldn't have to deal with me. He's here to have a nice time.'

Astrid shoved Sullivan in the back, propelling him in Vincent's direction. It was their entire relationship exhibited in a ten-second pageant: Astrid pushing Sullivan to be a better man than he really was.

She shoved him so hard that he knocked several elbows on the way past and spilled a woman's drink.

'Sorry, sorry, sorry,' said Sullivan.

And then it was too late. Vincent had noticed the kerfuffle so Sullivan was now too close and too exposed to pretend he hadn't been seen. He took two steps forward until he was in front of Vincent.

'Hello.'

'You look so different, I wasn't sure it was you,' said Vincent. 'But then I saw a guy knocking into people, spilling wine on the floor and mumbling "sorry" over and over again so I knew it must be Sullivan Moss.'

Sullivan attempted a smile but it went limp in the face of Vincent's severe expression. Vincent's mother was Korean and his father was Brazilian. The result of that genetic mix was a man so intriguing people tended to stare when he came into a room.

Vincent was a high-school geography teacher who'd stuck it out in tough schools for a decade and then accepted a cushier post in a selective school. He and Pete were together for eighteen years, through the majority of Pete's medical training, through his first bout with melanoma at the age of twenty-two, through Pete's doctoring stints in the Northern Territory, through a few failed attempts at having a baby with Vincent's sister and finally through the awful year once the melanoma had metastasised and got busy destroying Pete's body.

Sullivan inhaled, scrambling for whatever words he could say to this man now, but Vincent put his hand up in a stop gesture.

'I don't want to hear one word,' he said.

Sullivan clapped his mouth shut and nodded. Fair enough.

'I always saw you as a harmless creature. But when Pete was in the hospice, trying to call you, really hoping – for some unaccountable fucking reason, you were important to him. Even if you didn't have the decency to visit him, one phone call, one email would've been something. But apparently even that was beyond you.'

Vincent pressed his lips hard together as he fought tears. Then he turned towards the side exit door.

'Vincent, please don't leave the party because of me. I'll leave. I'll go now. I'll make myself scarce. I'll leave.'

'Don't flatter yourself, Sully. I was about to go anyway.'

Vincent slipped through the party crowd and outside into the alley at remarkable speed. Sullivan felt his whole body go cold and his insides freeze-dried. He was heading for the exit too when the music cut out and there was a hand on his shoulder.

It was some guy Sully didn't know, saying, 'You can't leave now, mate. Tim's about to do a speech.'

Juliet watched Tim adjust the microphone stand to speak. At the same time, he was leaning down from the stage to flirt with a pretty woman in her late twenties, a trader who used to work in his department. Not that Juliet was worried he had done or would do anything sexual with this girl. Tim had a solid, rather self-righteous commitment to fidelity in marriage. But she could see the option was there for him. And that was why Juliet would never leave Tim no matter how miserable she was. If she left him, he would take up with some young woman like this and possibly be happy. The notion that Tim would find happiness after all the years of misery he'd caused her – well, that prospect was so galling, she had to do everything to avoid it happening. Even if that meant staying put in their toxic household.

Tim was too drunk by the time he gave the speech. Many of his sentences dribbled off into chuckles and he seemed liable to slide into one of his syrupy moods, which Juliet had come to find repugnant.

The occasion of his fortieth inspired an attempt at grand talk about life. He raved about 'promises broken' and 'hoping our lives add up to something worthwhile'. And similarly mawkish shite.

He talked about old friends and managed to pick out Sullivan in the sea of faces.

'That's my oldest mate Sully right there,' said Tim. 'Those of you who know him, know he's been a fuckwit. Those of you who don't know him, trust me – he's been a fuckwit. But get this, people: Sully's gonna give away his kidney to a stranger. He's going to let doctors cut him open and take out his kidney for someone who needs it. So, I mean, fuck me . . . people can do things you don't expect. They can find chunks of goodness – fucking goodness you don't expect and that just . . . oh, that makes me think about our mate Pete . . . he died nine months ago.'

As Tim raved on about Pete, how much he admired him, loved him, missed him, Juliet felt a swell of compassion for her husband. Any kind of tender feeling for Tim made her ache a bit, like blood flowing back into a bruised area. But then a minute later, he started rambling on about how much he loved his wife and twins. Sentimental phoney bullshit. The disgust that coursed through Juliet was enough to kill off any momentary warmth she'd felt for him.

After Tim's speech, Sullivan had trouble reaching the exit because so many people wanted to talk to him about the kidney donation.

At first this caused discomfort because Sully was still stinging with shame from his encounter with Vincent. But as people continued to swarm around him, full of questions and praise and even flirtatious behaviour, he eventually allowed himself to bask in it a little. Yes, there was vanity at play but of a modest variety. And he was also using this opportunity, he told himself, to promote organ donation in general. He was sure that at the end of that night, several people would go home and tick 'yes' to donation on their driver's licence.

He was persuaded to stay on at the party by women who wanted more men to dance. Dancing sober was a new experience for Sullivan but he discovered he could use the rhythm and the physical pleasure of moving to drift into a euphoric state, equivalent to a lightly boozy high. Being clear-headed also had the extra benefit that he could enjoy a lovely eyeful of the women dancing around him without making it too obvious.

One of the dancing women was Paola, an actress he'd met when they both worked at the call centre selling wine. Paola had always been kind to him, even when most people had found him too exasperating to warrant kindness. As they danced now, she was raving on to him about a play she was going to be in at the Furniture Warehouse.

'You must come and see it. I'll Facebook you. Get you a comp,' she said.

Towards the end of the night, Paola danced quite close, occasionally letting her hips lightly brush Sully's. Maybe she was just tipsy and into the dancing so meant nothing by it. Then again, maybe he would go and see that play she was in.

Sullivan wound up being one of the late stayers at the party. He'd not managed to connect with Tim all night and by the time he did, Tim was so pissed and emotional that he was capable of nothing more than a clumsy hug and a few incomprehensible, weepy words.

Taxis were hard to find and handfuls of party guests were stranded on the street outside the Hammond Room. Some banker friend of Tim's had parked his Mercedes right in front of the venue but was now too drunk to drive it. Sully, being the only sober person left, found himself in the novel position of being the designated driver.

He drove the Merc – smooth, amazing, everything he would've expected – around the eastern suburbs, dropping people off one at a time.

'Thanks, mate. You're a lifesaver,' said one banker as he swung out of the back seat.

'You're the kidney guy, right?' said a tax lawyer as Sullivan delivered him and his sleepy wife to the gate of their Bellevue Hill palace. 'Good on you.'

The owner of the Merc lived in an apartment tower on the edge of Chinatown. He directed Sullivan down into the underground car park.

'Thanks. Right to my door. That's what I call service,' said the Merc owner. 'Can I call you a cab?'

'No thanks. I'm happy to walk from here,' said Sullivan.

As the Merc owner leaned against the wall waiting for the lift to his apartment, Sullivan took long strides up the ramp to the street and walked the few kilometres back to Glebe.

22

When Louis' team played their major semi-final, Sullivan Moss wasn't on the sideline to see them win.

'I think Sullivan's pretty busy at the moment,' said Natalie.

Louis nodded earnestly, as he yanked off his soccer boots and threw them in the car. 'Yeah, I bet he's got a heap of kidney stuff to do.'

So, Natalie was not required to lie to her son or offer up some awkward version of the truth. ('Mum and your friend Sullivan had an abortive attempt at a kiss and now it's all a bit weird and we might not see him much any more.')

Not that Louis let the matter go easily. 'Sullivan will want to know we won and how we go straight into the grand final and everything. Let me use your phone,' he demanded, wriggling sweatily in the front seat of the car.

Louis sent a text and Sullivan texted back straight away: *Go Louis! You're a star!*

The sign in the foyer of the Furniture Warehouse theatre stated that the play was only seventy minutes long with no interval. When Sullivan took his seat in the theatre he was full of energy but even so, he struggled to concentrate all the way through. The play, translated from German, used a cast of four – two young men, a woman in her sixties and Paola. Paola had emailed Sully after Tim's party and arranged for him to pick up a free ticket from the box office.

The actors spent most of the show standing with their legs slightly apart delivering seemingly unconnected monologues intercut with each other. Paola was proficient at performing in the required awkward style and with moments of intensity which suited the piece. In one section she displayed some impressive capital-A acting, gouging at her own sternum with a piece of broken glass. Sullivan would genuinely be able to praise her performance and that was a relief.

When Sully's attention wafted away from the show, there was plenty to occupy his mind. He'd performed two plays in this same theatre – impoverished indie productions in which cast members were only paid a share of the box office takings.

He remembered standing where Paola now stood, loving being part of the group putting on a show. He remembered forgetting lines on that stage thereby stuffing up several scenes and provoking the bad temper of his cast-mates in the tiny dressing room afterwards. It shocked him to think it all happened twelve years ago.

Eventually the German play stopped and Sullivan sat up straight to applaud vigorously. During the curtain call, Paola scanned the audience rows and spotted Sullivan. He grinned in greeting to her.

The hint of sexual promise from Paola at Tim's party had motivated Sully's theatre expedition but that motivation had faded for him. She was a lovely, sincere woman and he could certainly imagine enjoying sex with her. But it didn't feel right. He wasn't sure why. Maybe the project of husbanding his kidney demanded celibacy.

After the show, Sullivan positioned himself in a corner of the foyer behind a thick wooden post. His plan was to hang about long enough to say something positive to Paola when she emerged from the dressing room and then to scoot out of there quickly. He was leafing through the theatre program when he heard a subtle shift in the conversational burble around him. The crowd had shuffled apart slightly, creating a space in the middle of the foyer.

Sullivan craned around the wooden post and realised what was drawing the crowd's interest. Rory Wallace had walked into the building from the street.

Rory Wallace had been in a co-op production with Sully, here at the Furniture Warehouse, thirteen years ago when Rory was twenty-two, just out of drama school. The two young men hit it off right from the start, going drinking most nights after the show. Both of them would get stonkered, often staying out until mid-morning.

Rory moved on to a stint in a local TV series set in a coastal town but it wasn't long before he headed off to Los Angeles on the Aussie actor pilgrimage, trudging through a string of auditions for several years running. Sully happened to see him in an episode of an American TV show, playing the guy who appears to be the murderer but turns out not to be.

In a recent chat-show interview, Rory painted a picture of himself when he first arrived in LA: cash-strapped, sleeping in his car parked in a Santa Monica street, living off the free food samples in gourmet grocery stores. It was at that low point he scored a small-ish role in a well-regarded miniseries about the French Resistance. So many main characters were killed in the first season that when they went on to make a second series, Rory's character – a Hungarian Jewish doctor who smuggles stranded airmen across the Pyrenees into Spain – became one of the central roles.

That miniseries was Rory's breakthrough, landing him a BAFTA and an abundance of work offers. In *Boadicea* he played the Celtic queen's love interest and was required to bulk up, developing massive arms and a torso so ripped you could've hidden pencils between the corrugations of abdominal muscle. He used that same buff body to play a vigilante truck-driver in a huge budget futuristic action movie. Next he played an Iraq War veteran who becomes a scabby-faced crystal-meth addict.

Sullivan could see the theatre folk in the foyer working hard to be nonchalant about the fact that Rory Wallace was paying a nostalgic visit to his early acting arena. But their pupils were dilated, cheeks flushed and heads flicking about, apparently fascinated by the posters on the wall behind Rory's head.

Sullivan hung back behind the post and watched Rory operate. The guy was supremely comfortable in his own skin, seemingly oblivious to the excitement that vibrated around him at the same time as he soaked in its energy. When he turned to address someone, he fixed them with his gaze, giving them his attention so intensely the person would light up, as if the sun had just hit the surface of a pool of water. Lots of actors used such tricks of eye contact but Rory was a master.

Sully watched Rory do his thing on Paola as she emerged from the dressing room. He was clearly apologising for missing the show but doing it with such a bewitching smile that Paola was laughing, effervescent, her pleasant face suddenly made radiant by the beam of Rory's attention.

Sullivan could see Paola describing something to Rory, slapping a hand against her body in the rough location of her left kidney. Then she scanned the foyer, spotted Sullivan beside the post and pointed him out.

'Sullivan Moss!' Rory's deep, resonant voice cut through all the other voices.

Sullivan raised a hand, assuming a brief across-the-room greeting would be appropriate but Rory was already making his way towards him, making mock-growling noises like an excited dog.

'Mate! What an excellent surprise!'

Even though Sully was alert to Rory's charm methods, he was as much a sucker for them as anyone else in that foyer. When Rory reached him and grinned, Sullivan felt the sun hit him full in the face, blinding and marvellous. Rory grabbed him in a hug, holding the embrace a second or two longer than people customarily did. It was often that way with actors.

'I am glad to see you, Sully.'

Sullivan was confused by the importance Rory was attaching to their previous limited relationship but he was still flattered. Before he had a chance to reach Paola to say 'Thanks for the free ticket' or 'You were great in the play', Rory was bundling him out of the theatre into the street.

'Let's get out of here and go drinking,' said Rory.

Rory hailed a cab and directed the driver to a narrow laneway in Surry Hills where a new hidden-away bar had opened the week before.

The entrance to Lenno's was via an industrial steel door, then down rusted factory stairs to a basement saloon. The interior was resolutely eclectic – a plush Art Deco bar with panels of inlaid wood and chrome detailing, Mexican Day of the Dead figurines, sixties lounge furniture, a couple of red leather seating booths and so forth. The lighting was caramel soft, perfectly judged to make the fixtures look even more luscious and make the patrons – all of whom were attractive and/or stylishly eccentric – look even more attractive than they would in the lighting directed at regular folk.

The other occupants of the bar were laid-back about Rory's presence. Then again, his celebrity presence must have registered because when Rory scanned for a seat, the prime position in a private corner became vacant for him, thanks to the magical force that hovers around the famous.

'So what do you want to drink, Sully?' Rory asked. 'They have, like, three hundred different whiskies and forty different mezcals in this place.'

'I'll have a lime and soda,' said Sullivan.

'Right, yeah! You're not drinking because of the kidney thing! You've got more strength than me, brother.'

Rory laughed and shook his head, impressed, in a way that made Sullivan feel rather good about himself.

'I had to quit drinking for a few months once,' Rory explained.

'When I was getting into shape for the woad movie.' The 'woad movie' was what Rory called the Celtic warrior film for which he had first developed those abdominal muscles. 'Mate, I lived on chicken breasts and asparagus for so long. Nearly killed me.'

When Rory's double whiskey arrived, he clinked his glass against Sully's. 'Lucky I ran into you.' He raved on about how much better it was to spend time with a 'civilian' instead of exclusively show-business people.

'Not that I don't have some good friends in LA,' he said. 'But my mates are in the business too and you always end up with those sticky moments when people get the shits about who's worth more in the industry, you know?'

'I can't say I know from direct experience,' said Sully. 'But I've been developing my imaginative powers lately so . . .'

'Ha. You were always a smart guy. Even when you were wasted. I remember that. So! Can we talk about something other than movie business?'

Scrambling for topics that might interest Rory, Sullivan offered up a couple of stories about his asbestos job.

'That is fascinating shit,' said Rory. 'Hey, could I come out and watch you guys work one day?'

'I can probably make arrangements for that.'

Rory went to the gents and on the way back stopped to chat to the barman who handed him two shots of mezcal and a plate of orange slices sprinkled with spices, urging him to try them. Within seconds a small group gathered around Rory and it was clear he had them all captivated. Did Rory attract people to him because of his fame or had he become famous because he'd always had a charisma which made people want him to like them?

Of course it was partly about looks. Rory was a very handsome man. But there were plenty of good-looking people around so it must be more than that. There was something sexual about him, as if the guy was semi-tumescent most of the time. Was he literally semi-tumescent? Or was it a metaphorical semi-tumescence? Sullivan decided it was both. There was an energy that hummed off Rory Wallace's person that was simply exciting to be near.

At one point Sullivan realised all four of the people with Rory were looking over at him. Feeling exposed, he averted his gaze and feigned an overwhelming fascination with a Mexican dancing skeleton on the wall.

When Rory sat back down opposite Sullivan, he flicked his head to indicate the group at the bar. 'They couldn't believe it when I told them about you donating a kidney. Disbelieving, then amazed, then impressed.'

'Oh well . . . I didn't decide to do this to impress anyone.' Which was true. But would it remain true if people happened to be impressed and Sullivan let himself enjoy that?

'Mate, in my life,' said Rory pointing both hands at his own head emphatically, 'I am surrounded – I am *immersed* – in a world of wankery where people get themselves worked up about stuff that *does not* matter. That's why what you're doing – a simple act that will make a measurable difference and mean something and help someone and shake people up a bit about the bullshit they fret about and —'

Rory stopped and grinned. 'I'm ranting at you. Sorry.' He downed the two shots of mezcal. 'Let's get out of this masturbatorium. Three hundred fucking types of whiskey, Day of the Dead tat in the middle of Sydney. Can you believe this wankfest?'

They headed back out to the top of the laneway and Rory immediately found a passing cab. Vacant taxis were apparently drawn to him too. Sullivan imagined a fleet of cabs cruising around Sydney, until Rory had need of them, each driver hopeful and fizzy like a teenage girl waiting to be picked to dance.

'Come and check out the place I'm staying,' said Rory.

The place was a cliff-top house in Tamarama, around the headland from Bondi. At street level, the only visible structure was a long wall, painted gunmetal grey, with a discreet security door and a garage door.

On the other side of the wall was a courtyard that provided another layer of privacy, like an airlock. The interior of the house was colour-consulted and elegant in an unobjectionable way. It made Sullivan think of a plush bunker, blockaded from the street, with windows that overlooked nothing but cliffs and ocean. Sullivan assumed the level of privacy was the reason Rory's Australian handlers had leased this particular house for his hometown stay.

'It's next door I want to show you.'

Rory grabbed a laptop and a torch before leading the way down some internal stairs to the rear courtyard. He aimed his torch-beam at the side fence where a stepladder created a makeshift stile.

'We're climbing over?' asked Sullivan. 'Who owns that place?'

'I do.'

The major renovation of the property next door had stalled in the wake of the vicious divorce and financial collapse of the owners. Rory liked the place. He bought it.

Guided by the torch, Sullivan clambered up several concrete ledges to get inside. Rory then switched on builders' work-lights so Sullivan could appreciate the house. Or rather, so he could appreciate Rory's vision for the house this shell of a building would eventually become.

From the street, it appeared no different to the other expensive houses in the row, with a high lime-washed wall, similar to the fortified exterior of the place Rory was staying. But the interior was a different story – it had been gutted, as if a bomb had blasted off the rear half. Through the enormous cavity where the back wall should have been, Sullivan could hear the surf and make out the white smudges of the waves.

There were stacks of building materials and other evidence that builders had restarted work. Even so, the floors and most of the walls were still just raw concrete, with pipes and hanks of ragged wiring hanging out of holes.

Rory turned on the laptop to show Sully the plans for the house – first the straightforward architectural drawings, then the 3D computer renderings he'd commissioned so you could swoop through the imaginary rooms and outside into the yard.

'What big fun is this!' said Rory. 'It's like having a Steadicam snaking through your house before it's even built.'

The new living area would step some way down the cliff in open-plan spaces, ending in a terrace that jutted out, overlooking the ocean. The lower level housed a self-contained flat, a steam room and a gym, with access to the lap pool. On the upper storey were guest bedrooms and a colossal master suite with its own terrace. Every design element was gigantic or dramatic or both, from a kitchen bench as large, black and glossy as a stretch limousine to a home theatre bigger than many art-house cinemas.

As Rory raved about the plans, he was even more magnetic a figure than usual. He strode around the space, drawing shapes in the air with his arms, eager for Sullivan to envisage where the doors and stairs and decks would one day be.

'I am so pumped about this place. There's a chance I'll have to sprint back to LA sometime soon – for a role that might happen – but half the time I'm wishing it doesn't happen so I can stay here and get this joint done.'

Sullivan could understand the impulse. There was something about the bare casing of the house in this spectacular location that ignited an urge to complete it.

'Fucking hell, Sully, you know what just occurred to me? If I have to leave in a hurry, you could be a caretaker, oversee the building for me while I'm away.'

'Sorry?'

'The self-contained flat downstairs should be liveable soon. You'll have to move out of the dead guy's place when they sell it, won't you? You could move in here and be my building supervisor.'

'I don't know anything about building,' Sullivan pointed out.

'You're a smart guy. And I trust you. That's the important thing. Oh, the more I think about it – yeah, yeah, yeah, this is a good idea, yeah?'

'I've got Mack. Remember I told you about the dog I'm looking after.'

'No problem. I love the idea of a dog living here. Bring the dog, yeah?'

Rory grinned at Sullivan, his eyes and teeth shining in the dim space. He was boyishly excited but with the assurance of a grown-up who was accustomed to getting things. To say no to him would have felt like saying no to some irrepressibly positive life force.

23

The sharp tips of the chicken wings poked into Natalie's calves through the plastic, as she carried the bag up to Frank's building. She was already in a testy mood. There seemed to be a gritty substance rasping away at her neck and shoulders.

When Gordana lurched out of her front doorway and onto the landing, Natalie had a spike of annoyance – certain, for one mad instant, that Gordana was the person who was sprinkling gritty stuff into her bones.

'Hello, Natalie,' said Gordana, holding a green supermarket bag with empty bottles clinking inside.

'Yes. Hello.'

'How are you?'

It was the second time that week Gordana had appeared on the landing in front of her, as if by chance.

'How does this work?' Natalie squinted at her. 'Do you peer through the spyhole, waiting for me, so you can pop out like this?'

'What? No. I have bottles to take to the recycling.'

'Really? Because it feels like you pounce on me.'

'I don't pounce,' Gordana insisted.

'And why? Is this some kind of surveillance? Or are you warning me off? I already told you, I won't dob. I won't get you into trouble.'

'I know that.'

'Good. Well, that's good.'

Gordana clomped past and out the side door towards the recycling bins. Natalie was immediately remorseful. Why was she such a nasty cow to that woman? Was she simply annoyed and petulant that Frank hadn't told her about their liaison? If so, that was childish, ridiculous.

Natalie was in a generally foul mood, stirred up by the usual culprits – Judy, work frustration, lack of sleep – with the added embarrassment about and crankiness towards Sullivan Moss.

After three weeks without seeing Sullivan, she had received a voice message from him: 'Listen, Nat, very very sorry. I'm out and I can't get back to Frank's to feed Mack this evening. Is there any chance you could feed him? Sorry.'

The request itself was reasonable. The man was allowed to have a life and ask for favours with the care of the dog. But he'd asked twice more in the week after that. He was strangely coy about why he was suddenly neglecting his duties with Mack. He was 'busy', 'out of normal routine', 'caught up'.

Eventually Natalie injected a note of irritation down the phoneline. 'Look, Sullivan, if you're having second thoughts about taking on the dog, tell me now so I can —'

'No, no, no!' Then Sullivan sighed and was obliged to explain himself. 'An old friend's blown into town.'

'All right, so . . . is this old friend of yours likely to stay around for a while?'

'Uncertain. It's Rory Wallace,' said Sullivan finally.

'Oh. I see,' said Natalie. That was why he'd been evasive. Sullivan was a person who wouldn't want to boast about his famous mate.

Natalie knew Sullivan knew that Rory Wallace was one of Louis' favourite actors, having been entranced by him in *Boadicea*. Natalie herself thought Wallace was wonderful as the troubled doctor in the French Resistance drama. But she was careful to keep her tone neutral on the phone, with no gushy fandom in her voice. 'Well, what fun for you. But you need to let me know if —'

'Please don't worry. I'm not turning my back on Mack. Looks like I'll be moving into a flat underneath the house Rory is renovating. He's really happy for the dog to live there with me.'

'Well, sounds terrific. Just keep me informed. Bye.' Natalie hung up quickly before the conversation could go on any longer.

She stepped inside her father's flat and Mack was thrilled to see her, even before he gave his attention to the chicken wings. She fished a couple of wings out of the bag for him, this generosity merely adding to the dog's appreciation of her as a glorious creature. He chomped through the chicken in two bites apiece, then galloped back to receive more pats from Natalie. It was a blessedly simple relationship.

Rory Wallace's Australian agent, Mel, was in her early sixties, powerful on the local scene and with a few international heavyweights on her client list. Mel projected a jaded air, as if she were over the whole business, but it was clear to Sullivan that behind her weary sighs, her mind was sharp and she was still loving the game.

She was big, always dressed in floaty silk garments and lots of jewellery, her policy being that she might as well make use of her sizeable surface area by hanging lots of decoration on herself.

Sullivan had spent a bit of time with Mel in the last couple of weeks, thanks to Rory. He was not only one of Mel's most important clients but also a personal favourite. She handled him with a combination of astringent candour and motherly coddling, Rory wallowing happily in both.

'Good Lord,' Mel groaned when she saw the emerald-green 1959 FJ Holden parked outside the Tamarama house. Rory had hired it as his Sydney car.

Rory reached out to tickle Mel's forearms, jangling with bangles. 'It's so voluptuous. Feast your eyes on it.'

Instead Mel rolled her eyes.

'Sully can be my designated driver when I wanna be the designated drunk,' said Rory and flashed her his naughty-boy smile.

Mel thwacked him in the face like a lioness cuffing her cub.

Rory went out most nights of the week – to restaurants, bars, screenings, parties. The bulk of his day was spent sleeping off his hangover, working out with his trainer, surfing, skim-reading scripts. By late-afternoon, Rory was ready to play and Sullivan had become one of his chief playmates.

'Why me?' Sullivan had asked several times.

'Don't put too low a value on yourself, princess,' said Rory. 'Why wouldn't I want to hang out with a no-bullshit operator who makes me laugh and who gets why I'm so stoked about my house?'

Rory loved dropping in next door to discuss the build with any tradesmen working on the site and he was always keen for Sullivan to join him on these visits.

'It's like we're playing with a huge crate of customised Lego!'

After a bout of enthusiastic design talk, Sullivan would often accompany Rory on some evening outing. At these events, Sullivan kept a low profile, happy to function as the safe zone to which Rory could return when he needed to extricate himself from an unwelcome social entanglement. Then on the way home at the end of the night, Sullivan would try to make Rory laugh with his commentary on the social manoeuvrings he'd witnessed.

In Rory's orbit, there was always distraction on offer and Sullivan was less likely to miss Natalie and Louis. He could relax into his position as an adjunct to Rory Wallace's life. After all these months of steering himself, having to generate his own purpose and make his own decisions, it was a relief to hand over agency to someone else for a while. Sully regarded this period as a kind of rest before facing the final ordeal of the surgery.

Being one of Rory Wallace's playmates did entail frequent late nights – a problem, given Sullivan still had daylight duties to take care of. He jumped out of bed early to put in a day's work with Jose Luis, then would dash back to Frank's place and take Mack for a long walk to compensate for providing him less company in the evenings.

Sullivan did let Jose Luis down more than once. There were days he was significantly late for work and several shifts he missed entirely. Knowing Sullivan was facing major surgery soon, Jose Luis was very understanding. 'Enjoy yourself while you can, my friend. Hopefully you can come for lunch next Sunday. Liliana misses you.' Sullivan hadn't made it to a Sunday lunch at his boss's house since Rory had shown up.

When Mel arrived at the Tamarama house this morning, she nodded hello to Sullivan, by now used to his role as one of Rory's courtiers.

Rory ushered her inside. 'Let me make you some Turkish apple tea.'

'Lovely,' said Mel and then in a stage whisper to Sullivan, added, 'Persuade him to stick with apple tea all night, can you?'

Curbing Rory's substance use was one of Mel's chief concerns. She was like a stern but affectionate boarding-school mistress who earned commission from the handsome young man in her care.

In fact Rory was realistic about the obligation to keep his body looking a certain way for professional purposes. He was required to stay lean, muscled-up and not let the ravages of recreational drugs show on his face. He occasionally allowed himself what he called 'Substance Nights' when he'd hang out with certain mates and avail himself of whatever substances were on hand. Sullivan wasn't invited to Substance Nights.

'You've got a kidney to look after,' Rory explained. 'I'm not gonna be responsible for tempting you away from your wholesome quest.'

In truth, Sullivan would have found it much easier to resist pills or powders than the high-quality alcohol Rory splashed around in front of him but the demarcation made sense to Rory so Sully went along with it.

There were other nights when Rory's focus would be on a woman and no playmates were invited to hang about. Several times Sullivan arrived at Rory's rented house in the afternoon to discover some ridiculously attractive early-twenties female lolling on the furniture. Sullivan never saw the same woman twice.

As Sullivan, Mel and Rory sipped on apple tea, a mobile phone started to buzz, jerking itself across the kitchen counter. Rory checked the caller ID and winced.

'Can you get it for me, Mel?'

'Is it the Waif?' she asked.

Rory nodded and made exaggerated pleading gestures.

Mel groaned but picked up the phone. 'Hello, Whitney. It's Mel here. How are you, darling? Rory's out in the surf right now.'

Whitney Todd Harrison – dubbed the Waif by Mel – was calling from LA. She'd started acting at the age of thirteen, when she looked young enough to play the eight-year-old daughter of the main characters in movies. Now twenty-three, she was intent on being taken seriously as an adult performer. Whitney had been Rory's girlfriend for almost a year now.

Rory beckoned Sullivan to follow him out onto the deck. Behind them, they could hear Mel handling the call with wave after wave of reassuring excuses.

But only a few moments later, Rory puffed out a breath and headed back inside, indicating to Mel that she should hand him the phone.

'Oh, here he is, Whitney,' said Mel. 'Still all wet and salty from the surf.'

Rory took the phone. 'Hey, baby.'

Sullivan could hear Whitney crying through the phone line as Rory coaxed her down from whatever emotional ledge she'd got herself onto. Sully felt sorry for Whitney. He felt sorry for Rory too – he knew how lousy it felt to make a woman cry that much.

The newspaper article was Rory's idea.

'Sully, what you're doing, your altruistic act, it should be an inspiration to people. Yeah, it's stupid that we need to use my name to get the media interested. But you have to work with reality.'

'I can't do an interview about it. The whole idea of non-directed donation is that it's anonymous,' Sullivan had countered.

'So we make sure they don't show your face or use your name. A piece on what you're doing could get people thinking about organ donation. You can't knock back an opportunity to do that, can you?'

And so now, Sullivan found himself shaking hands with Bec the journalist and Arpad the photographer at Rory's front door.

To be available for the interview, Sully needed a day off work. He had felt bad asking again, having let Jose Luis down so much lately. So he put off asking until he had no choice but to phone the night before the interview.

'Hi, Jose Luis. Something's come up tomorrow that I have to do.'

'Is it because of the kidney transplant?' asked Jose Luis.

'Mmm, yeah,' said Sullivan which wasn't a direct lie. The interview was indeed because of the kidney donation. Of course Jose Luis meant some necessary medical procedure. Sullivan just didn't correct him.

'I can manage, Sullivan. You do what needs to be done,' said Jose Luis.

The photos were taken in a cliff-top park near Rory's house. As agreed, Sullivan's face would not be shown in the picture.

Then they all trooped back to Rory's place to drink Turkish apple tea and conduct the interview. Bec the journalist was so mesmerised by Rory that she could hardly register Sullivan's existence. Sully didn't mind.

Rory stayed on message, steering Bec away from talk about his career or personal gossip, always bringing the conversation back to the importance of people appreciating the valuable gift of organ donation.

24

Tim brought the Sunday papers in from the front yard. He wasn't sure why they still had them delivered – rubbishy publications that offered little more than wrist exercise while flipping through the vacuous pages.

The Sunday rags used to be part of a ritual. He would peel the plastic off the papers, take tea upstairs and climb back into bed with Juliet. But they hadn't done that ritual for – well, quite a few years now. Juliet said she'd rather have the extra sleep.

So Tim stayed downstairs and flattened the newspapers onto the kitchen table. In the features section, he flicked to the 'Between Us' page and there was a photo of Sullivan's actor friend Rory Wallace. Next to him was a man with his head out of frame, pulling up his shirt to show his torso, while the grinning movie star pointed at the guy's abdomen. Sullivan's abdomen.

He was only identified as 'Rory's mate'. With no face or name, at least Sully wasn't extracting personal publicity from it. Wallace on the other hand – that smug show-pony – was quoted at length, banging on about raising awareness of organ donation. The journalist was clearly panting over Wallace, as if he were the one giving up an organ and Tim felt a twinge of indignation on his friend's behalf. He also felt a twinge of resentment about Sully's friendship with Rory Wallace.

He was aware the two had been hanging out quite a bit. One

evening, in a silly attack of man-jealousy, he'd driven past the Tamarama house Sully said Wallace was renting. He had spotted the garish green vintage Holden parked outside before driving on.

Tim was just getting to the end of the newspaper piece when Juliet came downstairs, dressed for running, with her shoes in her hand.

'Sully's made the paper,' said Tim and spun the paper round on the table for her to read.

She scanned the article. 'Do you think he's really going to do it?'

'Looks like he might.'

They both pulled mock-horrified faces and laughed.

'Good on him, I guess,' said Juliet.

'You're right. Good on him.'

Juliet looked up and they shared a smile.

'I just boiled the kettle,' he said, nonchalant, not wanting to wreck this small soft moment by pushing it too hard.

'I'll have tea.' Juliet sounded equally casual but she must have felt the significance of the moment too.

Tim decided to make a proper pot. They both used to make the effort with leaf tea. While it brewed, they chatted about Sullivan's strange new friendship with Rory Wallace.

'It's like something out of *Entourage*,' said Juliet.

'Exactly,' said Tim.

Juliet watched Tim put out good cups and pour the tea through the strainer. He was still the confident, friendly, competitive, sentimental, energetic brainbox she'd first met, before they'd both made a series of bad choices which had locked them together in what was always destined to be a foolish pairing.

Tim could not be blamed for everything. And they used to have a lot of fun. Right now he was being quite sweet to her.

They sat at the table with their tea and Juliet thought it'd be nice to meander through the Sunday papers together. But within seconds of sitting down, Tim flipped open his laptop.

That image – Tim sitting across from her but with his face directed at a screen, numbers reflected on his eyeballs – was very familiar. It pierced the little sacs of vitriol that sat in Juliet's belly, which then began to leak resentment all through her.

She looked at him across the kitchen table and willed him to talk to her. Amazingly, for once, this silent invocation seemed to work.

'Y'know, I've been thinking a lot about Pete and Sully,' said Tim, not shifting his eyes from the screen.

Yes, this scene was familiar too: Tim ignoring her, then suddenly having a paroxysm of nostalgia.

'Well, the speech at your fortieth made that clear,' she said. It hurt her that Tim talked as if his real and best life was all in the time before her. But she would never give him the satisfaction of knowing how much it hurt.

'And now – this,' said Tim, staring at the newspaper photo. 'Sully's been going on about making a contribution and now he's really doing something.'

'Even I am beginning to have some respect for him,' Juliet conceded.

At least what Sully was doing was better than bloodless charity. Juliet had given the charity thing a go. But the other people – during school hours, it was mostly women – were boring or gullible or fraudulent or self-righteous or some combination of the above.

'Yeah, it's got me thinking about ways we could make a contribution, that is if you think you might let – hear me out,' Tim began.

Juliet bristled. 'Oh, is this going to turn into a dig at me? Are you going to sic Astrid onto me again?' At Tim's urging, Astrid had tried, with her galumphing goodness, to get Juliet involved in her various good works, back when the twins started high school.

'What? Why are you talking about Astrid now?'

'I actually like Astrid. Whatever you think.' And Juliet really did think Astrid was one of the few genuine do-gooders she'd met. 'But let me tell you, Mr Man, I do not want to hear Astrid's views on what I should be doing with my life ever again.'

'I know you think you can read my thoughts, Juliet, but you can't, okay?'

'How could I since you hardly say a fucking word to me for days at a time.'

'And fuck knows why that would be, you sweet-tongued angel.'

'Okay. Okay.' Juliet made a show of tying up her shoes to go. She yanked at the laces very hard to demonstrate to Tim how quickly he had pushed her from sweet to angry. She yanked them so hard it sent a stabbing pain across her instep. Which was also Tim's fault, since he'd ruined her good mood in the first place.

'Come on Juliet, I didn't mean —'

'What the fuck did you mean?'

'This thing with Sullivan's got me thinking.'

'It's got you soul-searching over the Sunday papers. That's where most people seek moral guidance.'

'Okay, now you sound like a sour bitch. Is that what you're aiming for?'

'Remember I've known you for a long time. Not as long as Pete and Sully but long enough. I've seen you have spasms of virtue plenty of times before. A lot of saintly bullshit talk that never goes anywhere.'

Tim did his head waggle – a maddening gesture he employed when he didn't know how to answer but wanted to let her know that her worthless mouthings didn't matter one tiny scrap to him. She wanted to rip his waggling head off his stupid neck, feeling the vertebrae and nerves tear apart in her hands.

Juliet hated having her mind filled with images like that. She had to get away from Tim and his waggling head and his blowhard, hypocritical soul-searching. She ran out the door and started jogging at warm-up pace.

She passed one of their neighbours picking up the newspaper from his driveway. He was shirtless, just wearing pyjama bottoms, and you could see he was bald on top but hirsute everywhere else. Hairy Shoulders Man ran his eyes up and down Juliet's body with his trademark leer. He was one of those men who was constantly transmitting a signal which said *I'm available*. He nodded hello but she ignored him and ran on.

Juliet had considered becoming one of those women – she knew a few – who had a series of affairs. She was fit, still not bad-looking and she genuinely liked sex which she understood was a sought-after characteristic. But when she looked around at the men in her world, they were an unappealing lot. She did have a one-night stand once with a man she met in a hotel bar in Melbourne when she was on a shopping weekend with women friends. But that encounter had been more awkward than satisfying.

She thought about Tim sitting there at the kitchen table, brooding over the newspaper photo. At least Sullivan Moss was honest about what he was worth – that is, not much. Sully was offering up the one bit of himself that was worth anything to other people. A body part. Good on him.

Tim was deflated for a moment after Juliet slammed the front door. The two of them managed to destroy good moments with a speed that left him baffled, ashamed, angry. These days he understood there were undercurrents in an exchange with Juliet that he missed. But that understanding didn't help him to prevent those nasty implosions.

The mistake he'd made this morning was to mention the idea of making a contribution before he had anything worked out. In fact, he'd flipped open the laptop at the kitchen table because he was already doing some calculations on their finances, seeing what the options might be. But he knew Juliet hated him burying his face in a computer screen and he realised now that was an error.

Looking at the photo of Sully's stomach, Tim rallied himself. He was not a person who liked to give up on things and Sullivan's radical act was a useful example. The best way for Tim to fix his life would be to embrace the idea of a radical change. Not by giving up an organ but having a similarly fundamental rethink.

He would do the numbers and once he had a decent plan, he would present it to Juliet in a way she could believe. How much money did he need to service his existing commitments? What financial structure could he establish that would generate sufficient income to live comfortably if he got out of the market? How much capital might he then have available to set up a new venture of real value? Why not do something interesting and constructive and – yes, fuck it – altruistic?

It could be fun. Rejuvenating. It could be the best way for him and Juliet to reconnect.

The day the newspaper article came out, Sullivan found himself torn between wishing Natalie had seen the article in the hope she might think about him and wishing she hadn't seen it for fear she might think less of him as a publicity-seeker. That night, he tagged along with Rory to a party in a converted Alexandria warehouse.

Rory was in an ebullient mood. 'Meet my headless friend, Sully,' he said to everyone they encountered. 'I can prove it's the guy from the article. Look.' Then he would lift up Sullivan's shirt to reveal the same torso as the one in the photo.

Being the focus of attention for a noble act was not entirely unpleasant. And Sullivan particularly enjoyed holding the attention of an attractive woman at the party who was laughing at his jokes more enthusiastically than they warranted. As the night progressed, he ended up in a dark corner with her.

'Show me exactly where they cut you to get the kidney out,' she said, lifting up Sullivan's shirt.

He guided her hand to a spot on his abdomen. 'Somewhere around here.'

'I see,' she said and then slid her hand down his jeans, brushing past his cock.

It felt very good, and Sullivan was thinking he would like to pursue this when he noticed Rory signalling to him across the room. *Let's get out of here.*

'Unfortunately, I have to go,' Sullivan said to the woman in a tone he hoped would indicate how reluctant he was to end their discussion.

'Wait one sec,' she said. She reached her hand into Sullivan's pocket, not wasting the opportunity to brush his cock again, and fished out his mobile. She tapped her number and *Jess* into his phone.

On the drive back to Tamarama, Rory was checking messages on his phone when he suddenly turned to Sullivan. 'Shit, I just thought – that woman you were yacking to – did I blow a chance for you, son? Sorry.'

'I've got her number. Don't worry about it.'

'Well, I am worried about it. Want me to ring her?'

'If you ring her, she'll want to fuck you,' Sullivan pointed out.

'I don't think so. I reckon she was hot for you, the Organ Donor.'

They both laughed.

Sullivan parked the FJ Holden in the garage and then, armed with torches, they climbed over the side fence from the rented house into the half-built house.

Rory had purchased two pool loungers so they could sit on the concrete shelf that would eventually become the top-floor terrace. It felt very high, ten metres above the hole where the pool would go.

Rory swigged a beer, flopped in a lounger next to Sullivan. 'Hey – tell me about what was going on in your head when you stood on that roof about to jump off.'

Sully did his best to answer the barrage of questions. 'Were you emotional in the moment or were you peaceful once you'd decided?' 'Did you feel scared at the point you were about to go over?' 'Did you look down at the ground?' 'Did you close your eyes?'

Sullivan realised Rory was gathering details to store in his mental bank as an actor. If he were ever to play a man about to jump off a rooftop, he could make use of these details. It was a legitimate form of salvage. If one day down the track Sullivan saw bits of himself harvested and employed in a performance, that would be okay.

'I love you, mate,' said Rory. 'I hope you know that. Hey, when's your surgery happening?'

'I'm waiting for them to tell me the date.'

'Right. Right. Whenever it is, afterwards, when you're feeling like shit, I'll be here. Come and live here afterwards, yeah?'

'Oh. Excellent. Thanks.'

Sullivan could get used to that idea. Being Rory's Australian gofer could offer him a place and purpose while still providing a home for Mack.

The two men sat on the half-built terrace for another hour. Rory insisted Sully stay the night in the guest bedroom of the rented place.

As Sullivan drifted off, he decided he felt okay. It was good to sleep. It was good to inhale the smell of frangipanis from the glass bowl in the guest ensuite. It was good to recall the sensation of that woman's hand on his cock and to know her number was tucked in his phone. It was good not to ruminate as much on Pete or Natalie or his messed up life. And it was good to feel slightly giddy like this – tapping into the energy Rory generated.

Sullivan was woken at nine by a call from Diane Milton.

'Shit, Diane . . . I got your message yesterday. I meant to call back but – sorry.'

'You've always been such an eager beaver about returning my calls, I wondered what had happened to you. Is there a problem?' asked Diane.

'No problem. I've been having fun. Sober fun.'

'Okay. You're allowed to have fun, Sullivan. The main thing I wanted to tell you is that we have your match for transplant.'

'It's a good match? How many compatibility markers?'

'Six out of six markers. We've set your date for surgery.'

'That's . . . that's exciting.' Sullivan was genuinely excited.

'One week from now. The twenty-ninth,' said Diane. 'Is that going to be okay?'

'Yes. Yes. Great.'

As Sullivan registered the date, a calendar page flashed up in his mind. That's when it struck him that he had forgotten Louis' soccer grand final. The game was yesterday. He'd missed it.

25

On the drive to the airport, Louis was quiet. Natalie assumed it was because he was nervous about travelling to Kuala Lumpur on his own for the first time. She suspected he was also still brooding over yesterday's grand final.

The game had been close – three goals to two. Afterwards, walking from the field to the car park, Louis was mud-spattered and glum, mostly about the loss, but Natalie knew there was also disappointment about Sullivan's failure to show.

'You played so well, Louis,' she'd said. 'You were fast and you never gave up and you followed the play in a really smart way. That cross you did at the start of the second half was really —'

'Saying that stuff won't make me feel better,' he muttered.

'I'm going to say it anyway.'

Natalie went on for a few more minutes about how valiantly his team had played, the achievement of making the grand final at all and other heartening, wise observations. Louis sighed loudly and refused to be cheered up as a matter of honour. Fair enough. Natalie hoped the words would sit on the edge of his brain and soak in sometime later when he was ready.

Now, Monday, on the way to the airport, the grand final was indeed on Louis' mind.

'Did Sullivan know the day the grand final was on?' he asked. 'He could've got mixed up because they put it on a Sunday instead of a Saturday.'

'Well, I texted him the date,' said Natalie.

All through the week, Louis had pestered Natalie to call Sullivan and check he would be at the game. She did ring a few times but got his voicemail and wavered over the wording to use in a message. By the Thursday, she gave up.

Should she have persevered and forced Sullivan Moss to appreciate how much it meant to the boy? Well, she didn't persevere, so in the end, she allowed him to forget his grand-final promise. Not that this absolved Sullivan of responsibility to keep his word to an eight-year-old. Even so Nat knew her motives were questionable. There was a protective urge towards Louis – maybe it would be just as well if the man disappeared from their lives – but that was mixed with her own wounded pride, that Sullivan had chosen to disappear from their lives so suddenly. Natalie's reticence about calling was really an act of quiet sabotage on her part.

Louis sighed. 'Maybe there was something wrong with Sullivan's phone. I should've gone round to Grandpa Frank's place and reminded him when it was on.'

'Well, maybe,' said Natalie but it rankled her that Louis was taking on responsibility for the negligence of a grown-up man. He had already absorbed enough let-downs from his father in his eight years on earth. 'Sometimes people make promises and then don't end up keeping them. Don't think it's your fault if —'

'I know. You've done that speech before.'

Natalie gulped a breath to fight the urge to say more.

'You know,' said Louis more brightly. 'I bet Sullivan couldn't come to the grand final because he had to go to the hospital for tests and stuff. His operation is gonna happen really soon.'

'Maybe that's it,' said Natalie.

'You know what? It's good he didn't come. Heaps of the parents had colds. If one of them sneezed on him and he got their germs, it might mess up his kidney.'

Natalie nodded. She envied his ability to convert disappointment into a more palatable narrative.

When she handed Louis over to the airline staff, the procedure for unaccompanied minors struck her as an absurd act of faith: to trust that a lanyard hanging around her child's neck would act as a magic talisman, guaranteeing his safety as he flew thousands of kilometres to a strange city choked with diesel fumes and people who spoke a different language.

'Your dad said he'll be waiting for you at the gate lounge.'

Louis rolled his eyes. 'You said that seventeen thousand times.'

'We'll skype every day. And text me whenever you think of something funny or something I'd be interested to hear about.'

Natalie hugged him in one long squeeze, trying to lock in the memory of his little body, then a few seconds later he was gone, through the passengers-only gateway.

Walking back through the airport without Louis, Natalie felt weightless and peculiar. Before she could face returning to her car and the world, she needed a period in limbo to get accustomed to being childless for the next seven days, so she roamed the airport shops.

Seven days as a single, unencumbered person. This was an opportunity she should make the most of. Nine months ago, on the day Frank died, she had vowed to have sex with another human being in the next year. That deadline was approaching rapidly.

Natalie sat at one of the tables in the food hall with a coffee. As an exercise in libido stimulation, she observed the men walking past. Any man between the ages of twenty and sixty she imagined naked. If a man possessed any skerrick of attractiveness to her, she imagined fucking him.

In an astonishingly short space of time, she was turned on. There was one guy – the way he walked, the line of his body in jeans, his forearms – who inspired Natalie sufficiently to let the sexual fantasy run on for some time, until she found herself making a small involuntary *mmm* sound out loud. If Astrid was right about the atrophy of sexual apparatus from lack of use, Natalie was attempting to treat the problem before it was too late, feeling neural and vascular pathways reconnecting in her pelvic region moment by moment.

Male friends had described their discreet perving habits to her – how they would sometimes mentally undress women walking past and imagine having sex with them. Natalie could see why men were tempted to do this – it was compelling. But it was also so distracting that it compromised other brain activity.

Natalie was wondering how to switch off this libidinous thought stream when her phone rang. She didn't recognise the caller's number.

'Natalie Dennis speaking.'

'Hi, Nat. It's Sullivan. I'm so sorry about missing the grand final.'

'Oh well, don't – uh . . .' Natalie began and then stopped herself from letting him off the hook too swiftly.

'How did they go?'

'They lost. But it was a great game and Louis played really well.'

'I bet he did. Good on him,' said Sullivan. 'Thing is, Natalie, I feel so bad about not showing up, I've been trying to think of a way to make it up to him.'

'Look, don't feel any obligation to —'

'I know Louis is a big fan of Rory Wallace. Rory was wondering if Louis would like to come and hang out with him one day this week. See a movie or go surfing or something.'

'I'm sure he'd love that. But he's just got on a plane to Kuala Lumpur to spend time with his father. He'll be away all week.'

'Oh right . . . I should've called earlier. I mean, Rory might still be in Sydney a week from now but you can never be sure because he's – you know . . .'

'Unpredictable.'

'Yeah, but look, I still want to make it up to you guys for stuffing up and . . .'

Sullivan put his hand over the phone, conducted a conversation with someone else, then came back on the line.

'Nat, let's organise something when Louis gets back but before then, what if Rory came in for an interview on your breakfast show? Would that be good?'

Wallace was supposedly not doing any publicity on this holiday in Sydney so securing an interview with him would be a coup for Natalie.

'Yes, that would be good.'

The junior breakfast producer ushered Rory and Sullivan from the foyer, up in the lift, to the radio studio. Rory asked if it might be possible to peek into the control room to see what went on. He punctuated this with a melting smile and the young producer duly melted.

Sullivan could see Natalie through the glass panel of the control room door. She was swivelling back and forth in her chair at the panel, hands flying over keyboards and switches, gaze darting across a battery of monitors. The producer sitting next to Natalie tapped her on the shoulder and she swung round to face the door.

It was the first time Sullivan had seen her in more than five weeks. The first time since their abortive kiss. He held his breath – not confident he wouldn't blurt out something inappropriate – but did manage to smile and wave hello.

'Good morning, gentlemen,' Natalie said as she swung open the door, then shook Rory's hand. 'Lovely to meet you. Thanks so much for coming in to do this.'

'No worries. Thank *you* for looking after my mate Sully a few months back when his need was great.'

Natalie did a mock grimace, flicked her gaze to Sullivan and away again. Was she embarrassed because Rory said that? Should Sullivan be embarrassed?

'We had your interview scheduled for twenty to, but since you're here early, we can pull it forward.'

'No, no, don't muck up your running order,' said Rory. 'I'd love to just sit here if we wouldn't be in your way.'

'That's fine.' Natalie's attention was already taken by the monitors and blinking phone lines. 'It's turning out to be a big morning.'

Sullivan and Rory sat on the small sofa at the back of the control room and watched Natalie steer the show, coordinating with the technical producer beside her and the junior producer who was darting in and out.

Two things had happened in the hours before the breakfast show went to air. Blues legend TJ Letourneau had died and a hotel building had collapsed in Rome, killing a number of people, with rumours that some Australians were staying there.

Checking Twitter, Natalie figured out there was an archaeology conference in Rome that week and the hotel was one of the conference accommodation options. She flipped through her contact book and rang an archaeology professor who then gave her the mobile number of an academic attending the conference.

Meanwhile, whenever there was a gap between tasks, Natalie was relaying other instructions for the junior producer to scribble down.

'Let's cut a package on TJ Letourneau to play after the news heads. Heather did a terrific interview with him a few months ago. About three minutes in TJ talks about working with John Lee Hooker. Oh and he describes his house being flooded when he was a kid. Get twenty secs of that, then play a grab of "The Levee". That track's in our system, I'm pretty sure.'

The junior producer nodded but was clearly flustered, so Natalie added, 'Use your judgement. You'll be fine.' Then she laughed – in a manner that said 'high-pressure morning but we're in this together'. The young producer responded with a nervous laugh and seemed partially reassured as she hurried away to cut the package.

A second later, Natalie got through on the phone to the archaeology academic in Rome. The woman had been inside the hotel as it collapsed but managed to scramble onto the roof of a neighbouring building. And now Natalie was talking to the woman, who was at that moment perched on a terrace, waiting to be evacuated.

Natalie's legs were jiggling with the urgency of the moment but she kept her voice calm, uncoercive. 'So Jennifer, are you safe where you are right now? Would it be okay if I put you through to talk to Heather live on the radio? Great. Wait one sec for me.'

The traffic report was playing, so Natalie spoke directly to Heather over the intercom.

'Jennifer Metcalfe on line two. Details are on your screen. She's safe, waiting on the roof of the building next door. No one else has this. News channels are still only saying there *might* have been Australians in the hotel.'

Heather widened her eyes, impressed, and went to the call while Natalie immediately rang the Canberra political correspondent to check he was ready for his upcoming segment. At the same time, she typed information about the Rome story onto the screen for Heather as more details came through online, while also fielding calls from listeners in a manner that managed to be simultaneously rapid and courteous.

Sullivan had always known Natalie was clever and capable but seeing her in full flight like this – Jesus, she was spectacular. For some time he was entirely lost in watching her, intoxicated. He didn't trust himself to stand up from the sofa because if he did, he would likely crumple to his knees at her feet.

Heather wound up the call to Rome when the academic was about to be lifted off the roof by a rescue team. 'Thanks for speaking to us, Jennifer.'

Natalie turned to Rory. 'Sorry to keep you waiting. We're ready if you are,' she said and escorted him to the studio.

Unsurprisingly, Rory was a fantastic interviewee. He flirted with Heather just enough to make her light up but not so much that it undermined her professional dignity. He began the segment by expressing his concern for the people trapped in the Rome hotel and his admiration for the archaeologist who had spoken to Heather from the scene 'with such composure and amazing eloquence'.

He went on to speak about his sadness at the death of TJ Letourneau.

'Have you ever heard the song he wrote for his wife?' he asked. 'Oh Heather, you've gotta have a listen. It's called "Honey". One of the best love songs ever. Not to mention saucy.'

Only after paying respect to Letourneau and the disaster victims in Rome did Rory allow Heather to swing the interview around to himself. He offered brief amusing anecdotes and came across as earthy and humble without being nauseatingly disingenuous.

Natalie swivelled to Sullivan who was sitting on the sofa behind her. 'Your friend Rory is very good at interviews.'

'So it would seem.'

'Thanks for organising it for us.'

'You're very welcome,' said Sullivan. 'Least I could do.'

When Rory's interview wound up, Heather mouthed 'thank you' to him before she had to turn away to take another live cross to Rome. As Rory slipped quietly out of the studio, he signalled through the glass to Sullivan – *Meet you outside?*

Sullivan wanted to offer his thanks and more apologies to Natalie – if only for the chance to speak to her – but she was in the middle of yet another urgent phone call so there was only time for a farewell wave.

'Sorry I'm late,' Sullivan said to Jose Luis. The journey from the radio station to the job site had taken way longer than he'd expected. And seeing Natalie again had unsettled him more than he'd expected.

'It's not a problem,' said Jose Luis. He'd put up with a fair whack of lateness from Sullivan, assuming it was related to the transplant preparation.

'Shall I get cracking?' Sully reached for a bundle of black plastic. 'You want to squeeze a few more litres of sweat out of me, don't you, boss?'

For Sullivan, this was his last day at work before his hospital admission. For Jose Luis it was the start of a three-week job, stripping asbestos from a warehouse before demolition. He'd taken on three extra guys to handle such a major operation and was hoping to score more contracts from the demolition company.

Through the day, Sully fumbled with the screwdriver and the vacuum, as clumsy as he had been right back at the start.

'Where is your brain today, my friend?' Jose Luis smiled. 'Are you already under the anaesthetic?'

Sullivan dropped his head jokingly, allowing the respirator and hood of the blue suit to conceal his expression.

When they decontaminated at the end of the afternoon and face-masks came off, Sullivan felt Jose Luis watching him, concerned. Sully made his best effort to produce a smile as he made his goodbyes.

Daramy explained the situation to the new guys in barely audible Khmer, then stepped forward to shake Sullivan's hand solemnly. 'Good luck. We'll see you soon.'

'Yes! How long until you come back?' asked Rickie.

Sullivan hesitated and Jose Luis jumped in to reassure everyone. 'Just a few weeks. He'll be back with us as soon as the doctors say he's allowed, even if he can't do the lifting work straight away.'

Rickie and Daramy nodded, happy with this.

'Are you scared, man?' asked Rickie.

Sullivan shrugged. 'It'll be all right.'

Jose Luis gave Sullivan a lift to the bus stop, as he often did. But this time he pulled over into the bus bay and they both hopped out of the truck.

'Liliana and I will visit when they say you can have visitors.'

'Don't worry about it. You're busy. The warehouse is a big job. You don't need to —'

'Are you arguing with me? Don't argue with me. We will visit.'

'Okay.' Sullivan nodded, more to end the discussion than in real assent.

Jose Luis pulled Sullivan into a strong hug. 'I hope all goes well, my friend.'

The next day, the Saturday before surgery, Sullivan spent the morning packing up his belongings into a couple of Frank's old suitcases, then did a thorough spring clean of the flat, glad to have uncomplicated physical tasks to perform. Mack followed him from room to room, plonking himself on the floor to watch the activity.

Disappointment about Natalie was dragging in Sullivan's belly. What had he imagined would happen after the radio interview? Had he hoped she would be so grateful to him for brokering the Rory Wallace interview that she would suddenly say, 'You know what? I love you, Sullivan Moss. I want you.' That was never going to happen. And it was scummy to think in those terms – he had done her that simple favour to make amends for letting Louis down. It was small-minded to give a gift only because you expected something in return.

When there were no more jobs to do, Sullivan and Mack headed out on their favourite walk by the harbour.

'Hey, Mack.' The dog looked round, listening, as he loped along. 'This is our last chance to do this walk on a regular basis. After today, you and me'll be living near the beach.'

Rory had offered to look after Mack at the rented Tamarama house while Sullivan was in hospital, and afterwards, Sully would join him there to convalesce. Once the downstairs flat in the new house was liveable – any day now – Sullivan and the dog would move in there on a long-term basis.

'Don't worry though, mate,' he assured Mack. 'I'll find out which beaches allow dogs. We'll have an excellent time no matter what.'

They strolled on until it was dark and gradually made their way through the night-time streets back to Frank's. Sullivan tried watching a couple of DVDs but it was hard to concentrate. He was marking time, wishing he could just go to sleep and wake up in the post-op recovery room.

Rory's FJ Holden was parked in Frank's garage spot so Sullivan could use the car to transport luggage to Tamarama the following day. Maybe he should take a load round there right now. The prospect of spending a night listening to Rory Wallace talk his diverting, self-absorbed bullshit was mighty appealing. He tried calling Rory.

'His phone's off,' Sullivan explained when Mack cocked his head expectantly. 'He's probably dodging a call from Whitney.' Sometimes Rory turned his phone right off so the Waif could not accuse him of seeing her name on the caller ID and dodging her calls.

Sullivan drove across town and parked the Holden in Rory's garage, hauled the suitcases out of the boot and used the door that led directly into the kitchen. It was only midnight but few lights were on and the house was quiet. Perhaps Rory had gone to bed unusually early. Then Sullivan spotted a woman's shoes on the floor in front of the big sofa. So it was one of Rory's woman nights.

Sullivan moved round the sofa to park his suitcases in a corner, intending to slip quietly back out through the garage. Then his eye fell on a jacket on the far side of the sofa. It was unmistakably Natalie's.

26

Rory Wallace's mouth moved from Natalie's lips, down her neck and onto her breasts in a perfectly judged zigzag.

Some hours earlier, Nat had been on the floor in Louis' room, cleaning out the festy accumulation of shoes and toys in the bottom of the wardrobe. She could hear Judy clacking down the hallway in the heeled slippers she wore around the house. If Nat went out there she would have to endure a stream of opinion about the damage being done to Louis by his separated parents or whichever subject was Judy's Topic of the Day. She imagined her mother's words fluttering down over her like ashy fall-out from a chemical weapon attack, seeping through her skin to eat away at her guts. She needed to leave the house.

On Friday afternoon, Natalie had scooped up a stack of the invitations that came into the radio station. Maybe there was something that could get her out of the house. Flipping through the pile now, it was clear she'd missed the RSVP date on most of them. The best of the current invitations was a press screening of an indie Australian film. That would be okay.

Nat texted Astrid and a couple of other friends to be her plus-one for the screening but Saturday afternoon was too late-notice. Maybe she should forget the whole thing. Saturday night in the city on her own was a pretty sad look. But was it sadder still to stay home when her kid was away and she was free to go out on the spur of the moment? She should go somewhere, if only to demonstrate that she could. Nat wasn't sure for whom she would be making this demonstration. For the benefit of some hypothetical tribunal examining her life? Anyway, she would go. No matter what the film was like, at least it would be in one of the plush screening rooms with armchairs and publicity staff offering glasses of wine.

In the lounge area outside the screening room, she showed her invitation to the publicity girl who was smiling so hard Nat worried her face would split in half.

'Natalie!'

She spun around to see Rory Wallace in the corner, pouring mineral water into a pre-chilled glass.

There was a volley of mutual thanks and compliments about the radio interview the previous day. Rory explained that he was the person who'd brought in the invitations to this screening and asked the junior breakfast producer to put them on Heather's desk. The film was directed by an old mate and Rory was keen to garner some media attention for the guy.

'Not sure what the film's gonna be like,' he admitted. 'But you being here is a surprise bonus.'

From that first moment outside the screening room, Rory Wallace flirted with her. She knew flirtation was the default setting for a guy like him, so there was no way to be sure if he was really coming on to her or just flirting for practice.

During the film, Rory glanced at her in significant moments and afterwards seemed genuinely keen to hear her opinion of what they'd just seen. (A pedestrian but amiable movie about a country town football team.) In the post-screening drinks, he chatted dutifully to a number of people before turning to Natalie with a conspiratorial murmur, 'Let's get out of here into the fresh air, shall we?'

They ended up walking across the city, talking. Ordinarily, Natalie would have felt awkward with someone like Rory Wallace, possibly even tongue-tied, but the nature of their meeting had short-circuited that. They'd met in the control room when she was too busy to be self-conscious. Now she was surprisingly at ease with him, responding to his stories and musings on various topics.

When it grew dark and too cold for walking, Rory hailed a cab to take them to a laughably chic basement bar called Lenno's.

Once they were ensconced in a red leather booth at Lenno's, Natalie played along with the pretence of trying different kinds of mezcal out of 'interest', knowing the unstated goal was for the two of them to get drunk quickly. Each round of mezcal came with a couple of orange slices dipped in spices. She enjoyed the sweetness of the orange in combination with the smoky burn of the mezcal. And she remembered the way neat spirits could whoosh straight through the roof of her mouth to dissolve all the tension in her scalp.

Scanning the people in the bar, Natalie was conscious of her age and relative lack of glamour. 'My God, is every female in this place a twenty-year-old model?'

Rory laughed. 'Come on, Natalie. You and me are the same age. And look at yourself – beautiful.'

With mock bossiness, he signalled that she should turn her head and regard her reflection in one of the mirrors beside their booth. The narrow rectangle of mirror sat in a metal frame in the shape of a skeleton in a sombrero. Natalie could only see half of her face, soft and golden in the flattering light.

Rory smiled. 'And can I say – slap me if this is too intimate coming from a virtual stranger – there's something sexy about the idea that your body grew a baby.'

Natalie did not slap him. She usually found compliments hard to absorb but she was happily soaking up every drop of Rory's flattery. By now, the plate in front of her was piled with orange rinds sitting in a slurry of juice streaked with reddish spice mix. She must have downed a significant number of mezcal shots.

'And Natalie, in that studio yesterday – you were extraordinary.

Do you not realise, do you not know how hot that is?'

Any question of whether Rory was truly coming on to her was answered in the cab back to his place when he leaned across to kiss her with the sureness of a man used to be being desired.

A blast of sobering cold air hit Natalie's face as they walked from the cab to Rory's front door. In that brief moment of clarity she interrogated her motives for having sex with this man. Was it simply because he had picked her and no one had picked her for a long time? Or did she regard Rory Wallace as some kind of trophy in a dreadfully shallow way? Maybe so. But in the end she decided she should have sex with him because it would be straightforward, with no emotional residue. Also, she really wanted to have sex with someone tonight and the guy leading her through the courtyard was unquestionably attractive.

Now, on the bed, both naked, Natalie was acutely aware of her normal-person body against his leading-man body. At first she made some effort to suck in her belly but that didn't last long. She was so pissed and so lustful that she kept forgetting. Blessedly, Rory didn't seem to notice any imperfections and Natalie threw herself into the business of enjoying this.

It was once they started fucking that Natalie realised why Rory wasn't fussed about her imperfections or otherwise. He was constantly glancing at his own reflection in the oak-framed mirror next to the bed. But he wasn't doing it in a spicy way, watching their bodies entwined. He was actually making eye contact with himself. Natalie flashed back to their time in Lenno's and recalled how often he had glanced sideways at the skeleton-in-a-sombrero mirror beside his seat. He'd been looking at his own face while he talked to her. His principal interest was himself and right now his interest lay in watching himself fuck the smart woman from the radio.

Unlike most people – who fantasised about sex with another person while they were masturbating – he was a guy who fantasised about masturbation while having sex. Rory Wallace was the most arousing thing Rory Wallace could imagine. That thought made Natalie laugh aloud and she had to cover up the laugh noise as a sexual grunt. Rory didn't seem to notice anything unusual.

A few seconds later, the whole scenario struck her as depressing rather than comical and she regretted being in bed with such a man. The trouble was, the man in question was inside her right at that moment.

There was no dignified way she could extricate herself from their current sexual position, like two docking space craft disengaging. She would have to stay and make the most of a rare opportunity to have sex with a handsome man, even if it was depressing in practice. At least she'd be able to tell people she'd had sex with Rory Wallace. But when she imagined telling people about it, she sounded like a sad thirty-something star-fucker and it didn't seem like a great boasting opportunity at all.

Next, she tried imagining the man on top of her was Jakov, the character he played in the French Resistance miniseries, and that helped a little. But the trouble was, Rory was not in fact a Hungarian doctor who rescued stranded airmen. It would be a mistake to fold all Jakov's pain and virtues into this person, this body on top of her.

In the end, Natalie closed her eyes, focused on herself and worked at extracting whatever physical pleasure she could, as if she were masturbating. Which was pretty much what Rory was also doing. In truth, they were both using each other as sex toys, sex toys that conveniently operated at body temperature.

Afterwards, Natalie lay awake, calculating how soon Rory would be deeply enough asleep for her to sneak out unnoticed. But then the combined effect of the mezcal and sleep deprivation overwhelmed her and she drifted into unconsciousness too.

The moment Sullivan realised Natalie and Rory were having sex, he should have left – for the sake of politeness and self-protection. Instead of leaving, he took off his shoes and moved noiselessly down the hall towards the bedroom until he was close enough to hear the sound of two people breathing hard, limbs sliding along sheets and the occasional murmurs of a female voice. Natalie's voice.

Sullivan felt his body splice into incongruous segments – his head crumbly like stale cake, his throat tight in a spasm of anger and his cock stiffening with an unwelcome lust reaction. In the end, his legs made the decision, walking him back down the hall into the living room, away from the epicentre of pain, and sitting him down on the sofa.

He closed his eyes, scrunched up tightly, as if the awareness of his own foolishness was a sudden too-bright light. He should have realised this had always been a possibility. If Sullivan found Natalie attractive as he observed her in the radio studio, then it was quite likely Rory felt the same way. Still, Sullivan was surprised. From his observations, Rory's taste in women ranged from twenty-year-old not-very-bright models and actresses to twenty-three-year-old not-very-bright models and actresses. Natalie did not seem to be Rory's type.

Next, Sully tried to console himself with the thought that it was nice for Natalie to be the object of Rory's attentions. She deserved to feel desirable. He should be glad on her behalf. But no, Sully could not sustain that thought. He couldn't squeeze out that much generosity of spirit from any part of his soul. Fuck Rory. Which was what Natalie had chosen to do – fuck Rory instead of him. So as far as Sully was concerned, Natalie could get fucked.

When the anger subsided, Sullivan sank back into misery. He urged himself to stand up, to leave and stop torturing himself. Did he imagine that by staying here in this house he could prevent something he didn't want to happen from continuing? Should he run in there and make a formal protest? He should probably make himself scarce before Natalie came out and found him sitting there like a sad voyeur.

He probably deserved this wallop of pain. Once Sully started to calculate his many low acts, especially towards women, he reckoned he definitely deserved it, but that didn't stop him also feeling sorry for

himself. The same brew of self-laceration and self-pity had left Sullivan
Moss paralysed on lumpy couches in share houses on many occasions
in the past. But tonight, he was more clear-headed and with more of
himself invested than before, and that familiar pain was sharper, powerful enough to really skewer him, pinning him to the leather sofa. He
didn't move from that spot – not immediately and not for the next
seven hours.

At seven forty-five, the doorbell at the front security gate rang.
The bonging sound roused Sullivan from his stupor and brought
Rory running down the hall, pulling jeans up over his bare arse.

Rory was disoriented, bleary from sleep. He clocked Sullivan sitting on the sofa and frowned – *what are you doing here?* The two men
stared at each other for one second but there was no time to process
this. Rory had to deal with a more urgent problem than Sullivan's
presence.

Rory was holding his phone like a grenade with the ring already
pulled. 'It's Whitney. She texted me from the cab – on her way here
from the airport.'

'What?' Sullivan looked at Rory's phone as if it would offer more
by way of explanation.

Rory waved his phone towards the gate where Whitney was currently waiting for someone to buzz her in. 'Text says she wanted to
surprise me. Came in on an early flight from LA.'

The doorbell rang again. Rory buttoned his jeans and composed
his face. 'Mate, can you do me a favour? Take Nat out the back and
next door?'

At that moment, Natalie appeared in the hallway. She was wearing
a shirt and underpants, holding her shirt front together with one hand
and clutching her bra and skirt in the other. Sullivan didn't think he
could bear to make eye contact with her but he need not have worried. Natalie was so flushed with embarrassment, there was no risk she
would look directly at either Sullivan or Rory.

'Can you do that for me, Sully?' Rory asked again.

There didn't seem any other choice, or not one that declared itself to Sully in that moment.

'Sure.'

He scooped up Natalie's shoes and jacket while she grabbed her handbag off the coffee table. He moved directly down the stairs and she followed a couple of metres behind him. From upstairs, he could hear Rory buzz the security gate open and call into the intercom, 'Whitney! Hey, baby!'

Sullivan led the way down and across the courtyard, hearing Natalie's bare feet pattering on the tiles, then he hopped over the stile to the other side of the fence. He realised that both Natalie's hands were occupied holding her clothing, so the climbing might be tricky. He turned to help, supporting her forearm, as she hoisted her body over. Again, they both resolutely avoided eye contact but the softness of Natalie's skin made him giddy for a moment. Women really were so lovely and soft – including this woman who had, only hours before, torn out his heart.

As Nat climbed down into the yard of the half-built house, Sullivan could see goosebumps on her bare legs. He had an urge to fold her in his warm arms but an equally strong urge to slap her hard across the face.

They climbed up into the shell of the building and picked their way across the rough concrete of the terrace, both of them barefoot. Once inside, Natalie shoved her bra in her handbag, buttoned up her shirt and yanked on her skirt. When she bent down to put on her shoes, Sullivan could see her breasts swinging under the fabric of the shirt and that sent a stab of pain through his chest. He turned away.

'There's a working toilet and hand basin on the left there,' he said, pointing down one of the passageways. 'This is the house Rory is having remodelled.'

Natalie nodded and fumbled to do up the buckles on her shoes. Sullivan listened to the tiny scraping sounds of her heels on the building grit underfoot. He listened to his own breathing and the noise of the surf on the rocks. Then they both heard the rumble of male voices moving down the side of the building.

'The builders. Here to start work,' Sullivan explained.

Natalie looked panicked. 'On a Sunday?'

'Rory's paying extra to get the job done fast.'

'Well, shit . . . is there some way I can get out without them seeing me?'

'They're coming round the side. You can get to the street through the front gate.'

Natalie hurried towards the door, turning her head only slightly so she wouldn't have to face Sullivan as she said, 'I'll find my way out. You don't have to follow me.'

He didn't follow her.

27

When Sullivan dragged himself up the back stairs into Rory's kitchen to fetch his shoes and keys, he found a tiny young woman peering into the fridge.

He had seen Whitney Todd Harrison on screen but in the flesh she was smaller and younger, with a child-like body and a face made pretty more through the absence of flaws than the presence of any particularly lovely feature.

'Hello. I'm Sullivan.'

'Oh! Sullivan!' She spoke so astonishingly loudly that it made him wince. 'Hi. I'm Whitney. Rory's partner,' she added in a more modulated tone.

'Great. To meet you. Finally.' Words jerked out of Sullivan's mouth in odd fragments. His neurones were fried, misfiring, out of sync. 'I was – uh – downstairs. Hunting for shoes.' His attempt at coherent speech trailed off as he prowled the living room looking for his shoes. 'I must've . . . here they are . . . yeah . . .'

'Rory's in the shower,' she said. 'I'm making French toast!'

Sullivan managed to nod.

'I really surprised Rory when I turned up at his door this morning!'

'Uh . . . yes – you must've.'

While Sullivan laced up his shoes, Whitney sliced fruit and chattered on, relentlessly perky, as if this were a TV commercial about a young woman preparing breakfast for her husband. She was claiming her place in this house, her place as Rory's partner.

'I had to make this trip a total surprise,' she said. 'Otherwise Rory would've talked me out of it.' She did a strangled version of an Australian accent to speak as Rory. 'Oh no, Whitney baby, you need to stay in LA. Too many important things about to happen for you.' She flashed a smile. 'But taking care of our relationship is important too, don't you think?'

'Mmm.'

'It's so hard when we're separated. I mean, this time we've been apart for two months,' she explained. 'Rory's a very sexual guy, so for him two months is . . . well, that's why I had to pay my baby a visit.'

Sullivan made an ambiguous *hmm* noise. To relieve Rory's sacrificial celibacy, Whitney had decided to parachute herself into Sydney like a sexual care package.

'Sullivan, I almost forgot!' Whitney was looking at him with her tiny features scrunched up with curiosity. 'Rory told me about your kidney donation. Good job!'

'Oh. Thanks.'

Rory called out as he came down the hall, dressed in board-shorts and a singlet, hair wet from the shower. 'Hey, hey, hey, I'm smelling sweeter now.'

Then he saw Sullivan and stopped. Sully didn't want to make a scene in front of Whitney so he endeavoured to keep his facial expression neutral. 'Hey, Rory.'

Rory handled him gently. 'Mate, I thought you were going to – uh . . .'

'Yeah, going for a walk. Came back up here for my shoes.'

Before Rory and Sullivan could finesse their way out of this, Whitney piped up. 'Sullivan should have breakfast with us!'

'Right. Okay. Great.' Rory put his hands on Whitney's waist as she beat eggs in a bowl but he kept glancing at Sullivan who was pacing around the living room as if the floor were red hot.

She whispered to Rory at what she must have imagined was a low volume but Sully could hear every word. 'From the way you described him,' she murmured, 'I thought Sully would be cute and small, like a chimp. But he's not at all.'

Rory hushed her but Whitney went on in her clear stage whisper. 'Is he high on something? No? I guess he's nervous about the kidney surgery. Even so, he seems disturbed. Oh sweetie, I love that you're so supportive to your poor friend.'

She twisted away from the eggs to kiss him, overcome with admiration for Rory's devotion to his mentally ill mate.

When she came up for air, Whitney had an idea that she expressed at full volume. 'Hey, we should give Sullivan a brilliant last day!'

'Sorry?' asked Rory.

'Well, you said this is his last day before he goes into hospital! You and me should make it special for him. After breakfast, we could go on the harbour in a boat or something. Maybe a speedboat. Do you like speed, Sullivan?'

'Hey, Whitney,' said Rory. 'You're talking a bit too loud.'

She flinched at Rory's rebuke. It was clear he had deliberately poked at a tender spot. She went back to the food, dipping slices of bread in egg and frying them in a pan of frothing brown butter.

Sullivan tried not to stare at Rory. He flashed on the image of himself punching the guy in the balls, bellowing, 'Why did you fuck Natalie?' While Rory writhed on the floor in pain, Sullivan would then turn to Whitney and declare, 'As you rang the doorbell, he was in bed with another woman. A woman I happen to adore. He asked me to smuggle her out the back then he took a shower to wash that other female off his faithless cock while you cooked him French toast.'

But if he'd done that, Whitney would end up weeping and broken like a hollow-boned bird. It wouldn't be fair to upset her for his momentary satisfaction.

Sullivan was still scrambling to understand why Rory – who had chosen this scrawny girl as his partner – would have ended up in bed with a woman like Natalie. The only way to understand Rory's choices was to look at them through the narcissism filter. What image of himself was a certain action designed to demonstrate? In what way would sex with Natalie Dennis satisfy Rory's vanity?

In the last week, Sullivan had made a few teasing cracks about Rory choosing the company of very young and not especially clever women. So most likely last night's sexual conquest was to reassure himself that he could be a match for a smart thirty-five-year-old woman.

As the three of them ate French toast with sliced fruit, Whitney kept talking, her voice growing loud as she became excited about an idea, then suddenly hushed to a self-consciously softer tone. Rory kyboshed all her plans for Sullivan's Special Last Day, plans that included helicopters, paraffin wax pedicures and a sake bar she'd read about in the inflight magazine.

Whitney was digging in her heels about having 'a special dinner for Sullivan' that night. 'That's what we're doing, okay? I'm not gonna let you be a boring grumpy old —'

'Too loud, Whitney. Too loud,' countered Rory.

The pain on her face, caused by this comment, incited Rory to be even harsher with her. 'You're giving me a headache,' he said. 'Forget tonight. I'm going out anyway. You can stay here.'

'Huh? You're . . . what?' she bleated.

'I've got plans. I didn't know you were going to land on me, did I.'

'I'm only here to see you!'

'You're seeing me right now,' Rory shot back.

Whitney suddenly cranked up to a piercing volume. 'It's a woman! You're seeing some other woman tonight!'

'No. There's stuff I'd already arranged.'

'No, no, it's some other woman you're having sex with so now you're trying to —'

'Now I'm trying to stop the sound of your voice perforating my eardrums.'

Whitney's face contorted like a toddler's and she ran, sobbing, down the hall to the bathroom.

Rory hooked a strawberry into his mouth, sounding quite calm. 'She's gone to vomit up the French toast.'

Sullivan didn't look at him, not wanting to collude in any snideness about that girl.

Rory was matey, intimate. 'Thanks, Sully. Thanks for helping me out this morning. What a mess, eh. Thanks for not saying anything.'

Sullivan didn't respond to that. Instead, he said, 'Rory . . . none of my business . . . but maybe you shouldn't've been so harsh to Whitney just now.'

'Eh?'

'Look, I think —'

'What? You're giving me a serve about – oh, hang on. Sully . . . Jesus, I'm an idiot.'

'I'm not saying you're an idiot. I just think —'

'Are you hot for Natalie? Oh, you are. So me fucking her was – shit, sorry mate. You should've said.'

Anger burned through Sullivan's chest but he forced himself to take a deep calming breath. 'That's your business. And Natalie's business.'

'But come on, you obviously —'

'I'm not talking about that. I'm just saying Whitney flew all this way to be with you and you should treat her decently.'

'Don't "should" me, Sully. You're being snarky because I happened to fuck the —'

'No.' Sullivan closed his eyes so he wouldn't have to look at Rory at that moment. 'I'm saying we shouldn't treat people badly. We should be better men than that.'

'Oh and you're a better man now, are you?'

'No,' said Sullivan. 'But I know what it looks like from here.'

'You self-righteous prick. Don't dump this on me.'

Sullivan put his hands up in a pacifying gesture. He didn't trust himself to behave decently with Rory right now. He didn't want either of them to say things they would regret. 'I'll head back to the flat. Give you and Whitney some privacy to sort things out. See you later.'

Tim rode the pod lift to his floor of the bank. The office was the place he felt most confident and in control. Today, being a Sunday, there would be none of the distracting regular activity, leaving him free to think beyond the constraints of his existing life.

Knowing Sullivan was going under the knife tomorrow morning was galvanising. Sometimes you had to use a symbolic moment to make the leap to a better choice, rather than sink into the ooze of inertia. Today, he would finish the proposed new strategic plan and print out a straightforward version to show Juliet this evening.

By Tim's calculations, once he resigned from the bank, he could extricate himself from any leveraged positions and then set up investments that would cover the twins' education plus his and Juliet's eventual retirement. (A slightly more modest retirement than they might have imagined but hardly a life of austerity.) They would then be left with a fund to use for whatever purposes they decided on.

The majority of the spare money could be given away straight up. Tim had sought information from Vincent about the Indigenous health program Pete had been working with in central Australia before he got too sick to continue. That would be worth considering.

Once the financial stuff was sorted, that left open the decision of how Tim and Juliet would then make a contribution to the world. They could go for a radical option – for example, both work on the ground for an NGO in some malarial country – but he couldn't imagine either of them operating at their best in those conditions.

Tim's preferred scheme – though he must be careful not to bully Juliet into it – was to set up a music venue to support new bands, eventually expanding into recording and helping musicians with promotion. When they found the right venue, Juliet could handle the interior design and maybe run the place.

No matter what path they decided on, he and Juliet would be able to spend lots more time together once Tim quit the bank. Hopefully she would see the potential for them to give each other that time and rebuild their relationship.

Tim found he was smiling as he sat at his desk. He was picturing Juliet swanning around some derelict pub, concocting ways to turn it into a brilliant music room, and felt a surge of love for her.

28

When Sullivan walked away from Rory's house, he hauled himself up to Bondi Road, then continued weaving through side streets. If he stopped for any length of time, he felt his belly pitch and roll with something like motion sickness, so he started jogging.

By eleven a.m., he was sweaty, lungs burning, and needing to drink water, if only to keep his kidneys plumply hydrated. He should find a bus back to Frank's place. He didn't want to leave Mack on his own for much longer.

As Sullivan fished in his pockets for coins to buy a bottle of water, his hand wrapped around his phone. He had turned it off during the night, so phone noises wouldn't alert Rory and Natalie to his presence a few metres away from their sexual activities.

Turning his phone on again, Sullivan saw a missed call from Tim.

Spending time with Tim on the day before the kidney surgery seemed like a healthy choice. Something Anthony would approve of. A healthier choice than bashing Rory or screaming abuse at Natalie or obliterating himself with booze.

Tim's house was only a kilometre downhill from where Sullivan now stood, panting and sweating. He could get a glass of water there. Maybe even a lift home. He turned and jogged down the hill.

'It's Sully,' he said to the intercom panel and the wrought-iron gate into the front garden swung open.

Juliet opened the front door of the house.

'Oh. Hi, Juliet. Sorry . . . I'm really sweaty,' he said, as if perspiration explained why he wasn't hugging her in greeting. In fact they both knew their relationship was too strained for physical affection.

'I can see you're sweaty,' she said.

'I've been running.'

'So have I.' Juliet was in serious running gear, her hair pulled back in a ponytail and damp with sweat. There were trickles of perspiration in the hollow of her throat. 'You need to drink something. Come in.'

Sullivan followed Juliet through the large entrance hall into the kitchen. He hadn't been welcome inside this house for more than two years.

She poured two tumblers of water from a filter jug in the fridge and they both leaned against the kitchen bench, guzzling.

'Tim still lazing around in bed?' asked Sullivan. Tim loved the weekend newspapers.

She shook her head. 'He's out. Did you want to see him about something in particular?'

'No, I just missed a call from him. Thought it might be good to . . . I dunno . . .'

'Good to hang out before you go into hospital for the big operation?' suggested Juliet.

Her faintly charitable tone emboldened Sullivan to meet her usually uncharitable gaze. 'I guess so.'

'It's tomorrow, isn't it? So this is your last day before all that pain. Are you scared?' she asked.

'Trying not to think about it.'

Juliet scrutinised him. 'You look scared. No, you look rattled.'

'Oh. Ha. Overdid the running.'

'No, it's not that,' she said confidently. 'You're upset about something.'

Women were so good at sniffing out emotional mess, especially when you didn't want them to.

'Nah,' he said to throw her off the scent. 'Guess I'm nervous about being sliced open.'

Juliet asked, 'Is it like the cosmetic surgery you see on TV shows? Do they draw the incision line on your body in marker pen?' Then she ran her finger along his waist as an imaginary pen.

Sullivan wasn't sure if Juliet's sultry tone and the touching were the same kind of fake flirtation she had aimed at him at Tim's birthday party. There was a good chance this was sarcasm, nasty, luring him into making a fool of himself. But in that moment, Sullivan didn't care enough to second-guess. He felt like fucking Juliet. If she was going to look at him like that and run her finger along his stomach, he would call her bluff. If it was a mocking trick and he was about to be more humiliated than he already was, so be it.

He put down the glass on the bench, then grabbed Juliet round the waist and pulled her into him with some force, kissing her hard on the mouth.

He was ready for her to slap him. Or push him away and laugh disdainfully. *Gotcha, you pathetic fool. Did you think I was seriously coming on to you?*

But in fact Juliet kissed him back urgently. She slid her hands up under his shirt and down inside his jeans, not caring that his clothes were damp with sweat. They ended up pressed against the kitchen bench kissing hungrily for several minutes until Juliet pulled back.

'Not here. The twins are upstairs,' she said, then grabbed her car keys and moved to the door.

Driving across the city in Juliet's BMW was deeply strange. If they'd stayed where they were and rutted on the kitchen floor, they could at least have said they were overcome in the moment and it was an unthinking act. But the drive to Glebe gave them both time to reconsider. Juliet turned the music up loudly so there was no need to talk. The enveloping music operated like a movie soundtrack – they were two characters travelling in a car on their way to have sex.

He glanced at Juliet's strong thighs as she pressed the clutch down.

He saw her slender, manicured hands on the steering wheel. Those hands would shortly be all over his body. He remembered this particular thrill: the heady minutes when you know you're definitely going to have sex with someone, and it was just a matter of getting to a place to do it.

He didn't know what was going through Juliet's head as she drove, and better he didn't know. Sullivan himself seized on one idea: he should have sex. It wouldn't be because of Natalie. No, it wouldn't be done out of spite and sexual humiliation. He should have sex because this was his last day before kidney donation. What if he turned out to be one of the small number of people who died in surgery? He was like a soldier on the eve of battle, throwing himself on the mercy of a kind-hearted woman, begging for one last knee-trembler in an alleyway before marching off to face the guns of war. Juliet was not a kind-hearted woman but she certainly seemed to be up for it.

Walking into Frank's home with Juliet's hand in his and half an erection in his jeans felt unnerving and wrong, so he pulled Juliet quickly through the lounge room towards the bedroom. He could see Mack in the garden, running up to the sliding doors, tail wagging, thrilled to see Sullivan and a visitor.

Sullivan darted over to let Mack inside and then followed Juliet into the bedroom, shutting the door firmly behind them.

He pulled his clothes off quickly. Juliet peeled off her tight-fitting running gear as if removing her outer skin. Sullivan's skin was slightly tacky from dried sweat and so was Juliet's. Didn't matter. She was still delicious to touch.

Early on, an image flashed into his mind – that Natalie was the woman kissing him on this bed – but he quickly pushed it aside.

It was pretty clear to Sully that Juliet enjoyed sex. She pushed his fingers and his mouth exactly where she wanted them and he liked that. She ran her hands over him with straightforward appreciation, demanding, almost greedy. Having a woman grab at his body with such appetite was glorious. When Juliet came with his mouth on her, he felt fantastic. It felt like an achievement.

Juliet wordlessly directed him to get on top and the sensation was extraordinary, like fucking for the first time ever. Well, it was Sullivan's first time in over a year and it was his first time completely sober in a very long while. He'd always loved sex but this was uncommonly pleasurable. He used to fancy himself as good in bed but now, with his freshly healthy body and the extra levels of sensitivity that came with sobriety, he was even better at it. This is what he should be doing with himself for the next eighteen hours before surgery. He should beg Juliet to have sex with him as many times as possible. He should ring Jess – the woman who had put her hand on his cock and her number in his phone. He should ring Paola too. Maybe he should even risk the ultimate rejection and put in a plea to Natalie. His body was built for having sex. He was put on the earth to do this.

Leaving Rory's place, Natalie had hailed a cab on Bondi Road for the journey back to Judy's house. Thank Christ her mother wasn't home, having left a Post-it note on the kettle. *Out until midday. Mystery shopping.*

Working as an undercover customer in the home-ware stores was a task way beneath Judy's status as head of human resources but she chose to do it periodically. There was nothing Judy found more satisfying than catching out lazy, stupid or thieving employees, and she didn't trust anyone to do the surveillance as scrupulously as she did.

Natalie took a long shower, then dressed and headed straight back out again. She didn't want to linger in that house where she might even *imagine* Judy's eyes on her. She parked herself in a cafe, ate eggs and drank three coffees in a row.

Whenever she thought about Rory Wallace her face burned. She reminded herself that he was as irrelevant to her as she was to him. A misguided one-night stand wasn't the end of the world. But the indignity of the experience was too fresh for common sense to assert itself.

Natalie splashed around in self-loathing for some time. What unspeakable bad judgement – allowing paper-thin flattery from an attractive man to mess with her head, letting a ludicrous self-imposed sex deadline direct her into bed with a narcissistic arsehole (an actor!). She had participated in lousy sex and then offered herself up to the extra humiliation of being bundled out of the man's bedroom, half-dressed, then handed over to one of his cronies (Sullivan Moss, of all people) to be smuggled out through the backyard into a building site, so his pubescent poppet movie-star girlfriend wouldn't be confronted by the sight of the rumpled, hung-over, thirty-something woman he'd rooted the previous night.

Even by the standards of Natalie's previous bad judgement record, this was pretty special. It seemed that in her mid-thirties she was still capable of engineering a hot mess, if given the slightest opportunity to do so. From now on, it was better if she kept her life simple – just work, socialising with selected anodyne friends and looking after Louis. There should be no attempts at a love life or any steps into a realm of existence where she could possibly exercise her poor judgement.

By the third coffee, the waves of shame were all about Sullivan Moss. Natalie would never have done anything if she'd thought he would find out. She hated the idea of him thinking badly of her or suffering unnecessarily.

What if Sullivan died under the anaesthetic tomorrow? Before then, should she offer some kind of apology? 'Sorry for sleeping with your friend after rejecting your romantic overture. If it's any consolation, the sex was shithouse.' Possibly that would make Sullivan feel worse. So not that. But she should at least wish him well for the surgery. Make it clear she cared about him very, very much. Or maybe it was better if she made contact but they simply discussed arrangements about the dog and Frank's flat, pretending nothing had happened. The main thing was: she needed to make things okay with Sullivan before his operation.

She tried calling but he didn't pick up, probably because he saw her name on the caller ID. So she drove to Glebe.

Natalie rang the buzzer for 1A a few times but there was no response. She was just about to give up and walk away when she heard the crackle of the intercom.

Sullivan's voice. 'Hello?'

'Oh. You are there. I'm coming up,' she said without giving him a chance to fob her off. She didn't want Sullivan to avoid her out of awkwardness. She needed to make things as right as she could. She used her own key.

Sullivan was hurrying to get to the door of the flat as Natalie let herself in. He was flustered, buttoning up a shirt.

'Natalie. Hi.'

He looked so upset it made her feel even worse. He was clearly too fragile to speak directly about what had happened. Luckily, Natalie was holding a bag of chicken necks so the pretence of dog arrangements would play more smoothly.

Natalie strode straight into the kitchen to deal with the chicken. The bathroom door swung open and a small wiry woman stepped out, with one of Frank Dennis's green bath towels wrapped around her naked body.

'Oh. Hello,' said Natalie. 'I'm here about the dog.'

The woman nodded, as if that was the explanation she sought, then indicated she was going into the bedroom.

Natalie turned to Sullivan but he seemed incapable of speech. Mack ran into the kitchen and started licking chicken blood off Natalie's hand, so she was stranded there for a moment.

'Hello, Mack.' Natalie kneeled down to give the dog a cuddle with her clean hand.

Moments later, the woman emerged from the bedroom wearing one of those black jogging outfits, carrying running shoes in her hand and heading for the door.

From inside the kitchen, Natalie heard Jogging Outfit Woman say, 'I . . . uh . . . I must go.'

Sullivan finally found his voice. 'Okay. Bye, Juliet.'

Juliet. The wife of Sullivan's best mate Tim. Toxically miserable, supposedly unpleasant Juliet who Sully had talked about, always describing her to Natalie with trepidation or pity.

When Nat heard the front door close behind Juliet, she stepped out from the kitchen. 'Tim's wife?'

Sullivan nodded.

'Right. Far out.'

Determined to keep her cool, Natalie carried a bowl of chicken necks into the garden for Mack. When she came back inside, Sullivan was waiting for her.

'Listen, Natalie, I'm sorry if – shit . . .'

'No. No. Don't apologise. You've done me a favour. I don't have to feel so tacky now. Because you've managed to out-tacky me, Sullivan.'

Her heart was pounding but she made a stab at a dry smile, seeking a way to make this endurable for both of them.

'Well, you certainly managed to surprise me,' he said, spiky.

Natalie toughened her voice a little but still hoped it would play jokily. 'Sorry, was last night not part of the plan? You deliver Rory Wallace to me at the studio and I was supposed to fall into *your* arms in gratitude?'

'That might've been nice,' he said. 'Better than you fucking him.'

Sullivan found the judgement in Natalie's eyes so unbearable, all he could do was convert the shame into rage. Anyway, he was furious with her. She must have realised he loved her but she still chose Rory. He wanted to blast her with scalding anger, anger that could burn away any other feelings.

She said, 'I don't think you have any right to —'

'No, sure. I only organised the interview for you. Didn't realise you wanted to nail the guy too.'

She flared up to his level of anger very quickly. 'Well, since you just nailed a woman in my father's bed, I hardly think —'

'Seriously? You want to play that?'

'An affair with your best mate's wife. What a prince.'

'Hey. Hey. I am not —'

'How many other women have you had sex with while you've been living here? No, actually, don't answer. Don't lie to me like you lied to Astrid for years.'

The thing escalated at a giddying speed.

'And how was it fucking Rory?'

'Shut up. You don't have any idea —'

'Sounded like you were both enjoying yourselves.'

'What? You were sitting outside listening all night? What?'

'Yeah, sorry, I didn't get the text warning me you guys'd be going at it. So, was he great?'

'You tell me. You were the pervert sitting outside listening.'

Sullivan heard how revolting his voice sounded as he shot back, 'I'm sure Rory performed as well as he does with all the other women he brings home.'

'Oh, I get it. You hide and listen to your famous mate fuck women. Is that how you get off, is it?'

'Well, you seem to think I'm —'

'Did you set me up?' She was yelling now. 'Is that one your duties as his flunky?'

'What? Set you up? I didn't *make* you have sex with the guy! Oh, no, no, no, I see. You wanna play poor Nat the victim, trapped in her terrible life. Your mother, your ex, your boss – not enough people to blame so now you're gonna cast me as some —'

'Fuck you,' Natalie spat back at him. 'You think the kidney thing gives you a free pass to be a treacherous shit.'

'I don't think that.'

'I think you do,' she snarled. 'Oh, hang on, was I another one of the unhappy women you sidle up to? You tell me your kidney story, listen to my problems and then offer me a mercy root?'

'What? Do you hear yourself? Jesus, that says more about your screwed-up . . . You are a sad case.'

'And you are a fucking parasite.'

'Yeah, yeah, yeah, I've been called a parasite before so don't think —'

'I've been one of your stupid host organisms.'

'Not for much longer. I'm moving to Rory's place today.'

'Mmm, easier that way for you two,' she sneered. 'You can move his women from room to room more discreetly. Avoid sleazy mix-ups like this morning.'

Sully had been here before: a woman chucking mouthfuls of loathing at him. He hated that this time the woman was Natalie.

He tried to pull things back closer to civil. 'Listen, I'm taking Mack round to Rory's this afternoon.'

'What?'

'We agreed he could live there with me while I'm —'

Natalie almost growled the words at him, 'You're not taking my father's dog anywhere.'

'He can't stay here alone.'

'It's not your business any more.'

'Natalie, Natalie, things got out of hand a minute ago. Let's not —'

'I want you out of here. How long will it take to pack up your junk?'

'Oh – uh – I've already moved most of my stuff.'

'Hurry up and pack the rest. Then get out.'

'Sure. Okay. Listen, listen, I'm sorry if —'

'You know what I think is the saddest thing about you,' said Natalie.

'Oh well, a big list of things competing for that spot so —'

She cut him off. 'Shut up. Don't waste your self-loathing party act on me. You giving your kidney to a stranger is proof that you think – you really believe – there'll never be anyone important in your life, no loved one who might need saving one day. That's fucking sad.'

Natalie was shaking as she walked out into the garden, slammed the sliding door closed and sat on the grass with Mack.

Sullivan shoved his last remaining belongings into supermarket bags. When he was done, he held the keys to the flat up in the air and made sure Natalie saw him leave them on the dining table.

29

Juliet tried to ignore Tim when he walked in the door with a smile on his big stupid face, holding a sheaf of papers like a kid busting to show off a good school report. She kept her gaze fixed on the television but he stood in front of her with such ceremony that she was obliged to pause the DVD.

'Juliet. I've been doing a lot of thinking. I know you don't like who I've become and maybe I don't like who you've become. But people can shift the patterns they've fallen into.'

Juliet imagined him practising this speech in front of the mirror and it made him ridiculous to her. But under the circumstances, she should probably indulge him.

'I've been doing some calculations,' he went on. 'Seeing what our options would be in terms of certain radical changes, which include me quitting the bank. I don't want you to freak out, Jules.'

He was obviously nervous about her reaction, anticipating her being the obstacle blockading the path to some majestic new life-plan. Tim had always liked to blame her for the fact that he never followed through on those noble vows he'd made to Pete, the vows to get out of the money market by this age or that age and do something more worthy. But that wasn't her fault. She'd never stopped him. He'd devoted years to his career at the bank for his own vain reasons and how the fuck dare he blame her? She had a sour taste in her mouth, but given where her mouth had been recently, she controlled the urge to say anything sour.

'What about the kids?' she said.

'Don't worry. This plan would provide for them – for their education and later a leg-up to buy property. But it's better if the twins don't get a cushy ride, so they have to earn their own —'

'I'm not talking about money. You can't measure everything in terms of money.'

'Exactly right!' Tim was beaming, smug, assuming he'd persuaded her to this point of view. Which was bloody rich, seeing Tim was the one who had always measured his success as a man in dollars. Juliet only regarded money as compensation for misery.

'That's the whole point of us coming up with a new plan,' he said, brandishing the papers as if they were the magic key to life's mysteries. 'You'll see – once I go through the numbers with you – we'll be free to go anywhere in the world and devote ourselves to whatever worthwhile project we think is —'

'But we can't go off to work with poor children in Africa while we have Pia and Justin here. We messed up our offspring so they're our responsibility. Have you even thought about the kids?'

'Yes. Yes. I have absolutely been thinking about the kids.'

Juliet knew he hadn't. She could see the signs of him scrambling to cover his position.

'In fact, this is about setting a good example for them,' he said.

The pomposity was too much for Juliet. She had been holding her tongue out of remorse for the infidelity, but really and truly, the man needed a fucking wake-up.

'For a guy paid millions of dollars for his brain, you're a naive idiot,' she said. 'Taken in by Sullivan's bullshit nobility.'

Tim puffed up his chest in some absurd male display. 'I'm not ashamed to say Sully's choices have been an inspiration.'

'Why don't you give away your kidney then? Mind you, it'd be far more efficient to work two more weeks at the bank and use the buckets of money you earn to pay twenty poor Indian people to give their kidneys away.'

'Fucking hell, Juliet – look, maybe now isn't the best time to discuss this.'

Juliet pictured them both standing there having this conversation and it filled her with disgust. 'You know what, Tim – if you've been doing your sums and looking for a way to invest in do-gooding, here's a thought: the most efficient thing is if you give someone *my* organs.'

'What?'

'Well, you've fed me for all these years, paid my way, and I don't add anything of value to the world. So your contribution to good causes could be —'

'Please don't talk like that,' he pleaded. 'I don't think that way and you shouldn't either. You could do something with your life. No, sorry . . . that came out wrong. I want us to do something *together*.'

Juliet couldn't bear to look at him so she turned her back. She could hear him laying the sheets of paper out on the dining table. Did Tim think that if he made a performance of giving a bit more money to charity that it would make up for the greedy years? Or make up for the cruel stuff he'd said to her and all the years of her life he'd ruined? Did he really believe Sullivan Moss had become a different man? Or that either of them could change in any benign and meaningful way? Maybe the healthiest thing was to blow up the whole enterprise and compost what was left.

'Tim,' she said.

He looked up from the pages on the table, his face hopeful and self-righteous and needing a good hard slap.

'Sullivan dropped round today. I gave him a lift back to his flat where we then had sex.'

When Sully walked away from Frank's flat, the Thirst came on him powerfully. He was struck by the unfairness of being yelled at and hated on by a woman he hadn't even slept with. But that was nothing compared to the anguish of knowing he would never see Natalie again.

His task now was simply to endure until seven in the morning when he would present himself at the hospital and submit to a general anaesthetic. The best way to burn time and suspend thought was to watch a big loud dumb movie.

Sullivan went to two movies in a row, purchasing both tickets up front so he could swing from one cinema to the other without passing through the bar area and facing the temptation to get hammered. He carried the supermarket bags with his belongings between the cinemas and let the hours unspool.

When he stepped out into the street again, it was dark. He had to get a good night's sleep pre-op, so he would have to drag his sorry carcass back to Rory's house. He was in no position to be self-righteous or judgemental with Rory after the way he'd behaved. When the mood was right, they could talk through what had happened. Anyway, he had to go to Tamarama tonight. He had nowhere else.

Sullivan caught a bus across town and trudged from the bus stop towards Rory's place. He peered along the dark street and noticed the garage was open. Rory must have taken the Holden out. Whitney would most likely be inside on her own and, to avoid awkward conversations with the poor girl, Sullivan would retire to bed very early, using the surgery as his excuse.

Closer, he realised there was no glow of lights from behind the security wall. Perhaps Rory had relented and taken Whitney out with him for the night. Perhaps Sullivan's call to be a better man had had some effect, even if he'd proved himself a hypocrite within hours of uttering it.

Then Sully saw the glint of something shiny in the darkness. It was Mel's chunky silver and turquoise necklace catching the street-light. Rory's agent was coming out of the front door, lugging a box.

'Good. It's you,' Mel said when she recognised Sullivan on the footpath. 'You'll need these.'

She dumped the box and reached just inside the front security door to heave out Sullivan's two suitcases.

'Oh, well, Rory's letting me stay here after my surgery.'

Mel shook her head. 'Not any more. As we speak, Rory's on a flight back to LA with the Waif.'

'What?'

'Easiest option. We had some media sniffing around and Whitney was likely to have an attack of the screaming habdabs in front of a camera.'

'Right. But is Rory going to be back soon?'

'He'll be over there for the foreseeable,' explained Mel. 'We're giving up the lease on this place. So, I'll need your key back. Oh, and the spare key to that ludicrous green car.'

Sullivan pulled the keys out of his jeans pocket and handed them to her.

'Cheers,' Mel said. 'As usual, Rory's left me to clean up after the party.'

She smiled grimly, seeking a moment of fellowship with Sullivan as another of Rory's abandoned courtiers.

Sullivan waved his hand in the direction of the property next door. 'What about the building project?'

'Putting it on hold,' she said. 'I fully expect a phone call in a couple of days, asking me to sell it. Ridiculous whim, buying that place. Rory doesn't live in this hemisphere in any meaningful sense.'

'Did he leave a note for me or a message or anything?'

Mel shook her head. 'This is what he does. It's not personal, Sullivan.'

Sully nodded dumbly. He thought he'd had no illusions about who Rory Wallace was, thought he'd always been clear-eyed about the ephemeral and mutually convenient nature of their connection. But in fact he must have gradually fallen for the matey bluster they'd both sprayed around, must have invested some hope in the idea of a genuine friendship, because now here he was, feeling wounded and foolish.

'Will you be okay?' Mel asked, with a tinge of the motherly tone for which Rory paid her thousands of dollars a year. 'You've got somewhere else to go, haven't you?'

Well, Sullivan at least had a hospital bed to go to first thing in the morning, so he nodded.

'Can I give you a lift somewhere?' she asked.

'No, thanks. I'll be right.'

'Good. All the best, Sullivan.'

Mel seemed relieved not to have yet another Rory loose end to tie up. She pulled the security door shut behind her, carried the box to her car, which was already loaded up with Rory detritus, swung her large silk-draped body behind the wheel and drove away.

Sullivan wheeled the two suitcases along to the half-rebuilt house. It was easy to yank aside the sheet of marine ply between the side wall and the fence.

Once inside, he found one of the builder's work lights and a torch Rory had left there. He brought one of the pool loungers down from the upstairs balcony and used clothes from his suitcases to serve as bedding.

Tim had been driving around for hours.

When Juliet first told him, she didn't seem remorseful or upset. She fired the information at him like a hit man two hundred metres away with a telescopic rifle. At first it knocked the air out of his lungs. So unexpected. So shitful. So hard to fathom, but then a few seconds later, so horribly easy to picture. He gulped for breath, expecting Juliet to follow up with volleys of vicious words, but she was surprisingly muted.

Tim barked a series of questions at her. She answered each one in a defeated tone.

Was she in love with Sullivan? Christ, no.

Had it been an ongoing affair? No, just the once and never again.

Was Sullivan good in bed? Yes, good.

Was he better than Tim? Not comparable.

Had the two of them talked about Tim? No.

Was this a pattern? Had she fucked anyone else? A guy a few years ago in Melbourne. It was only that one time and otherwise no one.

Juliet didn't attempt to justify herself, didn't blame Sullivan, didn't attack Tim. Lack of retaliation from her meant Tim's anger didn't have enough oxygen to burn for very long. He felt his rage sputter out, until he was standing there an impotent and pathetic figure. If he remained in that room, in front of Juliet, for a moment longer, his last scrap of dignity would be burned to nothing, so he walked out of the house.

Once in the car, Tim realised he didn't know where to go. He didn't want to contaminate the office or a mate's home or his gym by turning up in any of those places nursing this double betrayal in his arms. If he pulled over and stopped the car, he would have to sit with the excruciating fact of it. If he wasn't required to keep his eyes focused on the road, he might picture Sully and Juliet fucking. So he kept driving.

Tim wasn't a suffer-alone type of guy. He was happy to vent and cry and rave drunkenly to thrash out a problem with friends. But in a situation as heavy-duty as this, there were only two people he would ever consider turning to – Sullivan or Pete. Sullivan was the person who'd betrayed him and Pete was dead. So there was no one.

After some time on the road, it occurred to him that confronting Sullivan would at least be a thing he could do. A thing that might bolster his dignity. Tim didn't know the address of the flat where Sullivan had been living. He considered ringing Astrid to ask but he might betray emotion on the phone and he didn't want Astrid's scrutiny on his marriage right now. He then remembered that Sullivan had been planning to move into Rory Wallace's house. Tim was pretty sure he could find that house again if he drove round Tamarama for a while.

When he turned into a street that snaked around the headland, it looked familiar and there was the unmistakable grey-painted wall.

Definitely the spot he'd seen that kitschy green FJ Holden parked. This was the place Wallace was renting and most likely where that scumbag Sully would be.

Tim rang the bell at the security door. He rang it repeatedly, ramming the heel of his hand against the button. For a moment he imagined Sully and Rory Wallace inside, watching him on a security camera, laughing at him. But eventually he accepted there was no one home.

Turning back to his car, Tim noticed a sweep of light – the trace of a torch beam in the dark area behind the massive whitewashed wall of the place next door. He thumped on the door and yelled over the top of the outer wall towards the house.

'Sullivan! Are you in there? Let me in!'

A few moments later he heard Sully's voice yelling back. 'Gate's locked. Come round the side.'

Tim used the light from his mobile phone to pick his way along the fence-line then saw the spill of light from a side doorway and climbed inside.

The white glare from a builder's light made the concrete shell of the house look even starker. He was surprised to see how little of the renovation had been completed. It was more building site than house but you could still envisage what a huge and impressive place it was going to be.

'Tim.'

Sullivan stood next to a pool lounger piled with clothes. Tim hadn't determined what he was going to do when he confronted him – probably just yell a lot – but then Sully opened his mouth.

'I'm sorry, Tim. You gotta know I'm sorry,' said Sullivan. So he must've guessed from Tim's face that Juliet had confessed. 'I wasn't thinking and I . . . fuck, I am so sorry.'

Those piss-weak apologies shot Tim to an instant blistering rage. He kicked aside some suitcases on the rough floor and in two strides he was close enough to punch the guy. His fist connected with Sullivan's cheekbone and the edge of his eye socket. Sully staggered sideways and would have hit the floor if he hadn't landed on the lounger, which broke his fall as he tumbled onto a tangle of shirts.

Tim's hand was throbbing. He'd punched very few people in his life and he'd forgotten how much it hurt to do the punching.

Sullivan stayed down on the floor, using a shirt sleeve to dab blood from where the skin had split beside his eye. 'You're right,' he said, breathless from the pain. 'There's no point me . . . there's nothing I can say.'

Tim stood over him. 'Do you know what friendship means, you shitbag?'

Sullivan opened his mouth to answer but then stuck with saying nothing.

'I trusted you,' said Tim. 'All your years of unbelievable crap, but I still trusted you with my – I told you about my marriage *as a friend*. And what, you thought you could use that . . . swoop in when my marriage is disintegrating and get yourself an easy root? Do you know who Juliet is? She's not a happy woman but I guess you thought you could . . . Fuck you. I thought you'd actually changed, Sully. What a naive dickhead I am. This whole thing's been a con job.'

Sullivan hauled himself to his feet. 'Tim, listen, can I just say —'

'No. I've heard bullshit streaming out of you for the last thirty years.'

'Fair enough. But please —'

Tim lunged forward, shoved Sully backwards and rammed him up against a wall, hand around throat. As Sullivan braced himself against the concrete, Tim could feel there was considerable strength in the guy now. He was lean and muscled, more powerful than he'd been since high school. In the past, Tim would never have had any trouble demolishing Sullivan Moss in a fight, but now he wasn't so sure.

In fact Sullivan was passive, not exactly limp in Tim's grip but not fighting back. His body was tensed, guarded for the next blow, but steadfastly not retaliating, prepared to take whatever punishment was about to be inflicted.

Tim loosened his hold. He was sure he could still pulverise Sullivan if he chose to. But instead he took a step back.

'Part of me wants to pound you to a bloody mess but I'm not gonna do that. Not for your sake, you loathsome fuck. But I don't want to damage the kidney inside there. Whoever's getting that kidney deserves to get one in good shape. So you're not worth beating up.'

Tim felt empowered by his own restraint, with just enough of his personal command restored that he could walk out of that house with a crumb of dignity.

30

Gordana took a bag of rubbish down to the bins. Her hands were still sticky with marzipan from baking almond cakes, ready for Mirko when he got home from night shift. The almond ones were his favourite and she felt those small kindnesses between them were worth maintaining.

Mirko could be a distant man, almost cold, but never nasty. They had encountered each other in the mess of Vukovar, both having recently lost their families. They had detected a certain strength in each other – the strength a person would need (along with a large quantity of luck) to survive the fighting, the march out of the city, the detention camp and then to reach someplace decent to have a life. She and Mirko had helped each other through the process and for that alone, Gordana owed him her loyalty.

They had agreed not to have children. Gordana harboured a fear that she would be a bad mother, bound to infect any offspring with her own darkness, and she suspected Mirko felt something similar. In recent years she had doubted this decision. Maybe a child would have been a good thing, a softening influence. Maybe a child could have been a way to replace the many people they had both lost. Then again, people shouldn't have children for those kinds of selfish reasons. And anyway, she was too old now.

Yes, she owed Mirko her loyalty and whatever kindnesses were possible and welcome. He was a hard worker, an honest man and they had built a good, safe life here. Which was not to say she didn't miss Frank Dennis. There was a softness in Frank and a playfulness that could make even Gordana feel wonderfully silly for a moment. He had appreciated her company in a way that surprised and delighted her. The age difference had never bothered her. She missed him a lot.

As Gordana was returning to her unit from the rubbish area, she heard sobbing sounds from Frank's flat. Was Sullivan upset, anxious about the big operation tomorrow? In Gordana's opinion, he should abandon the whole misguided plan. There were enough gruesome things that could happen to a person without volunteering to undergo bleeding and pain.

She knocked on the door. She could spare one of Mirko's almond cakes if that might cheer Sullivan up.

The voice from inside was female. 'Who is it?'

'Gordana. From the unit across the hall.'

The door opened and there was Natalie, clearly upset.

'Oh. Hello,' said Gordana, guarded.

'It's Mack,' said Natalie and opened the door wider so Gordana could see the problem.

The dog was lying on the carpet having some kind of seizure, his one eye staring blankly. Gordana took a step back. She was frightened of the dog, even in this state.

Natalie knelt back down and held onto Mack's twitching legs. 'I should do something for him but I just . . .' She was too upset to finish the thought, paralysed with distress.

'Do you want me to ring someone?' asked Gordana.

'Yes, I should take him to the vet. I'm scared they'll put him down . . . Don't know if I can face it.'

The poor woman. No husband and her father dead. Gordana understood that the dog – it was obviously dying – was one loss too many. She didn't blame Natalie for going to pieces but the animal was suffering. Something must be done.

'Really, I think —' began Gordana.

'Yes, poor Mack. I must take him. Can you help me carry him down to the car?'

Gordana went cold with panic at the thought of touching the dog, especially when it was twitching and staring out of its one eye like that. She shook her head.

'Sullivan can help,' said Gordana and reached for her phone.

Natalie didn't object. She just stayed on the floor, holding the dog's hind legs as if she could prevent him toppling over the edge of a cliff.

Twenty-five minutes later, Sullivan walked into Frank's flat. He'd taken a taxi straight over, using the travel time to ring around and locate a vet surgery that would be open this late. He must have had a recent accident because Gordana saw his cheek was swollen and the area next to one eye was bruised with a small fresh scab. He acted as if nothing had happened so she didn't question him.

When Sullivan first saw the dog on the floor in a terrible state Gordana knew he was heartbroken. But he contained his emotion in order to do what needed to be done.

'Why don't you get some shoes on,' he said to Natalie. His tone wasn't unkind but firm enough to rouse her from the daze she was in.

Next, he fetched Frank's old bathrobe from the bedroom and wrapped it around Mack's body. 'Frank's scent might be a comfort, don't you reckon?'

Natalie nodded.

'Got your car keys?' he asked her, then turned to Gordana. 'Could you get the door for us?'

Gordana held Frank's door open, standing as far away from the dog as possible, while Sullivan lifted Mack up in his arms.

'Come on, old son,' he murmured to the dog. 'You're not too good, are you mate. Don't worry. We're gonna get you to the vet.'

Gordana then ran to hold the main door open so Sullivan could carry the dog outside into the street. Natalie hurried ahead of him to clear the back seat of her car. It was a distressing sight – an animal in its

death throes and two wretched people – but at the same time Gordana
was impressed. Sullivan was a man doing what needed to be done.

Sullivan drove Natalie's car, heading straight for the after-hours vet-
erinary practice on Parramatta Road. Natalie sat in the back seat with
Mack swaddled in the bathrobe, his head on her lap. Sullivan could
hear her murmuring gently to the dog.

Because it was so late, the clinic staff was mostly made up of
vet students. The dog was first examined by an earnest Chinese guy
who, despite appearing no older than fourteen, was very thorough.
Eventually a more senior vet came in – a kind, sturdy woman – to
confirm the diagnosis.

Mack had a brain tumour. That had caused the seizure and evi-
dently the cancer was extensive. There would likely be more seizures
and even if those could be controlled, Mack could be in considerable
pain, with very little physical and mental function left. Natalie was
crying softly, being given tissues and a back rub by the vet.

Sullivan stared at the dog lying on the surgery table. Had he been
negligent? Was it his fault Mack was dying?

'Should I have realised he was sick and brought him in sooner?' he
asked the vet.

'Had you noticed any changes in him? Weakness, balance problems, lack of appetite, tremors?'

'No, none of those,' Sullivan said, then half turned to Natalie.
'Did you notice anything?'

Natalie shook her head.

The vet smiled kindly. 'Well, there was nothing you could've done.
Sometimes it just goes like this.'

Sullivan nodded. So this wasn't his fault. But it was still shit.

'Mack's a lovely, very old fellow who's had a great life,' said the vet,
stroking Mack's head. Sullivan wanted to kiss her for being so sweet
with the dog. 'You could see it as a good thing this was quick, without

him enduring horrible symptoms for ages.'

It struck Sully that Natalie had been wrong before, when she accused him of not having a loved one to whom he would donate an organ. He would give part of his body to Mack right now, if that would save this beautiful dog who had saved him.

He couldn't save the dog but he still had a duty to perform: Sullivan needed to be calm, present and anything else he could be that might ease this terrible night for Natalie.

The vet explained there was no hope of recovery. Euthanasia was the only real option. She looked at the two of them, waiting for confirmation that they understood and agreed. Sully felt the decision was up to Natalie, since Mack was her father's dog. But then she threw him a look – *what do you think?* – and Sullivan nodded to her, solemn, decisive.

Natalie's voice came out in a husky whisper, 'Okay, we should do it.'

'Do you two want to stay with Mack while I give him the needle?' asked the vet.

Sullivan glanced at Natalie. 'Do you want me to leave or . . .'

'No, please stay,' she said.

The vet prepared the needle, a syringe full of strangely bright green liquid. Mack was already far gone, not moving, unconscious.

Natalie squatted down beside the table so she was face to face with Mack and stroked his ear the way he liked. Sullivan kneaded the loose fur around his neck and crooned, 'Hey, Mack. Sorry you're having a rough night, mate. But it'll all be over soon. Vet's going to give you the Green Dream needle and you'll drift off to sleep. You're a great dog. You're a great dog.'

As the bright liquid went in, Sullivan felt the life go out of Mack. It really was as peaceful as people said. Rapidly, there was just a furry shape on the table, still warm, but Mack himself had departed. Natalie made a whimpering noise and then took a huge shuddering breath.

In the office area, Natalie paid the bill, her voice broken by tearful hiccups.

'Do you need a lift somewhere?' she asked.

'No, I'm fine,' said Sullivan. 'Bus stop's right there.'

She nodded. 'Thanks for helping.'

'Thanks for letting me be there with Mack.'

Sullivan's entire self was screaming with the impulse to fold her in his arms but he knew that would be unwelcome. Natalie stepped outside and walked to her car with Mack's collar and Frank's bathrobe in her hand.

Tim used the hotel key-card to get into one of the standard rooms at the Four Seasons and threw a plastic shopping bag onto the armchair. He'd stopped by the late-opener Kmart and bought a shirt, socks and undies so he could go straight to work without having to engage with Juliet or anyone else.

He was tired through to his bones, his punching hand still aching. He fell onto the bed fully clothed and wondered if he should let Juliet know he was okay. Possibly she didn't give a flying fuck about where or how he was. But if the situation were reversed, he would want some basic message. He texted.

At 4 Seasons. T.

Natalie wasn't up to facing her mother. If Judy were to say one dismissive thing about Mack or make the smallest acerbic facial expression about the dog, it would be unbearable.

Instead of going home, Nat stretched out on the couch at Frank's place. She wrapped herself up in the bathrobe which held the scent of her father and Mack. She knew she wouldn't sleep but it didn't matter much. She had to be on her feet and heading to the airport to collect Louis first thing.

Natalie lay there for the next few hours, missing her dad with a ferocity that frightened her. She lay very still. If she didn't, the feeling would engulf her.

*

It was close to midnight as Sullivan walked up Parramatta Road. In the last twenty-four hours, he had staggered from one dizzying mess to another without the chance to regain his balance in between.

He continued walking until he found himself one block away from the Chippendale pub where he'd spent the afternoon of Pete's funeral. On that terrible day, Tim had been leaving messages, hassling him to come to the crematorium. Sully turned his phone off but just knowing Tim's voice was beaming into it was unbearable. He had chucked the wretched thing in a drawer and escaped to the pub.

After his first few tequilas, he'd struck up conversation with Travis, a guy he ran into there sometimes. As they drank together, Sully was mesmerised by the carotid artery visibly pulsing under the spider-web tattoo on Travis's sinewy neck, as if it were the heartbeat of the little blue spider tattooed there.

Sullivan raved about how bad he felt to have ducked the funeral, and Travis reckoned he understood where Sully was coming from. He couldn't remember whose idea it had been – his or Travis's – to hike round to Pete's house. Either way, the idea was: if Sully could be at the house, ready when the mourners arrived from the crematorium for the wake, that might be better than nothing.

Pete and Vincent had bought their narrow Redfern terrace fifteen years ago, when the area was unfashionable and considered dangerous by many people. They'd done the place up in their characteristically modest, homey but elegant way.

Sullivan knew where Pete hid a spare key in the back courtyard so he and Travis had hopped the fence from the back lane. Sully was hunting under terracotta pots for the key when he heard the smash of glass.

'Here we go,' said Travis, reaching through the broken pane to unlock the back door.

In the kitchen, the caterers had left large platters of canapes, covered in cling wrap. Seeing those little savoury doodads made Sullivan realise how long it had been since he'd eaten anything. He could peel the plastic wrap off one platter, hook out a few bits of finger food and rearrange it so no one would know. Trouble was, that clingy stuff was a bastard to handle and Sullivan's fingers, clumsy with tequila, knocked both trays of food onto the floor. He did his best to reassemble the canapes but it was a lost cause. It looked as if scavenging animals had been through the place.

Flustered by his food disaster and sweaty from the long walk, Sully decided a shower was the best idea. Yeah, he could cool off, freshen up and be in a clearer state to face Tim, Vincent, everyone.

He stripped off and got into the shower, blasting his head with water. Better. But when he stepped out, he felt dizzy and feverish. He lay down on the tiled floor for a moment to cool off and steady himself.

He came to when he felt something land on him. A towel. He looked up to see two dark shapes looming over him – Vincent and Tim in their funeral suits.

'Get dressed,' said Tim.

Tim bundled him downstairs into the cab and delivered the news that Travis had robbed Pete's house while Sully was passed out naked on the bathroom floor.

Sullivan spent the weeks after that mostly in bed, either asleep or drunk. But there wasn't enough booze in the world to drown the shame of that day. When he finally got out of bed, he managed to organise a few things, such as leaving the envelope of cash for Astrid. Then he caught the lift to the roof of what he judged was a sufficiently tall building.

Now here he was, outside that Chippendale pub again, still incapable of moving through the world without creating mess.

Some things were clear. He was a worthless piece of shit. There was no remedy. The idea that donating his kidney would solve anything was laughable, self-aggrandising, possibly obscene. If he was doing it to be a good person, that had clearly failed. If he was doing it to assuage guilt about Pete, that was misguided.

When Sullivan reached Pete and Vincent's house, there were lights on and music playing. Someone inside was still up.

Standing on the doorstep, Sullivan felt his chest wall splay open, exposing all his innards, wet and soft and glistening in the night air, without any covering. He was afraid Pete would appear at the front door and pass judgement on him. Impossible, of course, but the image was still unbearable.

Vincent had obviously seen Sullivan through the spyhole so when he opened the door, his expression was set hard. He remained in the doorway, making it clear Sullivan would not be invited inside.

'What happened to your face?'

Sully ignored the question about his black eye and spoke in a determined burst. 'Sorry to bother you so late, Vincent. I know you don't want to hear my apology for letting Pete down but I need to say it. Yes, yes, yes, Pete's the one I should have said sorry to . . . should've said a lot of things to, should've returned his calls, should've been by his side. But I can't do any of that now. So that just leaves you. And I need to . . . I don't know exactly . . .'

Sullivan realised tears were streaming down his face as he spoke. 'I'm sorry I'm crying. I'm not crying to put pressure on you. Some things have happened and I'm just . . . Please ignore the crying.'

When Sullivan took a moment to steady himself, Vincent took the chance to interrupt. 'Aren't you supposed to be in hospital donating your kidney? Tim mentioned —'

'Yes, but . . . well, that's why I'm here now.'

'Are you planning to lay your kidney down on our doorstep as an offering to Pete's memory?'

'If I could do that, I would.'

'I've got a sharp Japanese knife. I could carve a big enough hole in you to get the thing out.'

Vincent hated him. Hated him so very much. Sullivan knew that but facing it was still difficult.

Vincent softened his tone a fraction. 'I accept that you're sorry. But for fuck's sake, don't expect the spirit of Saint Pete to offer you absolution in exchange for your kidney.'

'I don't expect that. Well, I probably did before but now . . .'

'Stop using my dead boyfriend as a stick to beat yourself with. Why would I want to listen to that?' demanded Vincent.

'Sorry. I can see that must be . . . sorry.'

'Do you know what it was like to live with Pete? Someone everyone thought was a saint?'

'Are you saying he wasn't —'

'No, I'm not saying – he was . . . I don't know. He was just built that way. The rest of us can't be as good as him. It's like wishing you were taller.'

'But does that mean —'

'Can you imagine what it's like to be with a partner you will never feel worthy of?'

'Yes. I can,' said Sullivan.

Vincent frowned and then nodded, conceding Sullivan might have an inkling.

'Look, Sullivan, I don't know what you expect me to do for you.'

'Nothing. Well, just to listen to my apology, which you've done. I'm here now because I was going to do this thing for the wrong reasons. That's why I'm not going to donate my kidney any more.'

Sullivan's plan was to ring Diane Milton first thing in the morning and explain he was calling off the transplant.

'Well, up to you,' said Vincent. 'But if you've gone this far . . .'

'I know, I know. Trouble is, it was meant to be this pure act but it can't be because . . . Maybe it was always a childish idea. Whatever, whatever, now I've contaminated it. Contaminated the whole process with bad behaviour and vanity and messed-up —'

'My God, you are such a wanker. Does it have to be a symbol? It's a fucking kidney.'

'But if my reasons for doing it are fucked up then —'

'Who cares about your reasons? I mean, the person who gets your kidney won't care if it comes via your vanity, will they?'

Sullivan's head was spinning. Maybe it was the ultimate vanity *not* to do it for fear of vanity.

Vincent shrugged. 'A kidney is a kidney.'

Sullivan was scheduled to meet Diane Milton at the hospital admissions desk at seven in the morning. He made it just in time, having spent the rest of the night walking around the city until his legs ached. The staff at the twenty-four-hour Macca's let him sit for an hour or so without ordering food once he explained he was on a pre-operative fast. At six a.m., he found a convenience store where he bought some cheap pyjamas, toiletries and a nylon bag, so he wouldn't show up at the hospital empty-handed.

'Sullivan, what happened to your face?' Diane asked when she found him at the desk.

He put his hand to his puffy cheek. There was some bruising and a small patch of broken skin from Tim's fist. 'I whacked myself with some framing timber at work. Nothing serious. I'm fine.'

Diane frowned, hesitated for a moment but then opened the folder of pre-op paperwork they needed to fill out together. Sullivan could see she was keyed up. This must be a satisfying moment for her. After months of planning, after all those occasions when things could have slid apart and led to nothing, finally here was the day when her patient efforts would amount to something.

Diane had told him once that the situations in which they packed a kidney off for transport to another hospital were pleasing. But the miracle of the whole process – an organ taken from one living person and given to another – was more potent when both donor and recipient were in the same hospital, as they were today. Which meant that right now, you could describe Diane's mood as bubbly – well, as bubbly as Diane Milton would ever be.

When the final forms were signed, she turned to Sully. 'I'd like to offer my personal thanks, Sullivan, for what you're doing today and the months of commitment leading up to it.'

He felt uncomfortable to have her look directly at him. Could she see that he had almost reneged? Only hours before, he had planned to pull the plug on the whole thing. She shouldn't be looking at him as if he were some wonderful person.

Sullivan certainly didn't want to hear any more of Diane's speech – a spiel she presumably gave to all donors – so he put his hands up in a gesture to indicate *Enough*.

She respected his wish to leave it there. 'You look tired, Sullivan. Let's get you settled in your room.'

Sully was installed in a room on the urology ward. Post-operatively, the recipient of his kidney would be cared for on a different floor, to avoid the risk of people running into each other and anonymity being compromised.

Gowned up, hospital wristband attached, cannula inserted, blood pressure taken, Sullivan numbly submitted to the process. While a series of nurses and doctors poked at him and asked the same battery of questions, Sully kept his eyes closed, as if meditating, so none of them would be encouraged to chat or engage with him as a person. He just wanted to be a body delivering an organ.

It was cold in the anaesthetic bay, a dry lifeless chill. Lying on the gurney, Sullivan was deeply tired. He'd been awake for two nights running but there was also a dragging tiredness from the last months of trying to become the useful creature he would never be. Let it be over now. Let him surrender to the drugs and rest now.

He relished the moment of succumbing to the general anaesthetic – someone flicking a switch to offer that clean simple unconsciousness.

Part Three

31

Natalie stood in the international arrivals area, watching for Louis. Family groups waited with helium balloons and grandmothers in fleecy tracksuits. A trio of twenty-something women still wearing last night's eyeliner chattered about the girlfriend they were meeting. A young man gripped a bunch of flowers so tightly he was crushing the stems. Women in hijabs held small babies while their husbands wrangled toddlers. Behind the friends and family crowd, the limousine drivers in dark suits stood in an almost-straight line, each holding the name of their pick-up passenger.

When Natalie saw the limo guys, she remembered joking with Louis that she might be at the arrivals hall holding a sign – *Mr Louis Dennis-Cook*. She should have done that for him. They would have had a laugh about it. It would have made Louis feel special. But she'd forgotten. For a fleeting moment, Natalie considered asking the cafe woman if she had a square of cardboard and a marker pen, but then realised she lacked the confident energy you would need to negotiate something like that right now.

Louis appeared at the top of the arrivals ramp, glimpsed behind clumps of adults with towering trolleys of luggage. But Natalie could locate the shape of her child at any distance.

Her initial relief – he was safely home – quickly gave way to uneasiness when she saw his small sweet face searching for her in the crowd.

What did he expect from her? Whatever he was hoping for, she was likely to disappoint him. She was so depleted. She had nothing left for her child.

Louis darted between the luggage trolleys and ran forward to throw his arms round her.

'Hey, gorgeous boy, did you have a good time?' asked Natalie.

She let him hold her tightly while the airline woman hurried to catch up with him. Nat signed the documents, encouraging Louis to bid thanks and farewell to the woman.

The boy looked at his mother's face, immediately detecting a mood that needed explanation. 'Has Sully had his operation? Did something bad happen?'

'I think he's having his operation today.'

'Can we ring up and make sure he's okay? And you have to ask when we can visit.'

Natalie made as non-committal a noise as she could without sparking more discussion.

'Cool,' said Louis. But still he wanted to decipher her mood. 'What's up?'

Natalie had not told Louis about the dog over the phone, not wanting him to handle the sadness while he was far away from anyone else who cared about Mack. Now, as they walked from the arrivals hall to the car park, she broke the news.

On the drive home, Louis wept and bombarded her with questions.

'Why didn't you wait so I could say goodbye to him?' 'Couldn't they do an operation and take out the brain tumour?' 'Did it hurt him?' 'Did Mack know he was going to die?' 'What did you do with his body?'

When Louis' initial shock was exhausted, he sat in the passenger seat, quiet and sniffly. Natalie reached over and squeezed his thigh in a feeble attempt at consolation.

In truth, she was relieved to have the excuse of Mack's death as an explanation for being so flat with her son. In his grief about the dog,

Louis didn't pursue the matter of visiting Sullivan. Just as well. Natalie felt ashamed of herself – using the death of a dog to cover her own inadequacies. You could think you'd reached your lowest point but no, you could always go lower, it seemed.

In recovery, Sullivan felt hands tucking blankets round him and taking his blood pressure. He heard the voices of the nurses, with their hearty sing-song. 'It's all over, Sullivan.' 'Are you warm enough, Sullivan?' But it was only once he was up in the ward that he was able to focus on a person's face – Diane Milton.

'It went really well, Sullivan. Let the nurses know if you have too much pain, won't you.'

He murmured assent as best he could with a dry throat. 'Rest up now,' said Diane and left the room.

Sullivan was dopey from analgesia, with the pain in his side sitting like a big lump underneath the layer of grogginess. Going under the anaesthetic had been good. Waking up again was not so good.

He didn't feel any more noble. Someone presumably had a working kidney now – which was a good thing – but Sullivan was still the same person he always was. Instead of being a fuckwit with two kidneys, he was now a fuckwit with one kidney and a urinary catheter.

It felt right to be in pain. He resolved to submerge himself in the pool of agony. But after a while the pain grew in intensity and he knew he wasn't the kind of stoic who could endure much. So Sullivan held his thumb down on the Patient Controlled Analgesia button, wishing he could medicate himself into oblivion.

Natalie phoned Astrid on the Tuesday. 'Do you know if Sullivan had his surgery?'

Astrid rang the hospital to check and then texted Natalie. *All well with Sullivan, A.*

Good. Natalie would be able to reassure her son Sullivan was fine and that would be the end of it. Well, no, it wouldn't be that simple. Louis would agitate to visit him and Natalie would have to come up with some plausible reason why they wouldn't.

She was relieved he'd come through the operation okay but there was no way she could face Sullivan Moss. She was angry with him but that wasn't the thing making her stay well away. That man had witnessed the worst of her. He'd heard the nasty thoughts that came out of her mouth. He'd seen the cowardly way she sat frozen on the floor, unable to help Mack. He knew the foolish selfish creature she really was. She could not bear to be in the gaze of someone who could see all of that in her.

Sullivan stayed on the ward for six days. The medical staff took efficient care of him, making sure his remaining kidney worked well (it did) and that the procedure hadn't damaged his overall physical health (it hadn't).

He didn't have many visitors. Few people knew where he was anyway. Rory was gone, of course. Gordana had an aversion to hospitals – she'd made that clear to Sullivan months ago – so he didn't expect her to come. Nor could he expect Tim or Natalie to visit.

Jose Luis came twice, first with Liliana and then on his own. Both times Sullivan feigned sleep.

The second visit, Jose Luis brought a container with Liliana's caramel flan.

'Please, can you put this in the fridge for him?' Jose Luis whispered to the nurse. 'I don't want to disturb Sullivan if he's resting.'

Sully was aware of his boss sitting in the chair by the bed for over an hour, quietly doing some paperwork for the business. Sullivan couldn't face him. Jose Luis regarded him as a nobler person than he was. All Sully could feel was the gap between Jose Luis' estimation of the person in the bed and the reality, that gap filling up with a constant ache, insistent, uncomfortable.

Listening to Jose Luis' accent, the rolled r's, the soft consonants, as he spoke politely to a nurse, Sullivan was struck by how much he loved this man. That reminded Sully how much he had loved Tim and Pete. And what good had his love ever done them? Better for Jose Luis if Sullivan kept himself well away.

Eventually, Jose Luis slipped out of the hospital room, whispering his gratitude to the nurses for the good care they were taking of Sullivan.

Sully was astonished to see his ex-wife stride into his hospital room.

'Oh. Astrid. Hello.'

'How are you feeling, Sullivan?'

'Ah, well, the body is an amazing thing,' he said with a joyless smile.

'Do you know how the transplant went for the other person?'

'It's anonymous so they don't tell you much. But they did say the recipient is doing well.'

'That's wonderful,' said Astrid.

Sullivan noticed she was unusually jittery. 'It's very kind of you to visit,' he said.

'I was in the vicinity,' she was quick to explain. 'Consultation with a fertility specialist in the building next door.'

'Oh, are you . . . ?'

'We're exploring the option of IVF. Grahame's always felt – well, he thought it would be unfair to burden a child with a father who has a degenerative illness. Which is typical of him – his sense of honour, I mean. And that's exactly why he would make a wonderful father. The point is, I had to respect his policy on children.'

Sullivan nodded cautiously, seeing how vulnerable Astrid was on the subject, talking too much and too quickly.

'But lately, I've been – the notion of a child's been scratching away in my mind. Grahame still has qualms but he cares so much about my potential happiness, he's – anyway, we're going to explore IVF.'

'Oh Astrid, I hope it works. You'd be a great mother.'

'Steady on. The success rate is very low. Grahame and I agreed we have to keep our expectations low and not pin our overall happiness on the process of producing a baby.'

'Very wise,' Sullivan agreed. 'But I do wish you well. You deserve a lot of happiness.'

'Anyway, I still have half an hour on the parking meter so I thought I'd pop in and check on you. You should be very proud of what you've done, Sullivan.'

Sullivan tipped his head to acknowledge the comment. 'The docs reckon I can be discharged today.'

'Really? You seem too zonked to be on the street. Are you sure you're ready?'

'I'm ready.'

'I don't agree. I should speak to the medical staff and see if —'

'Please don't do that. I want to get out of here.'

Sullivan's firmness obviously surprised Astrid but then she smiled kindly. 'I guess that's understandable. Grahame's always keen to come home after a stint in hospital. So, are you going back to live at Frank's place?'

'No.'

'By the way, Natalie rang me on Tuesday. I told her you got through the operation okay.'

'Right. Thanks.'

Astrid shifted her weight awkwardly. 'Look, I have been accused of being blind to the nuances between people but I'm wondering . . . I can sense there's some tension between you and Nat.'

'What?'

'Oh, Sullivan. Did you sleep with her?'

'No, I did not.'

'Well, I'm relieved. Natalie is a lovely person,' Astrid said. 'She's been hurt a lot in the past. You're the last thing she needs now.'

'I'm well aware of that,' he said.

'If you're not going back to the Glebe flat, where are you going?'

'Rory Wallace bought a house in Tamarama. I'm going there.'

'Well, lucky you. Celebrity accommodation.' Astrid didn't go to the movies or watch TV much but even she knew Wallace was famous. 'And is this movie star going to look after you properly while you convalesce?'

'I'll be fine. One small problem: Rory can't pick me up today. I'd happily get a cab to his house but the hospital isn't keen on discharging me without an escort. In fact, Astrid, could I possibly ask you for one more favour? I have no right to ask after everything that's —'

'For God's sake, Sullivan, just ask.'

'Could you give me a lift to Tamarama?'

Astrid dropped Sullivan off outside Rory's.

'This one? The one with the huge white wall?' she asked as she found a spot to pull in. 'Have you got a key or is there someone home to let you in?'

'I can get in round the side. No problem.'

'Let me carry the bag in for you,' she said.

'No, no, I'll be fine. Thanks, Astrid.' Again, Sullivan used a firm tone to dissuade her from escorting him inside and realising that the house behind the wall was in fact a half-built shell.

'Take care of yourself, Sullivan.'

32

In the bottle shop, Sullivan moved around the shelves gingerly. If he swivelled his torso too much, his surgical wound might split open. It probably wouldn't but it felt that way. With any quick movement, dizziness overwhelmed him and he had to grip onto the handle of the beer fridge.

There was a nineteen-year-old guy behind the counter, with a clump of bleached hair and several piercings nestled moistly in his acne-crusted face. While Sullivan slowly selected bottles and put them in the little trolley, the kid shook his head, assuming he was watching a sad drunk stocking up.

When Sullivan put the bottles up on the counter to pay, the kid made no effort to conceal his contempt. 'Big night for a Monday, eh mate.'

'Sorry?' said Sullivan, fishing cash out of his wallet.

'I mean, I shouldn't even be selling you this stuff since you're already pissed as,' the kid said.

'I am not pissed,' Sullivan responded then lifted his shirt to display the bandage covering his incision. 'I just donated a kidney, okay?'

'Yeah, whatever,' snorted the boy and accepted the money.

Sully took things slowly as he carried the bag of bottles back down the hill to Rory's house. During his week in hospital, the builders had collected their remaining gear from the defunct work site. Someone had also taken Sullivan's suitcases, but no matter. It was a shame the builders' work-light was gone because it would be dark soon. But then he found Rory's torch; that would suffice.

Sully walked through the shell of the house, looking for the best spot. It might be comforting to see the sky, so he climbed to the top storey and found the other pool lounger still on the balcony where Rory had left it. It was a relief to put the bottle-shop bag down on the balcony – the bottles were heavy and causing Sully twinges of fresh pain down his side.

First, he tipped the orange juice out of the two-litre container, over the raw concrete edge and into the hole for the pool way below. He then used the empty container as a mixing receptacle, pouring in an entire 750 ml bottle of vodka, most of the Midori melon liqueur and a few good slugs of the Zen green tea liqueur (the name was tartly amusing to him). He shook the cocktail up in the plastic bottle – his own Green Dream.

Sullivan took a swig of the mixture, sweet and powerful. Intoxication surged through him with surprising speed. Maybe his system wasn't used to alcohol after months of sobriety or maybe, being one kidney down, the sensation came on more swiftly.

He wondered what his father had been thinking the day he climbed down the rail embankment to put his head on the tracks. Sully had some memory of his dad but it was an unreliable picture made up of the egocentric memories of a seven-year-old, some images constructed from photos and others probably contaminated by things his mother had said.

He'd discussed his father a fair bit with Anthony, the shrink, but it had always seemed more a matter of intellectual curiosity than present illumination. It stood to reason that Sullivan had inherited some brain wiring from the guy – the tendency to substance abuse and self-annihilation – but what utility was there in knowing that?

In his teens and early twenties Sully had traded on having a suicide for a father. It impressed certain kinds of people, made him seem poetic and sad and interesting, and girls were more likely to have sex with him. It was disgusting he'd exploited his father like that. The poor bastard.

There was little hope of working out what had happened in his father's mind. Like examining a fossil record, Sullivan could see the outline of the man who was once there and could reconstruct a plausible model of how unhappy his dad must have been. But he could never know for sure, and anyway, what did it matter. The point was, Sullivan felt like shit. Sullivan wanted to go to sleep and not wake up.

The hospital had given him a supply of painkillers to take home – Endone, a type of oxycodone. He extracted all the pills from the blister pack and put them in a nest he made out of the bottle-shop bag. He scooped up half the Endone in one go, swallowing them with swigs of Green Dream.

It would be fitting to watch the sun set over the ocean so Sully dragged the pool lounger out to the edge of the balcony. He kicked his shoes off and let them drop over the edge. Then he lay down on the lounger and shifted around until he found a position that didn't squash the area around his incision. He drank steadily from the flagon of lurid green booze.

Nine months ago, when Sullivan was on that rooftop preparing to top himself, he had been better off than he was now, because back then, he had nothing to lose. In the last nine months, he had allowed himself the delusion that he might deserve to be loved by someone – a woman, a friend, a child, a dog, a stranger who would get his kidney. He had seen a possible good life and then destroyed it. He felt the lack of it like the wound where a limb had been torn off.

Nine months ago, when he'd made the decision to jump, he had been continuously drunk for a long time, unthinking, numb to himself. Now more of him was alive so it felt like more of a job to kill himself.

He took the rest of the pills and tipped the Green Dream down his throat, drinking as much as he could without feeling sick. He lay still, allowing his guts to settle so he wouldn't vomit, then drank some more.

As the oxycodone drew him down with its velvety fingers, Sully thought about Ken, the lovely, lovely, lovely man he'd met in the hospital cafeteria. At whatever time Ken decided to let dialysis go and sink into unconsciousness, his wife Leone would be there, massaging his restless legs, smoothing cream over his itchy skin, sitting by his bed as he faded away. That man would have a death with love around him, a death with some honour. Good on Ken.

As Sullivan took one last, floppy-armed swig of the Green Dream, he saw his own dead body being wrapped in double sheets of two-hundred-micron black plastic, the edges firmly sealed with duct tape. The parcel could then be dumped in the special section of the tip for such materials.

33

Natalie hit the button for the studio intercom.

'Good show, Heather,' she said. 'Loved the fish market call.'

'Thanks, Nat,' said Heather and they smiled at each other through the glass.

Gathering up papers from the studio desk, Natalie marvelled at how a person could go on functioning, doing her job, smiling at co-workers, helping her son with his homework, negotiating household duties with her mother and all the while show no signs of having drained away to almost nothing inside. Nat wondered how long she could continue in this moribund state. Maybe for a very long time.

Back at her own desk, she glanced at her mobile and noticed three missed calls from Louis. Before she had a chance to dial home, the office phone rang.

'Breakfast show. This is —'

'Mum.'

She heard the wheeze. It was loud, amplified in Natalie's skull, spinning up her heart rate within a second. Louis' asthma had been worse in Kuala Lumpur – the pollution – and had only just started to settle.

'Louis. Have you got your puffer?'

There was a fumbling noise on the line and then Judy's voice. 'He's fine. I thought he should try sitting it out without his puffer. He's got his puffer now.'

Judy talked on. There was a seesaw in her mother's voice – the tone she adopted when she was in the wrong but damned if she'd admit it – but Nat paid no attention to the words. She was focused on the sound of Louis wheezing in the background, gulping for breath, more and more panicky. 'Mum. I can hear this is a bad attack. Does he look blue around the mouth?'

'He's a bit pale. Oh, listen now. He's stopped making the awful noise. He'll be fine soon.'

No, you stupid fucking cow, it meant the opposite. It meant Louis was now so bad his lungs couldn't even manage to produce a wheezing sound. Natalie felt something ignite inside her, every cell in her body vibrating.

'Listen to me. I'm ringing an ambulance.'

She dialled triple zero on her mobile and gave details to the emergency operator. At the same time, she stayed on the landline, relaying instructions to her mother about keeping Louis calm and upright.

'Tell Louis I'll be with him soon.'

Natalie later had no memory of how she got out of the office, down in the lift and into her car. She was replaying a radio segment in her head, an interview Heather had done with an asthma specialist. Almost four hundred people a year died from asthma attacks in this country. It seemed so unlikely, so absurd, so monstrous. But it happened to hundreds of people. It was possible. Her hands on the steering wheel were tingling, her heart thudding hard.

Pulling up outside Judy's house, Natalie saw the ambulance in the driveway. The rear hatch was open and one of the paramedics was helping Louis to sit upright in the back of the vehicle, using a nebuliser. Out of the car and running closer she saw his face. Pale, bluish, struggling for breath, drowning really, eyes distended with the terror of a dying animal.

Natalie jumped in the back of the ambulance beside Louis for the ride to hospital. Above the facemask, his gaze latched on to her. *Save me.* To survive this, her boy needed to stay calm. In an instant,

Natalie's thrashing panic went still and all that energy condensed into a single solid core inside her. She took his free hand, holding it firmly in her lap.

At the hospital, Natalie strode alongside the gurney, through emergency department passageways and into the treatment room. There was one night in her early twenties when Nat had snorted several lines of cocaine that had rendered every sensation and every physical action stronger, heightened, more intense. Now, moving through the hospital with her son, the extra strength she was feeling, this sharpness, was coming from her own blood.

Nebulisers, oxygen, steroids. From the way the main doctor was moving and delivering instructions, it was obvious Louis' condition was precarious. But perceiving the danger only made Natalie more fiercely composed. She stayed by Louis' side, holding his hand whenever that was possible. She maintained her own breathing at a measured pace, silently urging Louis to fall in with her steady tempo. She murmured encouraging words in the same soothing rhythm, assuring him she was there, he would be okay, that he could just breathe. Watching his energy flag, his narrow chest exhausted from the effort to gulp air, she stroked his hand, transferring strength from her body into his.

Eventually, Louis responded to the drugs. His breathing steadied. Three hours later, he was doing so well that the doctor declared he wouldn't have to go to the ICU. Natalie finally allowed herself to shift down to a lower level of vigilance.

When Louis dropped off to sleep in the treatment room, Natalie left him to fill out paperwork for his transfer to the paediatric ward. She was searching for the correct administrative window when she spotted Judy sitting in a waiting area.

Natalie felt the power within herself to lunge across the space between them and tear out her mother's throat. But when she looked again at Judy, the impulse waned. Her mother appeared more dishevelled than Nat had ever seen her – the smooth helmet of hair was an unkempt mess, makeup smudged into a dark blur around the eyes, clothes rumpled. Judy looked old, her face sagging off her skull like a soggy dishcloth.

'How is he?' she asked in a small voice.

'Okay now. Do you understand that he could have died?' Natalie demanded. 'Nod to indicate that you understand that.'

Judy nodded.

'I am trying to blame your ignorance and not you,' said Natalie. 'But at this moment, I'm not capable of being that reasonable. So better if you go home now and I'll call you later.'

Natalie spent the night on a foldout cot beside Louis in their corner of a four-bed paediatric room. She didn't sleep, just dozed a little, always alert to his breathing. When a nurse came round the ward for her regular observations, she and Natalie nodded to each other, their eyes shining out of the darkness like watchful animals.

The next morning, Louis was worn out and still shaken. Even so, he made a show of being cheerful. Natalie knew it was bunged on for her sake but she played along. She sat up on the bed with him watching episodes of *Horrible Histories* on an iPad they borrowed from the boy in the opposite bed.

Judy visited in the late morning. She had reinstalled herself in her trim clothes, hair smooth, face neatly drawn on.

'Here's Nana,' said Natalie, then took a step back from the bed to allow her mother to have a moment with Louis.

Judy gave him a book about Vikings and a bag with a collection of his favourite lollies, treats she would normally have condemned. She was clearly chastened, so eager to please that Natalie let go some of the anger. Judy was who she was. No point getting spun-up about her limitations or her bullying.

And in truth, Natalie had dumped a fair bit on her mother, relying on their misshapen domestic situation to make her life work. Judy had taken on the burden without question, with staunchness if not with grace. That must be remembered and accounted for.

When a nurse came to check Louis' breathing again, Judy moved out of the way, closer to Nat.

'The staff,' said Judy in a snaky whisper, flicking her head towards the nurse. 'Have you noticed how many of them are fat? What sort of example of good health are they setting for these sick kids?'

Natalie glared at her mother – *shut up*. Judy wiggled her head and mouthed an insincere 'Sorry'.

Natalie drew a deep breath, drawing up her most reasonable self. 'Mum, how busy are you this afternoon?'

'Nothing I can't rearrange,' said Judy.

'There are a few errands I need to do. Could you stay with Louis for a couple of hours?'

Judy was so grateful to be asked, her eyes were wet with tears. 'Of course. Of course I'll stay with our boy.'

'Thanks. I appreciate it.' Nat could hardly bear to look at her mother appearing so needy.

She drove Judy's car out of the hospital car park. She should be shredded from lack of sleep but she wasn't. The chemical charge from the day before was still in her system like a fuel source.

She walked into the radio station and straight to Neil's office.

'Natalie,' said Neil, standing up at his desk the moment he saw her. 'How's Louis doing?'

'He's on the mend.'

'Good. Oh, that's good. Listen, you take off as many days as you need. We'll cover for you.'

'Thanks for that,' she said. 'But I want to make more of a substantial long-term change.'

'Sure, let's talk about . . . When you're back we can —'

'I need to move out of breakfast.'

'Right, right, right.'

Neil was nodding but then he opened his mouth to argue. Natalie jumped in swiftly. This wasn't going to be a discussion. She was making a declaration.

'You'll need a producer for afternoons once Rob leaves.'

The work schedule as afternoons producer would mean Natalie could take Louis to school in the mornings and pick him up from aftercare. They wouldn't need to live with Judy.

'Yes, well – uh – no, that could work – yeah,' stammered Neil.

'And just to let you know, I'll be applying for on-air jobs next year wherever they come up.'

Natalie smiled, a smile intended to punctuate the conversation firmly.

'I'll call you first thing tomorrow,' she said as she left his office.

When Gordana arrived home from her shift at the drycleaners, she heard thumping and dragging sounds coming from Frank's unit. Was Sullivan Moss back in there doing something peculiar?

The door opened a little and she saw the end of the light brown sofa being nudged into the gap.

'Hello?' Gordana called out cautiously.

'Can you get the door for me?' Natalie yelled from inside.

Gordana pushed the door fully open to see her in the process of pushing the sofa out of the unit. Frank's doona and a small floor rug were thrown on top of the sofa cushions.

Natalie was sweaty, her jaw clenched tenaciously, her eyes dark and a little bit frightening.

'My son and I are going to live here,' she said. 'Need to get all the dog hair out first.'

The two women heaved the sofa out through the foyer. They shared the weight equally, careful not to let the side swing against the wall, putting it down momentarily to wedge the main door open, then hoisting it up again. Gordana wondered if Natalie was reminded of the moment they had carried Frank's body together.

They deposited the sofa, the rug and the doona on the kerb out-side the building. Natalie wrote a note on the back of an advertising flyer and pinned it to the upholstery.

Please take. Good if not allergic to dogs.

Gordana helped Natalie roll up the large Persian carpet from the lounge room and they carried that down to the kerbside pile too.

Back in the flat, Gordana glanced around the bare room.

'Tomorrow I'll buy new rugs, new sofa, new bedding,' Natalie said. 'Do you happen to have a powerful vacuum cleaner?'

Natalie wielded Gordana's vacuum cleaner like a weapon, striding around Frank's unit, hauling aside furniture, intent on sucking every dog hair out of every crevice.

Gordana brought in a jug of iced tea and a plate of walnut biscuits from her own kitchen. She put the tray on Frank's marble-topped table. 'If you want any,' she said.

'Ah. Thank you.'

Natalie was breathing hard from her exertions. She devoured three biscuits one after the other, chewing vigorously like a hungry wild animal.

34

Sullivan had not expected to wake up. He was so disoriented, it took him a few minutes to realise he was back in the urology ward. There was mental haziness from whatever medication they'd given him and a stabbing in his side where he must have roughed up his surgical wound. One side of his face was tender to the touch, scratched and scabbed.

'How did I get here?' he asked a passing nurse.

'You came in through Emergency.'

'How did I get there?'

'Ambos, I think. Not sure.'

One of the builders must have found him and called an ambulance. Or perhaps it was a real estate agent, inspecting Rory's place.

The docs must have given him Narcan or pumped his stomach because as he lay on that bed, Sullivan felt completely emptied out.

He drifted off again and a few hours later opened his eyes.

'*Hola*, my friend.'

Sullivan lifted his head to see Jose Luis sitting by his bed.

'Hello,' said Sully. 'How did you know I was here?'

'The transplant coordinator, Diane, she phoned me. She had my mobile number in her files as your employer.'

Sullivan wondered if Diane had told Jose Luis about the overdose.

'She said you suffered a post-operative relapse and they put you back in here.'

So Diane hadn't told him about the overdose.

'Your transplant lady – she's pretty angry with you,' said Jose Luis. 'Whoa, yes, that lady is angry!'

He grinned to indicate he was being jokey but Sullivan nodded dully. 'Well, I guess Diane's angry because —'

'She's angry that you didn't take better care of yourself.'

Sullivan sighed heavily, exhaling from deep within his belly.

'Diane said there's a problem with your accommodation. You can't stay with your movie friend any more?'

'No.'

'And you can't stay at the dead gentleman's flat any more?'

'No.'

'In this case, you would be welcome to stay at our home.'

'Oh, Jose Luis . . . that's very kind but I have enough money for a place of my own.'

Jose Luis tipped his head. 'Well, I won't boss you around about that right now. But perhaps now is a good time to . . .' He drew the bedside chair a little closer and spoke in a measured tone.

'Sullivan. My plan was to leave my big request until you would be recovered from the operation but . . . I think . . . Here is the thing: Liliana and I would like, soon, to spend three months in Colombia, spend some time with our parents. But there is, of course, the business. So, if you – when you are well – if you got your supervising certificate, you could run the business for me during my absence. You know this would be a big help for me. It would make this idea possible for us. I trust you to run things and when I came back we think about expanding the —'

'I'm going to stop you there,' said Sullivan and sighed again.

'Have I chosen the wrong moment to raise this? I'm sorry, Sullivan. Here you are in a hospital bed after major surgery and now a relapse. It's selfish of me to ask this now and put pressure on you.'

'Listen,' said Sullivan, hoisting himself more upright with a small grunt of pain, 'you should know that I'm back in the hospital because

I took an overdose of the pills they gave me. Deliberately. I was trying to kill myself.'

Jose Luis nodded and was silent for a moment. 'I'm very sorry to hear that.'

Sullivan knew he had to be honest with Jose Luis, given the offer being made. Now the fact of the suicide attempt, the reality of who he was, was lying there in the space between them. He could see Jose Luis was troubled, rapidly wanting to backtrack from any proposal that relied on Sullivan's supposed strength of character. Sully was hardly the stable man you would trust as a business partner.

Jose Luis was shifting in the chair, unable to meet Sullivan's gaze, obviously trying to find a polite way to withdraw and get out of there. Before he had a chance to come up with anything, Diane walked into the room.

'Mr Rojas? Diane Milton.'

Jose Luis jumped to his feet and shook her hand. 'Yes. Good to meet you.'

'Thank you so much for coming,' she said.

'Not at all. Thank you for calling me. Oh, I brought some clothes for Sullivan, as you asked.'

Jose Luis patted a hardware shop bag that he'd placed in the cubbyhole of the bedside table. Sullivan noticed he didn't sit down again. Jose Luis would be able to use Diane's arrival as his opportunity to leave.

'Thanks for the clothes,' said Sullivan. 'And thanks for coming.'

Jose Luis was heading for the door but then he stopped and looked Sully directly in the eyes. 'Sullivan, please consider my proposal. It would be a big help to me. So think about it. Not now. Rest now and then think about it.'

The man was clearly upset and Sullivan was sorry to have been the cause of that distress.

When Jose Luis left the room, Diane didn't look up from the paperwork she was holding. 'He seems delightful. I can see why you always spoke highly of him.'

'Is that why you rang him?' asked Sullivan.

'I had to ring someone. It was Jose Luis or the psychiatric team.'

'I suppose it's not great for your records if one of your altruistic donors tops himself straight after the organ donation.'

'It's not great, no. Anyway, there are some forms I need you to fill out so . . .' she began, then dumped the papers on the bedside table and looked at him sternly. 'I wish you'd said something to me.'

'You probably would've cancelled the donation. At least this way someone got —'

'No. I'm not talking about that.' He could see she was really quite angry with him. 'I'm asking why you, Sullivan, didn't tell me, Diane, you were feeling so . . .'

She shook her head and gave up, pressing the heel of her hand into her eyes, which Sullivan could now see were teary. He was so shocked she cared about him in this way that he couldn't respond.

Diane's mobile buzzed with a text. She read it and began tapping a reply to whoever it was. 'I have to go.'

She walked towards the door, still typing on her phone, then added, 'Maybe you don't think it was good someone found you. But I happen to think it was lucky your friend stopped by that house.'

'What friend?

'The person who rang the ambulance.'

'Who?'

'He rang my office later, to check you were alive. Tim.'

When Astrid had called the previous evening, Tim didn't feel the need to tell her he was sitting in a room in the Four Seasons rather than at home with his wife.

'Sullivan's had his operation and been discharged,' she said.

'Oh. Right. Astrid, to be honest —'

But she didn't hear the injury in his voice and ploughed on in her hearty Astrid way. 'I know you and Sullivan have rebuilt your friendship so I wanted to check that you'll be keeping an eye on him. He was very flat today. Not himself.'

Tim didn't respond but Astrid continued as if he had. 'Yeah, you're probably right. I suppose he'll be okay. Always seems to land on his feet. Did you know he's staying with that movie star?'

'Rory Wallace?'

'Yes. I dropped him at the house. Not that you could see the house with that big white wall blocking it from the street like some kind of castle.'

When Astrid got off the phone, Tim's thought track was no more sophisticated than *So Sullivan Moss is flat. Well, he can go fuck himself flat as a pancake.* But when his jaw muscles released a little, it occurred to him that Rory Wallace had left the country. The house the actor had been renting was shielded by a dark grey wall. The enormous white wall was next door, outside the half-built house. Astrid had unwittingly deposited Sullivan at a deserted construction site.

Tim drove to Tamarama, parked outside Wallace's house and sat in the car. Was he an anxious idiot to be here, checking an empty building in the dark when Sully was most likely somewhere else, tucked up warm with some gullible person nursing him? Even if Sullivan was in the building rubble, alone and sick, was Tim a soft-headed idiot to be looking out for that scumbag?

Fuck it, he'd driven all the way here. If he didn't check and then something bad happened, he'd feel guilty. It was not worth feeling one iota of remorse over Sullivan Moss.

Tim fished a torch out of the glove box and grabbed a jacket from the back seat. It was a chilly night. He picked his way around the side as he had a week before on his previous mission to thump the man.

'Sully!' he called repeatedly through the concrete shell.

Finally Tim found him, up the top of the house. It looked as if he'd slid off the pool lounger, scraping some skin off the side of his face, and rolled close to the unguarded edge of the balcony. He was unconscious, unresponsive, cold to touch. Probably hypothermic, to the extent that Tim understood that stuff. There were empty pill packets and empty bottles of booze on the concrete.

Tim dragged Sullivan inside away from the edge and rang triple zero. He struggled to remember the CPR course he'd done years ago but then realised Sully was still breathing – shallow breaths but something. So no CPR then. Sullivan was barefoot, wearing jeans and a thin T-shirt, so Tim took off his jacket to provide some warmth to the top half of Sully's body.

He looked down at his old friend lying there and wasn't sure what he should be feeling. Better to just do what needed to be done.

Once the ambulance had gone and Tim pulled away from the Tamarama house, the thought of going back to the hotel room was so dispiriting he found himself driving towards home.

Juliet was in the lounge room watching a DVD, drinking red wine. When Tim walked in, she didn't make a big deal of it, acting as if he'd just come home in a regular way, after working late. She paused the DVD.

'The kids around?' asked Tim.

'Both staying over at friends' places. Our children – the most self-absorbed creatures on the planet – even they have noticed the atmosphere in this house. So they're accepting every invitation they get to be elsewhere.'

'Good luck to them,' said Tim.

He stood in the lounge room and told Juliet about his evening's activities.

'Sullivan's going to survive?' she asked.

'That's what the ambulance guys reckoned.'

'Good. So you rescued him,' she said.

'I guess I did.'

'You're shaking,' said Juliet, pointing out Tim's trembling hands. Then she lifted the wine bottle up from the table. 'Want some?'

Tim nodded and sat down as she poured him a glass.

'There's talk at work about looking for someone to run the Hong Kong office. I was thinking I might put my hand up for it. We could go together if you wanted to.'

Juliet tipped her head, thinking about it. 'If we both went, what would happen to the twins?'

'They have good international schools in Hong Kong. Or they could board back here.'

'I think they'd prefer that,' said Juliet.

'Yeah, probably.'

Juliet added, 'Maybe we should send them to one of those boarding schools in the bush where they make rich kids hike and chop their own firewood.'

That made Tim smile. Juliet smiled back. Unbelievable.

Tim had already relinquished his fantasies about quitting banking and becoming some kind of wandering aid worker. Such morally pristine paths were not really open to him. The unromantic reality was that Tim Wozniak could achieve more good in the world by continuing to earn huge money doing the work for which he had a knack – even if the work was of no intrinsic value and possibly destructive – and then give away a big chunk of that money every year to people who had the skills to organise immunisation programs and the like. Of course Tim was aware that if he thought about this moral position too hard it would fall apart in his hands.

He sat there drinking the wine. The Hong Kong move could be the chance for him and Juliet to reboot. But there was a struggle between his optimistic and pessimistic impulses. Without too much effort, he could picture Juliet sobbing in a Repulse Bay high-rise. It was possible the two of them would be locked in a wretched embrace forever, like marathon dancers dragging each other around the dance-floor until one of them died.

But Tim was by nature an optimist so he chose to focus on an image of the two of them laughing as they levered noodles into their mouths at an authentic backstreet food stall before going back to their Sheung Wan penthouse to make deeply connected love.

Seeing Tim stand there, trembling, telling the story about Sullivan, Juliet felt a little bit of tenderness for him, that aching bruise. Maybe they should try the Hong Kong option. Anyway, she didn't have the energy to start a relationship with anyone new. It was Tim or no one.

'I think Hong Kong's worth thinking about seriously,' said Juliet.

She didn't believe there were many people who could change in any significant way. Most of us occupied a tight space, like living inside a Tupperware container. There was a bit of room to slide and shift around inside the container but not much.

35

Sullivan looked inside the hardware-shop bag that Jose Luis had brought. On top was one of the red shirts Jose Luis liked to wear on Sundays and a pair of his light brown cotton trousers. The shirt was a reasonable fit around the chest but the sleeves were too short, so Sully rolled up the cuffs. He expected the pants would be at half-mast on him, given that Jose Luis was several centimetres shorter but when he pulled them on, he noticed someone (Jose Luis or Liliana) had unpicked the hems to make them long enough. Looking down at the white line of the old hem made Sullivan want to burst into tears.

At the bottom of the bag was a new pair of the protective gum-boots they wore on asbestos sites. Jose Luis had gone to the hardware store to buy a pair in Sullivan's size.

Louis fell asleep on top of the hospital bed in the afternoon, an innocent boy sleep. Natalie stared at his beautiful face. Sometimes her love for him was overwhelming, almost more than her body could handle, but right now, today, it was anchoring, warming.

Some process had started with Frank's death, stirring up a lot of sludge from the bottom. The last twenty-four hours had blasted her head clean again like high-pressure water jets. One of the notions clinging to the inside of her skull was that she would like to see Sullivan Moss again.

She thought back to the night Mack died. At the time, she was stumbling through it, vision too blurred by shame and anger to see anything much clearly. But now she re-ran the events in her mind and recalled Sullivan being so steady and strong and tender.

She allowed herself to imagine a potential scene – Sullivan and her taking Louis to a music festival somewhere. She imagined Louis running ahead to grab a good spot near the stage while she and Sullivan took their time strolling to join him. Sully had his hand on the small of her back.

Natalie shook that image out of her head for now. She would send Sullivan a text wishing him well. A no-obligation text.

Sully dressed and travelled down in the lift with the goal of apologising to Diane. And so he could thank her for everything. And possibly hug her if that was something she would like. And reassure her that he would not muck up the reputation of her non-directed donor program by killing himself.

Sully didn't recognise the young woman on the desk at the renal unit. She must be new.

He asked, 'Is Diane Milton around?'

'She's with someone right now but if you don't mind waiting . . .'

'I'll wait,' said Sullivan.

The only other person on the pastel chairs was a woman in her mid-forties who shot Sully a polite smile as he took a seat across from her.

The woman was flicking through stuff on her phone and readjusting the clip holding the tumble of dark hair off her face. She was wearing jeans, runners, a T-shirt, no makeup, no jewellery. Sullivan thought she looked tired.

The woman glanced up from her phone and, noticing Sully's industrial gumboots, she looked confused. Then she clocked his hospital wristband. He smiled, giving her permission to ask.

Eventually she did ask, 'Are you an inpatient for renal surgery or some procedure?'

'No. I'm an inpatient because I tried to kill myself.'

The woman made a small sound in her throat, embarrassed. A moment later, she blurted out, 'I'm sorry.'

'Oh well,' said Sullivan, not wanting her to feel obliged to continue the discussion.

But she did continue. 'My son received a donor kidney a week ago from someone not related to us, someone we didn't even know. Can you believe that?'

Sullivan gulped a breath. It was probably his kidney but there was no way to be absolutely sure.

'My husband died from polycystic kidney disease and it was, well —'

'Horrible,' offered Sullivan.

'Mmm. My son had the same condition. It's genetic.'

Sullivan nodded his understanding.

'He was going downhill.' She pulled a face. 'I have to tell you, I was a very bitter person. Very. Then a stranger comes along and gives Kyle a kidney.'

Sullivan wasn't sure what to say so he widened his eyes – *wow*.

The woman shook her head, laughing. 'It doesn't fit my world view. It's thrown me right off. Ha. Anyway, whatever is wrong with you – I mean, it's none of my business . . .'

She broke off when a young man, a skinny sweet-faced twenty-year-old, emerged from the consulting room. Her face lit up and Sullivan knew this was her son.

A moment later, Diane Milton followed Kyle out into the waiting room. When the woman began to introduce her son to Sullivan, there was a flash of panic across Diane's face. That's when Sullivan knew for certain.

He didn't want to incur Diane Milton's wrath so he jumped up, hurried straight out to the corridor and into the gents.

Just as he pushed through the swing door, he realised Kyle was following him in there. Well, he wasn't following Sullivan but happened to be making a visit to the gents at the same time.

Not sure how to face the recipient of his kidney, Sullivan ducked into a cubicle and locked the door. Kyle started pissing and Sully listened to the bold stream of urine hitting the metal trough with a resounding splash. That piss was passing through Sullivan's kidney, which was working splendidly. Kyle could again enjoy a satisfying vigorous flow just as Ken had yearned to do.

Sitting on the toilet, Sully wondered if he should fling open the door and out himself to Kyle. *Hello. I'm the dude who donated the kidney you now have in you.* The kid would be surprised and amazed and impressed. Kyle's gratitude would wrap around Sullivan and it would feel very good.

The pissing stopped and there was the sound of jeans being zipped up, then hands being washed. Sullivan gave it a moment for Kyle to leave the gents, before he opened the door. In fact, when Sully stepped out of the cubicle, the guy was still there, fiddling with his hair in the mirror. This was pleasing to Sullivan – pleasing to think this young man could now fuss about his hair on the assumption he would have a long-term future that might involve impressing romantic partners.

Sullivan went to the basins to wash his hands. He was startled to see his own reflection – one side of his face raw, peppered with scabs, as if he'd gone through a grater.

Kyle glanced at Sullivan and said, 'Sorry if my mum was raving on at you. She gets really – oh, you know . . .'

'She was fine. How are you feeling?'

'Good. Much better.'

Kyle smiled, awkward, sweet, full of nervous hopefulness. In that moment, Sullivan knew there was no way in the world he would say anything that might make this young man feel uncomfortable or beholden to him in any way.

Sully just said, 'Good luck with everything.'

Kyle walked out and Sullivan flopped against the tiled wall, enjoying the coolness on his back coming through Jose Luis' shirt.

He had chosen not to burden the kidney recipient with that piece of radioactive information. He'd made that choice for the sake of the young man, without thinking about himself at all. Now, once Kyle was gone, it occurred to Sully that the decision to keep quiet felt mighty good.

Sullivan leaned against the cool tiles and for one brief, tantalising moment, all his remaining organs were sitting comfortably in his body cavity, radiating love to everyone he had ever met or would ever meet.

Sully would use the savings he had accumulated to cover the bond and rent on a small flat until he was fit enough to work again. He would get his supervisor certificate to look after the business while Jose Luis and Liliana spent time with their parents in Colombia. He would book some sessions with Anthony the shrink but this time they would work without Sullivan having any kind of escape hatch in place. He would send a thank-you message to Tim but expect nothing back.

He even allowed himself to imagine Natalie and her loveliness. He indulged, for a moment, in a fantasy of living with her as her man. Every day Nat would go off to the radio station and Sullivan would go to his job removing asbestos. At the end of the workday, he would pick Louis up from school and take him to soccer training. They could get a Xoloitzcuintli dog that wouldn't cause allergy problems for Louis. Sully would cook delicious healthy meals for them all.

At night, after Louis fell asleep, Natalie and Sullivan would go to bed. Sully used the images he had tucked away in his mind – his memory of kissing her, the delicate skin on her neck, even the goosebumps on her bare legs as she fled Rory's place – to construct a fantasy of the glorious sex they would have.

Those images were so intoxicating that Sully thought he might well keel over. He needed to lie down for a while. He headed out of the gents and back towards the urology floor. He would talk to Diane Milton later, once Kyle was long gone.

As he waited at the bank of lifts, his mind was wafting around libidinous Natalie thoughts. The lift doors opened and Sully found himself face to face with Judy Dennis.

'Oh. You,' she said. 'Jesus Christ, you look appalling.'

Sullivan blinked hard a couple of times. An encounter with Natalie's mother was like having lemon juice tossed in your eyes. It didn't help that he was in the middle of a sexual fantasy about her daughter.

'Are you here to see Louis?' she asked as the lift doors started to close.

Sullivan slammed his arm against the doors to hold them open. 'Louis is here?'

Judy started to explain the asthma crisis. Her version of events was crusted over with defensiveness and criticism of the paramedics but Sullivan gleaned enough to know the boy had been in real danger. That meant Louis might need support now. He might need cheering up. He might need something.

'Excuse me,' Sully said, interrupting Judy. He released the door so she could take the lift wherever she needed to go.

Sullivan strode to the fire stairs which would take him up the two floors to the paediatric ward.

Acknowledgements

I would like to thank the people who helped in the writing of *Useful*.

Jane Mawson, transplant coordinator at Royal Prince Alfred Hospital, for being so generous with information about renal transplant; Dr Karen Oswald for help with medical matters; Dr Michele Franks for medical advice and volunteering to read an early draft; Steve Kennedy for allowing me to pick his considerable brain about the banking world; the teachers at Macquarie Fields TAFE and Bret Baker from Beasy Pty Ltd for help on asbestos removal.

My agent Anthony Blair for his enthusiasm and thoughtful reading. Huge thanks to Sophie Hamley for offering her insight, good humour and wisdom through the process.

Arwen Summers, Belinda Byrne and everyone at Penguin for their care with every aspect of the book. A special thanks to Ben Ball.

Matthew Kalitowski who resuscitated my joy in writing; Michael Wynne, my stalwart friend who listens to ideas, advises on drafts, but mostly importantly, can tease me until I'm thinking clearly again; Annabelle Sheehan for being the kind of good friend a writer needs and for believing in the story from the start.

And enormous thanks to my partner Richard Glover who listens patiently to half-formed scraps, reads messy drafts, offers smart advice and emotional support, and helps me feel it's worth persevering.